"I love Ruggle's characters. They're sharply drawn and vividly alive. I'm happy when they find each other. These are wonderful escapist books."
— **Charlaine Harris**, #1 *New York Times* Bestselling Author of the Sookie Stackhouse Series

"Sexy and suspenseful, I couldn't turn the pages fast enough."
— **Julie Ann Walker**, *New York Times* and *USA Today* Bestselling Author, for *Hold Your Breath*

"Chills and thrills and a sexy, slow-burning romance from a terrific new voice."
— **D. D. Ayres**, Author of the K-9 Rescue Series, for *Hold Your Breath*

"Fast, funny read, and a promising start to a new series."
— *Smart Bitches, Trashy Books* for *Hold Your Breath*

"The Rocky Mountain Search and Rescue series is off to a promising start."
— *RT Book Reviews*, 4 Stars for *Hold Your Breath*

"I cannot read these books fast enough. Waiting for the next book to see what happens is going to be pure torture. Is it October yet?"

"As this series draws to a close, the most fascinating of the heroines is introduced. Her story is both heartbreaking and uplifting at the same time. She's a sympathetic sweetheart who carries the reader along on her journey to emotional healing."

ALSO BY KATIE RUGGLE

ON THE CHASE

KATIE RUGGLE

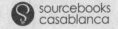
sourcebooks
casablanca

Published by Sourcebooks Casablanca, an imprint of Sourcebooks, Inc.
P.O. Box 4410, Naperville, Illinois 60567-4410
(630) 961-3900
Fax: (630) 961-2168
sourcebooks.com

Printed and bound in Canada.
MBP 10 9 8 7 6 5 4 3 2 1

To kick-ass women and girls everywhere.
You're the real-life heroines.

CHAPTER 1

"I DON'T TRUST HIM."

Kaylee stared at her friend—her apparently *insane* friend. "How can you not trust him? Haven't you seen his cheekbones? And those eyes? And pretty much his entire face? He looks like a freaking Disney prince. How can you not trust a Disney prince?"

"Pretty is as pretty does," Penny muttered, shoving dresses aside with a little too much force.

Kaylee snorted, reaching toward the rack despite the risk of losing a finger to Penny's violent sorting. She grabbed a dress and moved out of the closet so she could toss it on the growing pile on her bed. Not for the first time, Kaylee was grateful for her expansive walk-in closet. Not only did it hold her excessive amount of clothes and a truly extravagant number of shoes, but it also made it possible to give a wrathful Penny some space. The woman had pointy elbows and knew how to use them. "You're channeling your grandma Nita again."

Yanking another dress off the rack, Penny used the hanger to point at Kaylee. "She'd totally agree with me on this. You're blinded by hormones and can't see that your prince is actually the villain—or at least the semi-villain. I deal with men like him every day. I know what I'm talking about."

Crossing her arms, Kaylee leaned her shoulder against the closet doorframe. "Do you think that maybe, just maybe, the guys you come into contact with at work are making you a little bitter and jaded? I mean, it's an emergency women's shelter. That's a pretty skewed sample of the male population."

"I'm not bitter and jaded." Penny paused before adding, "Not yet, at least. And I'm really good at spotting a toad in prince's clothing. It's my superpower."

Despite her best efforts at keeping Penny's gloom and doom from darkening her mood, doubt tugged at Kaylee. Trying to hide her sudden frown, she turned to stare at the mound of dresses on the bed, a rainbow of silky fabrics and wonderful possibilities.

The California sun streamed through the window, making the entire room glow and turning the white bedding silver around the edges. When she'd been searching for a condo two years ago, Kaylee's top requirement had been light—a lot of it. After spending her childhood in a cramped Midwestern basement apartment, she couldn't get enough sunlight. Her condo was everything her home growing up had not been— warm and bright and clean. She'd spent too many years cold, poor, and helpless, and she wasn't going to go back to that…ever.

The scrape of a hanger against the rod brought her back to the present.

"It's been so long since I found a good guy," Kaylee said wistfully, keeping her gaze on the dresses. "They're out there, though, and I need to believe that Noah is one of them. After all, he invited me to his uncle's house, and the man pretty much raised Noah. A toad wouldn't invite me home to meet his family, right? You just need to give him a chance."

Risking another glance at Penny, Kaylee hid a half smile. She knew that scowl. It meant her friend was seconds away from caving. "Please? Let me have my fairy tale for a few more dates? If he turns into a complete ass, then I'll even let you say 'I told you so' while we throw darts at his picture—the really pointy, dangerous darts that they've banned in the U.S. because too many kids lost their eyeballs. *Please?*"

"Fine," Penny grumbled. Kaylee had known that she wouldn't be able to resist. Besides peanut butter ice cream and motorcycles, Penny's favorite thing in the world was being right—and getting to crow about it. Now if Noah could keep acting like the perfect boyfriend he'd promised to be, then Penny would be proven wrong, and Kaylee's story could have a happy ending. "Here." Penny thrust a dress toward Kaylee.

"Oh, Penny…you're the best!" As soon as she accepted the hanger, Kaylee knew it was the one. The dress was simple and elegant and just perfect. Pressing it against her front, she did a little spin, her happiness bubbling out of her. The dress felt silky and sinfully good under her hand, and she couldn't help but remember all the thrift store hand-me-downs she'd had growing up— all the thin coats and musty-smelling boots and scratchy blankets that never managed to be warm enough. The memory of that bone-deep cold was the main reason she'd fought so hard to be here in California, a place where winter never came.

Penny snorted a laugh. "What's with the dress-dancing? Are you trying to be an ethnically ambiguous

Sleeping Beauty right now? Since that makes me the helpful rodent, I'm not loving this theme."

"No," Kaylee huffed, although she couldn't hold a straight face. "You're the twittery bird." Grinning, she dodged Penny's mock punch and twirled around the bedroom again. "I'm just happy. Everything is going right. I have a job I love, a home I love, a Penny I love, a dress I love, a new boyfriend I…"

Narrowing her eyes, Penny warned, "Don't say it."

Even Penny's death glare couldn't dampen Kaylee's spirits, and she laughed merrily. "A new boyfriend I could really, really come to like. How about that?"

Penny made a skeptical sound. "As long as you don't let that 'like' blind you to any creeper warning signs."

"I won't," Kaylee promised. The sunlight soaked into her skin, warming her, and she wiggled her toes in delight. It was going to be an amazing night. She could just feel it.

"You really are a Disney prince," she blurted.

Noah's eyebrows drew together even as he laughed and leaned closer so the other guests around the table couldn't hear their conversation. "What?"

"I mean, your hair alone is pretty much irrefutable evidence." Kaylee fought the urge to reach over and muss it a little. It was gold and perfect, just long enough to frame his handsome face. Sure, credit could be given to a talented and expensive stylist, but Kaylee was leaning more toward princely genes. "And you open doors and pull out chairs and—"

"That's manners, not proof that I'm animated royalty," Noah interrupted, his mouth still curled in amusement. "If I really were a prince, I would've picked you up tonight. That was very unprincely of me."

Kaylee waved off his apology as she leaned to the side, giving the server room to place a delicate cup holding her after-dinner coffee in front of her. After thanking her, Kaylee turned back to Noah. "You had a meeting, *and* you offered to send a car. I don't think that qualifies as being rude."

With a playful frown, he said, "An offer you turned down. I hate that you have to make the drive back alone."

As smitten as she was with Noah, she had to roll her eyes at that. "It's a thirty-minute drive. I'll survive." Kaylee didn't mention that the seed of doubt Penny had planted had prompted her to decline. It made her feel safer to have her own transportation, just in case. *Not that I'll need to escape*, she thought, taking in Noah's warm smile and amused blue eyes.

Martin, Noah's uncle, cleared his throat, drawing her attention to where he sat at the head of the table, framed by the wall of windows behind him. Darkness transformed the glass into a mirror, reflecting the enormous room back at them—as if it needed to look twice as big. The house was huge, set like an island on lush, irrigated, and landscaped acres. Kaylee couldn't even imagine how much the sprawling LA property was worth.

As expensive as it must have been, the decorating scheme was a little too ostentatious for Kaylee's taste. It felt as if everything had been chosen to impress visitors with the owner's wealth, rather than to create a home. Although Kaylee had a healthy appreciation for financial stability, she was happy just to be able to pay her mortgage and buy food and have enough left over for some really nice shoes. The pushy glamour of Noah's uncle's home left her cold.

"So, Kaylee," Martin said, jerking her out of her thoughts. She gave him a polite smile. "You work at St. Macartan's College?" Although he put a lilt at the end of the statement, it didn't sound like a question. From the look in his eyes, Kaylee was pretty sure he knew perfectly well where she worked—and a whole lot more about her. Before inviting her to their gazillion-dollar mansion, Martin had probably had her investigated to make sure she wouldn't steal the silverware.

"Yes," she said. "I'm in development and fundraising."

"And how do you like that?"

"I love it." A warm glow of satisfaction filled her, as it always did when she thought about her job. "Scholarships made it possible for me to go to college." Scholarships and working her tail off, but Kaylee left off that part. It sounded too self-pitying. "Now I get to raise money so that other kids have that same opportunity."

"Sounds…noble." There was an off note to his tone that made Kaylee stiffen, even as she tried to define it. The expression on Martin's face was uncomfortably close to a sneer, with a wrinkled nose and curled upper lip that made him look like he smelled something foul. She knew that look, had seen it thousands of times as she was growing up, but she wasn't sure why Martin was wearing it now. She braced herself, ready to defend her job or her background or her worthiness to even be in the same room as his nephew, but Martin changed the subject. "Where did you go to school?"

"University of Minnesota for my undergraduate degree, and St. Macartan's for my master's." There was a hint of challenge in her tone, but Martin didn't take her up on it. Instead, he just asked what her major had been.

The conversation continued, so polite on the surface that it made Kaylee nervous. To be honest, Martin freaked her out a little. He had that crocodile-in-disguise manner, his eyes flat and cool even as he smiled. As soon as Martin turned his attention to an older couple seated next to him, Kaylee gave a silent sigh of relief and leaned toward Noah. "Restroom?" Martin had flustered her, and she needed a minute and some privacy to remind herself that she wasn't that helpless, needy child any longer.

Noah tipped his head toward one of the doorways. "Turn left, then right; it's the third door on the right. Want me to take you?"

"Oh no." She stood, making patting motions with her hands as if to keep him in his seat. "I've got it. My sense of direction is excellent." With a teasing smile, she excused herself to the rest of the guests. It was probably her imagination, but she thought she felt Martin's sharp gaze on her back as she left the room.

Within a few minutes, she was hopelessly lost.

Kaylee made a low sound of frustration. She'd followed Noah's directions, turning left and then right, but there had only been two doors on the right in that hall. Deciding that he'd left out a third turn, she'd made her way down another hallway, which only brought her farther into a twisted maze.

"Rich people and their ginormous mansions," she muttered, deciding to just start checking rooms. There had to be a thousand bathrooms in this place, so she figured she'd eventually stumble over one. She tried several doors, most of which were locked, and the rest of which were definitely not bathrooms. As she reached for yet another doorknob, male voices caught her attention, and she turned toward the sound. Rounding the corner, she saw two burly men enter a room at the very end of the hall.

"Excuse me," she called, hurrying as fast as she could on her impractical—yet very cute—shoes, but they'd already disappeared, closing the door behind them. When Kaylee reached it, she tried the knob. It was locked.

With a growl of impatience, she considered kicking the door, but refrained. Not only did she not know where a bathroom was, but she wasn't sure how to get back to the dining room. Annoyed with herself, she started trying doors again.

She yanked at one. The handle turned with the heavy click of an automatic lock. Kaylee frowned. Why did Martin have a room in his house that could only be opened from the outside? She pulled at it, curious. The door was heavy and resisted opening at first, but then it swung toward her. To her disappointment, it wasn't a bathroom. Instead, a flight of stairs descended to a concrete floor. She was about to allow the door to swing shut when she heard a sound.

"Hello?" she called, although her voice came out wispy. There was something about the blocky, utilitarian stairs and fluorescent lighting that gave the space an icky basement vibe. Her childhood home had left her with a special abhorrence for basements.

"Help!" someone called in a hoarse voice. The hair rose on the back of her neck. "Please help us!"

The words were so unexpected, so out of place in the glamorous mansion, that it took a moment for the plea to register. Her heart rate sped up. "Who's there?" Forcing her feet forward, she descended a few steps. The door started to close and, remembering the automatic lock, she wedged her clutch purse against the jamb before releasing the door.

Her shoes sounded too loud on the steps. "Who's there? Are you hurt?"

"Down here!" The voice was rough and scratchy, the urgent tone enough to make her stomach clench. How had she gone from fairy tale to horror movie in just a few hallways? Her gaze darted toward the door, and she briefly considered running up the stairs and escaping, but she told herself firmly that she was being ridiculous. This was Martin Jovanovic's fancy-pants mansion, not a haunted house. She clomped down the remainder of the stairs with forced confidence. She was the girlfriend—well, almost-girlfriend—of the perfect man. She'd been invited to a California dream home. She belonged here, damn it. There wasn't any reason for her to feel intimidated.

Then she saw the blood.

Oddly, the first thing Kaylee felt was exasperation. Now Penny would get to say "I told you so," because her friend had been right...again. The mansion, the boyfriend, the food...everything had been too perfect, so it was time for reality to kick Kaylee in the face once again. Her gaze followed the dark-red trail across the floor until it reached the source of the blood…so much blood. Then her brain shut off as horror swamped her, rushing over her in a black wave as her lungs sucked in a huge breath, automatically preparing for a scream.

"Help," a man—although he was barely recognizable as human—gasped, startling Kaylee into swallowing her shriek and turning it into a harsh croak instead. "Please."

There were three of them, tied to chairs and facing one another in a rough triangle. Her gaze darted from one battered, blood-soaked form to the next, unable to comprehend what she was seeing. "I was just looking for a bathroom," she whispered.

A wheezing choke—was it a laugh?—came from the man whose face was so swollen that it was hard to pick out his features. A slitted, glittering eye peered at her from the wreckage. Her lungs flattened and refused to take in any air as Kaylee stared at his battered visage. Someone had done that to him, had tied him up and tortured him…someone who could be coming back at any moment. "Good thing for us. A hand?" He tilted his head toward the table that sat in the center of the small room. When she stayed frozen, he added, "If you could grab something sharp and cut us loose, we'd appreciate it."

His words were oddly polite, but they held an underlying plea that jerked Kaylee into motion. It was hard to think, to understand what was happening or what she needed to do, and she seized on his gently worded request. *Cut them free*, she mentally repeated. *Cut them free*.

Sucking in a much-needed breath, she rushed toward the table, her heels clattering against the concrete. Her body felt foreign and awkward, and her movements were jerky, as if she were a marionette with someone else controlling her strings. She stumbled to a halt next to the small folding table, and a small, near-hysterical portion of her brain noted how the cheap metal stand didn't go with the rest of Martin's decor. No wonder he hid it in the basement.

Stop. Don't freak out. Just breathe.

She forced herself to focus on the task at hand. As her brain registered what the items on the table were, what horrific things the knives and pliers and hammer and— *oh shit*—the *ice pick* had been used to do, she couldn't stop from returning her gaze to the first man's ravaged face. He tried to smile at her, but the result was macabre.

"It's okay, sweetheart," he said, but tension lay beneath his soothing tone. "Anything with a sharp edge will work. Let's get out of here, huh?"

His last sentence echoed in her mind, reminding her that the people who'd done this could walk in at any time. With a hunted glance at the stairs, she grabbed a small but wicked-looking knife from the table, forcing her brain to ignore how sticky the floor was beneath her shoes, or the purpose of the other tools lined up neatly, ready to be used again in an instant. She kept herself focused as she started cutting the zip ties securing the first man to his chair.

"You're an angel," he said as the knife sliced through the binding around his wrist. The zip tie popped open, revealing a bloody groove where it had been. Her gaze fixed on his wrist, on that evidence that he'd struggled against his bonds. She was unable to look away from the gory sight until he cleared his throat.

Kaylee jolted at the sound, fumbling and almost

dropping the knife. Recovering her grip, she squeezed the handle tightly as she gave herself a mental smack. *Get it together, Kay*, she commanded, reaching for the tie on his other wrist. When she noticed how badly she was shaking, though, she stopped before she accidentally cut him.

"You've got this, angel," the man said, and his calm assurance helped. Taking a deep breath, she steadied her hand enough to slip the tip of the knife under the plastic tie. When she pulled up, it opened with a *pop*. His ankles were easier, and she cut his legs free in seconds before hastily backing up several steps. She almost felt like she'd opened the cage of a circus lion. Would he reward her help or just eat her?

"Thanks, angel." The man stood and immediately moved to the table. Although he stumbled, his legs wobbling beneath him, he managed to stay on his feet. Grabbing another knife—this one much scarier-looking than Kaylee's—he moved to the second man and cut his hands free. As he worked, she stared, wondering if she'd made a horrendous mistake. Two out of the three were free. What if they were dangerous criminals? What if they hurt her—or killed her? She was so worried about the return of the torturers, but what if the biggest threat was already in the room with her?

She pushed away the doubt. It was too late to worry about that now. If the men did try to hurt her, they looked to be in bad enough shape that she was pretty sure she could outrun them.

Kaylee forced her body into jerky motion. She headed toward the last guy, who was slumped to the side, only his bonds keeping him semi-upright. He was limp and still, his head lolling to the side as blood ran from his ear and across his cheek before it dripped steadily on the floor. Kaylee seized on the fact that he was still bleeding. Dead people didn't bleed, did they?

"Please be alive. Please be alive," she pleaded almost soundlessly. Kaylee sawed at the zip tie securing his hands until the plastic separated and released suddenly. His arms flopped to hang by his sides. Without the restraints holding him, he started to slide sideways, heading toward the floor.

With a squeak of alarm, Kaylee tried to catch him, but his dead weight—*no! His* unconscious *weight*—brought her to the floor with him. She put out a hand, trying to catch herself, but her palm slid across wet concrete. Her hip and then her head hit the floor painfully, and the man's limp body fell heavily across her legs, pinning her. For several seconds, she lay still, stunned.

Then the weight disappeared from her legs, jerking her back to reality. The first man was pulling his unconscious friend's arm over his shoulder. The second supported the unresponsive man's other side. Her gaze landed on his face, and she flinched so violently that the back of her head bumped against the floor again. There was a gory mess where one of his eyes should have been. Bile rose in her throat, forcing her to swallow several times. Barely able to keep from vomiting, Kaylee ripped her gaze away from the empty, bloody socket.

"Up you go, Angel." The man with the swollen face offered the hand not holding on to his unconscious buddy. When she grabbed it, he pulled her up, almost lifting her to her feet, and she scrambled to get her wobbly legs to support her. "Let's get out before our *friends* come back, yeah?"

Kaylee couldn't speak. The best she could do was a jerky nod as she moved to follow the trio. The stairs were too narrow for three big guys to stay side by side, so they were forced to turn sideways. The unconscious man's boots struck the edges of the treads, and each thud made Kaylee flinch as she climbed the steps behind them. Every sound seemed thunderous, too loud to not be heard everywhere in the mansion, and each step they made, each inch farther that the men dragged their unconscious friend, felt horribly, painfully slow.

When they finally reached the door, all the air left Kaylee's lungs so quickly and completely that her head spun. After a quick glance into the hall, the men slipped through the doorway. Kaylee hurried up the final few steps, not wanting to be left behind. The thought of being trapped alone in the bloody basement made her stumble forward, rushing to flatten her hands against the opened door.

The man with the swollen face glanced at her as he hitched the unconscious man higher. "Better not go back to the party like that."

Confused, Kaylee glanced down and saw that, on her hip, a white section of her color-block dress was now smeared with dark red. *Blood*. The salmon she'd eaten earlier threatened to climb back in her throat.

"You have a car here?" he asked.

She stared at him without seeing his face. All she could see was blood. It was only after he repeated the question that it finally penetrated. Kaylee nodded.

"Head that way." He jerked his head to the left. "Turn right at the T, and you'll get to some stairs. They'll take you to a back entrance."

"What about you?" Her voice was a husky imitation of its usual self. Her throat felt as rough and sore as if she'd actually been screaming the entire time, instead of just wanting to. "How are you getting out?"

His half grin contorted his abused face, twisting the cuts and bruises and making his eyes almost disappear. "We're going out the *other* back door. Good luck, Angel." He and the other man started making their painful-looking progress in the opposite direction, the unconscious guy slumped between them, his boots dragging across the polished hardwood floor.

The sight of them walking away, leaving her alone, sent a surge of panic through her. She had to bite the inside of her lower lip to keep from calling after them. They were strangers, but it had felt like they'd been on her side. Now she was on her own.

At the thought, the voice in her head screamed at her to get out of the nightmare house. As she moved out of the doorway, Kaylee stepped on something and stumbled slightly. She glanced down and saw her silver clutch. Her fuzzy brain wondered how it got on the floor, until she recalled that she'd used it to prop open the door. Automatically, she bent to grab it.

Once it was in her hands, she remembered that it held her phone. "I can call the police," she called in a carrying whisper to the retreating men.

They stopped abruptly. "Won't help," the one missing an eye said. His voice was raspy, too, and she wondered if he *had* been screaming. The thought made her shudder. "The Jovanovics have deep pockets and a wide reach. Just get out and get far away from these people."

It felt wrong, not calling for help, and Kaylee's fingers tightened around her clutch. Urgency was building in her, panic expanding like air inside a balloon, stretching her tighter and tighter. She needed to get out before she broke. Turning away from the men, she hurried in the opposite direction. It was hard to believe that Noah's family had the entire police force on their payroll, but she'd wait to contact them, just in case. Later, after the men had a chance to get out and she was safe, Kaylee would call. The thought of being out of this nightmare mansion, of being home, made her hurry her steps.

As she reached the end of the hall, she snuck a quick glance behind her. The men were nowhere to be seen. Sucking in a shaky breath, she turned right toward the stairs…and what she hoped was safety. She refused to think about how she'd gotten so terribly lost in the rabbit warren of a mansion just a short time earlier, or about how easy it would be to get turned around again. The thought of running through Martin's gilded house, frightened and trapped, made her throat close. There was a door right in front of her, but would it lead to escape or a continuation of her waking nightmare?

Turning the knob with shaking fingers, she didn't know whether to be grateful or scared that it wasn't locked. The door opened to a neatly kept yard, lit by an almost-full moon and discreet landscape lights. She was out. Relief flooded her, even as a hundred other emotions—fear and paranoia and horror—pounded through her veins. The cool night air felt good on her flushed cheeks, and Kaylee bent at the waist, trying to catch her breath and make her brain reboot. A revolving chain of images flashed in her mind—blood and knives and the one man's ravaged, empty eye socket. Her next inhale sounded like a sob, and she forced herself to stand up straight.

There was no time to fall apart. She was out of the house, but Kaylee definitely wasn't safe yet. Even though he'd been sitting innocently at the dining table with her and the rest of his guests all evening, Uncle Martin had to have given the order for those men to be tortured. After all, they were in his house. Her memory of his flat stare seemed even more menacing now, and she hurried to follow a flagstone path that led to the front of the house.

With every step, Kaylee's shocked brain was tuning back in to reality, her fear spiraling into panic. Surely they would've noticed her extended absence by now. What if the men's escape had been discovered? How fast would they put the two together?

Her breaths were getting quicker, louder, and she forced herself to slow. Hyperventilating until she passed out was not a good escape plan. In fact, it was a very *bad* escape plan. When the panicked haze had cleared slightly, she hurried along the path again. Her shoes were loud on the flagstones, and she shifted her weight to the balls of her feet.

The path ended at the entrance to what looked like a garage. Kaylee wasn't about to go through another unknown door leading to who-knew-what horrors, so she turned, stepping onto the grass and staying close to the exterior of the building.

Her heels sank into the soft, sprinkler-fed lawn, and

she shifted to her toes again. A light flickered to life right above her, and she froze, feeling like she was a cat burglar caught by a police spotlight. Clenching her jaw against the need to scream, she looked away from the glare, not wanting to lose her night vision.

No one yelled or chased her or shot her or did any of the horrible things she was expecting. Instead, the night remained quiet except for the chirping and buzzing of nocturnal wild things.

Must be motion-activated, she decided, and her pent-up breath escaped in a whoosh. All the creatures around her went silent, and she hesitated again, hoping her relieved sigh hadn't been loud enough to catch someone's attention. A small walkway peeked from around a corner, taunting her with its normalcy.

She forced her feet forward, heading toward the small paved path. As she rounded the corner, Kaylee could see the lights from the front of the estate. She was hit by concurrent feelings of hope and fear, the need to get into a populated spot warring with the panic that someone knew, that she would be grabbed as soon as she stepped into the closest puddle of light—grabbed and taken to that horrible basement room. This time, she'd be the one tied to the chair, the one with the swollen face and empty eye socket and—

It was too much. Kaylee turned off her brain and jogged toward the front entrance, silently praying as hard as she could. The valet startled as Kaylee walked toward him. She'd lengthened her stride and was trying to project confidence, although she didn't know if she was succeeding.

"Can I...help you?" the valet asked, his voice

squeaking a little in the middle, even though he looked many years past puberty.

"Yes, please." *Oh God, not the quivery voice!* Kaylee pinched her arm hard, trying to shove back the tears. All that did was make her want to cry harder. "Could you get my car? It's the Infiniti Q50. And hurry? Please?"

Instead of running off like a good valet, he visibly swallowed and took a step closer. "Are you okay?"

"Yes, I just…I need to leave." Her brain frantically grabbed for an excuse to explain why she was running out of Martin Jovanovic's mansion, shaking and near tears and streaked with blood—*oh God, the blood.* How could she explain the blood? Quickly, she shoved her hands behind her back and hoped that the stains on her dress wouldn't be that noticeable in the poor light. "My boyfriend's been cheating on me, so I broke up with him, but he'll be following me, and I need to be gone before he makes it out here and tries to convince me that he's the perfect guy that I thought he was, so if you could hurry, that would be great, and then you won't have to watch a really uncomfortable scene with yelling and tears and drama, okay?"

The valet blinked rapidly before turning and jogging away. Kaylee hoped he was heading toward the parked cars and not just running away from the crazy girl. Now that she was alone with only night sounds and the fading footsteps of the valet, she could hear her heartbeat pattering in her ears. She was breathing too fast, each inhale catching on a tiny bit of a sob.

"Calm down," she muttered. "Calm down, calm down, calm do—"

Someone grabbed her arm and yanked her toward the house.

CHAPTER 2

KAYLEE STUMBLED AS SHE WAS JERKED BACKWARD. SHE tried to get her feet under her, to get some leverage to pull away, but her heels and the force with which she was being hauled toward the door made it impossible. Sucking in a breath, she opened her mouth to scream, only to have a hand clamp over her face. The fingers around her forearm released, and she tried to twist away, but her captor caught her around the waist and lifted her off the ground.

They were headed for the front doorway, and she struggled harder as her panic boiled over. Images rushed through her mind—the tortured men, the blood on the floor, the instruments lined up so neatly, ready to be used. She couldn't go back in that house. If she did, she knew she wouldn't be coming back out.

Sinking her teeth into her captor's meaty palm, she squirmed and thrashed in his grip. Kaylee heard him swear, and she recognized Uncle Martin's voice. The knowledge that it was him, not hired muscle, not someone she could possibly convince to let her go, sent a fresh spear of terror through her. Ripping her arm free of his grip, she sent a hard elbow into his gut.

His breath wheezed out of his lungs at the blow, and she elbowed him again. This hit loosened the arm around her waist. The memory of a self-defense class she'd taken years ago rose in her mind, and she turned, bringing her fists up close to her face.

Martin was red-faced and panting, although she wasn't sure if it was from exertion or pain. His expression could only be called a snarl. It scared her, and she hesitated for the briefest second. His hands rose as if to grab her again, and the movement knocked her out of her paralysis.

Her knee slammed into his groin, and he yelled, his body folding in the middle as if to protect himself from another attack. Grabbing his head, she pushed it down as she raised her leg again. Kaylee felt his nose connect with her kneecap, felt it crunch and flatten, but it happened too fast for her to cringe away. Blood poured from his broken nose, and his eyes rolled up as if he were about to pass out.

With a groan, he fell to his knees, and Kaylee ran. The valet had just gotten out of the driver's seat of her car and was now frozen in place, his gaze locked on Martin struggling to his feet. Kaylee shoved the valet out of the way as she dove into the car, and he stumbled back a few steps, just far enough that she could shut the door.

"Stop her!" Despite the nasally edge to his voice, Martin's fury was obvious. Looking confused, the valet reached toward the door handle. Fumbling the gearshift into drive, Kaylee stomped on the gas pedal.

With a squeal of tires, the car shot forward, leaving an enraged Martin behind her.

Kaylee couldn't keep her leg still. It bounced up and down, betraying her nerves. If the room where the desk sergeant had brought her had been bigger than the tiniest of closets, she would've paced, but she'd scarcely be able to fit in two strides before running into a wall.

Shifting in her chair, she pressed both hands on top of her thigh, trying to physically stop the nervous twitch. It didn't work. With a shaky sigh, she gave up on keeping her jittery leg still and glanced around the room.

Besides her very hard chair, there was a small table— barely bigger than a kid's desk—and a second chair. A detective was supposed to come in to talk to her. As soon as Kaylee had mentioned the name *Martin Jovanovic*, the cop who'd brought her to the interrogation closet had said that Detective Grailley would want to speak with her. At least the cop had let her go to the bathroom first to wash up, and he'd given her a department hoodie that was warm and covered the worst of the bloodstains on her dress.

She wondered if there was already an ongoing investigation into Martin's activities. Kaylee hoped so. It would take some of the focus off her. She wouldn't have to be the main witness, the only source of information…Martin's main target. The thought of Jovanovic coming after her, seeking revenge and her silence, made her have to bite her lip to hold back a frightened sound. The tiny room felt claustrophobic, and Kaylee couldn't sit still anymore.

She shot to her feet just as the door opened and a uniformed cop entered. A little bit of tension left her body now that someone was in the room with her. Kaylee didn't think she could've taken waiting alone for much longer. The officer was young and very tall, with shorn, light-brown hair and an attempted mustache. His gaze fixed on her for a long moment before he looked over his shoulder.

Kaylee's skin prickled with heat before flashing cold, her initial relief overtaken by alarm. There was something wrong. Maybe she was basing her cop knowledge on too many TV shows, but Kaylee was pretty sure that a detective wouldn't be wearing a uniform. There was also a tenseness in the officer's posture, in the way he glanced behind him as if checking to make sure no one else was around. Her brain spun as she tried to think clearly, tried to figure out what she was going to do. All her instincts were screaming *Danger!*

He refocused on her, his light-blue eyes cold and strangely familiar. "Let's go."

"Where?" she asked, even as she reluctantly moved toward him. Although she wasn't sure what she was going to do, Kaylee knew she couldn't accomplish anything in this small room. With the creepy cop blocking the door, she couldn't escape it, either.

He didn't answer. Instead, he stepped back, allowing her to leave the room. As she passed close to him, her gaze dropped to the gold name tag pinned to his starched uniform shirt pocket.

L. Jovanovic.

Numb, Kaylee walked down the narrow hallway, followed closely by Martin's...what? Nephew? Son? Much younger brother? His hand latched around her upper arm, exactly where Martin had grabbed her earlier, and she flinched. Her breath wanted to come quickly, but she couldn't show her fear. Her lungs burned as she forced each inhale to slow, each exhale to come out silently, rather than in a terrified sob.

Right before they reached the end of the corridor, the cop steered her toward a door marked Stairs. Just as she'd known she wouldn't survive if she'd gone back into Martin's mansion, Kaylee knew, deep in her gut, not to enter the stairway with L. Jovanovic.

Forcing herself to stay outwardly relaxed, to stay compliant and pliable under his hold, Kaylee stepped toward the door, her hands reaching for the release bar. Before she pressed it, though, she wrenched free of his grip and sprinted for the next hallway. She needed to find other people, other cops. L. Jovanovic had taken her out of the room where she'd been trapped like a mouse in a tiny box. He was steering her away from cameras, away from somewhere they could be seen. He wanted to get her alone to do whatever he was planning, and Kaylee knew her survival depended on preventing that.

When she pulled away, he didn't shout, didn't call out after her, reinforcing her suspicion that he was trying to avoid drawing attention. The silence doubled her fear. She expected him to grab her hair or the back of her dress at any second. Dragging in ragged breaths, she ran faster.

At the intersecting corridor, she turned left without looking, tearing down the hall. She fought the urge to glance behind her, knowing it would only slow her down, make her stumble, allow him to catch her. Instead, she sprinted down the quiet hallway, desperately wishing for someone—anyone—to step into view.

As if she'd summoned them, two uniformed cops

rounded the corner. Kaylee tried to stop, but her momentum carried her forward. She would've crashed into one of the officers if he hadn't caught her by the shoulders.

"Whoa," he said, steadying her. "What's your rush?"

With the two other cops there, she risked a glance behind her and caught a glimpse of Jovanovic as he ducked back into the hallway she'd just escaped. Turning to the officers, she took a breath, ready to blurt out the entire story.

Before she could, the tortured man's words came back to her, and her mouth snapped shut. What if they didn't believe her? After all, they worked with Officer Jovanovic—maybe even were friends with him. Worse yet, what if Martin had them in his back pocket? Although the station was huge, employing hundreds of officers, it would be just her luck that these two cops were ones on the Jovanovic payroll.

"Sorry," she said, stalling for time. "I didn't see you there."

"No problem. I'm used to beautiful women throwing themselves at me." The other cop snorted, but the one holding her shoulders ignored the skeptical sound. "Were you here visiting someone?"

Kaylee seized on the excuse with both hands. "Yes! Um…I mean, yes. My boyfriend. But we started arguing, and…" Trailing off, she shrugged, and the cops exchanged a look. Sweat prickled along her hairline. It sounded so weak, but the fake explanation had worked on the valet, and her brain was too scattered to come up with a better story.

Even though she'd scrubbed her hands in the bathroom until they were raw, and the sweatshirt covered most of her bloodstained dress, she felt like everything she'd seen, everything she'd experienced, was written on her forehead. The cops would never believe her. They'd march her back to that tiny interrogation room and leave her there, vulnerable. If that happened, she was dead. Literally.

"Jovanovic?" one of them asked, and her whole body jerked with shock. *He knew!* Her body went hot and then cold, and her mind filled with panicked escape plans before all thought was overwhelmed with the need to run. "He's the boyfriend? No loss there. Pretty girl like you can do better than Logan." The two cops exchanged another glance.

"*Anyone* would be better than Jovanovic," the other one muttered.

The pounding of her heart slowed as their words registered, and she sucked in an audible breath, relief slamming into her. They didn't know. They'd seen Logan Jovanovic darting away, so they assumed he was her boyfriend. The cops were eyeing her curiously. Shaking off the remaining blanket of terror, she tried to piece together a sentence that made sense.

"I know." Her voice still shook. "I'm learning he's not the Disney prince I thought he was."

One of the cops turned away, obviously hiding a laugh in a cough, while the other fought a smile. Giving her shoulders a squeeze, he dropped his hands. "You're right about that. Logan's definitely not any kind of prince. Want us to walk you out?"

"Sure." Kaylee couldn't quite manage a smile. She was close, so close, to escape that it almost made everything more terrifying. "That would be great. Thank you."

The two cops fell in next to her as they walked through the maze of hallways. Although it was late, they passed quite a few people, both in uniform and street clothes. Kaylee was even more grateful for her escort; she would've never found her way out of the sprawling station otherwise.

"So, you're definitely dumping Logan, then?" one of her chaperones asked.

"Oh yes." An image of Noah flashed through her mind, but it was quickly replaced by the mental picture of the tortured men. "We're done."

The cop patted her shoulder blade. "Smart."

Kaylee didn't feel smart. She felt anxious and scared out of her mind and hunted. Everything she'd done so far had been based in stupid panic. She'd have to start thinking three steps ahead, or Martin Jovanovic was going to find her.

She needed to start being smart. Otherwise, she was dead.

The cops ushered her to the lobby, and she walked through it with purpose, pretending like she wasn't fighting the urge to hide behind the artificial ficus plant in the corner. As soon as she pushed through the doors, though, she darted for the closest patch of shadows. The parking area was well lit, the sodium bulbs spotlighting the few cars, including hers, scattered around the lot.

Martin would know what she drove. Logan Jovanovic would be able to pull up her license and registration, so they'd get her plate number and her vehicle description and her address. Logan could probably even put a BOLO out on her, could say anything—that she was wanted for questioning, that she had mental issues, that she was a danger to herself and others—to make it so that any cop in the city could pull her over and bring her to the station for questioning…to be served up on a platter to men who wanted her dead.

As she wiped clammy palms down the sides of her borrowed sweatshirt, Kaylee tried to think. She couldn't go home, and she couldn't stay in her car—at least not in the city, and maybe not even the county. How far did Martin's influence stretch? The tortured man had said that he had a wide reach. Did that mean she wouldn't be safe anywhere?

Her breaths were short, with an audible gasp at the end of each, and she clamped her jaw, trying to quiet them. A car turned into the lot, its headlights traveling across the building in a slow sweep. Kaylee froze, closing her eyes in an automatic, silly attempt to turn herself invisible.

Panic built in her chest until it was almost painful, pushing at her ribs and screaming at her to run. Her nails dug into her palms as she fisted her hands at her sides. Her eyelids stayed dark, though. When she forced her eyes to open, she saw the car had parked, and someone climbed out of the driver's side.

Kaylee watched as the woman strode toward a side door and used a key card to let herself in. Only when the door closed with a thud did Kaylee drag in a deep breath, her lungs aching.

She couldn't stay there. Someone would see her, and then the questions would start. Casting a frantic look around, she hurried along the front of the building, staying in the sparse shadows but still feeling horribly exposed the entire time. The sounds of not-too-distant traffic scraped against her raw nerves. She was used to the city, to the constant noise and movement, but now every sound made her flinch. She knew Martin Jovanovic was already searching for her. It was just a matter of time before he caught her.

Ducking around the corner of the building, she smelled the dumpster before she saw it. Her initial instinct was to move away from the cloying stench of rotting garbage, but she forced herself to slip into the darkness behind the trash bin instead. Kaylee crouched in the shadows, feeling incredibly exposed despite the hulking dumpster in front of her. Fumbling in her purse, she pulled out her cell. Her hands were shaking so badly that it took a few tries before she could tap the right name on her screen.

"Kaylee?" Penny's voice was rough with sleep. "What's wrong?"

It was so hard to say anything after what she'd been through.

"Kaylee?" The rising worry in Penny's tone helped Kaylee push out the words.

"I'm in trouble," she blurted out, her voice sounding too loud. "I can't come home."

"Do you need a ride?" All sleepiness was out of Penny's voice now, and she sounded like she was in the problem-solving mode she used for her job at the women's shelter. "Where are you? I'll pick you up."

"You can't." Her voice broke, and the second word came out soundless. Clearing her throat, Kaylee tried again. "You can't. I can't go home."

"What do you mean?" Under the practical snap was a thread of worry. "Of course you can come home. Just tell me where you are, and I'll pick you up."

The thought of Martin or Logan or any of the Jovanovic army spotting Penny helping her sent a fresh surge of panic through Kaylee, and her knees almost buckled. "No! No, Penny. He knows where I live. If he doesn't now, he will soon. Mom is gone, and I don't have any other family, so you're the only one he can use to get to me. Noah might tell him that, not knowing... You need to leave. Go see your mom in Texas, or stay at work for a few days—will they let you do that?"

"Kaylee. You're scaring me."

The hitch in Kaylee's breathing was back, but her mention of Penny's work sparked an idea. "What would you tell one of your clients if she said she needed to disappear?"

"Oh God, Kaylee..." Penny groaned, fear leaking into her voice. "How bad is it?"

"Bad. What would you tell her? You have to know a way out." Now that a slight hope had risen, Kaylee was almost frantic to hear Penny's answer. There had to be a solution. Kaylee couldn't accept that they'd find her and kill her. Penny would have a way to run, to hide. "Please, Penny? What would you tell her?"

"Does she have money? Any resources?"

"I can get it." Kaylee fingered the diamond pendant lying cool at her throat, grateful that she'd worn the entire set—necklace, ring, and earrings. Her car, too... Now that the Jovanovics were looking for it, it was useless to her.

There was a tiny pause, but it felt like hours passed before Penny spoke again. "I'd tell her to call Mateo Espina."

"Mateo Espina?" Repeating the name, Kaylee felt a

tiny tendril of hope worm its way through the terror that swamped her. "He can make me disappear?"

"He's good." Although Penny sounded stoic, Kaylee could hear the faint tremble in her friend's words, and that shake made tears flood her eyes. She blinked them back. It wasn't the time to cry, even if she was terrified and hiding behind a police station dumpster in a bloodstained dress. "The best disappearance expert that I know."

"Do you know a lot?"

"Just Mr. Espina."

"That's comforting, then."

At Penny's choked laugh, Kaylee really wanted to cry again. That short bit of banter made her painfully aware how much she was going to miss her friend. Squeezing her eyes closed, she fought against the need to curl up in a ball and sob her eyes out—either that, or ask Penny to pick her up so Kaylee could hide out in her condo and pretend the hellish night had never happened.

Sucking in a slow breath, she opened her eyes again. She couldn't do that to Penny. Her friend was in enough danger as it was. No matter how much it sucked, Kaylee needed to act like a responsible adult and take care of herself. She had to be brave and strong and smart. If she wanted to live, she needed to push past the paralyzing fear and save her own ass.

"What's this magician's number?"

CHAPTER 3

"No."

Hugh didn't think he'd ever seen Blessard so angry, not even when he'd discovered the Tight-Buns Tommy blow-up doll dressed in his uniform sitting at his desk. "But, LT, the Rack and Ruin MC will be passing through town in less than an hour. No question they'll be hauling coke from Denver to Dresden."

"I know this," Blessard snapped. "The question is, how do you know this? You're on mandatory medical leave. You have a goddamned bullet hole in your goddamned leg. Your radio is locked in my desk. Want to tell me, Murdoch, how you still know every word that comes out of the dispatchers' mouths?"

"Guess I just have a sixth sense for when I'm needed?" From the way Blessard's face went from dark red to purple, Hugh figured that the lieutenant didn't care for his answer. "Forget how I heard about it. The R and Rs are going to have twenty or so riders, plus support vehicles. Lexi's our only narcotic-detection dog, and there's not enough time to borrow a K9 from Denver. Even if they left now, they couldn't get here in less than an hour. Let us help, LT. My leg's fine. It's a waste having us sit at home, watching daytime television. Besides, there are only so many episodes of *Tattered Hearts* that I can stand without losing my mind."

His lieutenant's face showed no sympathy. "If you show up on scene, Officer Murdoch, I will arrest you." The corner of his mouth twitched. "And your little dog, too."

"Really, LT?" Frustration nipped at Hugh, making it hard to stay silent, even though he knew he'd lost the battle already. "*Wizard of Oz* jokes? Way to add insult to injury."

All hints of humor disappeared from Blessard's face. "Do not go to this call, Officer. You have three more weeks before we'll even consider letting you return to desk duty, and that's with a doctor's okay. Until then, if you even *think* about popping up at another call uninvited, I'm going to add another mandatory month to your leave. Got it?"

Blowing out a hard breath, Hugh resisted the urge to continue arguing. It was done. If he kept pushing, he knew he'd risk not only missing the next seven weeks of calls, but his job with the Monroe Police Department. "Fine."

"Now get out of my office."

As he drove away from the station, Hugh glanced at Lexi, who was riding shotgun. "Where are we headed? Home?" He grimaced at the idea. "Nah. I'd just pace and then bitch because my leg is sore. Besides, *Tattered Hearts* is a rerun today." Lexi turned her head, her attention caught by something in the VFW's parking lot. "Good idea, Lex. Let's go bug Jules. If she's not working today, we'll just get food. It'll be a win-win."

He parked in front of the VFW and turned off the

engine. Silence settled over the lot. The back of his neck prickled, and Hugh rubbed it, fighting the urge to turn and look out the back window of his pickup. He knew what he'd see if he did—absolutely nothing. Apparently, a side effect of getting shot in the leg was paranoia.

In the seat next to him, Lexi growled.

"Seriously? Are we having a mutual psychotic break, then?" he grumbled, although he followed his K9 partner's gaze across the VFW parking lot and saw exactly what he expected: *nothing*. Rolling down his window, he listened. The street was as still and quiet as it always was so early in the morning. All he could hear out his open window was the first twittering of dawn birdsong and the howling, ever-present wind.

Several businesses had already closed for the winter, and the buildings looked abandoned. The town emptied out every fall, occupants and tourists fleeing to ski towns or warm beaches to escape the cold and storms. Hugh couldn't blame them. As one of the few year-round police officers in Monroe, Colorado, he could attest that the place got pretty dull in the winter, when the few hard-core residents who remained got snowed in on a regular basis. With mountain passes bookending the town, the highway in either direction was closed more often than not.

The blackened ruin of the town diner a few buildings down from the VFW added to the post-apocalyptic feel. After an explosion destroyed it a few weeks earlier, the diner's owner had moved into the VFW temporarily so that the Monroe residents weren't forced to go without their morning eggs and coffee. She was planning to rebuild the diner, but the work wouldn't start until spring. The construction crews abandoned town before winter just as quickly as everyone else.

Hugh frowned at the front of the VFW. Things had gone to hell over the past month. He missed the diner. In fact, he missed a lot of things he'd taken for granted a month ago: sitting in his usual booth, going to work, being pain free.

After checking to make sure Lexi's window fan was on, he headed toward the VFW entrance. His scalp and the back of his neck began to prickle again, warning him that there were eyes on him. Slowing his stride, he surreptitiously glanced around, checking the surrounding buildings and the street.

No one was there.

Everything was silent, as if even the ever-present wind was holding its breath. The scuff of his boots against the pavement sounded too loud, and he stopped, this time not caring who saw him looking around. Nothing was moving, though. The entire town was still.

With a swallowed groan, he turned back toward the VFW. He'd been sensing these phantom stalkers for days now. Boredom and inactivity were obviously driving him insane. He'd only taken one more step toward the makeshift diner when Lexi started barking. Pivoting, he half jogged, half limped toward his truck. It was one thing to ignore his own instincts, but there was no way he was going to ignore Lexi's. His partner was never wrong.

At the truck, he hurried to attach her lead to her harness, clipping it to the ring he used when they were going to do a search. Lexi quivered with anticipation, already in drive and ready to go.

As soon as he stepped back and gave the command,

she was bounding toward the building across the street. It was a historic brick building that had been a bank at one point. Now, it housed a laundromat—closed for the winter—on the first level and several offices above.

When Lexi led him to the alley behind the building, Hugh was relieved. Without a uniform or a badge, snooping around the front of the laundromat was likely to attract suspicion from passersby. His relief disappeared, however, when Lexi led him to a back door and promptly sat, looking at him expectantly, waiting for him to open the door so she could continue tracking.

The door was locked. Hugh pulled his phone from his pocket but then hesitated. Everyone else was dealing with the Rack and Ruin bust. He wasn't chasing a suspect or following a confirmed tip; he wasn't even on duty. All he had was his K9 partner tracking an unknown scent. If this caused officers to be pulled off the drug bust, he could be endangering lives. They needed all the help they could get with that motorcycle club.

Dropping his phone back in his pocket, he pulled out his lockpick set.

His uncle Gavin had taught him how to open his first lock when Hugh was eight. It was the bathroom door, so it wasn't the trickiest of locks, but they'd moved on to the front door dead bolt next. After that, Gavin had shown him the trick to opening school lockers, handcuffs, and car doors before he'd advanced to disabling alarm systems.

Uncle Gavin was currently serving a six-year sentence at Colorado State Penitentiary for second-degree burglary. When Hugh was eleven, he'd been home when the cops had come for Gavin the first time. After the arrest, one of the officers had walked over to where a terrified Hugh had been watching on the front steps. The policeman had sat down next to Hugh, given him a rub-on tattoo of a badge, and explained the importance of leaving other people's stuff alone. When the cops had left with Gavin, Hugh had decided to become a police officer. After all, the front of the squad car seemed like a much better place to be than the back.

As Hugh casually glanced over his shoulder, checking to make sure the coast was clear, he gave silent thanks for Uncle Gavin's lessons. The dead bolt was a simple single-cylinder style, something he could've handled with a couple of bobby pins. With his professional torque and pick, it only took seconds for Hugh to gently press the keyhole pins into place and unlock the door.

After another quick look around, he turned the knob and slipped into a small, dim entry. Lexi brushed past his leg in her eagerness to get inside and immediately trotted up the stairs. Drawing his gun, Hugh followed, keeping his footsteps as quiet as possible.

At the top of the stairs, Lexi took a left. Hugh paused, looking at the three closed doors to the right. Someone could be hiding in one of those offices, and Hugh didn't want to turn his back until he checked them. His hand tightened on the leash as the impatient dog hauled against him in her hurry to follow the scent. An almost silent command brought her back to him, albeit reluctantly, and they headed down the hall to the right. Keeping an eye out for anything behind them, he listened as he walked softly toward the first closed door. All he heard was the click of Lexi's nails and the occasional creaks of the elderly wood floors under his weight.

The first knob resisted turning under his grip. Locked. He tried the second and the third. Both were locked as well. Only then did he allow Lexi to lead them down the hallway in the other direction. She surged forward eagerly and sat in front of the first door on the right.

This doorknob turned easily under his fingers. Pushing open the door, he stepped into the room in the same movement, gun up and ready, turning right and then pivoting to the left to check the entire space.

It was empty. The small area had been an office at some point, but now the only evidence of its former occupation was the cables that snaked out of the wall, the ends sprawled uselessly into dust and cobwebs. The dirty blinds were down, but the slats were at an angle, as if someone wanted to look outside without anyone being able to see in.

Lexi trotted to the window, sniffing along the baseboard. As he moved to follow, Hugh noticed the dust on the floor was smudged. There weren't any shoe prints that he could make out. Instead, it looked more like someone had knelt or sat next to the window. He walked to the spot where the dust had been rubbed away and looked around the room. There were other marks in the dust, including where his own boots had scuffed, but nothing as distinct as the area where he stood. Hugh crouched awkwardly, extending his injured leg out straight, and peered through the slats of the blinds.

He had a clear view of the VFW parking lot and the top of his pickup.

A door slammed. Shoving to his feet and ignoring the spike of pain in his thigh, Hugh ran out of the room. Lexi quickly took the lead as they tore through the hallway and down the stairs. Hugh shoved the door open, and he and Lexi tumbled out into the sunshine.

Squinting as his eyes struggled to adjust to the brightness after the dim, dusty interior of the building, Hugh swiveled his head back and forth, looking for whoever had just exited the building. There was no sign of anyone, no sound, not even a chirp of a bird. Lexi wasn't hauling on her leash. Instead, she made uncertain circles, facing one direction and then another. Hugh swore under his breath.

Whoever had been in that building, whoever'd been *watching* him, was long gone.

═══════════

This new life Mr. Espina had given her was a nightmare.

Sure, it beat getting strangled by a Jovanovic and being buried in a shallow, unmarked grave, but it still wasn't good. There was one bathroom. One single, solitary, *old* bathroom…for six people. It was as if all her struggles, all her hard work, had been erased, leaving her as poor and powerless and trapped as her twelve-year-old self had been.

And this time, there was no escape.

Turning from the ancient claw-foot tub, she found five pairs of eyes watching her with everything from friendly interest to deep suspicion. Kaylee forced a smile. "I like the lion feet."

"Me too!" the youngest, who had been introduced as Dee, blurted out, bouncing in place. She quieted quickly when the oldest boy—and the most silently hostile of the bunch—put a hand on her shoulder. Although Dee went obediently still, she snuck Kaylee a quick, conspiratorial smile.

As if she could read Kaylee's mind, Jules—the only adult there except for Kaylee—made a face. "I know. One bathroom sucks. We'll make it work, though. I'm up really early, and the kids are quick getting ready for school. Dee takes a bath at night, so that's one less person hogging the tub in the mornings. Did Mr. Esp— Uh, do you have any idea where you'll be working?"

"Not yet." Kaylee fought to keep her expression untroubled. After going over the new persona that Mateo Espina had created for her, Kaylee had wanted to cry. No, she'd wanted to scream and kick things and roll around on the floor and have a complete and utter tantrum like a two-year-old. The disappearance expert had stripped her of her six years of hard-earned college education, both her undergrad and grad-school work, and replaced it all with a GED. A *GED*. She didn't even get to keep her status as high-school valedictorian. All of those double shifts at the factory and sleepless nights spent studying had been for nothing.

She took a deep breath, reminding herself for the hundredth time that a life of minimum wage and limited personal space was a small price to pay for not getting tortured to death.

"I have to go job hunting," she added. Her tone was as flat as she felt.

"Okay, well, just let us know when you need the bathroom in the mornings, and we'll work around your schedule." One of the teenage twins made a sound of protest, but a look from Jules had him turning it into a cough.

"What'd you do?" the other twin asked.

Kaylee looked at him quizzically, but Jules must have understood his meaning, because she gave him a stern glare. "Tio, zip it."

It finally registered with Kaylee what he'd been asking. Although he didn't press the question, everyone except for Jules was staring at her with varying degrees of interest and wariness. Not for the first time, she wondered why Jules and her siblings had had to run. Mr. Espina had told her that they'd take Kaylee in because Jules owed him a favor. Kaylee figured that had to mean that he'd helped this family disappear, too. Had they witnessed something, like Kaylee had? They stared back at her, obviously wondering the same thing about her. From the wary looks they were giving her, she could only imagine what heinous crimes they thought she'd committed to be forced to change her identity and share their house.

"Nothing." Kaylee figured she'd better say something before they mentally convicted her of mass murder. "I just…saw something. Something bad that a powerful man didn't want me to see."

"Like a mob hit?" the other twin, Ty, asked.

Kaylee couldn't stop a wince when his words touched a little too close to home. "No."

"A drive-by shooting?" Apparently, the twins weren't going to leave it alone.

"An assassination?"

"Someone planting a bomb?"

"A kidnapping?"

Everyone went still, the air thick with tension, until Jules broke it with a clap that made every single person in the hallway flinch. "Sorry. How would you like to see your room?"

Honestly, Kaylee would rather not see her room, since she could only imagine what it would be like. It was in this collapsing house of horrors, after all. Jules looked so desperately optimistic, however, that Kaylee couldn't find it in herself to crush her hostess. Instead of allowing her true feelings to escape, she swallowed back all the emotion that had been building from the moment she walked into Martin's basement room.

"Sounds good."

Kaylee followed Jules to the base of the stairs, the kids close behind them. Since no one could see her face, Kaylee allowed her forced smile to drop. It probably just looked like she'd been baring her teeth anyway. Maybe once they'd shown her to her room, she could lock herself inside and have the shrieking, stomping, pillow-punching tantrum she'd been dying to have since her life had been stolen from her. The entire time Kaylee had been traveling to Monroe, Colorado, she'd been terrified. Everyone—from the gas station attendant to the woman in the next public bathroom stall—had been a potential associate of Martin Jovanovic.

A potential assassin.

Kaylee's foot had just touched the first step when the front door swung open, startling her into turning. There, framed in the doorway, backlit by the afternoon sun, stood a cop with a police dog by his side.

Officer Jovanovic's face flashed in her mind, and her head spun with instant panic. That had been so fast. She'd just arrived at the supposed safe house, and Martin had already found her. Kaylee grabbed at the banister to catch her balance. Her fingers felt thick and useless, but she managed to grip the wood. She braced, waiting for the shouting, for the cop or the dog to tackle her and handcuff her and put her in the squad car and drive her who-knew-where to her grisly death. Everything in front of her went gray.

"Viggy!" Dee ran to the dog, petting him as he pressed his head into her stomach. The cop smiled down at them.

Jules brushed by her as she headed for the cop. Kaylee sucked back a protest, wanting to scream for her to run, not to get closer, not to grab his hand and smile up at him in greeting.

Kaylee squeezed her eyes closed and then opened them again, but the scene in front of her didn't change. Jules and the cop were still making googly eyes at each other. Kaylee could almost see the cartoon hearts circling the pair. He didn't look like a cop on a mission to hunt down Martin Jovanovic's enemy. He looked like a guy in love.

Martin hadn't sent him here. She wouldn't be hauled away in handcuffs…not now, at least. As the realization sunk in, her panic retreated enough for her to pull in a shaky breath. Blinking several times, she managed to clear her vision, and her grip on the banister eased.

The officer looked at Kaylee, and his expression hardened. The muscles that had just relaxed ever so slightly stiffened again.

"Who are you?" he barked.

Her heart thundered in her chest, and she swallowed. *You're ready for this*, she reminded herself firmly. She'd repeated the name and backstory over and over to herself for hours as she drove across deserts and mountains. "Grace Robinson."

"Where are you from?"

"Most recently? Bangor, Maine."

"Why are you here?" The kids' heads turned with each question and answer, following the exchange like they were watching a tennis match.

"Theo," Jules broke in firmly. "Stop interrogating her. She's not one of your suspects. Grace was my friend in high school. She's going to stay here for a while."

For a brief moment, his too-intense gaze left Kaylee—*not Kaylee*, she thought for the umpteenth time, *Grace*—and landed on Jules. Grace took the opportunity to suck in a few long breaths and try to quiet her shaking hands. Too soon, that laser focus was locked on her again.

"Why don't you have an accent?"

"What?" Accent? Did people from Maine have an accent? Mr. Espina had let her choose her pretend city of origin, and Kaylee had chosen Bangor because it seemed like a nice place, a peaceful place. She hadn't realized there was an accent.

"You went to high school with Jules."

"Yes." The word came out slowly. Kaylee felt like she was stepping into a trap.

"In Arkansas."

Oh! That accent! "Just for a few years. My parents moved around a lot."

"Military?"

"No." Kaylee didn't have enough knowledge about the different military branches and rankings and everything else she'd be expected to know to pull off that lie. "They were just restless."

"Restless? Is that another term for avoiding arrest?"

"What? No!" She couldn't believe she was offended

for her imaginary parents. Her real mom had lived in the same horrible basement apartment for twenty-four years until she died of liver failure five years ago. Grace hadn't known her real dad. "They didn't do anything wrong." Neither had she, but she was paying for Martin Jovanovic's sins. A new surge of rage filled her, and she shoved it back. She could have her pillow-thumping tantrum later. Right now, she needed to focus on not making the cop suspicious…well, *more* suspicious than he already was.

"Why are you here?"

The jump back to his original question threw her off-balance, and her answer came out sounding hesitant. "Just visiting Jules."

He waited, watching her steadily.

Racking her brain for a reason he would believe, all she could think about was that room in Martin's house. Grace decided to go with the truth—in a somewhat altered form. "And I needed to get away from my ex-boyfriend."

By the way his face hardened even more, she knew right away that it had been the wrong thing to say. "He's dangerous?" he barked.

"No. Just a jerk." Noah wasn't a jerk, though. His uncle was—well, *jerk* was a very mild word for what Martin was—but Noah had been nothing but sweet to her. Although her common sense told her that he had to have known his uncle did very bad things, another part of her felt guilty for convicting him without even talking to him about it. Maybe he was ignorant of his uncle's true nature, or maybe Noah didn't know exactly how deadly Martin really was. Grace just couldn't believe that Noah—kind, considerate Noah—would be okay with having her killed. There was no way he could have hidden a monster of that magnitude under his perfect-boyfriend exterior.

"Will he follow you?"

Grace yanked her mind away from her real ex-boyfriend and refocused on her fake one. "No. He's lazy, as well as a jerk. He's a lazy jerk."

Jules ducked her head in a way that made Grace think she was hiding a smile. For some reason, that, plus the affectionate hold Jules still had on the cop's hand, eased a few of Grace's fears. Jules wasn't scared of him, and she wasn't acting as if he was one wrong answer from hauling Grace away to her death, so Grace allowed herself to believe that this conversation would end well.

And that was when the second cop showed up.

CHAPTER 4

As Hugh drove away from the VFW, his discovery ate at him. The last few days, he'd just dismissed the feeling that he was being watched as paranoia, so finding evidence that someone quite possibly *had* been spying on him was deeply disturbing. Lexi whined from the passenger seat.

"It's okay," he said, trying to keep his voice calm. By the dog's anxious expression, he wasn't succeeding very well. "It's probably nothing. After all, who'd want to stalk me? I'm just not that interesting." Drumming his fingers against the wheel with frustration and pent-up adrenaline, he frowned and glanced at his injured leg. "Especially lately."

His spare radio—the radio he was not supposed to have—beeped, and Hugh jumped. Immediately, he felt like an idiot. Since when did the radio startle him? He was normally calm and steady. This whole mess was turning him into a nervous, trembling Chihuahua. On the radio, Theo informed dispatch that he'd be taking his lunch break and gave his location as Jules's address. Without hesitating, Hugh made a U-turn and headed in that direction. If Theo thought he'd be getting some alone time with his hot girlfriend, then he was in for an unpleasant surprise. Hugh needed to talk to Theo about the situation immediately. He smiled a little. For some reason, ruining Theo's fun made Hugh just a little bit happier.

Lexi was staring at him from the passenger seat.

"What?" he asked defensively. "I need to talk to my partner about this whole potential stalker deal. Besides, I haven't seen Jules's rug rats in a while. I'm trying to be a good uncle Hugh, that's all."

The dog turned to look out the window.

"Whatever," Hugh grumbled. "You're always so judgmental."

Lexi ignored him, her attention focused on a Lab playing in a yard they were passing.

After bumping across the extremely long and poorly maintained driveway that led to Jules's house, biting back curses every time his leg was jostled, Hugh parked behind Theo's squad car. As he turned on Lexi's window fan, he saw Theo standing in the open doorway, facing in. Hugh bounded up the steps, ignoring the shooting pains in his thigh—as well as the unwelcoming glare Theo shot him—and tossed an arm over his partner's stiff shoulders.

"Jules wouldn't even let you in?" he asked in mock concern, taking great pleasure in Theo's obvious irritation. This was so much more entertaining than he'd expected. "Well, we all knew it couldn't last. I mean, look at her, and then…well…" Hugh dropped his arm so he could gesture at Theo's unamused form. "There's you. And you can't even say you have a good personality."

"Hugh, stop," Jules scolded, although he could tell she was holding back a laugh.

Hugh winked at her and then glanced at the crowd

of kids. His smile of greeting slipped away as his gaze locked on the woman standing on the stairs. He didn't know her.

If he'd ever seen her before, he would've remembered.

She was gorgeous, tall and sleek and just Hugh's type. Her hair was true black, the kind that showed blue highlights in the sun, and her tan skin emphasized the unusual light-brown color of her eyes. They were lioness eyes. Terrified eyes.

Eyes of a woman with a secret.

Hugh bit back a curse. Something wasn't right. He'd only recently agreed to quit looking into Jules's background, and now another mystery woman had landed in his town, with scared eyes and a gorgeous body and... no! The last thing he needed was to get sucked into this woman's mess, whatever it may be.

Shaking off the strange spell that had come over him, Hugh mentally hunted for words, even as he marveled at his tongue-tied silence. Hugh didn't *do* silence. Even in life-or-death situations, he'd never had words fail him before. Right now, though, with those lioness eyes watching him, he scrambled to find something to say until finally settling on the very lame "You're new."

"Yes." Even her voice was beautiful. Husky and low and hinting of late-night, sexy things.

Hugh cleared his throat. *Focus.* "That was a hint. For you to tell me your name."

"Grace Robinson."

Lie. He'd always been good at sniffing out lies. It was a useful talent to have as a cop. For some reason, though, when the lie came from her mouth, it stung. His eyes narrowed. If she wanted a battle, he'd give her one—and he'd win. "And where are you from, *Grace*?"

"Lots of places." She pushed her thick fall of hair over her shoulder without dropping eye contact, and Hugh had to fight not to get distracted. It was just that her hair was so *shiny*. It was like she'd stepped out of a shampoo commercial, all gloss and attitude. With a huge effort, he kept his gaze locked with hers and focused on the fact that she had just dodged his question.

Propping a shoulder against the doorframe, he gave her his best shark's smile. "That sounds fascinating. Tell me more. You can start with details, specific details."

She leaned her hip against the railing with an impatient huff. He wasn't sure if she was imitating him unconsciously or mocking him. Either way, the movement made his skin prickle with awareness. "Why do you care?"

"I'm a curious guy."

Grace cleared her throat while muttering, "Stalker."

"I prefer the term 'future friend.'" He smirked, getting a strange charge from the way she narrowed her eyes at him. "You're making this get-to-know-each-other phase much more difficult than it needs to be. Let me show you how it should be done. I'm Officer Hugh Murdoch, and I live in Monroe, Colorado." He held out his hands in a *ta-da!* gesture. "Now you go."

"My name is Grace Robinson." She bit off the end of each word. "And you can kiss—"

"Okay!" Jules interrupted in a loud, fake-cheery voice.

"Can I go next?" Dee asked. "I'm Dee—"

"Nope. Remember, we don't play Hugh's games.

They always end in tears." Jules shot a warning glance at Grace, who offered her an apologetic grimace in response. Hugh watched the interplay with interest. Whatever Grace's secrets were, he was sure that Jules was fully aware of them. From the expressions on the kids' faces, they were in the loop, too. If the *children* knew, then surely Hugh could figure it out. "Now that introductions are done, maybe we should move this out of the doorway?"

"We could," Hugh said, turning back to Grace. Every time he looked at her, her beauty kicked him in the face. "We could also continue sharing time."

Grace's shoulders drooped in a sigh as her gaze shifted to Theo. Hugh was instantly annoyed, and he opened his mouth to say something, anything that would bring her attention back to him. When that desire registered, he snapped his mouth shut. Why did this woman bring out the third-grade boy in him? What was he going to do next to get her attention? Tackle her in the sandbox?

The thought of tackling her, of feeling her under him, made his skin heat.

"As much as I'd love to do this whole interrogation thing again, could you just fill him in about me?" she asked Theo, sounding cranky. "I've been traveling for what feels like an eternity, and I'm tired. Jules, if you could just point in the direction of my room, I'd be forever grateful."

"I'll show you," Jules said, turning toward her. When she started heading Grace's way, Theo's grip on her hand brought her to a halt. With a gentle smile that Hugh knew Theo, the prickly bastard, did not in any way deserve, Jules squeezed his fingers before pulling free and heading up the stairs with Grace in tow. Hugh couldn't pull his eyes away until Grace was out of sight.

"What's the story?" he asked, when the most perfect rear view he'd ever seen had disappeared.

"Why are you here?"

"That's not the story." Hugh sighed with exaggerated patience, and he heard one of the twins give an amused snort. Ty, most likely. "I'm talking about Grace's story."

Although Theo still didn't look too happy, he relented. "High-school friend of Jules. Ex is a"—he glanced at the watching kids—"dirtbag."

"No accent."

"Moved a lot as a kid."

"Military?"

"Flaky parents."

"Most recent location?"

"Bangor, Maine."

"None of that's true."

Theo shot him a look that told him to shut it, reminding Hugh of their fascinated audience—their fascinated, *scared* audience. His jaw tightened. If the kids knew what was really going on, that meant Not-Grace was involved in whatever mess Jules and her family had escaped, which meant it all fell under the same no-digging rule as Jules. When Theo had told him to stop investigating Jules, Hugh had let it go, despite his inner cop's objections. He already knew that he wouldn't be able to do the same with the beautiful woman who called herself Grace. Their hostile, yet intriguing, encounter had lasted just a few minutes, but that had been enough. Hugh's interest was caught. He wouldn't be able to rest until he knew who she really was. "Nope," he said. "Not happening."

"A word." Theo jerked his head toward the door.

They descended the porch steps in mutual silence, as Hugh tried to hide the way pain shot through his thigh with each downward step. For whatever reason, going down stairs was even more painful than going up. They ended up next to Hugh's pickup, out of earshot of the kids, who were now watching from the doorway.

"C'mon." Hugh tried to keep his voice low. "How are we supposed to ignore that every word out of that woman's mouth was a big, fat lie? She'll be living with Jules and the kids. We need to know what her real story is."

"Agreed."

"Oh." He'd expected Theo to fight him on it, and the lack of resistance destroyed his momentum. "So, why'd you shut me down just now?"

"We were in front of the kids."

"Right." Hugh paused. "I'm going to go do some research."

"Let me know what you find."

"Will do."

Climbing into his truck, Hugh sent Lexi a grin. His blood buzzed with excitement, sweeping away the feelings of boredom and uselessness that had plagued him since the bullet had burrowed into his thigh. "We have a case, Lex."

"I'm so sorry about that," Jules said as soon as she closed the door behind them.

Grace looked around at the room. It was tiny, with a neatly made twin bed and a battered dresser filling the space, but it was just hers. The house might be a wreck on the verge of being condemned, but at least it was a *big* wreck. Jules shifted, drawing her attention back to the other woman. "Are you seriously dating a cop? If your situation was anything like mine…"

Jules winced. "I didn't mean for it to happen. He was just so…*sweet*."

"Are we talking about the same guy who was at the door just now?"

Pressing her hands to her flushed cheeks, Jules let out a puff of laughter. "Shockingly, he is. Although I have to admit that I noticed his hotness first. Then he was so helpful, and kind, and saved my life a bunch of times, and is wonderful with the kids…" Her expression became dreamy as she trailed away.

"Huh." In a contest of hotness, Grace would've crowned the second cop over Theo. From the top of his shaved head all the way down his massive form to the tips of his shiny boots, Officer Hugh Murdoch was gorgeous. Too bad he acted like he knew it. "Aren't you scared of being caught?"

"Terrified."

Confused, Grace frowned at her. "So why are you with him?"

"Oh, he's not what worries me." Jules waved her hand, as if dismissing the fact that dating a cop while on the run was a really, really bad idea. "I trust Theo. If it came down to it, and our secret came out, then he'd help us. The only reason I didn't tell him our story is that I don't think it's fair to make him have to hide that information. It's everything else that freaks me out. What if she… I mean, what if we're found? What if we have to run again? Worse, what if we don't have time to run, and we're dragged back…"

Grace stared at her, feeling tendrils of panic creeping back in to strangle her again. For a while, fatigue and quiet rage had muffled her fear, but now it was returning, as strong as ever. "You don't think we're safe here, then? Mr. Espina promised—"

"Sorry," Jules interrupted her. "Of course we're safe here. Well, as safe as we can be anywhere. It's just hard not to lie awake at night and think of all the very worst possibilities, especially when I'm responsible for my sister and brothers."

Grace's mind rewound the past twenty-four hours, trying to imagine how much more horrible things would've been if she'd had kids to worry about. She shuddered, feeling a dawning respect for Jules. "I don't know how you managed. Doing this myself was bad enough."

With a shrug, Jules said, "You do what you have to, I guess."

"Yeah." Grace looked around the small room, taking in the spare furnishing and the itty-bitty closet, thinking about the sad, lone bathroom, her five roommates, and her newly conjured GED—about Penny, sunny California, the job she'd loved, her light-filled condo, and Noah, who'd been so very close to perfect. "I guess you do."

CHAPTER 5

"READY?" JULES ASKED, IN WHAT SEEMED LIKE HER perpetually happy Southern drawl. Dee was leaning into her side, watching Grace with her usual mix of fascination and caution. Jules's brother Sam's expression, on the other hand, was pure wariness as he hovered over his sisters.

Ready to return to my old life? Yes, please. It had only been a day, and Grace had already had several moments when she'd been almost willing to face a whole army of Jovanovics if it meant she could return to her old life. Then she'd remember her terror when Martin had dragged her toward the house or when Logan had marched her through the empty hallway at the police station, and things in Monroe didn't seem so bad. "Ready for what?"

"To experience the wonder that is Monroe, Colorado." Jules spread her arms dramatically and then let them fall again. "There's actually not that much wonder. There *is* a thrift store, though, and a furniture store. Don't you want a bigger bed?"

As much as Grace disliked the old house, the idea of leaving it was surprisingly terrifying. It seemed too silly to say out loud, though, so she mentally hunted for excuses. "Will a bigger bed fit in my room?"

"We'll make it fit." There was so much determination in Jules's voice that Grace had a feeling she'd find a way to cram in a king-size bed if that's what Grace wanted. "Even if it takes the whole room. The bedroom next to yours is empty if you want to turn it into a closet."

Dee's eyes grew huge. "I want a bed that takes up my whole room," she said with breathless wonder.

Unable to hold back a smile, Grace said, "Let's wait on the walk-in closet. All I have are the clothes I arrived in." A quarter of the way through her trip to Colorado, she'd stopped by a Walmart in a flying visit to grab a pair of ill-fitting jeans, a T-shirt, and a pair of flip-flops. She'd changed in the bathroom on her way out, and ended up stuffing her bloodstained dress and the LAPD sweatshirt in the trash container. She kept the shoes, though. They were one of her favorite pairs, and she needed to have something from her old life besides her underwear.

"Any closet can be a walk-in," Tio said as the twins slipped past where the women and Dee were standing in the entry and flung open the front door. "If you try hard enough."

Ty laughed, shoving the back of his twin's head as he ran outside. "Bet you can't walk into Dee's closet."

His expression turning thoughtful, Tio asked, "Does it count as walking if I'm not fully upright?"

"Yeah," Ty said. "But you have to stay on your feet. No crawling or slithering."

Jules watched with a fond expression as the boys ran toward her SUV, pushing at each other to try to be the first one in. "Guess we're all going to town."

With a weak smile, Grace resigned herself to leaving

the safety of the house. Jules was right; she did need new clothes and toiletries and some furniture—all sorts of things, really—but she could barely force herself to walk to Jules's SUV.

Her head swiveled from side to side as she looked around. Despite the sunny day, there was a feeling of menace that she just couldn't shake. The house was isolated, the property surrounded by trees that blocked the view of any neighbors or nearby roads, but that almost made her paranoia worse. Anyone could be crouched in the shadows between the evergreens, watching her. Her legs shook with the desire to run back into the house, to tear up the stairs to her new room, close the blinds, and hide.

She paused by the SUV, debating what to do, but all the kids were watching her. Jules hadn't moved toward the driver's seat. Instead, she was hovering behind Grace, as if she could sense Grace's need to run back to the house and was ready to block her escape route— for her own good, no doubt. With a silent groan, Grace resigned herself to going into town. As tempting as it was, she couldn't hide in her room forever, and she did need more than one outfit...and toothpaste. She desperately needed toothpaste.

Dee gave her an encouraging smile and waved her forward. Grace almost groaned again. If a little kid was pitying her, then Grace was truly being pathetic. Stiffening her spine, she climbed into the SUV.

When she'd driven through town the first time, Grace had been hopped up on fear and gas station coffee, so she hadn't noticed much. Now, with Jules driving, Grace could look her fill. What she saw made her heart sink.

"Wow." Although she tried for an excited tone, her effort fell flat. "It's...um...quaint."

Instead of taking offense, Jules snorted. "You could say that. Or you could just say *small*."

It was small. With the mountains circling the town, and the intentionally Old West feel of the line of Main Street shops, downtown Monroe looked like a movie set. An abandoned movie set.

"It's so quiet," Grace said, scanning for pedestrians and not seeing any. Except for a few parked cars, the street appeared to be empty. Instead of reassuring her, the lack of people felt eerie. Martin could grab her in broad daylight, and no one would see. Grace's heart rate picked up.

"Theo told me that most of the residents are seasonal," Jules explained as she pulled up to the otherwise empty curb. Apparently, parallel parking was not a necessary skill in Monroe. "I guess the winters here can be kind of brutal. A lot of people spend summers in Monroe and the cold months in Arizona or Florida or other warm places."

Like California. Grace felt a pang of homesickness, but it was muted by her growing anxiety.

"It's almost October, so people are starting to head south before the first snowstorm hits. According to Theo, this place is like a ghost town during the winter. A lot of the businesses shut down, too."

The words jolted Grace out of her building panic attack. "Um...it snows in October? From what I remember, snow is supposed to be more of a December thing." What kind of frozen hell had she fallen into?

Jules laughed. "This'll be my first winter here,

too, so I'm the wrong one to ask. Theo could tell you, though."

Grace held back a grimace, and she rubbed her arm where the bruises from Martin and Officer Jovanovic still ached. As much as Jules trusted Theo, Grace just couldn't do it. She was going to do her best to keep conversation between her and members of law enforcement as minimal as possible. Making a noncommittal sound, Grace forced herself to climb out of the SUV.

"I figured we'd go to the thrift store first," Jules said, and Grace marveled that the woman could sound so cheery. Growing up, all of Grace's clothes had come from thrift stores and garage sales. She'd been twenty-four before she bought something new for the first time. Now—well, before the dinner party from hell—Grace had donated to thrift stores, but she didn't shop at them anymore. Owning clothes that had never been worn before was a wonderful luxury that she indulged in now that she could afford it...at least she had. In just a matter of days, her life had skidded off course, and she was right back to where she'd started.

Jules and the kids piled into the store. Reminding herself that she had to do what needed to be done to survive, Grace squared her shoulders and prepared to enter after them.

"Hey, there," a deep, too-appealing voice said from behind her. "Grace...right?"

Her body jerked at the unexpected greeting, and her heart took off at a gallop. Because of her initial fright, it took several seconds for the words—and tone—to register. The heavy sarcasm made Grace frown as she turned to face Hugh.

Cocking her head to the side, she put on her best confused face. "I'm sorry, but have we met?"

His grin grew a predatory edge. "How could you not remember? It was only yesterday that our eyes locked and our souls recognized each other from hundreds of lives before."

Keeping her expression as bland and uninterested as possible, she studied him for another few seconds before lifting her hands in a shrug. "Maybe your soul confused mine for someone else's? Because I can't imagine having to put up with you for one life, much less hundreds."

He grabbed his chest as if she'd stabbed him. "Ouch! Not-Grace can be vicious. If I really *were* your soulmate, I'd be running off to write extremely bad, angsty poetry right now."

"Why did you call me that?" she snapped, even as she warned herself to stay calm, to laugh it off and not make a big deal out of it.

That wolf-eyeing-his-prey look was back in his eyes. "Not-Grace? I guess you just don't seem like a Grace to me."

She stared at him, frozen. Could he know? The image of Logan Jovanovic rose in her mind, reminding her that Martin had at least one cop under his control.

"No comeback?" He leaned closer, watching her closely. "Trying to think of some new lies?"

He's fishing, she told herself firmly. If he were on Martin's payroll, he wouldn't be trying to provoke a reaction. Instead, he'd have arrested her or had her shipped back to California or at least given the Jovanovics a call after he'd met her yesterday. Tossing her hair over her shoulder, she lifted her chin and tried very hard to keep her voice from shaking. "What? No, I just zoned out for a minute. What were you babbling about?"

Instead of looking offended, he gave a surprised-sounding laugh. It was incredibly infectious. The corners of her mouth started to lift, and she realized how close she was to smiling. She dug her fingernails into her palms until she was able to control her expression again.

"Nothing interesting, apparently." Although he'd stopped laughing, his eyes remained crinkled at the corners, and there was a stupidly attractive dent in one cheek that flirted with being a dimple. "What are you all up to?"

"Shopping." The word was out before Grace could remind herself that she couldn't stand him, and that she didn't need to answer his nosy questions. Apparently, Cheery-Hugh was a little too appealing for her safety.

He lifted his eyebrows while crossing his arms, making his biceps bulge. Grace clenched her fists even tighter, relying on the grounding pinch of her nails to keep her gaze on his, no matter how much it wanted to check out his muscles. "Good luck with that, unless you're looking for groceries or nails. Not many places are still open."

"Nails?" Her brain instantly took her to manicures.

"Hardware store."

"Oh." She deflated a little. Was it too much to ask for Monroe to have a spa? She gave herself a mental smack. *Priorities*, she reminded herself firmly. *Life over facials*. She realized that Hugh was still eyeing her with that annoying mixture of amusement and suspicion, and all her frustration at the unexpected and unwanted turn her life had taken coalesced into a hardened ball in her stomach. "Why are you here?"

"I went to the post office." He lifted a handful of letters. "I heard they had free mail there."

The practical answer made her building indignation collapse, and she wanted to laugh at herself. What had she expected him to say—that he was stalking her? She scrambled for a response that was witty or even halfway coherent, but she had nothing. The way he was holding back a smile, making his cheek crease in that too-adorable way, wasn't helping matters.

"Okay." Jules poked her head outside, interrupting Grace's scattered thoughts. "Enough flirting with the new girl, Hugh. Go to the station and bug Theo and Otto for a while. I'm sure they're missing you."

Hugh turned his gaze away from Grace, and she was suddenly able to breathe again. "I've been banned from the station."

"Then go to the viner." Jules grabbed Grace's hand and started towing her toward the store entrance.

"The what?" Hugh sounded like he was about to laugh again.

"Viner." Jules was still moving away from Hugh, pulling Grace with her. "We got sick of saying 'the diner at the VFW,' so we started calling it the viner." She hauled the door open and almost shoved Grace through, calling "Bye, Hugh," right as the doors closed, leaving him outside.

"Thank you," Grace said. All of Jules's siblings were already scattered around in different sections of the store. Now that she was out of reach of his strange magnetism, Grace's original fears about Hugh came flooding back. She lowered her voice to just below a whisper. "Do you think he knows something?"

"About you? Based on the month I've known Hugh," Jules whispered back, "I'd say he's fishing. If he knew something, he'd act on it."

A flush of relief burned through Grace, and she put a hand on a nearby counter to steady her. "Good."

"Now are you ready to shop?"

Grace looked around the store, and her heart sank. "No?"

With a laugh, Jules grabbed her hand again, this time pulling her to a rack of heavy coats. "Too bad. Winter is coming, as they say. What do you think of these insulated coveralls?"

"No." Grace could deal with a return to thrift-store shopping, but she drew the line at insulated coveralls.

Still grinning, Jules exchanged the adult onesie for a down coat. "How about this, then?"

"You just showed me the coveralls to make the coat look better," Grace accused, but she was fighting a smile as she accepted the jacket to try.

"It worked, didn't it?"

Jules flipped through the rack, and Grace was vividly reminded of just a few days ago. When she and Penny had been looking through clothes, it was as if they'd been in a whole different world. The expensive, brightly colored fabric of the dresses, glowing like jewels in the sun, made the drab thrift store with its buzzing fluorescent lighting seem even shabbier and so very demoralizing. Grace had been so hopeful and happy and secure in her perfect future, and now... She glanced around the store, the familiar musty odor bringing her childhood back to life in full smell-o-vision, and bit back a sigh. Now she could only hope that she'd *have* a future.

Her face must've shown her thoughts, because Jules said softly, "Hey." Grace met her steady, serious gaze. "It gets easier."

Forcing a smile, Grace looked down at the coats to hide that her eyes had filled with tears. Setting her jaw, she forced them back. It would have to get easier. After all, how could it get much harder?

Except for a tiny, elderly woman sitting behind the checkout counter, they were the only ones in the store. It was eerie, this lack of people.

"What stays open?" Grace asked as Jules dumped an armful of clothes in her arms.

"What?" Jules added another pair of jeans to the stack. It looked like the pants were lined in flannel. That couldn't be flattering. "Go try these on."

Grace obediently started toward the dressing room, although she'd already decided the flannel-and-jeans was a no. Honestly, how cold could it get? "You said that a lot of the stores close in the winter. Which ones stay open?"

"Well, I'm getting this information thirdhand, so don't quote me on this, but I think the grocery store and the gas stations stay open. Like Hugh mentioned, the hardware store's year-round. The diner does, although it'll be at the VFW for most of the winter. Um...this thrift store." Jules sent her a sly grin. "Bet that makes you happy, huh? Let's see... What else is open all year? The post office, the drugstore, the library, Grady's General Store, the police department—although about half the cops are semi-retired and follow the hordes to

Florida for the winter—the liquor store, the taxidermy shop... Actually, the liquor store and the taxidermy shop are one place."

From what she'd seen of Monroe so far, this didn't shock Grace at all. "One-stop shopping," she said dryly, making Jules laugh.

"Indeed." Jules gave her a push toward a curtained cubicle. "And I'm sure there are more, but that's all I can think of right now, and you're stalling. Get in there and start trying on clothes."

Although Grace didn't want to try on flannel-lined jeans—or really any of the practical secondhand clothes piled in her arms—a huff of laughter escaped her as she moved into the dressing room. After sorting through the clothes, she had to admit that they weren't bad. She was just being stubborn because a part of her didn't want to get new things. There were perfectly good clothes sitting in her condo that she couldn't access because Martin Jovanovic had chased her out of her home, forcing her to share a bathroom with five other people and buy clothes at a thrift store that smelled ever so slightly of mothballs and mildew.

Stiffening her shoulders, she commanded herself to stop being a whiny baby. For now, she needed to suck it up. She was alive, and that was what mattered. Grabbing the jeans, she gave them a hard look.

"This isn't going to be fun for either of us," she told the pants, "but this is what needs to happen, so we're going to have to make the best of it."

She started to unbutton her hastily purchased Walmart jeans, but a sound made her freeze. The noise had been faint, just a slight hiss of breath, but it had come from the other side of the dressing room curtain—as if someone was pressed close, *listening*.

Without moving, she strained to hear more. There was only silence, but she swore she could feel someone's presence. In her gut, she knew someone was right outside her dressing room.

It's just Jules, she told herself, but she didn't believe it. Jules wouldn't linger like that, hovering so close and quiet. In fact, Grace was fairly certain that Jules was physically incapable of not talking for more than a few seconds. If Jules had been on the other side of the curtain, she would've been peppering Grace with questions about how the clothes fit and if she should grab a few more coats.

Grace's thoughts began to jump around like popcorn. Had Martin found her already? Was it one of his lackeys, ready to take her out the second she emerged? She wasn't sure if she could actually hear someone breathing, or if her imagination was determined to freak her out.

Buttoning the top button of her jeans again, Grace reached for the edge of the curtain. She had to look. It was far worse not knowing who—if anyone—was silently standing there, watching her. It annoyed her how pale and uncertain her hand looked as she extended it. Her fingers closed around the rough fabric, but then she paused.

Just open it, she ordered herself. *Rip it open and get it over with*. Taking a deep breath, she yanked the curtain to the side.

No one was there.

Her gaze scanned the open space, finding Jules on

the other side looking at books with Dee. The three boys were in a huddle around a table covered with hand tools. The woman at the counter looked as if she might be taking a quick nap in her chair. Grace took several steps out of the dressing room so she could see the entrance to the store.

The door was closing. Grace hurried to the front, jerking open the door and rushing outside, only to crash into someone. With a startled yelp, she tried to stumble backward, but the person grabbed her upper arms. *He's here! He found me!* Immediate panic hazed her mind, and she began struggling against her captor's hold.

"Grace, it's okay. You're safe. It's just me."

It wasn't Martin's voice. Her vision cleared and her heart rate slowed as her terror eased. Tipping her head up, she looked into Hugh's concerned face. Relief warred with embarrassment, and she stepped backward. This time, he let her go, although his hands stayed up, as if to grab her again if she looked like she was going to fall.

"You okay?"

"Fine." Flustered, she raised a hand to push her hair over her shoulder, saw how much her fingers were shaking, and lowered her hand back to her side. She suddenly remembered why she'd come outside before Hugh had scared the spit out of her. Looking around, she didn't see any other people except for the two of them. The street was just as deserted as it had been earlier, but her skin burned as if a thousand pairs of eyes were watching her every move. Sunlight reflected off the windows of the buildings across the street, making it impossible to see inside. Grace wrapped her arms around herself and turned back to Hugh. "Did you see anyone come out of the store?"

His gaze sharpened, changing from general concern to focused interest. "Just you, but I was putting some things in my truck, so my back was turned for a few minutes." He waved at a red pickup—one that looked old in a ready-for-the-junkyard way, rather than in a classic-car-show way—parked behind Jules's SUV. A shepherd-type dog sat in the passenger seat, watching them with huge, pricked ears. "Why?"

"No reason." A rustling sound made her jerk her head around, but it was only the wind making leaves dance across the road.

"Uh-huh," Hugh said, not sounding as if he believed her. "Was someone bothering you in there?"

She wasn't sure how to answer that. Although she would've sworn she heard someone outside her dressing room, she was starting to think that she was imagining things. After all, the past several days would've messed with almost anyone's sanity. Since she didn't want to consider that she couldn't trust her own senses, she changed the subject. "What are you doing out here?"

"Just…more errands." For the first time since she'd met him, Hugh didn't answer with his usual cocky confidence. Instead, his gaze darted to the side as he slid his hands in his pockets, looking like a strangely appealing combination of naughty boy and confident man. He snuck a glance at her, and she raised an eyebrow, making him huff and swing a hand toward the pickup. "My truck's right there. I had to walk by here to get to it."

"Uh-huh." She echoed his skeptical sound from earlier. "Do we need to have the stalking-is-bad talk again?"

"I'm a cop, not a stalker," he said with exaggerated patience. "I arrest stalkers."

"Might want to check out your house."

"What?"

She smirked. "It's looking a little see-through and glassy to me."

"What?"

"Glass house? Throwing stones?"

Lips pursed, he eyed her for several seconds. "You're not very good at telling jokes."

"I'm an excellent joke teller!" Grace huffed.

"Uh-huh."

The door opened behind her. "Grace?" Jules said tentatively. "You okay?"

As Grace turned toward the store, she realized that her fear had disappeared. Hugh might be one of the most aggravating people she'd ever met, but he'd made her forget for just a moment that her life was a terrifying, out-of-control horror movie.

She realized that Jules was still waiting for an answer, so Grace gave her a smile. "Sure. Should we go back in?"

Jules studied her for a long moment. As the seconds ticked by, Grace's apprehension returned, and she fought the need to scan her surroundings again, looking for Martin or one of his flunkies. Now that she didn't have the distraction of Hugh teasing her, all she could think about was how it wasn't safe outside. She needed to get back into the store. As if Jules could read Grace's thoughts, she held the door open wider, allowing Grace to reenter the thrift store.

Grace couldn't resist sneaking a look over her shoulder as she headed through the doorway. The only person on the street was Hugh, watching her with an expression that was a mixture of heat and suspicion and a deep determination that sent a shiver through her.

Despite the comfort and distraction he'd just given her, she needed to be careful. There would be no falling for a cop—especially not one as annoying and bullheaded and beautiful as Officer Hugh Murdoch.

CHAPTER 6

SHE NEEDED A JOB. DESPERATELY.

It had only been a week. Despite having taken over the cleaning and the cooking and the packing of school lunches, Grace was bored out of her mind. It was her own fault. There was no reason she couldn't have gone to town—to the library or to one of the touristy shops having closing-for-the-season sales, or even to have lunch at the viner. Part of the deal with Mateo Espina when she'd left California had been trading her Infiniti for another car—a Subaru—so Grace had transportation.

She just hated the thought of leaving the house. The idea of venturing into the quiet, ghostly town, with its lurking strangers and suspicious cops, made her shudder. Grace knew she had to do *something* else, though, because she couldn't wander around the creaky, ancient house any longer without going a little bit crazy. The kids wouldn't be home from school for a couple of hours, and Jules was working a double shift. Grace had gone from living a fulfilling, happy life to spooking at her own shadow and hiding in a house that wasn't even hers.

She couldn't even mess around on the Internet, since she didn't have a laptop, and her new phone was a basic-model burner. To find a job, she needed to shake off her paranoia and go to town.

Now. She took a determined step toward the front door. *I should go job hunting now.* As she moved toward the door, Martin Jovanovic's face popped into her head. What if he'd found her new town? What if, as she walked into the library, he grabbed her from behind, just like he'd done at his house in California? He wouldn't even need to grab her. He could hide in the shadows and shoot her dead. All the possible ways Martin could kill her filled Grace's mind, and she froze in place, unable to move even an inch closer to the entrance.

Tomorrow morning, then, she thought, almost running into the living room and plopping down on the couch. There would probably be more business owners around in the morning anyway. She could stop at the library to use one of their computers, have lunch with Jules, and make a whole day of it. That would work much better than trying to squeeze everything in that afternoon.

Ignoring the rational part of her brain that knew she'd be just as scared of Martin Jovanovic tomorrow, she reached for the remote and clicked on the television. It was small and old and only got a few channels, but watching it was better than peeking out the windows and imagining that she saw Martin Jovanovic hiding in the trees.

The theme song for a soap opera came on, and she groaned. She'd never watched much daytime TV before, and, after a week of her self-imposed house arrest, she understood why. Most of it was very, very bad. She lifted the remote to change the channel.

A knock on the door had her jolting from the sofa to her feet in an instant. She hesitated, her heart pounding, not sure if she should run out the back or answer

the door. It was probably nothing. After all, Martin
Jovanovic wouldn't knock. He'd just barge in and grab
her. Or maybe just shoot her. Or stab her. Or... Okay,
she needed to stop.

The knock came again, a heavy pounding that
sounded urgent and serious. She took a step toward the
door, but then hesitated. Her car was parked behind the
house, out of sight, so whoever was at the door wouldn't
be able to tell that she was at home.

An advertising jingle rang out from the TV, making
her flinch. Fumbling for the remote, she muted the television, hoping it wasn't too late. Had the visitor heard
the TV before she'd silenced it? The knocking had
stopped, though. Maybe they were leaving?

Her nerves calming at the thought, she shifted toward
the window, intending to look outside. Before she could
take more than a couple of steps, she heard the distinc-
tive squeal of the front door hinges.

Someone had just broken in.

Her heart immediately sped up until it was thrumming in her ears. Had she locked the door after the kids
had left for the bus stop that morning? Grace knew she
had. She remembered the feel of the dead bolt under her
fingers as she turned it. Whoever it was must have a key.
Maybe it was Jules, home early.

Even as she had the thought, Grace dismissed it. Why
would Jules have knocked first?

The floor in the entry creaked, reminding Grace of
her most urgent issue at the moment: *someone was in
the house*. As quietly as possible, she started backing
up. This was not a good room to be trapped in. The only
door was the one into the hallway—where the intruder

was. The large, central window was solid. The two smaller panes of glass beside it would reluctantly crank out a few inches, but definitely not wide enough to fit her entire body through.

Why had she hesitated when she'd first heard the knock? If she'd immediately headed for the back door, she'd already be far, far away. Now she was stuck.

Her gaze ran over the room, searching for hiding spots, but there weren't any good ones. The closet was too obvious, but it would have to do. Maybe they wouldn't bother searching.

As she hurried toward the small closet door, her heart thumped painfully against her ribs. It beat so loudly that it felt as if everyone still left in Monroe could hear the pounding.

"What are you doing?"

She whipped around, grabbing the first thing within reach to use as a weapon.

Hugh looked from her face to her hand with his usual expression of barely contained amusement—a look that aggravated Grace more every time she encountered him. Even the dog standing next to him looked entertained. "The mute button doesn't work on me. Trust me. Others have tried."

There was still so much residual fear flooding through her body that Grace had a hard time understanding what he meant. She followed his gaze to the improvised weapon in her hand and realized that she was pointing the television remote at him. As her panic started to abate, anger took its place, along with a healthy dose of embarrassment.

"What are you doing here?" she demanded, allowing her arm to drop back to her side.

"I could ask you the same thing," he said.

"What?" It was almost a screech. Grace blamed residual nerves…and the fact that Hugh was truly aggravating. "I live here!"

"Jules said you were job hunting today." She opened her mouth, but he spoke again before she could ask how that justified him breaking into her house. "Why didn't you open the door when I knocked?"

Her eyes narrowed. "You came in because you thought I wasn't here? What were you going to do? Go through my stuff?"

The guilty look that flashed over his face disappeared quickly, but she still caught it. "You were!" Another thought occurred to her, and she almost growled. "How did you get in?"

His expression of pure innocence just made her suspicions double. "What do you mean? The door was unlocked."

"No, it wasn't. I definitely remember locking—"

"Hey!" he interrupted, his attention on the TV screen. "Is this the *Tattered Hearts* where Tatiana realizes that Natasha and Jorge are scheming against her?"

"What? I don't know. I've never watched this show."

"You've never seen *Tattered Hearts*?" He grabbed her hand and pulled her to the couch. Bemused by the sudden topic shift, she sat. "You are missing out. It's the best show ever."

Hugh plopped his oversized self on the couch right next to Grace, jostling her. He was so big, a wall of heat and muscle and sexiness—*whoa*. She shut down that thought abruptly. His dog stretched out in front of them, her furry head resting on Grace's foot, which was comforting and kind of nice. She scowled and briefly considered telling Hugh to leave—although the dog could stay—but Grace was curious why he was so obsessed with this soap. Besides, as annoying as Hugh could be, arguing with him kept her mind off Martin Jovanovic. She honestly didn't want to be in this big, creaky house alone anymore, especially after having the snot scared out of her, so she settled in to watch.

"Wait," she said after a few minutes. "So the guy with the waxed chest—"

"Jorge."

"So Jorge is cheating on the woman with the scary eyebrows—"

"Tatiana."

"Jorge is cheating on Tatiana with the lizard-faced woman?"

"Natasha."

"Why?" Keeping her gaze locked on the television, Grace made a face. "Tatiana is so much hotter, and Natasha is all about the drama. That gets so tiring."

"I know." Hugh sighed. "Jorge's an idiot."

"Yeah. He is." Although she wanted to talk more about Jorge's poor life choices, Grace went quiet so she could watch the show. As the soap continued, she found herself leaning forward, fascinated despite herself.

"Oh. My. God." Grace clapped a hand over her mouth in shocked glee as a commercial filled the small screen. "Did Tatiana actually tell Jorge about the secret baby?"

"I know, right? Natasha knew all along, too." Hugh shook his head and tsked. "Just wait. Javier—"

"Stop! No spoilers!" Lunging toward him and laughing, Grace clapped a hand over his mouth. As soon as she made contact, she froze. His skin was warm—almost hot—and his cheeks as stubbly as his lips were smooth. Grace stared at him. What was she doing? This was Hugh, a cop who was so suspicious of her that he'd broken into her house to dig through her things. Why was she flirting with him?

Realizing that she was still touching him, Grace started to yank her arm back, but he caught her hand before she could pull it away. He gave it a gentle squeeze before releasing it.

"What—"

"The show's on," Hugh interrupted. "Hush, or you'll miss it."

Watching *Tattered Hearts* was more important than smacking him down for *shushing* her, so Grace settled against the sofa cushions and tried to ignore the annoying, muscle-bound cop sharing the couch with her. She couldn't deny how nice it was to have him there, though. It made her feel a little less alone.

Grace felt herself relaxing for the first time in over a week. With a relieved sigh, she let herself enjoy the warmth of Hugh's shoulder so close to hers and the comfort of his presence. She got caught up in the drama of Tatiana, Jorge, and Natasha, and forgot about anyone with the name Jovanovic for a little while.

―――――――――

"What are you guys up to?" Grace asked, flipping through one of the recipe books that Tio had picked up for her at the library. The kids had just gotten home from school, and there was tons of time before dinner, but

Grace had been at a loss after Hugh had left a few hours earlier. Meal planning gave her something to focus on, something that wasn't a burly, soap-opera-loving cop.

Dee paused in her rush to beat the twins to the back door. "We're going to play footer."

"Footer?" Grace echoed.

"You can play, if you like." Dee looked at her with hopeful eyes, even as Grace's chest tightened at the thought of leaving the house.

She cleared her throat, hoping that her voice would come out sounding normal. "Thanks, but I should do… uh, something in here." Gesturing at the cookbook, Grace gave her a weak smile.

Dee studied her for a moment, her expression too serious for a little girl. "That's okay," she finally said, patting Grace's arm before following her brothers outside. Grace stared at the door, feeling like the biggest scaredy-cat alive.

"Y-you sh-sh-should c-come outside."

Grace jumped, twisting in her chair to see Sam. "Oh! You startled me." She cocked her head, watching him curiously. Usually, he did his best to avoid her, only speaking to her when it was absolutely unavoidable. This was the first time he'd actually initiated conversation.

He looked at her in a way that was uncomfortably close to how his sister had eyed her, as if they knew exactly what she was scared of. "You sh-should p-play."

Grace's laugh came out sounding strangled. "I don't even know what *footer* is, much less how to play it."

"It's a m-m-mix of f-footb-ball and soccer. We d-don't know the rules, either. W-we j-j-just make them up as w-we g-g-go."

That time, her smile was real, although short-lived. She looked down at the cookbook. "I don't know…" She didn't want to admit her silly fear that Martin Jovanovic and his flunkies might be hiding in the woods, waiting for her to leave the safety of the house. It was irrational, and she knew it. She shouldn't be hiding as children tried to coax her to do simple, normal things, but that seemed to be her life now. *Thanks, Martin, you asshole.*

"It's ok-kay." Her gaze flew to his face. It was like he'd read her thoughts. "If whoever's af-fter you knows wh-where you l-live, it's t-t-too l-late anyw-way."

She stared at him in horror. If he was trying to encourage her, then he kind of sucked at it.

"Th-they're n-not g-g-going to f-find you j-just bec-c-cause you g-go outside."

It was her turn to study him as she considered what he'd said. "You're right." Shutting the cookbook with a slap, she stood abruptly. Even though he was several feet away, Sam still took a step back, looking alarmed. Grace wondered what had happened to him, what he and his brothers and sisters had gone through that had driven them out of their lives and into hiding. His expression became guarded, and she shook off her thoughts. "I'm going to play sockball or whatever you call it."

Her attempt at a bad joke was rewarded by a tiny smile from Sam. "F-footer."

"Footer. Right. I'm going to play footer. No, I'm going to *rule* at footer. Watch out, footer world, because I'm about to dominate!"

His smile grew, and Grace felt like she'd already won. Taking a deep breath, she shoved all thoughts of

Martin Jovanovic from her mind and followed Sam out the door. Screw being scared. It was time to play footer.

―――――――

"You don't have to fix breakfast every morning, you know," Jules said, the last two words muffled by a yawn. Shoving some dark strands of hair out of her eyes, she made a beeline for the coffeepot. "I mean, it's wonderful to wake up to the smell of sausage and syrup, but I'm starting to feel like a slacker."

Grace snorted as she flipped a piece of French toast. "Right. You're a total slacker. Getting up at five to work your cute little butt off at the diner, and then coming home to take care of your brothers and sister. Plus there are all those things you keep trying to fix with duct tape. You really do live a pampered life."

After a halfhearted effort at glaring, Jules gave up with a shrug. "It's too early to do this battle-of-wits stuff. Give me ten minutes and some coffee, and I'll think of an awesome comeback to that."

With an amused snort, Grace said, "I really don't mind cooking. It helps keep my mind occupied. In fact, I'm going to go job hunting today. All I do if I sit around is think about…things."

"I get it." Jules really did understand, Grace knew. Although they hadn't exchanged too many details, Grace was certain their situations were similar. "It might not be the best time to look for jobs in Monroe, though."

Grace made a face. "Yeah, I figured that. At least it'll give me something to do besides watch daytime TV."

"I'd offer to ask Megan if you could waitress, but with the diner blowing up and all…"

Head cocked, Grace studied her.

"What?" Jules asked.

Turning back to the French toast, Grace explained. "If you'd told me a week and a half ago that I'd be living with five other people in a small Colorado town, casually talking about a diner exploding, I'd have said you were crazy. My life has gone a bit sideways."

Although Jules laughed, she squeezed her eyes closed as if she were in pain. "Tell me about it."

The kids thundered into the kitchen, and the conversation turned to washing hands and setting the table and putting out the food.

"Oh!" Jules exclaimed, drawing everyone's attention. "Sam, didn't the cleaner at the kennel move back to Kansas?"

He eyed her with his usual wary expression before finally answering. "Y-yeah."

Jules turned to beam at Grace. "That might be a job possibility for you."

With everyone staring at her, Grace tried to hide her horror at the idea, but she wasn't sure how well she succeeded. She knew her options were limited in such a small town, especially with her new, sadly skimpy résumé, but cleaning? And not only cleaning, but cleaning a dog kennel at that. She had been hoping to find something more along the lines of sales clerk or barista or…well, pretty much anything that didn't involve poo. She realized that Jules was waiting for a response and jerked herself out of her self-pitying fog. "Sounds…promising."

Sam looked just as doubtful as Grace, and she couldn't blame him.

"Let's eat!" Jules's announcement broke the awkward silence, and everyone sat in a clatter of chair legs and teasing. Grace had just settled in her chair when she remembered the orange juice was still in the fridge and jumped up again to grab it. As she turned back around, she saw a cop in the kitchen doorway. She almost dropped the juice.

"Theo!" Jules jumped up to give him a kiss. The others called their greetings, and Grace took a moment to collect herself. It wasn't just a cop; it was Jules's boyfriend. He didn't have any nefarious purpose for being there, other than to score a kiss and breakfast.

However, her still-vibrating nerves caused a surge of annoyance. "Does every cop in town just walk into this house?" she muttered beneath her breath.

Theo must have had ears like a bat, since he glanced at her sharply. "Who else was here?"

Feeling a little sheepish, she waved her hand as if shooing away her words. "Just Hugh. Don't mind me. I'm just hangry."

"Hugh walked in?" Apparently, he wasn't going to let it go. "When?"

"Yesterday." Grace poured juice into the glasses so she could avoid his piercing cop gaze. "Really, it was no big deal."

"Was the door locked?"

"Um…yes? I mean, I'm pretty sure I locked it after the kids left for school, but he just walked in, so it couldn't have been locked, right? Unless Hugh has a key?" She really hoped he didn't have a key. The thought of Hugh roaming around the house at will while she was doing things like showering and having bedhead and wearing sweatpants perturbed her in a way she didn't want to examine too closely.

"He doesn't have a key." Theo's tone was odd, a mixture of exasperation and... Grace would've said amusement, except that, from what she'd seen, Theo didn't get amused. He exchanged a look with Jules, who started to laugh.

Confused, Grace eyed first Jules and then Theo. "Then how'd he get in?"

"He picked the lock," Tio said in his precise way as he cut his French toast into even squares. Ty, sitting next to him, stabbed a piece from his own plate and brought the whole thing to his mouth.

"Ty! Manners," Jules barked, although her correction lost some of its sting since she was still laughing. "You are not at the fair eating French toast on a stick. Cut it into bite-size pieces first."

He eyed the slice still dangling from his fork thoughtfully.

"I don't care if you can fit the whole thing in your mouth." Jules had apparently read his mind, judging by the disappointed expression on Ty's face. "I want the pieces to have a total area of no more than two square inches. Understood?"

Tio lit up and stood.

"Where are you going, T?" Jules asked.

"To get a ruler."

Jules stepped out of his way, and Tio rushed out of the kitchen. Ty immediately started eating the precisely cut squares on Tio's plate instead.

"Going back to the whole he-picked-the-lock thing," Grace said evenly—at least as evenly as she could manage.

With an apologetic, yet still amused look, Jules explained. "It's Hugh's thing."

"His 'thing' or not, he shouldn't be using it to get into your house." It didn't sound like Theo thought the situation was as funny.

As much as it surprised her to be allies with the perpetually cranky cop, Grace had to agree. "I second that."

"I'll talk to him," Theo promised grimly. "I'm sure he's going to pop up at the station or on scene in the middle of a call. That's his 'thing' now, too."

Laughing, Jules patted Theo on the chest, not looking at all intimidated by his threatening tone. "Don't come down too hard on him. I think he's just bored. He misses protecting people, especially you and Otto."

"You're awfully sympathetic to someone who just broke into your house," Grace grumbled, poking at her French toast. Once he'd settled in to watch the show, Hugh hadn't bugged her *too* much. In fact, she'd been a little disappointed when he and Lexi had left after *Tattered Hearts* was over. Sitting with him so close had been especially nice, in a confusing way. She hadn't totally forgiven him for reducing her to a state of helpless fear before she'd realized who'd broken into the house, though.

With a shrug, Jules leaned in to Theo, which seemed to make him immediately less cranky. "What can I say? I'm still grateful for him getting those Rough Rider handcuffs off me."

"Rough Rider handcuffs?" Grace repeated, but Jules

and Theo had locked eyes and were oblivious to every-one else in the room, even when Tio—ruler in hand—squeezed past them on his way back to the table. Theo was stroking Jules's wrists with his thumbs, and he lifted her hands one at a time to lay a gentle kiss where Grace had to imagine the Rough Rider handcuffs had sat.

Even after a mere eight days in the house, Grace knew it was no use talking to either Theo or Jules when they were in lovey-dovey land, so she turned to make a face at the kids. Dee giggled, Ty pretended to retch, Tio concentrated on measuring French toast, and Sam gave her the tiniest smile—which made Grace want to throw her arms up in victory. It had taken more than a week and an extended game of footer, but the kid might actually be warming up to her.

As she ate a bite of cantaloupe, she felt a tiny spark of… Was it happiness? Maybe her stay in Monroe wouldn't be the utter hell-sentence she'd expected. Then she remembered the possible kennel job, and her hint of a smile disappeared.

No. It *was* an utter hell-sentence. One that would most likely contain dog poo.

CHAPTER 7

THERE WAS A GRACE ROBINSON IN BANGOR, MAINE. Apparently, she had a little shoplifting problem.

"Got you," Hugh muttered, clicking on the link to bring up the first of several mug shots. He leaned forward as the computer hesitated, humming as it uploaded the picture. When the photo appeared on the screen, however, he slumped back. This Ms. Robinson was at least forty-five years older than his Grace. Wait. *His* Grace?

He pushed the thought out of his head.

Instead, he ran another check, but there were no other Grace Robinsons in Bangor—at least, none that had any reason to be listed in the police database. He widened his search to include the whole county. Except for the sticky-fingered senior citizen, he had no other hits.

Lexi shifted next to him, resting her head right above his knee. He gave her a quick rub behind her ears and then tried a few different search combinations. When Hugh's focus stayed on the computer screen, Lexi started to whine.

"I know, Lex." He gave the dog a sympathetic glance, aware that she was as bored as he was with their enforced inactivity. "Maybe we can go give Otto a hand at one of his calls later. It's possible that someone will run when they see us, and then you can catch them. That would be fun, right?"

Lexi sat up straight, already vibrating with anticipation from her pricked ears to her thumping tail.

"No."

Hugh jerked in surprise at Otto's voice, and then braced himself as a wave of agony bolted through his thigh at the sudden movement. "Hey, Otto." Although he tried to sound casual, Hugh knew he was breathless from the pain. "What's up? Lexi and I were just discussing you. About how you're our favorite cop pretty much in the history of the universe."

Instead of answering, Otto just walked over to look at the computer screen. Trying to act casual, Hugh exited out of his most recent search, hitting the escape key until he was back at the home page. Only then did he look up at Otto. Way up.

"How'd you sneak in here without me hearing you? You're so tall, but you move so quietly. It's like you're a cross between Paul Bunyan and a ninja." When Otto narrowed his eyes, looking more annoyed than he usually ever got, Hugh raised his hands and plastered on his most innocent expression. "A Bunja. Or a Ninyan?"

Otto's stone-faced stare didn't falter. "You can't be here. If LT sees you…"

The idea made Hugh wince, but he forced a shrug. "Don't worry. Lex and I are in stealth mode. Besides, it's three in the morning. The lieutenant's fast asleep. Unless there's a monster of a call, he won't be wandering in here until eight—actually, five after eight, since he'll get coffee first."

Closing his eyes for a second, Otto looked as if he

was in pain, too. When he finally opened them, he fixed his glare on Hugh. "You will go home. You will stay there for the next sixteen days. You will not show up on any of my calls."

With a noncommittal hum, Hugh decided that a subject change was in order. "Hypothetically, if I were to bring you a set of prints, would you send them to the state lab for processing for me?" At their next *Tattered Hearts* viewing, he'd snag Grace's glass or popcorn bowl or something he could lift prints from.

Even as he thought that, a tickle of guilt made him itchy. Watching the soap with Grace had been fun. Sitting so close to her on the couch, laughing at the cheesy parts, gasping at the shocking parts had made his favorite show so much better. He couldn't get involved with her, though. The woman was obviously trouble. He just had to ignore the urge he felt every time she looked at him with those gorgeous, scared eyes—the need to protect her, to comfort her, to take away that terrified look and make her laugh…or want to smack him. Any reaction was fine, as long as it distracted her from whatever made her so frightened.

Otto cleared his throat, bringing Hugh back to the reality of his partner's deadly glare.

"From the angry eyes, I'm guessing the hypothetical answer to my hypothetical question would be *no*?" He'd have to hit up Theo instead.

To Hugh's surprise, the scowl disappeared. Otto's face smoothed into an expressionless mask as he crossed his thick arms over his chest. "Hypothetically," Otto said in an even tone, "if I shoot you in the other leg, will you finally stay home?"

Okay, so the blank face and the calm voice were misleading. Otto was *pissed*.

"Fine," Hugh grumbled, logging off the computer and shutting it down. "I'm going home. But if I die of utter boredom, then it's on your conscience."

Otto didn't look too concerned about future guilt. Instead, he turned abruptly, crossed to the door, and opened it just enough to stick his head into the hall. Taking advantage of Otto's distraction, Hugh used the opportunity to stand, knowing that he couldn't hide how much it hurt to do so.

"Hallway's clear," Otto said in a low grumble, standing aside to let Hugh walk into the hallway.

A flash of gratitude took Hugh by surprise. He was lucky to have Otto and Theo and Lexi. His partners had risked their lives to carry him to safety after he'd been shot. If he was honest, Hugh knew that he'd be just as big of a nagging grandma if either Otto or Theo had been the ones injured. In fact, he had been just as bad to Theo after their fellow K9 officer, Don Baker, had committed suicide the previous summer. Although everyone in the department had mourned, Theo had been hit the hardest. He'd retreated into himself and turned off every emotion except for anger. Hugh would rather get shot in his other leg than watch Theo go through that again. He'd rather get shot *anywhere* than see his friends hurting at all.

As he passed, Hugh squeezed Otto's massive shoulder. "Thanks, Otto."

Except for a slight tip of his head in acknowledgment, Otto stayed silent. With Lexi at his side, Hugh strolled down the hall to the stairway. Only when the heavy fire door thumped closed behind him did he allow himself to limp heavily. The first step down almost brought him to his knees. As much as he hated to admit it, he'd been overusing his leg, and now he was paying for it. Using the railings, he balanced on his good leg and swung down four steps at a time until he reached the door to the parking lot. His key fob for the parking garage had been confiscated by the lieutenant, so he'd been forced to park in the public lot and go through the lobby. Luckily, the desk sergeant had let him pass after inquiring about his leg. Apparently, she hadn't known about the station-wide Hugh ban...yet.

Hooking Lexi's leash to the first ring on her harness—the one that meant they weren't working or tracking—Hugh pressed the door's release bar and stepped into the chilly mountain night. As they walked toward his truck, he tipped his head back. Despite the sodium lights illuminating the lot, the stars were bright. The moon was just a sliver, but it stood out sharply against the deep black of the sky. The color reminded him of Grace's hair.

The sappiness of that image ripped him out of his thoughts, and he faced forward, focusing on his pickup. There were only a few other cars dotted around the lot. After six years on the force, plus a lifetime in Monroe, the station parking lot was a familiar, comfortable place. Tonight, however, it looked different...foreign.

The ever-present wind was sliding half of a Styrofoam takeout container across the asphalt, making a scratchy sound as the box skidded beneath a car. Despite the lights, the shadows were deep, giving plenty of cover to whoever needed it. Hugh's skin prickled with that same feeling of being watched, and he held back a grunt of frustration. Why was he being so paranoid? No one was there.

He was almost sure of it.

It took a great effort to keep his steps measured—and an even greater one to keep them even. He didn't want to hurry to the truck, though, any more than he wanted to limp and show weakness to whoever was lurking out there. Even Lexi seemed infected by his mood. Her ears swiveled like satellite dishes, trying to pick up the faintest sound.

As they drew close to the truck, he dug his keys out of his pocket—but when he pulled them out, his fingers fumbled, and he dropped them. They hit the pavement with a discordant jangle that sounded too loud in the sudden stillness. Even the wind seemed to be holding its breath.

With a huff of annoyance, Hugh bent to pick up the keys, extending his bad leg to the side in an awkward pose he was glad no one was there to witness. As he rose, keys in hand, Lexi started to bark.

It wasn't her normal bark. There was a frantic, almost shrill edge to her yelps. Bunching her hindquarters under her, Lexi turned and bolted.

Within a second, she hit the end of the leash. Already off-balance, Hugh stumbled along behind her for several steps. When his startled brain began working again, he stopped, turning his head to look behind him, searching for whatever had spooked Lexi worse than he'd ever seen before.

All he saw were shadows before another jerk on the leash pulled him forward. He quit hesitating and started to run behind her. His confident—almost overconfident—K9 partner was so terrified that she was dragging him along at the end of her leash. If there was something so bad that it made Lexi bolt, then he should probably follow suit.

Before they reached the edge of the lot, there was a bright flash and a *thump* so loud that it echoed through his whole body. He went airborne as the night lit up around him. There were crashing sounds and a chorus of car alarms, but they were all muffled, as if his head was buried in a pillow.

Hugh hit the ground hard, his skull bouncing painfully off the pavement. His vision spun, the white light from earlier fading into darker oranges and reds. Confused, he pushed himself up onto his elbows, hardly even feeling the gravel that dug into his arms. He squinted, trying to focus his blurry, shifting vision. A pickup was on fire.

His pickup was on fire.

Fragmented thoughts filled his mind, and he tried to tie them together into some sort of coherent string. He needed to have Dispatch call Fire. What had just happened? He'd been looking into Grace's background. Beautiful, scared Grace... *Focus!* Otto had sent him home. He'd been walking out to his truck with Lexi...

"Lexi!" he yelled, and his voice echoed strangely in his head. He twisted, trying to come to his hands and knees, but his balance was off, and his thigh refused to support him, sliding out to the side when he attempted to pull his knees under him. "Lexi!"

A cold nose touched the side of his neck, and he turned toward his K9 partner, sliding shaking hands into her ruff.

"You okay, sweetie?" he crooned, his voice rough

with smoke inhalation and emotion. Sliding his hands over her, he checked for any injuries, but she didn't seem to flinch from his touch. Instead, Lexi leaned into him, her weight throwing him off-balance. Unable to catch himself in time, he toppled onto his back.

The stars, hazy from smoke, seemed to squiggle in random patterns that made his head start to throb. He was suddenly so cold. Hugh felt a shaking Lexi pressed against his side, and he welcomed her warmth.

Suddenly, Otto's face was there, blocking the stars. His mouth was moving, but Hugh couldn't make sense of any of his words. Otto looked scared, though, more scared than Hugh'd ever seen him look before. Vaguely, he knew that he needed to tell Otto what was happening. What *was* happening? *Oh right*. Now he remembered.

"Some asshole blew up my truck," Hugh slurred, and then there was blackness.

"Seriously?" Now that the light wasn't stabbing knives into his eyeballs anymore, Hugh allowed them to open wider. "Didn't I just get out of this place?"

"Yes." Theo looked pissed—more pissed than Hugh had ever seen him, and that was saying something. His partner was an angry guy. "You did."

Hugh shifted, wanting to sit up, but simultaneous jolts of pain from his leg and his head made him suck in a harsh breath and freeze. If moving hurt that much, then he would just stay very still.

A silent Otto stepped forward and pushed a button so the bed rose, tilting Hugh into a more upright position.

Hugh thanked him, hating the rough sound of his voice. Without responding, Otto offered him a cup with a straw, and Hugh took a drink.

Shifting back, hiding a wince at the throbbing in his skull, the earlier events shuffled into place, and he sat bolt upright again. This time, he ignored the pain. "Lexi!"

"She'll be fine," Otto said, gently pressing him back with a hand to Hugh's shoulder. "Dr. Hellman has her."

Ignoring his partner's attempts to calm him, Hugh barked, "If she's fine, why's she at the vet?"

"For observation." Theo's voice was almost a snap. His bedside manner was a little rougher than Otto's. "She's got some bruising and is nicked up, but only one cut was big enough for staples." When Hugh started surging against Otto's hand again, Theo clarified. "Three. Just three staples. So quit Hulk-ing out."

Hugh gave him a hard stare, trying to determine whether Theo was softening the truth, but Theo just met him glare for glare. Subsiding against the bed, Hugh asked, "What the hell happened?"

"Someone put a bomb on your truck, blowing it—and almost you and Lexi—into fucking tiny pieces." That was Theo, as blunt as possible. It was a relief, though, not to have to pry the details out of someone who thought Hugh was too weak or injured to handle them.

Then the meaning of Theo's words actually hit Hugh. The explosion had been intentional. Someone had tried to kill him.

"Shit."

Otto snorted. Apparently, he trusted that Hugh wasn't going to try to run to Dr. Hellman's to check on Lexi, because he dropped his hand and pulled a chair up to the bed, settling his bulk into it. There was a second chair, but both he and Hugh knew that Theo would never sit. In fact, just standing still was an achievement. Watching Theo practically vibrate with tension, Hugh figured his partner would start pacing at any second. *Three…two…one…*

Pivoting, Theo took three choppy strides toward the door before turning around and stomping back to the bed. Hugh had to hold back a smile before reality hit again, wiping his expression free of humor. He wondered if his inability to think in a straight line was a symptom of his concussion. He wondered if even *wondering* about that when his truck had just exploded proved the theory. When he shifted, an unexpected bolt of agony shot from his thigh, and he couldn't hold back a grunt of pain.

Otto leaned forward again so he could point. "Push this button for pain meds."

"Forget it." Hugh didn't even look where Otto was indicating. "I'll be fine. Pain meds make me puke."

"Just push it."

"No."

"Then I will."

"Don't—" He reached to knock Otto's hand away, but it was too late. Hugh glared at Otto's defiantly smug expression and fought back the urge to yell at him. The big lug was concerned about him, and Hugh would probably—okay, *definitely*—do the same in Otto's place. Hugh gave his partner a final scowl and then refocused on the explosion that had put him in here.

"Who?" he asked, knowing that he'd skipped a few questions in between, but Otto and Theo would follow his train of thought. His parked truck wouldn't have exploded on its own. Someone had to have helped it along.

"Who has a grudge against the MPD and plays with bombs?" Theo asked, his voice heavy with sarcasm. Hugh didn't take it personally. Anger was pretty much Theo's default emotion when he felt scared or sad or helpless. Hugh's multiple trips to the hospital had to be messing with both Theo's and Otto's heads.

Once again, he forced himself to focus his straying thoughts. After all, it was important to figure out who had tried to blow him—and Lexi—into pieces. "Gordon Schwartz? You think he's still around after skipping bail?"

"Probably holed up in his militia compound," Otto said, stretching his feet in front of him. Although he looked relaxed, Hugh knew he was just as frantic about what had happened as Theo. The two men just displayed it differently.

Focus, Hugh ordered his brain, which sent a zigzagging spear of pain through his head in response. "Yeah. That would make sense. There's probably a whole underground-bunker village beneath his property. Why me, though? No offense, Theo, but Gordon's got to hate you more than he hates me. His girlfriend wanted to hurt *you*; I was just the expendable sidekick."

"You're not *expendable*," Theo gritted out, and Hugh waved a hand to brush away his partner's comment.

"To Sherry Baker I was, and that's the current theory, right? That Gordon—our own local bomb fairy—wants to get revenge for Sherry blowing herself up?" A wave of nausea made Hugh tighten his jaw against the need to hurl, but he wasn't sure if it was due to the meds or the concussion or the memory of the disturbed stranger that Don's daughter had become.

"Norman Rounds might know something, but we haven't been able to locate him since he got out of the hospital," Theo grumbled.

"Can't really blame him." Hugh felt like he was sinking deeper into the bed even as his stomach protested. The drugs were working their way through his system. Hopefully, he'd pass out before the urge to vomit got too strong. Puking was going to hurt. "He tried to stop Sherry, after all. Gordon can't be too happy with him."

With a grunt that could've been agreement, Theo turned and paced the other direction.

"This is speculation," Otto grumbled. "We should wait for LT."

Exhaustion and the dose of pain meds were pulling Hugh down, and the thought of sleeping and escaping his painful reality for a while was tempting. If the lieutenant didn't hurry, Hugh probably wasn't going to be awake for his visit. "He's investigating?"

"Last I heard, he'd ordered a perimeter put up and was waiting for the Denver bomb squad to arrive. He wanted to make sure the scene was safe before investigators started crawling all over it."

"Right." Hugh's eyelids were sinking, despite his best efforts. "Makes…sense."

Pacing back to the side of the bed, Theo crossed his arms over his chest. "Go to sleep. But you have to knock off this almost-getting-killed bullshit."

All Hugh could manage was an upward quirk of his lips and a slurred "I'll do my best." Then the darkness took him again.

CHAPTER 8

GRACE LOOKED DOWN AT HERSELF AND SIGHED. IT WAS JUST as bad as she'd imagined it would be. Worse, even. After all, there were *coveralls*. Between those and the knee-high rubber boots that were two sizes too big, Grace knew she looked more unattractive than she ever had in her entire adult life.

At least no one except Nan, the kennel owner, would see her like this. Telling herself to suck it up and be thankful that she was still alive, Grace tromped over to the power washer, passing one of the overhead doors. Both were open to let in the sunshine, and Grace could see the dogs playing in their various exercise yards. Despite the coveralls, she had to admit that some parts of the job weren't that bad, such as watching the dogs, especially two six-month-old puppies that romped and tumbled over each other. Cleaning up what they'd left behind, however, was not fun...not fun at all. She'd never had a pet as a kid. She *liked* dogs just fine, but taking care of them had never really been a part of her reality.

Now it was. And a dirty, stinky reality it was.

The empty, smelly kennels weren't going to clean themselves, though. Resigned, she gave one last mournful thought to her wonderful job at the college where she could dress up in pretty clothes and work her fund-raising magic and change people's lives. Then she lifted the power washer and got to work.

A squad car pulled up outside, and Grace held her breath. When Otto climbed out of the driver's side, however, she relaxed and ignored a silly pang of disappointment. He lifted a hand, returning her wave, before heading toward one of the exercise yards where a shy and scared Belgian Malinois huddled against the fence. Nan had told her that the dog was Otto's special project.

Grace caught movement out of the corner of her eye. She returned her gaze to the squad car and felt a rush of excitement that refused to be squashed. Hugh must've been in the front passenger seat, because now he was standing, leaning on the car and watching her. After hearing about the explosion, about how he almost *died*, she hadn't been able to stop thinking about him. She stared at him, unreasonably glad to see him in one piece. Her gaze rose to his face. Even from a distance, she could see his annoying smirk, and her relief dispersed, aggravation taking its place. She resisted the urge to make a rude gesture.

Determined to ignore him, Grace turned away from the squad car, momentarily forgetting the stream of water still jetting from the power washer. It hit a corner of the kennel wall and reflected right back at her, soaking her through in an instant.

With a bitten-off shriek, she turned off the water. Although she didn't even want to know, Grace couldn't stop herself from glancing down at her now-drenched coveralls. It was bad. Patting her loose bun, she tried to shove wet, bedraggled strands out of her face, but she knew that was a futile effort, especially when she heard a muffled laugh coming from one of the open doors.

"Shut it," she growled.

Hugh spread his hands in a gesture of pure innocence. "I haven't said anything yet."

How she wished she held a regular hose spray nozzle, rather than the power washer. After all, she didn't want to damage him; it just would've been nice to wash that annoying grin off his face. "Let's keep it that way."

He laughed. "What fun is that? Talking is one of my favorite things to do."

"Obviously," she muttered. He couldn't have just stayed quiet, swallowed his smirk, and walked away. He was Hugh. Obviously, the explosion hadn't damaged him too much if he still felt up to teasing her. Her next words tumbled out of her mouth without her permission. "How's your head?"

His smile dimmed just slightly before returning to full wattage. "Still where it's supposed to be. I might have lost a few brain cells, but there were plenty to spare."

Grace rolled her eyes. Of course he would joke about almost dying. Forget that she hadn't been able to sleep or think about anything else for the past five days since Jules had told her about the explosion. She didn't know why she cared, why she worried about him, why the idea of him almost dying made her heart hurt. It wasn't like they were friends. Every time they saw each other, they argued. Even now, seeing Hugh all happy and smirky and healthy-looking, she felt her worry turn to annoyance. "Have you found out who planted the bomb yet?"

"Can't talk about an ongoing investigation," he said lightly. "You know what we can talk about, though?"

"What?" she asked warily. He was just a few steps away, and she realized that she'd been moving closer without even realizing it. *Stupid feet. Don't they know he's an ass?*

Hugh gestured at her soaked coveralls. "This incredibly fashion-forward look you have going here."

Her finger hovered close to the trigger. So maybe he'd lose a little skin if she gave him a quick spray. Really, it was what he deserved. With a great effort of will, she kept the washer down at her side.

"You like it?" Posing with her free hand on her hip, she gave him her best sultry-model face. If she had to be stuck wearing wet coveralls and too-large rubber boots, then she was going to own the look.

He chuckled, although his gaze heated as he took her in. "Oh yeah. It's kennel chic."

"Right." Dropping the pose, she frowned at him, trying to figure out why he was looking at her like he wanted to eat her. There was nothing appealing about her at the moment. She knew this even before she glanced down again, confirming the horrid state of her appearance. "I miss wearing pretty things."

Immediately, his gaze sharpened. "Pretty things? Like what you used to wear to work? What did you do before in…Bangor?"

That slight pause reminded her that he was a cop—a cop who thought she was a liar. Tipping her head, she gave him a flirty look. "You want to know something?"

"Yeah. What?" He moved a half step closer, his inquisitive expression shifting to something a little… hungrier.

She smiled and leaned toward him. His gaze dropped

to her lips. "I'm beginning to understand why someone would want to blow you up."

To her surprise, he laughed. It made him even more stupidly attractive than usual, and Grace found herself unable to look away. "I'm told that a lot."

Thrown off guard, she scrambled for a witty retort. "Maybe you should, you know, work on that."

"Work on fixing my personality?" He leaned against the wall, and Grace gave a silent sigh. It looked as if he was settling in for a chat. As much as she welcomed an interruption from kennel cleaning, Hugh wasn't her first pick. Whenever he was around, she felt strange, unsettled, almost jittery. He'd pop into her head at odd times, and just the thought of him sent a rush of adrenaline through her veins. It was…uncomfortable.

She realized that he was watching her with a tiny, knowing smile, and she tried to remember what they'd been talking about. "Whatever." Grace figured that would cover most potential topics. "Why are you here?"

"Otto's working with his latest project."

"That explains why *he's* here. Why are *you* here?"

He smirked. The man was impossible to offend. "I was bored, so I tagged along. It's a good thing, too. We haven't talked much lately. I was going to stop by to watch *Tattered Hearts* with you again, but Theo gave me a little lecture about the importance of keeping my lockpicks in my pants."

"What a shame," she said flatly, proud of herself for not giving in and smiling. It was hard to resist Hugh's easy charm. "Well, this was a nice chat. We'll have to do it again sometime…or not."

His grin grew, and it became harder to keep her

deadpan expression in place. "Oh, our visit isn't over. Otto won't be done for a while yet. So tell me, Not-Grace, how long did you live in Bangor?"

"Almost two years."

"And before that?"

"Austin, Texas."

"For how long?"

"Eight months."

"Before that?"

"Portland."

"Maine or Oregon?"

"Oregon."

"Do you ever tell the truth?"

"Why do you think I'm lying?"

He smiled at her—a long, slow, easy, predatory baring of his teeth. "I can tell when someone's lying. It's my superpower."

Grace shivered and immediately hoped he hadn't noticed. By his expression, however, he'd seen it. He looked like a smug house cat, ready to pounce on a trapped mouse. "It's none of your business. So I've moved around a lot. That's not a crime. I haven't done anything wrong."

"Then why are you lying?"

"I told you." To her annoyance, she couldn't hold his gaze. Turning her head, she stared at one of the kennels. "I'm not lying. Go away. I have to get back to work."

She started spraying down the kennels again. The entire time, she felt his gaze on the back of her neck, as hot as sunburn on her skin. It made her crazy that he could bring out such a reaction in her, when she was just a suspect to him. Every time Hugh was nearby, her skin

buzzed and her blood flowed faster, and when he left, she
felt let down and lonely. He was a cop, and an annoying
one at that. Why did she allow him to affect her like this?
When she reached the end of the row, she couldn't take it
anymore. Turning, she huffed, "Would you please just…"

He was gone.

She glanced around, but she was alone. Moving
over to the door, she looked out and saw Hugh limping
slightly as he made his way to the squad car.

It was her turn to watch him. Crazily enough, she felt
slightly deflated now that he'd left. Shaking off her idi-
otic thoughts, she firmed her jaw and turned back to the
kennels. *Forget Hugh*, she told herself firmly. *There's
poo to clean.*

Even so, she couldn't resist a final glance out the
open door.

"Do you hate working there?"

Grace opened her mouth to tell the truth, but what
came out was the complete opposite. "No."

The relieved look on Jules's face made the lie worth
it. "Oh, I'm so glad! Nan loves you already, said you're
such a good worker and that she is already hoping that
you'll keep working there forever."

With a forced smile, Grace mentally hunted for
something positive to say. "Nan's nice." *True.* "And the
dogs are cute." *Also true.*

Jules beamed at her, giving her arm a pat with the
hand that wasn't holding the coffeepot. "That's wonderful! I'm so glad you found a job you like."

It took considerable effort for Grace to keep her false grin from turning into a grimace. "Sure is." Her cheeks were starting to ache from the effort. "I think that family over there is trying to get your attention."

After glancing over her shoulder, Jules turned back to Grace. "I'd better actually, you know, *work*. You'll be okay?"

"I'll be fine." Her smile became a little more genuine. Jules was just so sweet. She never seemed bitter about giving up her life to move to this pokey little town to play mom to her siblings and keep their disaster of a house upright using only strength of will and duct tape. Sometimes, Jules would make a joke that reminded Grace of Penny, and she'd miss her friend so much that it felt like her heart was being yanked out of her chest. "Go on. They look hungry."

With a final arm pat, Jules headed for the family's booth, and Grace could finally slump down and wallow like she'd wanted to do since she'd started her new, poo-filled job several days ago. One of the hardest things about living with five other people—four of them kids—was that she couldn't just mope around the house after work, eating ice cream and watching trashy television and fully indulging in a flat-out *my-life-sucks* sulk. Her room wasn't much of an escape. When she'd tried to hide the previous night, Dee had knocked, asking if Grace was okay, if she was *sure* she was okay, if she was *absolutely positive* she was okay, sounding more and more worried until Grace had plastered on a smile and emerged from her room to prove she was indeed *okay*. Dee had then talked her into playing one game of checkers that had turned into four.

Shortly after Grace had escaped, one of the twins had pounded on her door, saying that they'd been playing a modified game of curling in the dining room, during which there had been an incident with one of the broom handles, and now there *might* be a *tiny* hole in the ceiling that they *really* were hoping to fix before Jules got back from a parent-teacher conference.

After a semi-decent attempt to fix the dining room ceiling that involved homemade papier-mâché and some of Dee's white poster paint, Grace had ended up watching television with the kids for the rest of the night. It had all been so very…domestic.

Staring into her coffee cup, Grace wondered how this had happened. How had she gone from her wonderful, sparkling life to where she was now, sitting in a VFW-turned-diner in the shrinking town of Monroe, Colorado, and dreading her upcoming shift at a *dog kennel*?

"What's wrong?"

No. Please, no. Grace pushed her coffee out of the way so her forehead could hit the counter with a thump. *Why do you hate me, God?*

"Are you sad because Oliver's evil twin cheated on Constance with Tatiana?"

"Stop!" Sitting up abruptly, Grace covered her ears and glared at Hugh. He looked all amused and hot and cheerful sitting there on the stool next to hers—*right* next to hers—and that made her even crankier. How could he look so good when she was always such a mess around him? "Quit it, you nasty spoiler!"

He lifted his hands, palms out, as if to protect himself from her eye daggers. "Sorry! That was yesterday's episode, so I assumed you saw it. Oh, wait... That was during coverall fashion-show time, wasn't it?"

Since she could still hear his stupid voice, even with her ears covered, she dropped her hands and reached for her coffee again. She sipped it, pretending it wasn't as cold as Hugh's rotten, spoiler-y heart. Maybe if she ignored him, he'd go away.

With a groan that Grace knew was for dramatic purposes only, Hugh stretched out his leg. Since their stools were so close together, that put his foot right under hers, which were hooked on the bottom rung of the stool. For some dumb reason, her heart rate sped up.

From rage, she told herself, even as she recognized the lie. *Sheer rage*.

He shifted, and his knee bumped hers. When she transferred her glare from her coffee to his face, Grace caught the tail end of his smirk. That little knee touch had been intentional. "Respect my personal-space bubble, please."

"Did I...nudge you?" His eyes widened with completely unbelievable innocence. "So sorry. My leg—the one that was shot, you know—was feeling a bit stiff."

Her eyes narrowed, and she saw the corner of his mouth quiver. Even after knowing him for such a short time, she was perfectly aware that he was holding back a laugh. "So sorry your *leg* is *stiff*. Maybe you should walk a little to loosen it up." She gestured toward the door. "How about that way?"

He laughed, and Grace turned her gaze back to her now disgustingly cold coffee so she didn't reveal how much she liked the sound. "So, Grace Robinson... what's your birth date?"

"Why?" The seemingly random question made her glance at him again. "Are you planning to steal my identity?"

That look of fake innocence was back, but this time there was a harder edge hiding beneath it. "Of course not." He absently rubbed his thigh, and Grace wondered if his leg really was hurting. Three people—Dee, Jules, and Ty—had told her the story about how Hugh had been injured while heroically rescuing Sam during a school shooting. "Just wanted to make sure I knew when to bring over a birthday cake…and how many candles to put on it."

"That's okay. You won't be invited to my birthday party anyw—You weasel!" It had taken her several confused seconds to realize why he wanted to know her birth date. The ass wasn't just trying to get her to spill her secrets; he was actually *investigating* her! A reflexive surge of anger quickly morphed into fear. A *cop* was looking into her background, possibly checking databases and whatever other tools police had at their disposal. What had he found out about her? What did he know? Did Monroe share information with other police departments? Would Officer Jovanovic figure out that "Grace Robinson" from a small Colorado town was actually Kaylee Ramay from Los Angeles? Grace had no idea how police searches worked. All she knew was that she was screwed.

"I have to go." She twisted off her stool so quickly that she lost her balance and was forced to stumble back a few steps. "I'm late for…" It was like her anxiety had made her brain shut off. She couldn't be acting any more suspiciously if she'd tried. "Whatever. It's none of your business anyway." Her attempt to put more snap into her words failed when her voice quavered. It was time to walk away from this disaster before she made it worse.

"Hang on," Hugh said, but the need to escape overwhelmed Grace. She couldn't even pretend to act calm and unflustered. If she stayed, she was going to give herself away—even more than she already had.

Pivoting in a half circle, she scanned the viner for Jules, raising a hand in farewell when she caught her eye. Grace ignored Jules's *stay-there-I'll-be-over-in-just-a-minute* hand gestures and speed walked toward the door.

"Wait, Grace." Hugh was behind her...*right* behind her. If she walked any faster, she'd be flat-out bolting, so she went for plan B—the women's bathroom. The door was right next to the exit, so it only took her a few hurried steps to dodge inside. "Grace!"

The door closed behind her, shutting out Hugh. After quickly pushing in the button lock, Grace leaned back against the tiled wall. It was a tiny space without any stalls, just a sink and toilet. Grace's stomach fell when she didn't see any windows. It wouldn't have helped, though. If she crawled out a restroom window to escape from Hugh's questions, she'd only look guilty—guiltier.

A knock on the door made her jump. "Grace?" When she ignored him, the knocking increased in volume.

"Give me a minute!"

Thankfully, Hugh went quiet. She dreaded leaving the bathroom and facing him. The memory of how she'd checked him out, how his laugh had warmed her and her heart had sped up at his proximity, how comforting it had been to sit next to him while watching a soap opera, how stupidly safe he made her feel, brought an embarrassed flush to her cheeks. He was *investigating* her as if she were a criminal, at the same time that she was thinking how attractive he was. It was humiliating.

The seconds ticked by, and Grace knew she had to leave the bathroom, had to walk past Hugh and get to her car. Taking a deep breath, she pushed away from the wall and took a step toward the door.

The doorknob jiggled. She was opening her mouth to tell what was most likely a woman needing to use the bathroom that she'd be out in a second, when the button lock popped out.

Grace stared at it, horrified, as the knob turned and the door began to open. Suddenly, she was back in that bloody basement, watching the stairs. The torturers were coming back, they were here, and she was trapped. They were going to tie her up, and cut her, and beat her, and rip out one of her eyes, leaving a gaping, bloody socket—

"You okay?" Hugh asked, sticking his head and one burly shoulder through the opening.

Just like that, she jolted out of her waking nightmare, and her fear switched back to anger. "No! I'm not okay!" Her words came out in a screech. "You just *picked* the *lock* on the women's *bathroom* and stuck your big, stupid head inside while I was *in here*!"

He shrugged, one corner of his mouth turning up. "It's just a button lock. A two-year-old could've opened it. And it's not like your pants are off or anything." His gaze flickered down, and rage flared so strongly that her skin tingled. With a sound that came close to a roar, Grace shoved past him and stomped to the viner door.

"Grace," Hugh called after her. The ass sounded like he was trying not to laugh. She didn't even bother turning around, but slammed outside instead. The morning sunshine blinded her, and she stopped, blinking rapidly.

I'm not crying, she told herself, pressing the heels of her hands against her eyes. *It's just the sun. Hugh Murdoch is* not *getting to me.*

The door opened behind her, bumping into her back and pushing her forward a couple of steps. Knowing exactly who was standing behind her, she whirled around and glared.

Her glare must've been on point, because Hugh actually stopped right outside the door and winced. Laughter was still there, though, bubbling just under the surface of his contrite expression, and that brought Grace's rage up another notch, burning away any residual tears.

"You," she said through gritted teeth. Her jaw actually ached from how hard she was clenching it.

Taking a step closer, he let the door swing shut behind him. "Yes?"

"You are the most *aggravating* person I have ever met!"

"Really?" Although he looked relaxed, there was a sharp edge to his gaze. Grace couldn't tell if it was interest or excitement or just the look of a bloodhound on a trail—her trail. "Most people find me rather soothing."

"Liar."

With a shrug, he took another step. Although Grace wanted to stand her ground, she wasn't sure what would happen if he were within reach. Her hands itched to either punch him or grab him. Both would end badly, so she retreated a step.

The gleam in his eyes intensified, and he moved closer. As desperately as she wanted to bolt, she knew it would just make him chase her. "I have to get to work," she said, turning away and walking as casually as she could toward her car.

"Now who's the liar?" He was just a half step behind her. Even though she was running away in slow motion, his predator instincts had apparently been triggered. "You don't have to be at the kennel until eleven today."

Stopping abruptly, she whirled to face him. "How do you know my schedule, *stalker*?"

"I keep telling you, I'm not a stalker." Turning around had been a mistake, Grace realized. They were just inches apart. If she took too deep a breath, there would be chest touching. "I'm just…well informed."

With the way his face was tipped down toward hers, she could actually feel the warmth of his breath against her lips. Unexpected heat roared through her, and she rocked back. Unwilling to take a step away and give up ground again, Grace crossed her arms over her chest in an attempt to create a barrier between them. It didn't help; Hugh was still much too close for comfort. She scrambled to catch the thread of their conversation. "Well, stop being informed."

Even before he grinned, she knew that hadn't made any sense.

"About me. Stop informing yourself about me." That was even worse. Struggling to find her usual composure, Grace shifted back a step. That gave him the advantage, but she couldn't think with him so near. Stupid Hugh with his stupid, muscly body was distracting her.

"Sorry, Grace." His grin took on a shark-like cast.

"I'm not planning on stopping. You're a puzzle, and I don't like things to go...unsolved."

The last of her equanimity disappeared, evaporated with the knowledge that he wasn't going to quit investigating her. Beneath her anger and the anxiety about what he'd discover, there was a hard kernel of disappointment. She didn't want to be interesting to Hugh because she was some sort of unsolved puzzle. Despite herself, she wanted him to be interested because she was fascinating to him.

A tiny, dumb part of her wished that he was as attracted to her as she was to him.

When she realized she was just staring at him, thinking silly, useless thoughts, Grace abruptly turned and walked—well, stomped—toward her car. She was parked on the other side of the building, and she cursed herself for not picking one of the front spots instead. If she had, she'd already be inside, away from Hugh's looming presence. Having her car sitting exposed, for anyone to see if they drove past, bothered her, though, so she tended to pick the most hidden spots she could find. It didn't matter that the car wasn't registered to her real name. Maybe she was being paranoid, but she just didn't want to take any chances. One screwup, and she would be dead.

She turned the corner. Although she couldn't hear footsteps behind her, she knew he was there, and close. Shooting him a narrowed-eyed look over her shoulder, she snapped, "Don't you have something better to do than follow me?"

"Not really." Although his words were light, the usual humor wasn't there. Instead, he met her gaze with an intensity that made her whip her head around so she was facing forward again. Jokey Hugh was one thing, but smoldering Hugh could be a serious problem.

"Grace." He caught her hand, bringing her to a halt. Although her feet stopped moving, almost of their own accord, she kept her gaze focused on her car. "Grace, look at me."

She couldn't do it. If she looked at him, she wouldn't be able to think. It wasn't good that the man who had the drive to discover her secret made her incapable of rational thought. A tug at her hand made her realize that she was stuck. Until she met his eyes, Hugh was going to stay there.

I can do this. She'd faced worse than Hugh over the past two weeks.

Setting her jaw, she turned around. Her gaze traveled up his solid chest, over his serious face, and locked on to his gaze.

"Why are you running away from me?" he asked, sounding completely sincere. "You can trust me."

Unable to look away, she just pressed her lips together. She couldn't trust anyone. Martin Jovanovic's reach was too extensive. She'd made that mistake already, and it had left her hunted and crouching by a dumpster.

"I can help you." He tugged her closer, and her traitor body gave in to his pull. His head tipped down, and air from his words brushed her cheek. Her breath left her in a shuddering rush as her eyes closed. He felt so safe, so solid, so strong…

"What's your name?" he asked softly, directly in her ear. "Your *real* name?"

With a frustrated sound, she jerked her hand away.

He was playing her, using her attraction to him to get the information he wanted. "You are such an ass!" She started to stomp away, but Hugh caught her again, around the waist that time. He pulled her tightly against him, her back pressing against his front.

"It would make things a lot easier for both of us if you'd just tell me the truth." The rasp in his voice and the way his breath brushed her ear distracted her, tempting her to sink into the heat and strength of him—but then the meaning of his words hit her.

Clenching her teeth to hold back a frustrated scream, she yanked out of his grip and spun around. "I am not your puzzle to solve," she gritted out, poking him in the chest with each word. "I'm not one of your suspects. You do not get to interrogate me."

He caught her jabbing finger in a firm but gentle grip. Their eyes met, and his were hot and shockingly hungry. "You're so beautiful when you're yelling at me."

Her mouth fell open, but she couldn't say anything else. Was he serious this time, or had that just been another way to distract her, to disarm her? "Quit trying to butter me up. It's not going to make me tell you anything."

"I mean it." His expression was completely earnest. There wasn't a hint of laughter to be seen.

She stared at him, fury and anxiety and desire all swirling together in a molten mixture that burned her from the inside. This man was going to be the death of her. "You are so…"

"I'm so…what?" His gaze dropped to her mouth. "Hot?" The lilt of humor had returned to his voice.

"Arrrgh!" She started to turn away, fully prepared to stomp to her car, after which she would perhaps run him over several times, but his fingers closed around her arm, tugging her back around. Grace opened her mouth, ready to tell him off, but then her gaze collided with his. All amusement had been erased from his expression. The heat, the hunger burning in his eyes erased all thoughts of their latest argument and lit an answering inferno inside her.

Then his lips were on hers, and Grace was lost.

CHAPTER 9

THERE WAS NO HESITATION, NO MOMENT OF SHOCK. FROM the second their mouths met, Grace was kissing him back. All the anger, all the worry, all the aggravation she'd been feeling just seconds before were burned away by heat and need.

Hugh yanked her against him, and she went willingly, clutching at his shoulders. She'd never felt anything so intense, so incredible, as the feel of his mouth on hers. He kissed her hard, taking control. Sliding a hand behind his head, she nipped his lower lip and bossed him right back. They traded, giving and taking, back and forth, as if one of their arguments had transformed into a kiss — and it was wonderful.

She couldn't stay still, wanting to feel all of him at once, her hands greedily roaming over his shoulders and up his neck to the back of his head and then down again. Her fingers clenched around handfuls of his shirt, bunching it in her fists so she could use her grip to drag him even more tightly against her. She felt as if she couldn't get near enough, couldn't kiss him hard enough, couldn't hold him tightly enough.

With a grunt of pleasure, he pulled her even closer, his kiss deepening until she forgot to breathe. His hands roved over her as if he would die if he couldn't touch her, sliding over her back and then down to grab her hips. His squeeze sent a shock of desire through her, so intense and unexpected that she lurched forward, knocking them both off-balance. Hugh took a step back to catch them, never letting go of her. She loved how easily he caught her and held both of them upright.

There was a sharp *thwack*, the sound so close that her eardrum buzzed. A spot on her cheek stung sharply, like she'd been poked by a needle. Hugh's arms turned into hard bands of steel around her as his entire body stiffened.

Before she could manage to make a sound, she was on the ground with Hugh on top of her, no longer kissing. Her brain, still lost in the kiss, tried to catch up with what was happening. As her thoughts spun and her cheek throbbed, Hugh's weight ground her shoulder blades painfully into the pavement.

"What?" she tried to ask, but shock and Hugh's bulk pressed all the air out of her lungs. Before she could figure out how to breathe again, Hugh yanked her to her feet and gripped her arm, half pulling and half carrying her the short distance to her car.

"Get down," he barked, yanking her into the narrow space between her Subaru and the dumpsters. He had his gun out, gripped in the hand that wasn't holding on to her. As they crouched next to the car, he scanned the buildings around them.

Her shocked confusion was fading enough for her to fumble for her phone. "What's happening?" she asked, keeping her voice low. Her fingers were shaking, making it hard to dial, but she managed to punch in 911. Somewhere in the back of her mind, she realized that she'd been reduced to huddling by a dumpster again. This time, at least, Hugh was with her.

"Someone took a shot at us," he said. He didn't sound like Hugh, or even look like Hugh at that moment. It was as if someone had replaced the sarcastic cop with someone else—someone harder, sharper. It took a second for her to understand what he was talking about, and her gaze flew over to the wall where they'd just been standing, locked together in a kiss.

There was a large chunk of brick missing from a spot right where their heads had been. If she hadn't lurched forward at his touch, making them lose their balance, one of them would be dead.

Martin Jovanovic had found her.

Even before terror washed over her, regret and guilt hit her hard. Hugh's arm circled her, keeping her below the window line while, at the same time, keeping her close to him. Even though Grace knew she didn't deserve it, that it was her fault this innocent man had almost been killed, she was grateful for the heavy, comforting weight of his arm and the warm shelter of his body. Even as her heart pounded, as every muscle tightened in anticipation of the next gunshot, she leaned into his warmth, soaking in the rare feeling of being protected.

Guilt seeped in, though, pushing her to tell the truth. She opened her mouth to apologize, to confess that she'd nearly gotten Hugh killed, but the dispatcher answered before she could.

"*Nine-One-One Emergency*."

"Someone—oh God—someone shot at us!" Grace stammered out a mixed-up version of what was happening and where they were. Too much was tumbling through her head, though, and she kept losing her train of thought. She stared across the street, trying to figure out what Hugh was focused on—if it was the shooter—but all she saw was an empty building.

"Ma'am? Ma'am, are you still there?"

"Sorry!" Realizing that she'd missed one of the dispatcher's questions, Grace put the phone on speaker.

"Was anyone hit? What is your status?" The dispatcher's voice echoed from her phone speaker, sounding too loud in the tense silence.

When Hugh paused instead of answering, Grace glanced at him and found that he was staring at her cheek, scowling fiercely. She touched the spot, pulling her hand away so she could look at it. There was a small smear of blood on her fingers. She remembered the sting as the bullet hit the wall, but her cheek didn't hurt anymore. She assumed her face had been scratched by a chip of dislodged brick or something. "It's nothing. I'm fine."

Although his frown didn't lessen, Hugh told the dispatcher, "No one was hit."

"Is the shooter still in the area?"

"I don't know." Tensing, Hugh focused on the building across the street again. "There haven't been any other shots fired since the first."

As the dispatcher continued asking questions, Hugh clipped out the answers, still sounding like a cold, brusque stranger. Despite that, Grace tucked herself a little more tightly against him. Stranger or not, Hugh felt safe. His arm tightened, and she felt another surge of regret. If he knew that she was the reason they'd been shot at, that she'd let him blindly risk his life while she knew that someone as dangerous and far-reaching as Martin Jovanovic was trying to kill her, he wouldn't be offering her comfort.

"I'm so sorry."

"What?" Hugh asked, even as he kept scanning the area. "Why are you sorry?"

"For almost getting you killed."

This time, he looked at her, just a quick flash of surprise before his attention turned back to searching out the threat. "What are you talking about? It wasn't your fault." His brow furrowed. "I'm the one someone is trying to shoot…or blow up."

The reminder that his truck had exploded—and that *he'd* almost been inside it when it had—made Grace choke with remorse. That had to have been her fault, too. There was no way it was a coincidence. After all, Hugh was a good-natured cop—and an injured one, at that. Who would want to hurt him? Maybe Martin had seen them together. It could be a warning to Grace, or he'd wanted to hurt her by killing Hugh, or…who knew what. All Grace knew was that Martin Jovanovic wanted her dead. If bombs and guns were going off in this sleepy town, odds were that she was the target.

"No." After working so hard to keep her mouth shut, to sell the story of Grace Robinson, most recently from Bangor, Maine, it was painfully difficult to tell him the truth. "I'm…"

Sirens interrupted her, reminding her that the dispatcher was still on speaker and that it was probably not the best time for a confession—especially since someone was *shooting* at them. She would tell him as soon as they were safe. Her messy, dangerous life was threatening Hugh, and he deserved to know what was going on. He couldn't protect himself if he didn't know who was gunning for him...literally.

She followed Hugh's gaze to the building across the street from the VFW. The sun reflected off the windows on the second floor, hiding whatever—or whoever—was inside. Someone could be watching them right now, or even aiming a gun at them, ready to take a second shot, one that wouldn't miss this time. With a shudder, Grace crouched lower behind the dubious safety of her car, even as she imagined a bullet passing right through the Subaru and into her or Hugh's vulnerable body.

The sirens got louder, and then went silent, replaced by the sounds of slamming doors and urgent commands.

"*Officers are on scene.*" The dispatcher's voice made Grace jump and almost drop the phone. "*I'll let you know when they give the all clear.*"

"Copy," Hugh responded, still staring at the building across the street. "Tell them to check the offices above the laundromat. I'm pretty sure the shot came from the center window."

"*Copy.*"

The phone went silent again. From Grace's position, she couldn't see what was happening, and her feet were falling asleep. When she tried to stand slightly to peek through the car windows, Hugh tightened his arm around her, keeping her in that low, crouched position. Not knowing what was happening was driving her crazy, so she decided to settle for secondhand information.

Twisting her head to look at Hugh, she asked, "What's going on over there?"

"They're searching the building." Even though his

voice sounded more relaxed than it had a few minutes earlier, he kept scanning the area around them, and he didn't put away his gun. "Doubt they're going to find the shooter, though. I'm guessing he ran right after he took the shot."

"He's gone? Then why can't I look?"

"Just be patient. They're almost done." His hold relaxed as Hugh reached up and patted her on the head. Her mouth dropped open. He actually *patted* her on the *head*. Like she was an obedient toddler or a puppy who'd learned to sit on command. After the all clear, she was so going to punch him. Hard. In his stupid, too-appealing face.

Then she remembered that this whole thing was her fault, and that he'd almost gotten a bullet in his stupid, too-appealing face, and all of her righteous indignation drained out of her. "Hugh..."

Something in her voice must have caught his attention, because he interrupted his scan of the street and actually looked at her.

"I know who he is. The shooter."

"You saw him? Did you recognize him? Can you describe him?" The rapid-fire questions made Grace flinch, and Hugh visibly forced himself to calm. "Sorry about that. I just really want to get this guy." His arm tightened around her shoulders, and he stared at her for a long moment before turning his attention back to the building. When he spoke again, it was in his normal, jokey tone. "I really loved that truck he blew up."

Grace would've felt slighted if he didn't have her snuggled tight against him as if he were afraid to let her go. "It might not be him. I don't think he does his own dirty work," she said, aware that the words weren't coming out in a logical, understandable way. Everything that had just happened—the kiss, the gunshot, Hugh's side hug, her realization that she was the cause of them almost dying—was muddling her brain. She just wanted to go home, lock her bedroom door, and pull a pillow over her head. Either that, or burst into tears.

"It might not be who?" Hugh spared her a quick glance before scanning the lot again. "Are you thinking your ex is responsible? Because this doesn't have an angry-boyfriend feel to it. That's more direct confrontation and punching, not blowing up beloved trucks and taking aim from an upstairs window. I'm pretty sure this is work-related—on my side, not yours. Not that there aren't unbalanced dog owners, but the likelihood—"

"Hugh!" Grace interrupted, pinching his side. To her annoyance—and grudging fascination—there was nothing to grab. He was as hard and unpinchable as a rock. "Would you shut up for five seconds and let me get this out?"

"Only if you quit pinching me." Although he twisted away from her hand, he kept his arm locked protectively around her, so he wasn't able to get far. "Don't you think we've seen enough violence today?"

If he hadn't been holding a gun, and if she hadn't been reluctant to lose the comfort of his warm body, Grace would've shoved him, hard. "It's like you're physically incapable of being quiet for five seconds. Oh my freaking God, I've known kindergartners with untreated ADHD who are better listeners than you."

"That's a bit harsh—"

This time, it wasn't Grace who interrupted him.

"Would you knock this shit off?" Theo demanded, stomping around to their side of the car with his K9 partner, Viggy, next to him.

A little abashed, Grace turned toward him. "Sorry. I forgot what was happening. It's just that he would not stop talking."

"What? No." The grooves in Theo's forehead deepened along with his frown as he glared at Hugh, who let her go as he straightened to his full height. "I wasn't talking about that. You need to figure out who you've pissed off so we can go take them down. I'm sick of this near-death bullshit."

The dispatcher cleared her throat over the phone. "*All clear.*" She sounded as if she was trying not to laugh. "*I'm going to disconnect the call now.*"

"Thank you," Grace said absently, standing up. She couldn't stop looking at the building across the street, feeling vulnerable without the car between her and the spot where the shooter had been. Her feet prickled painfully as blood rushed back into them, and she put her hand on the car to catch her balance. Hugh reached out as if to steady her, but then he hesitated and withdrew his hand. She missed his comforting touch, but, now that the immediate danger had passed, she knew she had to stand on her own two feet again.

Hugh holstered his gun, although he still was glancing warily around them, as if he hadn't accepted that the threat was over. "Tell me about it. This is getting old. Grace was almost hit just now." There was an un-Hugh-like growl in his last words, and she raised her eyebrows, surprised. He caught her gaze and then cleared his throat. His voice came out lighter. "And I really did like that truck."

"This isn't a joke," Theo almost snarled, taking a step closer to Hugh as his hands balled into fists. "Who's doing these things? We need to catch this asshole."

Grace glanced back and forth between the two cops. Theo looked like he was about to punch Hugh, and, although part of her could appreciate the sentiment, she wanted information before they went off on another tangent. "You didn't find him?"

Theo glanced at Grace. "No." Although he appeared snarly, Grace was pretty sure it was at the situation and not her. "Looks as if he took the shot from that center second-floor office, like you thought, but he was gone when we got there. Viggy tracked him out the back door and a half block east down the alley before he lost the trail."

"Left in a car, probably," Hugh guessed, and Theo jerked his head in agreement.

"The LT has people going door to door, checking to see if anyone saw an unfamiliar vehicle." Theo let out a frustrated huff. "Not many people are left in town, so it's a long shot."

"Have to ask, though," Hugh said. "We need to get this guy."

"Who'd do this? First, your truck explodes, and now this?" Theo asked, glaring at Hugh. "Who'd you piss off so bad they want you dead?"

Grace's shoulders sagged under the weight of her guilt. "Hugh didn't piss off anyone. It was me."

CHAPTER 10

"I TOLD YOU IT'S PROBABLY NOT YOUR EX-BOYFRIEND," Hugh said.

"I know it's not him." When Hugh opened his mouth as if he was going to interrupt again, she rushed out the rest of the words, needing to say it, to get confession time over with. "It's his uncle."

"His uncle? Whose uncle?" Theo had his gaze locked on her, his expression set in harsh lines. He'd softened toward her since she'd arrived in town, but any hint of friendliness was now erased. "Why is he trying to kill Hugh?"

"Martin Jovanovic," she said. "I think he's trying to get to me through Hugh."

As she said Martin's name, both men went perfectly still. If Grace hadn't been so eaten up by guilt, she could've appreciated the fact that she'd finally stunned Hugh into silence. Their expressions were telling, however. Not only did they know the name, but they knew just how bad it was to be Martin's enemy. She tried to swallow, but her throat seemed to have closed.

"You're dating Martin Jovanovic?" Hugh asked, his voice low and deadly serious.

Grace's chest tightened. "No. I was dating his nephew. We were at his uncle's house in LA—that's where I live...*lived*—when I got lost searching for a bathroom." Her laugh was rough and humorless. Her entire life had been destroyed because Noah gave bad directions. "I found these three guys..." The scene played in her head, as vivid and terrifying as ever.

"Hey." Hugh cupped her face, tilting her head so she met his eyes. "Tell me, Gracie."

She stared at him, taking comfort and strength from his touch and steady gaze. Although she was vaguely aware of Theo's silent presence, she focused on Hugh. He was the one she needed to share her nightmare with. "They'd been tortured." Her voice shook, but she managed to keep talking. "Tied up and tortured. One guy was unconscious, and another's face was so swollen that he didn't even look like a person anymore."

A memory of the empty eye socket flashed through her mind, but she couldn't talk about that. For some reason, of all the terrible things she saw that night, that visual still horrified her the most. "I helped free them, and they escaped." She hoped they had, at least. It kept her up at night—wondering where they were, if they'd gotten out of the house, if the unconscious man had survived.

"How'd you get away?" Hugh's voice was harsh, but his hand on her face was gentle.

"I almost didn't." Even though the bruises on her arms had faded to yellow, she could still feel Martin's hold on her. "I went out a back door and snuck around to the front. The valet was getting my car when Martin grabbed me and tried to drag me inside."

With a sound that could only be called a growl, Hugh wrapped his arms around her and pulled her against his chest. "I'm going to kill him. This is my new life goal, to end Martin 'Fuckface' Jovanovic."

Even though he'd sounded completely serious, his words still made Grace choke out a laugh.

"How'd you get away from Jovanovic?" Theo's question reminded Grace of his presence, and she turned her head to look at him without pulling away from Hugh. She needed his arms around her if she wanted to get through reliving that horrible night.

She lifted her shoulders in a movement that would've been a shrug if she hadn't been squashed against Hugh. "A lucky shot to the groin, and then a knee to his face."

Hugh's arms tightened around her. "Nice. Good job, Kick-Ass Gracie."

"I went to the police, but he had a guy there." Officer Jovanovic's expressionless face flickered in her mind, and she shivered. Hugh stroked her back. "I ran. My friend…" Her voice quavered on the word. She missed Penny so much it hurt. "My friend works at a women's shelter. She gave me the number of a guy who helps people start new lives."

"Who?" Theo asked.

She wasn't about to rat out Mr. Espina, not even to the good guys. She already felt guilty enough about involving Jules and her family in her mess. "He helped me. Why does it matter?"

"No," Hugh corrected. "He means who's the dirty cop in LA?" Theo nodded grimly.

"Logan Jovanovic." Even just saying the name made her nervous. She stepped out of Hugh's hold, and he reluctantly let her go. A feeling of vulnerability, of being watched, hunted, swamped her. "Could we go somewhere else? Somewhere private? Not so... exposed?"

Theo and Hugh exchanged a look before Theo moved away from her car. When she started to follow, Hugh held her back with a gentle hand on her forearm.

"I'll protect you." His tone was completely serious, and he said the words as if they were a pledge. After studying his face for a long moment, allowing the warmth of his offer to spread through her, she nodded and moved to catch up with Theo. Hugh rested his hand on her lower back, and she welcomed the comfort of it. She told herself not to get used to it, though. Saving people was his job. She couldn't read any more into his actions than that, or she'd just be asking to get hurt. He'd protect her from Martin Jovanovic, but it was up to Grace to keep her heart safe from Hugh.

"Station?" Theo said in a low voice.

"Nope. If LT sees me there..." Hugh didn't finish his sentence, but from Theo's acknowledging grunt, he didn't have to.

"My house?"

Hugh snorted. "Is a closet imitating a house. Let's go to my place."

"What time is it?" Grace asked. It felt like hours had passed since she'd stormed out of the diner with Hugh in pursuit. "I have to go to work at eleven."

"You're not going anywhere by yourself until we get this situation figured out."

His resolute tone made her automatically balk, and she opened her mouth to tell him that he was not the boss of her—although in a slightly more mature way— when reason reasserted itself. If Martin or one of his minions was taking shots at her, she didn't want to be alone. "I can't ask for a round-the-clock police escort."

"Ask or not, you're getting one."

"You?" A mixture of pleasure and exasperation coursed through her at the thought of being with Hugh twenty-four hours a day. They would most likely kill each other.

"Me."

As he shot them both a sideways glance, Theo almost looked amused. "At least it'll keep you busy and off our calls. LT will be happy."

Hugh's response—a rude one, judging by his expression—was cut off when Jules came running from the front of the VFW. Barreling into Grace, she grabbed her in a hard hug. "Grace! Oh my goodness! Are you okay? The cops made us stay in the viner until they gave the all clear, so I couldn't see what was going on. Were you hurt?"

Something about the honest concern in Jules's voice made tears rush to the surface, and Grace blinked rapidly, forcing them back. There would be no crying on her part until she was safely ensconced at the house with her head under a pillow. "I'm fine," she lied.

"Are you sure? Did someone actually shoot at y'all? What about you, Hugh? Were you hit?" Jules's gaze ran over them frantically, as if searching for blood and bullet holes. The realization of what a close call it had been finally hit Grace, and she swayed slightly. Hugh must've felt it, because he moved his hand from her lower back to her far hip and tugged her into his side. It was weak of her, Grace knew, but she couldn't help leaning against him.

"I'm fine, Jules," Hugh said with a *pbbtt* sound. "So I got shot at again. It's happening to me so often lately that it's sort of becoming old. I wish the people trying to kill me would change it up a little. You know, get creative."

"Like use an explosion?" Theo asked pointedly. Despite his crabby expression, he reached over and took one of Jules's hands and tugged her toward him.

"Nah," Hugh said with a faux-casual shrug. "That's getting stale, too. Why doesn't someone come at me with nunchucks next time? Or a chainsaw?"

And that was it. Hugh joking so casually about getting killed made something inside Grace snap. In vivid detail, she saw the table of horrible tools, the bloodstained floor, the tortured men's battered, swollen features. Now, though, they all had Hugh's face. Her locked-down tears burst free.

"For goodness' sake, Hugh!" Jules scolded, rushing to put her arms around Grace and pull her out of Hugh's hold. "Why do you always have to make everyone cry?"

"What?" Although he let Grace go, Hugh patted her awkwardly on the back and shoulders. "I do not make everyone cry! When have I ever… Okay, so there was that one other time, but twice doesn't mean *always*."

Ignoring his protests, Jules started to usher Grace toward the VFW entrance. "C'mon, sweetie. Let's go inside."

"We need to talk to her." It was Theo's turn to protest.

"Besides"—Hugh stayed right next to them—"I have to stick with Grace. Wherever she goes, I go."

For some reason, those words brought forth a fresh round of sobs. Each time she thought things couldn't get any worse, life laughed and then punched her in the face. Martin Jovanovic had found her, and now she was endangering Hugh. Apparently, the threat of death wasn't enough to keep the guy away.

Even though she couldn't decide whether she wanted to argue with Hugh or kiss him again, she did know one thing: the thought of him being killed gutted her. They'd been lucky today, but the next bullet could easily find its mark...right in Hugh's head.

She'd never survive that.

"It doesn't make any sense." Frowning, Hugh leaned on the handle of the mop he was using. All three K9 cops had come with Grace to the kennel for her shift. To her surprise, Hugh and Theo had pitched in to help clean. It was amazing how quickly the work got done with their help.

Grace was the slowest moving, thanks to Lexi, who couldn't seem to get close enough to her. Several times, she'd almost tripped over the dog after Lexi had parked her furry self right next to her. It was as if the dog knew that Grace was the one in danger, so Lexi had appointed herself Grace's personal guardian.

"Except for the fact that I'm a cop handling a dog trained in narcotics detection," Hugh continued, "there is no reason for Martin Jovanovic to want me dead. He doesn't even know about me...or Lexi. Why would he try to kill us?"

"Also, you survived both times. From what I know of Jovanovic, he's not incompetent." Theo tied off the top of a full garbage bag and then lifted it out of the container without any visible effort. Although the play of his muscles didn't fascinate Grace as much as if Hugh had been the one flexing, she couldn't help but watch. A balled-up paper towel hit her on the side of the head, bouncing off harmlessly.

Grace turned narrowed eyes on Hugh. "That better have been clean."

"It was. Mostly. Now stop drooling over Theo and pay attention to me."

From his spot in a desk chair by the door, Otto cleared his throat. "Or we can pay attention to this Jovanovic situation." Instead of helping to clean, Otto had brought out the dog he was training. From what Grace had seen, the Belgian Malinois had a long way to go. Every time someone even thought about moving, the dog flattened herself against the floor in fear. She was currently wedged under the desk next to Otto, who didn't seem discouraged by his trainee's antisocial behavior. Every time the dog stuck out her head to peek at them, Otto slipped her a treat.

"I'm sorry." It was the umpteenth time Grace had apologized since spilling the whole ugly, terrifying story. "If I'd known he would find me so quickly, I'd never have led him here."

"I don't think it's him," Hugh said. "If it—" Tones from the portable radio on Theo's duty belt interrupted Hugh. Everyone went quiet, listening as the dispatcher requested backup for a traffic stop. Otto and Theo immediately headed for their vehicles.

"Why is Otto going?" Grace asked, watching as he returned the scared dog to her kennel. "He's not on duty right now."

"C'mon." Instead of answering, Hugh grabbed her hand and started towing her out of the kennel after them. She immediately tripped over Lexi, who'd stretched out in front of Grace, and stumbled forward a few steps before catching her balance.

"Hang on." When she leaned back against his hold, he stopped, looking impatiently at her, as if she was being unreasonable by not blindly following wherever he decided to go. "What are you doing? You're on leave, and I'm working."

With an impatient huff, he released her so he could yank out his cell phone and poke at the screen. "Nan? Hugh. There's an emergency, and Grace is my ride. The kennel's clean, so we're going to take off. That okay with you, boss lady? Good. We'll be here day after tomorrow at eleven."

The "we" both irritated Grace and made her feel incredibly relieved that she didn't have to deal with the Jovanovic situation alone anymore. Any gratitude she felt toward Hugh disappeared, however, when he grabbed her hand again and rushed them to her car with Lexi tagging close behind.

"Wait! At least let me lose the coveralls," she said.

Hugh opened the back door for Lexi to hop in and waited impatiently as Grace stripped off to her street clothes. Once she'd stuffed the coveralls into the back of the Subaru, Hugh headed for the driver's seat.

"Uh…no." Using the pointiest part of her elbow, she prodded him aside so she could get behind the wheel. "My car. I drive."

The corners of his mouth turned up in that ever-present smirk. "Yes, Ms. Cavewoman." Without any argument, he rounded the front of the car and hopped into the seat next to her. "Just drive fast."

"I will. As soon as you tell me where we're going and why."

"We're going to the traffic-assist call. Because we're helpful like that."

"Aren't you on leave?"

"Technically."

"Then why are you going on this call?"

His casual tone took on a serious edge. "Because the assist is actually the responding officer's way of saying that the Rack and Ruin motorcycle club is about to pass through town—and *not* on the day we expected them. Those MC guys can be so inconsiderate."

"So…?"

"So, the highway through Monroe is the most direct route to the ski town of Dresden, known for its scenic views and wealthy vacationers, some of whom really like their high-end drugs. The R and R guys, being the givers that they are, would love to help those tourists in need." He looked at her and then at the ignition, but Grace didn't start the car.

"That doesn't explain why *you* need to be there." The thought of confronting a bunch of dangerous, drug-toting motorcyclists made her cringe. "Or me. My new-life resolution is to avoid scary bad guys, not chase after them."

All humor dropped away, and he met her gaze evenly. "Lex is the only narcotics-detection dog we've got. I just want to be close by in case…well, in case we're needed. You have to come along because I'm not leaving you alone, now that I know Jovanovic is gunning for you." That irrepressible upward quirk of his lips reappeared.

Grace had known he wouldn't be able to keep it down for long. "Also, you're my ride. Since my truck blew up and all."

She studied him. It didn't sound so bad when he put it like that. They'd be staying a safe distance away from the Rack and Ruin traffic stop, but close enough that Lexi would be there if they needed to use her drug-sniffing skills.

Grace still hesitated, though. The man was good at getting his way, and his way seemed to lead to trouble a lot. Despite that, she trusted him. It probably was an indicator of mental deficiency on her part, but it was still true. Something inside her told her that Hugh would keep her safe, even if it killed him.

She turned on the car. "Don't make me regret this."

"Or have to turn this car around," Hugh joked.

"Damn straight."

═══════════════════

Silence fell over the car as Grace turned off the kennel driveway and onto the county road that led down the mountain to Monroe. Hugh watched her drive for a few seconds, enjoying the opportunity to look his fill without her snarling at him. Then he started to miss the snarling.

"How old are you, anyway?"

Grace gave him a sideways look before refocusing on the twisting, narrow road. Her hands gripped the steering wheel tightly enough to whiten her fingers. Clearly she wasn't that comfortable with mountain driving. "Is this another attempt to figure out my birth date?"

"No." Hugh put as much innocence as possible into his expression as she shot him another suspicious glance. "This is an attempt to figure out why you're driving like you're ninety years old. I figured it was possible you might actually be an elderly person with really good genes. Or an excellent plastic surgeon."

"If I didn't have to keep both hands on the wheel so we don't drive off the cliff and plunge to our fiery deaths," she responded in a conversational tone, "I'd punch you so hard, Hugh Murdoch."

He couldn't help it; he laughed. Settling back in his seat, he prepared himself for a lengthy drive to town. At least he got to stare at her. Grace was startlingly beautiful, even when—or maybe *especially* when—she was making violent threats against his person. That kiss outside the VFW ran through his brain. Until someone shot at them, it had been incredible, and so intense that it had wiped his brain of every logical thought.

Her hair was caught up in an untidy bun, and the lines of her neck and jaw looked so vulnerable. Now that he knew she wasn't just dodging a scumbag ex-boyfriend— which had been bad enough—but was actually running from the likes of *Martin Jovanovic*, his protective instincts had kicked into high gear. Although he'd never met Jovanovic, the name was unpleasantly familiar to every member of law enforcement. After all, Jovanovic was like the king of criminals, heading up a crooked empire from his castle in California. The man seemed to have his finger in every sordid pie, from human trafficking to drug running to illegal weapon sales.

When he looked at Grace and thought about how Jovanovic wanted her dead, Hugh was unable to breathe.

The weight of it settled heavily on his chest, making it nearly impossible to draw in air. He must've made a sound, some kind of strangled attempt at an inhale, because Grace shot him another glance. This time, it was full of concern rather than irritation.

"You okay?"

"Fine." The word came out rough, but he cleared his throat and ignored it. When he glanced out the window, searching for a distraction from Grace, her hotness, and her ruthless enemy, Hugh saw that they were approaching Baker Street. The Rack and Ruin stop would be six blocks east. "Turn left."

To his surprise, she did what he asked without question.

"Pull over next to that house with the cedar siding."

"That's every house on this block."

It probably had been too much to ask for her docile streak to last. If he was being honest, he didn't really want it to. He liked her sassiness. "Not every house. There's a gray one."

"That one is gray because it has really *old* cedar siding."

"Fine. Just pull over next to that one up there."

"Which one?"

"The one with the mailbox."

"Are you kidding me right now?"

He kind of was. It was just so much fun to bait her. "Of course not. Is it my fault that you can't follow simple directions?"

In response, she snarled at him. If her expression was any indication, she was thinking about punching him. It probably wasn't in his best interest to provoke her.

A mental image of that earlier kiss jumped into his head, and he shifted in his seat. On the other hand, maybe he did need to get her riled up, if another kiss like that was the result.

Grace pulled the car to the curb with an annoyed lurch. "What next?" she asked.

Abruptly reminded of the reason they were lurking on Baker Street, Hugh reached for his door handle. As soon as he opened his door, he could hear the rumbling of unmuffled motorcycle engines. Even though he wasn't part of the bust, adrenaline still flooded through him, making everything sharper and brighter. He surged out of the car.

His leg chose that moment to protest, and he had to grab the top of the door to keep from sprawling on the street. He scowled down at his thigh, mentally cursing the injury. Because of that stupid gunshot wound, he was on the sidelines of what could be a huge bust. Frustration warred with caution, and caution lost. It usually did with him. "Let's get a little closer."

Ignoring Grace's *is-that-really-a-good-idea* look, he leashed up Lexi. By her eager, ready posture, the dog was obviously feeling the same excitement he was. As she climbed out of the car, Grace looked significantly less enthused than Lexi. She locked the doors, and Hugh snorted.

"What?" Despite her aggrieved tone, she fell into step with him.

"City girl," he teased, even as thoughts of where he could see the action while still keeping Grace and Lexi out of harm's way coursed through his mind. There was a squatty printing shop right off Main Street with a sturdy, climbable tree right next to it. The view from the shop's roof should be perfect if the other officers had stopped the R and R convoy where they'd been planning to do the bust a few days earlier. "We don't lock our cars around here."

"Then what's to stop people from stealing loose change out of my cup holders?" she asked with mock seriousness. Hugh loved that she could banter with him, that she didn't ignore him or get offended, but gave it right back to him. "I'm a minimum-wage earner now. Every penny I get from cleaning up dog poo is precious."

"See that house?" He tipped his head toward a—what else—cedar-sided house. The almost scarily perfect condition of the yard distinguished it from its slightly sloppier neighbors. "That's Mr. Wu's house. If anyone even dared lay a hand on your car, much less steal a literal dime from your poo stash, Mr. Wu would be in his front yard, taking video on his cell phone. It doesn't matter if it's two in the morning. Mr. Wu takes his neighborhood watch duties very seriously."

"Makes your job easy," Grace said, although he noticed that she didn't make a move to unlock her car doors.

His grin broadened. "That he does. I wish every neighborhood had ten Mr. Wu clones. This way."

Grabbing her hand, Hugh turned on Deacon Avenue, moving faster and faster until they were almost trotting. His thigh gave a warning throb, but he ignored it. Although Grace was right next to him, he didn't release her hand. It was pathetic of him, but he was willing to take any opportunity to touch her. Hugh was inordinately pleased when she didn't try to pull away.

He started to weave through yards and between houses, making his way closer to Main Street. The motorcycle engines were much louder here, hiding any other sounds. He slipped through the weed-strewn lot behind the print shop. There was the tree, with low, thick branches that just screamed, "Climb me!" Even better, there was only a single, dust-covered window on the back side of the store, and Hugh knew the owner was pushing ninety and never wore her hearing aid. Any accidental thumps or stomps as they climbed onto the roof should go unnoticed, especially if the printing equipment was running.

Hugh sent a quick glance in Grace's direction, wondering what the best way would be to share his genius plan with her. "Ready?" he asked.

"For what?" Suspicion drew her eyebrows together. Even scowling, she was the most gorgeous person he'd ever seen.

Hugh gestured toward the tree. "We need to get into position."

Looking back and forth between his face and the tree, Grace frowned harder. "Tell me that *position* is not in that tree."

"It's not," he said honestly, then paused. "It's on that roof."

She stared.

"Up you go!" he said cheerily, trying to pretend that her silent, deadpan expression was not having any effect on him at all.

She didn't even blink. "No. This is a stupid plan."

"It's an *excellent* plan, and we're missing all the action."

"Missing action, when we're talking about *action* involving a dangerous, drug-toting motorcycle gang, is actually a good thing."

"No, it's not. Ignorance is never a good thing."

"But life is a good thing. I'd like to keep mine, thank you very much."

"It's perfectly safe. A baby could climb that tree."

"Then maybe you should've brought a baby with you."

"Chicken."

"You could've brought one of those with you, as well, although I'm thinking that even a chicken would see the flaws in your brilliant plan."

"I dare you."

She froze, and indecision flickered across her face. Apparently, the d-word was her weakness. Hugh filed that away in the back of his mind for possible later use. "You're evil."

He smirked, extending the silence and letting his words hang in the air.

"Fine!" Without hesitating, she boosted herself into the first crook of the tree.

Hugh watched as she climbed from branch to branch, her body moving in an athletic, easy way that threatened to hypnotize him.

Clearing his throat, he focused on Lexi, who'd been waiting patiently next to him. "Ready?"

She crouched, muscles bunched, just waiting for his command.

"Okay."

Lexi jumped onto the low, wide branch closest to the ground.

"Hang on," Grace said from her spot ten feet above his head. "Is your dog seriously climbing this tree?"

Just to rile her, Hugh gave Grace a "duh" look. When she visibly bristled, he ducked his head to hide his grin. "Of course," he said slowly, as if explaining something to an especially thick person. "How else do you think she'll get on the roof? She's a dog, not a flying squirrel." He could feel Grace's glare as he concentrated on helping Lexi scramble onto the second-lowest branch. If he looked at Grace, if he saw the offended glower, he knew he'd lose it and start laughing. She was just so easy to tease, and he enjoyed it way too much.

With an audible huff, Grace threw her leg over the next branch up and began sliding toward the building. The tree limb extended over the flat roof, making it the perfect bridge. Hugh swung up to the first branch, using Lexi's harness to steady her as she climbed ahead of him. A few times, he had to lift her bodily to the next branch. Between that and the pain tearing jaggedly through his injured thigh, Hugh was sweating a little by the time he reached the branch Grace had used to move above the building.

As he straddled the tree limb, Lexi in front of him, Grace swung down so she was dangling by her hands, her feet just inches from the roof. Letting go, she landed softly with bent knees. Without shifting her feet, she raised her arms above her head, as if she'd just finished a tumbling routine in front of a cheering audience. Turning, she let her arms drop as she shot Hugh a triumphant grin.

The sight brought a surge of admiration, along with a hefty dose of amusement. When her gaze turned quizzical, he realized he was staring, but he didn't care.

Lexi gave a faint whine, jerking him back to reality.

"Walk," he told the dog, and she navigated the branch with the ease of a mountain lion. He followed much less gracefully, scooting along the branch until his feet were dangling above the roof. Getting a firm grip on Lexi's harness, he called quietly to Grace, "Catch."

"Wha—?" The dog jumped, and Hugh caught her weight, lowering her into a startled Grace's arms. Although she was on the smaller end for a Malinois, the dog was still a solid forty-five pounds, and Hugh hurried to swing down onto the roof so he could help Grace.

Instead of struggling under the dog's weight, however, Grace had a solid grip. She was giggling, trying unsuccessfully to dodge as Lexi licked her face. Another surge of admiration hit Hugh. When he'd first met Grace, she'd struck him as a bit of a princess, but here she was, cleaning kennels, climbing trees, jumping onto roofs, holding an armful of heavy, wiggling dog—*his* wiggling dog—and laughing. If she was a princess, then she was a fun one, one who could take all of his teasing and give it right back to him, one who had a core of steel under that soft-looking exterior. In fact, she'd ruined him for all non-Grace princesses.

He took Lexi, lowering her to the rooftop without looking away from Grace. The memory of their earlier kiss returned for the hundredth time, and his blood ran hotter and faster through his veins. Her laughter dried up as she met his gaze, her lips parting slightly as she stared back at him. Grace looked as hungry for him as he felt for her, and he sucked in a hard breath through his nose. He'd never felt like that before, as if he had to kiss her, had to touch her, or he'd explode. Hugh leaned closer, drawn like a magnet. She gave an almost silent gasp and shifted, tipping her body forward as if she felt the same pull. They drew closer, until her breath brushed against his lips, sending a bolt of need so strong that it felt as if he'd been donkey kicked in the gut.

Just before their lips made contact, a revving motorcycle engine broke the spell, jerking them out of the world where only the two of them existed. Startled, they both pulled back. Grace looked away, visibly breathing hard, and Hugh had to give himself a firm, mental slap across the back of the head. Now was not the time for shenanigans—well, for the sexy kind of shenanigans, at least.

"C'mon." His voice was rough, and he cleared his throat, focusing on moving around the mechanical equipment and capped flues until he was at the front edge of the roof. Another tree, this one in front of the print shop, offered some concealment from the people in the street below. Just as Hugh had thought, the other cops had made the stop just a half block down from the print shop. He and Grace would be able to get a perfect view of the bust.

Although he didn't glance over at her, he knew exactly when she joined him. It was like she radiated heat or...*something* that made him ultra aware of her. They watched without speaking for a few minutes. It seemed as if everyone on the department—everyone except for Hugh, at least—had shown up for the party. He quickly found Theo and Otto in the crowd. Otto was talking to one of the R and R riders, while Theo was listening to something the lieutenant was saying. Although Hugh tried to determine if what LT and Theo were discussing was good or bad, Theo's everyday scowl was firmly affixed, not giving anything away. Shifting his gaze away from the pair, Hugh scanned the rest of the group.

The R and R riders looked outwardly cooperative,

despite a few wearing resentful expressions. There was a strange feeling, though, a tension, that made Hugh's muscles tighten in preparation for a fight. Next to him, on the opposite side of Grace, Lexi was alert as she eyed the crowd, her ears tipped forward.

Grace leaned closer to ask in a low voice, "Do you think they found anything?"

Hugh wasn't sure why she was speaking so softly. The rumble of engines would've covered her loudest outside voice, but he wasn't about to complain about her whispering if it made her lean so close to him. She smelled really good, like warm, sweet things. He wasn't sure how she managed that after the messy day they'd had, but she did. He shifted closer, pretending it was so he could hear her, rather than so he could breathe her in.

She was looking at him curiously, and Hugh dragged his brain back to her question. "Doubt it. See, they're just talking, running IDs. If they'd found something, there would be a lot more guys getting cuffed."

"What about him?" When Hugh followed her gaze, he spotted a burly guy with ratty blond hair and beard, his hands secured behind his back, being escorted toward one of the squad cars.

"That's Orv Beaumont." As he watched Orv get into the backseat, his face twisted into a scowl, Hugh had to grin. Even if they didn't find so much as a joint, this bust had been worth it just to bring in that jackass. "He's got an active domestic violence warrant."

Grace turned to look at Hugh and then back at Orv. "That's good. That he's caught now." The squad car door closed, shutting the biker inside. A smile curved

Grace's lips, and it was so satisfied that Hugh felt another jolt.

Seriously, this woman was perfect for him.

CHAPTER 11

As she watched the pissed-off biker get arrested, Grace understood how being a cop could be incredibly rewarding. Opening her mouth, she turned to say something to Hugh, but the look on his face knocked all the words right out of her head. Instead, all she said was, "What?"

"What?" he threw back at her. Of course he did. Because having a conversation with Officer Hugh Murdoch was like trying to discuss things with a twelve-year-old. And, for whatever strange reason, it turned her right back into a twelve-year-old as well, fighting the urge to stick out her tongue or kick him in the knee.

"Why are you looking at me like that?"

"Like what?"

"Like that."

"What?"

"That... Okay, this is stupid." She didn't even know what her initial question had been anymore. There were more important things to discuss, anyway. "Now that you know all is well, and no drugs were found, can we go before someone catches us up here?"

"You're with the police. What are they going to do if they do catch us? Call the... Hang on." He grinned at her. His gaze turned to the street below, and the grin slipped away. "Uh-oh."

"Uh-oh?" That wasn't reassuring. "Why uh-oh? What's wrong?"

"Nothing serious."

Not believing that for a second, she followed his gaze to see Theo glaring directly at them. She froze, feeling like a teenager caught sneaking out by her parents. The cop that Theo had been talking to started to turn, as if to see what caught Theo's attention, just as Hugh grabbed her by the arm and hauled her away from the edge.

"Time to move," he said.

As Grace started to turn, she saw someone else was looking at them. "Hugh," she said.

"What?"

"One of the bikers is staring at us."

He stepped behind her, looking over her shoulder at the crowd beneath them. "The ugly ginger guy?"

"No." Not wanting to point, she put her hand on his chin to direct his gaze. The light scratch of his stubbled cheek made her insides tighten in a too-pleasant way. "The ugly bald guy."

"Huh." Although Hugh's voice stayed casual, she could feel tension radiating from him. "Don't know him. That's another good reason to leave." Turning, he ushered her toward the back side of the building.

Grace snuck a final look at the biker, but he'd disappeared. "Where'd he go?"

Hugh turned to look, and his frown deepened. "Let's go." He slid feetfirst over the edge of the roof.

"What are you doing?"

"Making an ice-cream sundae." He grunted as he dangled for a moment before letting go, falling about four feet before his feet hit the ground. "What does it…

oof…look like I'm doing?" As he landed, his right leg crumpled beneath him. He stumbled, then regained his balance and stayed on his feet. Once he was steady, he looked up at her with his usual smirk in place, but a slightly green cast to his skin gave him away.

Peering over the edge of the roof, she frowned. "Faker. How badly does your leg hurt right now?"

"I'm fine. It takes more than jumping off a roof to slow me down. Lexi, here."

With total trust, Lexi jumped off the edge of the roof, and Hugh caught her with outward ease. If she hadn't been looking for it, Grace wouldn't have noticed his wince, since it disappeared so quickly. He bent to place Lexi on the ground before moving closer to the wall.

"Your turn. Turn onto your stomach and slide over the edge. I'll help you the rest of the way."

She did, her shoes scuffing against the brick wall as she lowered her body over the edge of the roof. There was a second when she dangled from her hands, hanging in empty space, and panic roared through her. Her fingers tightened painfully, and she kicked out, her feet trying to find purchase on the wall.

"Ow!" Hugh yelped, right before he wrapped his arms around her thighs. "Not the face!"

Now that he was gripping her, holding her steady, her fear faded. Grace felt a little sheepish. "Sorry."

"It's okay. You didn't make actual contact." He sounded amused, so she couldn't have damaged him too much. "If you had, it would've been karma in action. I'm sure I've done something to deserve being kicked in the face."

"Yeah, you have. There was that time you—"

"You can let go now," he interrupted.

She released her grip on the roof edge, and his arms immediately tightened, lowering her to the ground.

Lexi gave a low growl. Grace looked at the dog and saw that the hair was raised over Lexi's neck and shoulders as the dog stared at the corner of the print shop. Tugging Grace behind him, Hugh started backing toward the opposite corner.

"Should we call for help?" Grace whispered.

"They won't hear us back here over the bikes," he responded, his voice low. "Lex. Here."

Lexi swiveled an ear toward them. After holding her defensive stance for another moment, the dog reluctantly turned and moved to Hugh's side. Grace was impressed by Lexi's bravery. She'd been willing to face off with whomever was about to come around that corner, while Grace was cowering behind Hugh, her brain screaming at her to run away. She dropped a hand to Lexi's back, taking courage from the feel of her warm fur. Without taking her attention off the far corner, Lexi thumped her tail against Grace's leg in response.

"Is it the bald biker, do you think?" His flat stare flashed through her mind, and she tensed even more. "He was staring at us."

"It's not Theo," Hugh responded grimly. "We know that much."

Her heart pounded, and it suddenly became hard to breathe. Not knowing who was around the corner, who Lexi saw as such a threat, was worse than facing someone straight on.

"We'll go in the back door and cut through the shop," Hugh said very quietly while keeping his gaze forward. "Once we get out front, there'll be plenty of backup."

As they rounded the corner to the back of the building, they all turned and hurried toward the door. Even with Hugh and Lexi at her back, Grace felt vulnerable. The urge to look over her shoulder, to check to see who was chasing them, was almost overwhelming. Fighting it down, Grace rushed forward and turned the knob. Her stomach clenched when the door refused to open. It was locked.

She turned to Hugh, whispering frantically, "Can you pick it?"

His tools were already in his hands as he crouched in front of the door. "Oh, so all of a sudden you like my lockpicking skills?"

Lexi's growl ramped up a notch, her body stiff and pointed toward the corner they'd just rounded, and Grace gritted her teeth. "When you're not using them to walk in on me when I'm in the bathroom, yes. Why are we even talking about this at this moment? Can't you just do your lockpicking thing quietly without—"

"Got it." He opened the door. Grabbing her hand, Hugh ducked through the doorway, tugging her along behind him. He had to hiss a command at Lexi before she abandoned her self-appointed post and followed them into the shop. As soon as the dog's tail cleared the entry, Grace closed the door and turned the lock that Hugh had just opened.

It took several seconds to become accustomed to the dim shop after the bright sunshine outside. The sole window, set next to the door they'd just entered, was filthy, which didn't help. Her eyes finally adjusted, and the shadows lightened, revealing large machines that crowded the room. Just one was running with a rumbling roar, spitting out large sheets of paper into a receiving tray every ten seconds or so. Scattered boxes filled the rest of the space, leaving only a couple of narrow pathways. One went to the front door, and the other crossed the room to what looked like an office, judging by the little Grace could see through a half-opened door.

Hugh leaned down to speak directly in her ear. "The owner spends most of her time in there." He gestured toward the office. "She's almost completely deaf, so we should be able to slip through here without her ever knowing we took a detour." Despite the circumstances, she shivered when his lip grazed her ear. *Stop it,* she told herself firmly. *There's a time and a place to get all lusty, and this isn't it.*

She followed Hugh, Lexi at his side, as he moved quietly toward the front door. Glancing nervously over her shoulder, Grace eyed the back door. What had seemed like an insurmountable barrier just a minute ago seemed flimsy now that it was the only thing between them and danger. As she started to turn back around, a movement caught her attention. She refocused on the door, trying to figure out what—if anything—had shifted. To her horror, the knob turned.

She slapped a hand over her mouth to muffle her squeak of alarm, but it was still loud enough to make Hugh spin around. She waved frantically at the door, and his expression turned ferocious. He caught her hand and tugged her forward. They wove through the boxes and printers toward the front door, moving quickly.

There was a smashing sound, loud enough to hear

over the printer, and Grace ducked, swallowing a scream. Twisting around, she saw the butt of a gun retreating from the new hole it had just made in the windowpane next to the back door. A gloved hand slipped through the opening, reaching toward the door lock.

Hugh ducked behind one of the bulky machines, pulling Grace and Lexi with him. He crowded them toward the wall, keeping his body between them and the path. They crouched in the dust, the smell of oil and hot paper thick around them, and Grace tried not to think about huddling behind that dumpster by the police station or next to her car after the shooting. Once again, she was hiding, thanks to Martin Jovanovic and his army of killers. Rage began to burn away the edges of her fear.

Hugh swore under his breath.

"What's wrong?" Her words were barely a whisper.

"Nothing we can't handle." He gave her a conspiratorial look.

She frowned at him. Her heart was beating so hard it felt as if it were about to break out of her chest, and he was doing his jokey-Hugh thing. "I'd still feel better knowing what you were swearing about."

"No gun." He shrugged, but the tension in his body showed that he wasn't as nonchalant as he was pretending. "Didn't think I'd need it at the kennel."

Lexi crouched, ready to spring, and growled. Grace strained her ears, listening for any sound, wishing for Lexi's keen hearing. All she heard was the mechanical thump of the printer and muted rumbles from the motorcycles outside. There was no way to tell if the man had managed to get inside, or how close he was, or if he was right on the other side of the printer, ready to pounce...

If he'd followed the path toward the door, he'd see them. She knotted her hands into fists, fighting the urge to grab the back of Hugh's shirt. Clinging to him wouldn't help.

"Stay here," Hugh said so quietly that she could barely make out the words.

Grace's stomach tried to turn itself inside out. What was he about to do? It made her want to grab him even more, although this time, it would be to hold him back. He was going to get himself killed, all because he was trying to protect her.

Before she could protest, the huge, bald, leather-clad man stepped forward. He visibly started when he noticed them, but recovered quickly, swinging around to point a silver revolver at them. Hugh launched forward, his shoulder hitting the man right in his potbelly and driving the air out of the biker's lungs in a *whoosh*. They collided with another machine before falling to the ground, the gun hitting the floor with a clatter. Hugh twisted as he landed, ending up on top of the other man. He got in two punches before they rolled, and the biker got the upper hand. As the two men wrestled, faces red and muscles straining, Lexi barked wildly, circling the pair on stiff legs.

Grace knew she needed to help, but how? She stared at the interlocked figures, trying to think of some way to assist Hugh, but they were so close together and moving so quickly that any kick or punch would just as likely connect with Hugh, rather than their opponent. She scanned the area for a heavy object she could use as a weapon, and she saw the gun lying just feet from the bad guy's hand. She rushed toward it just as the men rolled, tripping her. Landing on all fours, she ignored the sting of her hands and knees and scrambled to grab the gun. As her fingers closed around it, she heard a yell from the fighting men, and her wrist was caught in a cruel grip.

"No you don't," the biker snarled, his grip tightening until she cried out.

With a roar, Hugh flipped them over, knocking the stranger's hand loose in the process. "You! Don't! Touch! Her!" He punctuated each word with a punch to the biker's face. Clutching the gun, Grace scrambled back until her back pressed against a stack of paper boxes. She aimed the pistol at the stranger, but Hugh blocked her aim. He had the upper hand, anyway, and she was intensely relieved that she probably wouldn't have to use the gun.

As she watched, her heart pounding fast enough to make her head spin, Hugh hammered his fist into the biker's face one last time. The other man didn't swing back, didn't try to turn them over again. Instead, he had his hands up as if to protect his face. Hugh, his expression furious, pushed up to a crouch and manhandled the biker over onto his stomach.

"Who hired you?" Hugh demanded, but the man didn't respond. Blood trickled from a cut next to his eyebrow, reminding Grace of the tortured men's blood-streaked faces, and she had to look away.

"Police!" Theo's shout was the best thing she'd ever heard. The cop ran to help Hugh, yanking a pair of handcuffs off his duty belt.

"Good timing." Although he was breathless, Hugh sounded almost back to his normal self. Grace, on the other hand, was pretty sure she'd burst into tears if she tried to talk. "I don't have my cuffs on me. I would've had to MacGyver something from a piece of twine and a couple of paper clips."

After he and Theo hauled the dazed-looking biker to his feet, Theo hammering the guy with questions that went unanswered, Hugh moved over to Grace and helped her to her feet much more gently than he'd handled the handcuffed man.

"Want me to deal with that?" he asked, looking pointedly at her hand.

"What?" Her voice shook, and Grace hated that. Following his gaze, she saw the gun still clutched in her hand. "Oh. Yes, please." She held it out, careful to keep the barrel pointed away from him. It suddenly felt impossibly heavy.

Hugh gently took it and cleared it with efficiency born from lots of practice. "Good job, Gracie."

"Thanks." She stared up at him, resisting the urge to topple forward against his solid chest. After everything that had just happened, she wanted to lean on him, take in his wonderful Hugh scent, and hide from the universe until it stopped taking a giant dump on her life.

"What the hell are you doing here?"

Rudely snapped out of her Hugh daze, Grace snapped her head around to look at Theo.

"Visiting local businesses?" Hugh offered, but Theo just glared. "Getting some ice cream?" That was the second time he'd mentioned ice cream in the past hour. Hugh must be getting hungry. He handed the gun and the bullets he'd removed from it over to Theo, who deposited them in his pocket without dropping his scowl. "Finding a quiet place to make out?"

Grace flushed and was instantly annoyed at herself

for turning red. She wasn't normally a blusher. Hugh just seemed to bring out unexpected reactions.

"You need to get out of here before LT shows up," Theo said, his face grim. "If he catches you here, you're done."

Grace felt her eyebrows shoot up. What did Theo mean? Would Hugh actually get fired for showing up at the call?

"I need to talk to this guy." Hugh jerked his head in the biker's direction. From the rage bubbling under his words, the conversation wasn't going to be a friendly one.

Theo started walking toward the front of the shop, towing the handcuffed biker along with him. "You *need* to go. I'll question him and let you know what I find out later."

"We'll go to my house," Hugh said, although he didn't look thrilled about it. "You and Otto meet us there once you're done here."

"I promised I'd make dinner for Jules and the kids tonight," Grace protested. Even to her own ears, she knew it sounded silly. Someone was gunning for her, almost killing Hugh in the cross fire, and she was worried about meal preparations. Still, she was scrambling for any hint of normalcy in the sea of hit men and bullets and exploding trucks.

"No." Theo stopped, turning that too-intense gaze on her, and she struggled not to look away. "If Jovanovic is after you, then I don't want you anywhere near Jules and the kids."

"But..." Once again, her life was spinning out of control. After the world's worst dinner party, all she had was a tiny bedroom in a dilapidated house that she shared with a surprisingly endearing family. Now, the threat of Martin Jovanovic was going to take even that away from her. Of course she didn't want to endanger Jules or her siblings, but that was supposed to be her safe house. Now, she was cut adrift again, and this time, there was no safe place.

Her voice came out embarrassingly small. "But that's where I live."

It wasn't until Hugh's arm circled her that she realized how close he'd gotten. Although a part of her figured she should step away and put some distance between them, a much larger part of her wanted to lean against him and take advantage of the comfort he offered.

Although a flicker of sympathy softened Theo's expression for a moment, his tone remained firm. "We'll find somewhere else for you to live until we figure out what to do about Jovanovic."

The "we" surprised her. "You're going to help me?"

"Yes," both men chorused.

"Thank you." Despite the whole wretched mess, Grace felt a flicker of hope.

"We're cops. Helping people in trouble is what we do. Now get out of here before someone else tries to kill you." Theo hauled the biker toward the front door. The handcuffed man turned his head and gave Grace and Hugh a blood-streaked sneer, mouthing, "*I'll get you.*"

Grace stared back at him as impassively as possible, trying her best to hide her shiver.

"No." Hugh's voice was abrupt and cold. "You won't. You'll get some time in prison, but you'll never get Grace."

At Hugh's words, Theo snapped his head around to

glare at the biker. "Face front," he barked, giving the man's arm a jerk that pulled him off-balance. The biker stumbled forward a few steps as Theo yanked open the door.

"Found this one trying to hide in the print shop," he called to someone outside as he stepped into the sunshine, biker in tow.

"What happened to his face?" asked a male voice Grace didn't recognize.

Theo said flatly, "He pulled a gun." The door swung shut behind them, cutting off the other person's reply. The gloom settled over Grace and Hugh again.

Glancing at the half-open office door across the shop, Grace gave a huff of laughter.

"What?" Hugh asked, grabbing her hand to lead her toward the back door. Even once Grace was headed in the right direction, he kept hold of her. Honestly, she didn't mind.

"The owner didn't hear any of that?"

"When I said she was mostly deaf"—he released her hand and bent to pick up Lexi—"I meant that. Theo will talk to her about the broken window."

Glass crunched under Grace's feet, making her realize why he was carrying his dog. He didn't want Lexi to cut her feet. Grace's heart softened even more at his consideration for his K9 partner. "Why did that guy come after us? Do you think Martin hired him?" she asked.

Hugh glanced at her. "Could be." He didn't sound convinced, though.

"Why else would he want to kill us?" Her voice was thin. It was bad enough to have one killer on her trail. She didn't think she could handle another.

"Not sure, but I'd like to have a chat with him."

Grace opened the door. "A couple of weeks ago, a crisis in my world was a long line at the coffee place."

He grinned at her as he carried Lexi through the doorway. "Sounds boring. Aren't you glad you moved here?"

"No. Not really."

He chuckled and put Lexi down, closing the door before reaching to grab Grace's hand again. She had to admit that, amid all the fear and death threats and panic, this small Colorado town did have a few perks. Shaking the bemused thought out of her head, she focused on crossing the rocky, weedy yard without tripping.

Bullets and scary bikers trump a hot guy, she reminded herself sharply.

Then Hugh snuck an all-too-obvious peek at her out of the corner of his eye, looking so stupidly adorable that her heart accelerated just a tiny bit.

She had to roll her eyes at herself. *Fine. So he's a perk*.

From the second she stepped through his front door, Grace loved Hugh's house. It had all the cuteness of a cabin, but the lofted ceilings and large windows made her feel almost like she was outside. Despite everything that was going on, she felt her shoulders relax for the first time in weeks.

Lexi's nails clicked against the hardwood floors as she trotted past Grace and into the kitchen, which was only separated from the living area by an island and several stools.

"You hungry?" Hugh asked.

Her stomach was such a mess of anxiety and leftover adrenaline that she had no idea whether she was hungry or not. She had a feeling that she'd regret trying to eat at that moment, though. "Not really. Would you mind if I took a shower? It's been a busy, dirty day."

"Go ahead." His eyes flicked over her body. "Do you need something to change into?"

It struck her that she was back to the same desperate place she'd been a couple of weeks ago, with nothing but the clothes she was wearing and the contents of her purse, running from Martin Jovanovic. A sense of futility hit her, bringing with it a wave of despair so strong that she swayed as the world blurred around her.

"Whoa there." Strong hands gripped her shoulders, steadying her. "Sure you don't want to reconsider eating something first?"

Blinking, she brought Hugh's face into focus. He'd leaned in close, and she noted absently that, even after crouching in dirty parking lots and cleaning dog kennels and climbing roofs and beating up a biker, he still smelled really good. Kind of warm and spicy and... something she couldn't identify.

His eyes narrowed and heated, and she realized with a start that she'd been getting closer and closer until they were almost kissing—again.

Grace jerked back as far as she could, which wasn't that far, since he still had hold of her shoulders.

"You okay?" he asked again. This time, his voice held a little more gravel, and she wondered if he was just as affected by the almost-kiss as she had been.

"No," she blurted out honestly. "Not really. I'm homeless again, for the second time in two weeks, and this time I don't even have my Walmart jeans with me. Just today, I've been kissed, shot at, cleaned up dog poo, climbed on a roof, and almost killed by a biker. So I've had better days. Why are you smiling? What part of my really sucky day is making you smile? Because that stupid smile will probably go away if I hurt you."

Instead of showing the appropriate fear and intimidation, Hugh actually chuckled. His hands slid down to her upper arms and then back to her shoulders in a gentle caress. "You're so cute. You actually said *poo*."

And just like that, all her righteous indignation disappeared, and she was fighting a return smile. As annoying as Hugh was, he was also charming. That made it very difficult to stay hostile, especially when he was touching her.

When her anger left her, so did the last of her strength. Her legs wobbled, just from sheer fatigue, and she wasn't able to stop the forward lean that plastered her front against his. He wasn't comfortable. His chest was too hard for that. Despite that, it was still an amazing feeling to be pressed against Hugh. Grace didn't want to move—ever.

"Poor Gracie." His arms wrapped around her, enveloping her in a bear hug, and Grace decided that was even better than the massage thing he'd been doing earlier. Cuddling her against his chest, he kissed her temple. His mouth stayed close, and she felt his next words brush across her skin. She shivered and then decided that, for her own mental health, she would just pretend that she hadn't reacted, that Hugh was not attractive, and that she didn't find him stupidly appealing. "What's your real name?"

"Kaylee." It felt strange to say it aloud now.

"Kaylee," he repeated, as if trying it out. "Hmm. I like Grace better."

"Too bad," she grumbled, although she wasn't annoyed enough to move yet. "I'm not going to change it just to make you happy."

"Grace fits you. You're very graceful."

The compliment made it hard to build up much indignation, so she just shrugged, the motion moving her body against his. "Whatever. Grace is fine."

"Oh." He sounded disappointed. "It doesn't annoy you?"

"Not really." She couldn't hold back a yawn.

He hummed. "That's not fun, then."

She raised her hand to smack him, but it was half-hearted at best. "Jerk." Her arm fell back to her side. "I don't care what I'm called. I just want this to be over."

"I'm kidding. Kaylee's a pretty name, too." His arms tightened around her. "I promise we'll get Jovanovic put away so you can go back to your life."

"Grace is good. I'm used to it now." She ignored the rest of what he said. As much as she wanted to be free of Martin Jovanovic's death threats, she wasn't sure if she wanted to give up Monroe, Colorado. The harsh truth was that, right now, the thought of her LA home didn't bring the same melancholy feeling as it had a few days ago. At this moment, Grace was completely content to stay right where she was, wrapped in the warmth and safety of Hugh's bear hug.

"You still with me, Grace?" he asked. Even the underlying thread of teasing humor wasn't enough to force her to pull away. She knew that once she stepped out of Hugh's embrace, she'd have to return to reality, and reality had been a little too full of near-death experiences lately. "You're not glaring at me or telling me how annoying I am. This new docile side has me worried."

"Docile?" she repeated, jerking her head back so she could scowl at him. "What am I? A cow?"

Hugh gave her that innocent, wide-eyed look that was more aggravating than any of his other rage-inducing habits. "I would never call you a cow, Gracie."

As she eyed him, waiting for whatever punch line he was coming up with, she realized that he still had his arms around her. With a reluctance that she wished she didn't feel, she stepped back, and his hold loosened and then fell away, leaving her cold and vulnerable.

His smile turned from devilish to wry, as if he knew fun times were over. "Let me make you some food, and we'll eat on the deck. The view from there is pretty nice."

"Shower first."

After giving her a measuring look, as if to reassure himself that she wasn't about to collapse from low blood sugar, Hugh waved toward the stairs. "Bathroom's the second door on the left, and my bedroom is the first. Feel free to raid my dresser and take any clothes you want." He faked a frown. "I don't have any Walmart jeans, though, so I can't help you there."

Grace seriously considered making a rude gesture, but she didn't have the energy. Her arms suddenly felt incredibly heavy, so she settled on ignoring his attempt at humor. "Thanks."

"Need help?"

"With finding something to wear?"

"Sure." He took a step toward her. "Or getting up the

stairs, or undressing, or…" When his voice trailed off into silence, they both stared at each other, and the air got thick and warm.

"Um, no." Her voice sounded several notes deeper than it usually did. She cleared her throat. "I'll be fine climbing the stairs. And with…everything else." She couldn't say *undressing* without turning bright red. Although she normally wasn't a blusher, there was something about Hugh that brought heat to her cheeks, as well as to other places she wasn't going to think about at the moment. They both had enough going on— like being chased by killers—without this stupid crush making things awkward.

She hurried away from him. Despite being distracted by the way Hugh watched her until she was out of sight, she noticed that the stairs were amazing. The heavy cross-sections of logs were held in place with curled wrought iron that looked almost delicate. The design gave the illusion that every step was floating. It was beautiful and unique and fit perfectly with the rest of the house. Her first impression had been that his house was rustic and homey, but the longer she was there, the more careful details she noticed.

When she was in Hugh's room, though, she tried not to notice any of those details—not the slightly mussed bed that looked like he'd just rolled out of it, or the way the room smelled faintly like that spicy, stupidly good scent that clung to his skin. Hurrying across the space, she fixed her eyes on the dresser. She needed to get some clothes and get out quickly, before she gave in to temptation and sniffed his pillow or something.

Yanking open the top drawer, Grace stared at the

stacks of underwear for a second before jamming it shut again. The second drawer was more helpful. She pulled out some athletic shorts and a T-shirt before closing the drawer and escaping to the bathroom.

The shower felt amazing. Tipping her head back into the hot, needling spray, she closed her eyes, only to snap them open a second later when she started to tip sideways. Although she'd heard of the saying "falling asleep on your feet," she'd never actually done it before. She seriously needed some rest. After briskly finishing washing and rinsing, she turned off the shower.

His clothes were huge on her. The T-shirt was fine, except for wanting to slip off one shoulder or the other, but the shorts were a challenge. Grace finally tied a knot in the waistband, which kept the shorts from falling around her ankles. A glance in the mirror made her groan quietly. She looked like a kid playing dress up. Tugging the T-shirt away from her sides, she decided that at least two normal-sized humans could fit into Hugh's clothes with her. He was just that massive.

"Grace?" His voice coming from behind the closed door made her jump. "You okay?"

She sighed, allowing the fabric to drape around her body again. "Fine. I'll be out in a second." She paused. "Don't pick the lock."

She heard a huff, but she wasn't sure if the sound was amusement or offense. Shrugging off Hugh's reaction, she turned back to the sad figure in the mirror. Her drooping shoulders made Grace give herself a mental slap. Considering how the past couple of weeks had gone, too-large clothes were such a minor problem that they shouldn't bother her. It was just annoying that Hugh had seen her in so many unflattering situations—the coveralls, her Walmart jeans, her post-roof-climbing outfit.

Abruptly, Grace cut off the mournful thought. She didn't—couldn't—care what Hugh thought of her.

Gathering her discarded clothes, she opened the bathroom door, and Hugh stumbled in, apparently having been leaning on the door. Once he recovered his balance, he took in her tentlike apparel and opened his mouth.

"Don't say a word if you want to live," she growled, pushing past him into the hall.

With a choked cough that sounded suspiciously close to a laugh, Hugh raised his hands in a gesture of innocence. "I was just going to tell you that the food's ready."

"Uh-huh." It was getting harder and harder to hold her irritation at him. Instead, as she headed down the stairs, she was struck again by how beautiful his house was. Although it was vastly different from her own decorating style, the interesting mix of elegant and cozy made her feel immediately at home. When she reached the bottom, Lexi trotted over to greet her, shoving her furry head under Grace's hand.

"Go on out to the deck," Hugh said from right behind her. "I'll bring out the food."

Walking toward the sliding glass door, through which she could already see a breathtaking view of the mountains, she felt a flicker of regret for her snarkiness. "You didn't need to cook for me."

He laughed. "I didn't. During your five-thousand-year shower, Otto stopped by to see for himself that I hadn't been dismembered by bikers. Knowing that all I have in my fridge are aging condiments, he took pity on us and brought food from the diner… Well, the VFW posing as a diner, I guess."

Stopping, she turned so she could give him her best glare. "You shouldn't joke about that. You could've died. It's serious." Even though she wanted to keep her stern tone, she couldn't keep from adding, "And we've been calling it the viner."

"Viner. I like it. And I know it's not a joking matter." Despite his words, a residue of amusement still lingered in his expression. "Otto said that, too. He was slightly annoyed that I'd been at the traffic stop today, and more than slightly annoyed that I'd dragged you along."

It seemed that, along with the bald biker, everyone on the police department had spotted them on the roof. Apparently, the camouflaging trees had been pretty much useless. "He saw us, too?"

"Nope." Although Hugh made a face, he didn't look too irritated. "Theo, the huge blabbermouth, told him. I knew he'd tell Otto. At least I got food with my lecture."

At the reminder, Grace crossed the last few feet to the door. She slid it open, marveling at how the deck jutted into space. The cliff fell away beneath them, plunging to a river that had worn a deep groove in the mountain. It was beautiful and, despite the severe, vertigo-inducing drop, calming. As she stepped onto the deck, Lexi brushed by her. The railing slats weren't very far apart, definitely not wide enough for a good-sized dog to squeeze through, but Grace figured she'd check, just in case. "Is it okay if Lexi's on the deck?"

"Sure," Hugh called back from the kitchen. "Just leave the door open so she can come back in if she wants."

Leaving the door open as instructed, Grace moved

to look over the railing. Her head spun. The cliff face plummeted to the river so far below that it looked as if someone had drawn the water using a dark-blue Sharpie. The dramatic plunge made her stomach lurch, and Grace took a hasty step back. Even though she didn't usually have a fear of heights, this was different. It felt as if she were suspended above nothingness, and looking straight down at the drop made her feel as if the deck was shifting under her feet.

Moving back another step toward the door, Grace focused on the view straight ahead of her. It didn't matter that she was no longer looking down, though. It still felt as if the deck was swaying beneath her. Frowning, she turned toward the door. Eating in the security of Hugh's kitchen suddenly seemed like a good idea.

There was a *crack*, and then another, and Lexi let out an uneasy whine. Grace froze, trying to identify the sound. Her first thought was that someone was shooting at them again, but the noise was different. Besides, there was nowhere to shoot from, unless the wannabe assassin was a rock climber, as well. Despite the improbability of a cliff-scaling killer, Grace looked around, but saw nothing but silent mountains and the setting sun.

Her instincts screamed at her, telling her that something was terribly wrong, and she took a step toward the door. "Lexi." The dog looked at her, tail tucked and her body slightly crouched. Her posture confirmed to Grace that, shooter or no shooter, they were in danger. "Let's go inside."

With a final squealing groan, the deck collapsed beneath her feet.

Too shocked to even shriek, Grace grabbed for the

edge of the open door, catching it with one hand just before she began to slide across the almost vertical surface. Her arm wrenched painfully as her entire weight pulled against her hold, but she managed to keep her grip.

Lexi yelped, making Grace twist her head to see the dog sliding toward the far railing. The dog's nails futilely fought for purchase as she skidded across the now-slanted deck.

"Grace!" Hugh shouted, sprinting toward the door. She opened her mouth to answer, but all she could do was suck in rapid, panicked breaths. Another yip caught her attention, and she watched in horror as Lexi collided with the tipped railing. One hind leg slid off the edge, and the dog scrabbled to pull herself back on the deck. Her second rear paw slipped over the top board, so that her entire back end hung over the railing, dangling over a terrifying, deadly drop.

The dog's muscles bulged as she strained to pull herself to safety, her eyes wide in terror, the whites showing clearly. If Grace didn't help her, didn't do *something*, Lexi was going to fall. As Hugh reached to seize her hand and pull her to safety, Grace knew she couldn't let that brave dog die. She released her grip on the door.

"No! Grace!" Hugh shouted. She slid, faster and faster, grabbing at the smooth deck flooring, but it didn't provide any handholds. All her efforts at stopping her free fall didn't even slow her down, and she crashed hard into the railing next to Lexi. The wood bowed at the impact, and every one of Grace's muscles braced in anticipation of the slats breaking, sending her plunging into the chasm below.

The railing held. Grace sucked in a sobbing breath,

opening eyes she hadn't even realized she'd squeezed shut. Immediately, she wished she'd kept them closed. The cliff next to them dropped straight down, leaving only air beneath them. They were dangling above nothingness. If the railing broke, she'd plunge hundreds of feet until she hit the rocks so, so far below. Only then would her fall—and Grace herself—be broken.

The drag of nails against the railing supports yanked Grace's attention away from the endless emptiness below and back to Lexi. Lunging toward the dog, Grace managed to grab her harness. Her fist closed around the nylon strap just as Lexi slipped over the edge of the railing.

With a yelp, Lexi fell. Her weight jerked Grace's whole body down against the railing. Her shoulder screamed in pain, but she clung to the harness desperately.

"Hold on, Grace!" Hugh shouted from the door. He'd tied a rope around his waist, and he was rappelling down the almost vertical deck floor toward them. If Grace had been able to spare any oxygen to yell, she would've screamed at him to hurry, but the only thing she could manage was to suck air in quick, panicked gasps.

Lexi flailed her legs as she dangled in the air, jerking on Grace's agonized shoulder. The railing slats pressed painfully against Grace's front, and she prayed that they continued to hold. Her fingers were numb from the tight clench of her fist, but she managed to grip the harness even tighter. She couldn't let Lexi go.

When Hugh was just a few feet away, the deck shuddered and dropped again. It only fell a few inches, but it was enough to jar Grace. For a fraction of a second, she was suspended, weightless, in the air, and then she connected with the railing—hard.

One of the supports under her hip gave a sharp crack and broke. The slat under her ribs splintered next. With a sobbing breath, she felt her body lurch against the too-few remaining supports. Her back stiffened as she tried to keep from dropping through the newly formed hole, and she wrapped her free arm around a post.

"I'm almost there, Grace. Just keep holding on."

She wasn't sure if Hugh was talking about holding on to Lexi or keeping her grip on the wooden post, but Grace was determined to do both. Just as the thought passed through her mind, the slat supporting her shoulders snapped, and she was plunging through the railing.

Vaguely, she heard Hugh's panicked shout, but everything was a blur. Her body jerked once when her downward drop was halted by her grip on the post, and a second time when Lexi hit the end of her short free fall. Agony shot from Grace's fingers all the way up her arm and through her shoulder, but still she didn't let go.

"I've got you, Gracie." Hugh's hands were on her, and she'd never been so relieved. He pulled her back through the hole in the railing, Lexi's weight a painful drag on her shrieking muscles. Grace welcomed the pain, though—it was so much better than numbness. If she couldn't feel the nylon strap burning her palm and cutting into her fingers, she wouldn't be sure that she still had the dog safe in her grasp.

As Hugh hauled her toward him, her feet struggled to find purchase, but the broken bits that remained of the railing supports cracked off like Popsicle sticks. Grace finally managed to stand on a post—the same one she'd been clinging to just a second earlier. As soon as she found her balance, Hugh reached down and grabbed

Lexi's harness. In one motion, he slung the dog over his shoulder.

"You can let go," he said, but the words didn't make any sense. She wasn't about to release her grip on Hugh's shirt. It was only when he gently worked her fingers free of Lexi's harness that she realized she still clutched the strap. It almost hurt worse to release her grip than it had to hold the dog suspended in the air, but her fist finally unclenched. As soon as Hugh let go, her arm dropped to her side. It felt like the entire appendage was on fire, and Grace wasn't sure if she could even lift her arm.

"Ready to get off this?" Hugh asked. Although he sounded steady, almost teasing, she could feel how tightly drawn he was, how he shook slightly under her clutching fingers.

There was no way she could speak, so she just gave a jerky bob of her head. He turned around, and she gasped as she was pulled with him by her one-handed death grip. Immediately, he stopped and looked at her.

"Get on my back," he said, crouching slightly. The command was a relief. Her body moved to obey him even before her brain could start doubting if she could manage it. She climbed on piggyback style, wrapping her legs around his waist and hooking her good arm around his shoulders, careful not to strangle him accidentally. In that position, Lexi was right next to her, and Grace turned her face into her furry shoulder. Small, continuous shudders ran through the dog.

Step by laborious step, hand over hand on the rope hooked around his waist, Hugh climbed the steep slope of the broken deck. Grace clung to him, shaking harder than the dog. On Hugh's fourth step, there was a low groaning sound and the deck listed to the right. His foot slipped, and he lurched sideways with a pained grunt, the rope holding all three of them going taut with the strain.

Swallowing a shriek, Grace tightened her grip on Hugh and focused on breathing. *In and out. In and out.* They would make it back into the house. Hugh wasn't going to let them fall.

"I've got you," he grunted, as if he could hear her panicked thoughts. She felt his chest expand as he took a deep breath, and then he was moving again. His breathing was rough, and Grace remembered that he'd been shot just weeks earlier. She could only imagine the agony he was in. Despite that, he held strong, hauling them closer and closer to the sliding glass door.

They were so close. If she hadn't been clinging to Hugh for dear life with her one usable arm, she could've reached out and touched the doorframe. The muscles in his arms and shoulders were straining as he surged up and forward, finally landing one foot inside the house. As he pushed off with his other leg, there was a loud, splintering noise followed by several explosive cracks. The deck dropped, falling out from under them, and Hugh lunged through the doorway, throwing all three of them to the blessedly solid and horizontal floor.

For endless seconds, they lay there in a panting, shivering heap. Lexi was the first to shift, wriggling out from where she was half pinned by Hugh's shoulder. Immediately, she pressed close to them, as if seeking comfort.

The dog's movement brought Grace back to reality,

and she realized that she was sprawled across Hugh's back. A vague pang of guilt pricked her through the foggy haze of shock. He'd saved them, and she'd plopped her entire weight on him as thanks. She rolled off him—at least she tried. Before she could land on the floor next to him, Hugh had turned over and snaked out an arm, hooking it around her and pulling her back to him, on his chest this time.

Too dazed to fight and not really wanting to be away from him anyway, Grace relaxed, allowing him to hold her against his chest. Lexi burrowed in, pressing her head into Grace's side.

"You okay?" Hugh's voice was gravelly, sounding as if he'd been screaming for hours.

"Yes." Her first try was soundless, and a sharp pain shot through her right shoulder, making the answer a lie. Taking a deep breath, she tried again. "Not really." Although her voice didn't even sound like her, at least it was audible.

Hugh pushed himself into a sitting position, letting Grace slide into his lap. With a whine of protest, Lexi shifted until she was plastered against both of them again. "What's wrong?"

The question almost made her laugh. Tipping her head forward, she pressed her forehead against his collarbone. "Besides almost dying? Again?"

"Yeah. Besides that."

"My arm doesn't seem to want to move."

His hands were instantly on her, running from her wrist to her shoulder. "Where does it hurt?"

"My shoulder, mostly." As he started manipulating it, she flinched. She'd been automatically stroking Lexi with her other hand, but she stopped for a second so she could shove against his chest. "Ow. Stop it."

His face set and serious, he didn't react to her push—or stop moving her shoulder. "It's not dislocated. If it were, or if it were broken, I'd be peeling you off the ceiling right now."

"Are you done with your sadistic science experiments now?" she asked, although her sarcasm was thinned by the quaver in her voice. Now that her shock was wearing off, and the realization that all three of them had survived was slowly starting to sink in, Grace wanted to laugh or cry or maybe dance around wildly, if only her shoulder wasn't hurting so badly.

Hugh carefully lowered her aching arm to her side before reaching for Lexi. "How about you, partner?" he crooned, running his hands over her furry body. With a sound that was more sigh than whine, Lexi lay down next to them, not flinching at Hugh's probing touch until he reached the area just behind her front legs. When Grace started to move out of his lap so Hugh could reach the dog more easily, he wrapped one arm around her and brought her firmly back down onto his thighs.

"Okay," he said, finishing his examination of Lexi with one hand, since the other was busy keeping her snugly against his chest. "Hospital for Grace, and vet for Lexi."

Any objection that Grace had about going to the emergency room disappeared when she shifted and accidentally jarred her injured arm. A wave of pain—so sharp she could taste it—flooded her. "*Oh*. Yes. Hospital, it is."

Hugh shot her a look so full of concern that it made her want to cry again, but she clenched her teeth and forced back the tears. If she started, it would be big and ugly, with a ton of snot and racking sobs. She needed to wait until she got back to her new room and…

The thought trailed off as she remembered that she couldn't go back to her safe-house bedroom, not without endangering Jules's whole family. The tears rushed back, and Grace had to bite her tongue hard to keep them contained this time.

Hugh shifted her off his lap onto the floor next to him, and she instantly missed the comforting warmth of his hold. As he hauled himself to his feet, he kept his injured leg straight, hopping a few times on his good leg before he caught his balance. She watched him, concerned. Hugh always hid any sign that his injury was bothering him. If he was showing her that he was in pain, then he had to be in *agony*.

"How bad is your leg?"

He shrugged, concentrating a little too hard on untying the knotted nylon rope around him. "I'll live."

"I'm only going to the emergency room if you promise you'll let them look at you, too."

He eyed her sharply, but she held his gaze without flinching. "Fine," he grumbled, throwing up his hands. The movement made Grace notice his palms, and she sucked in a harsh breath.

"Your hands!" Scrambling awkwardly to her feet, she rushed the few steps to him. Grabbing one of his wrists, she gently turned it over. His palm was raw and bleeding. Her gaze moved to the yellow rope, several feet of which had been stained a rusty color.

Following her gaze, he made a wry face. "Didn't think to grab a pair of gloves."

A laugh burst out of her. "So between us, we have one working hand? Good thing I don't drive a stick shift."

His grin, the one that usually infuriated her, was now the most beautiful thing she'd ever seen.

CHAPTER 12

"THAT'S IT!" THEO SLAMMED THE EXAM ROOM DOOR. "I'M sick of this shit."

Hugh hushed his partner, but it was too late. Grace, who'd finally dozed off five minutes earlier in a very uncomfortable-looking chair, had already startled awake. She winced, probably because the movement hurt her strained shoulder. Curled up in the chair, she looked so fragile, so delicate, that it was hard to believe she was the tough woman who'd saved herself and Lexi. Hugh watched her closely while absently responding to Theo. "*You*'re sick of it? I'm the one who keeps bleeding. All you have to do is visit me."

Turning his head, he saw that Theo was vibrating like a tuning fork—a rage-filled tuning fork. Hugh couldn't help but smile again. He knew that Theo would take every bruise and burn and bullet hole for Hugh and Otto and Jules and the kids if he could. The same went for Otto. Hugh's partners were his family.

From the look on Theo's face, it seemed that Hugh's happy expression was just cranking up his anger, but that was fine. If Theo did give into temptation and punch Hugh in the head, at least they were already at the hospital.

"It's not a joke," Theo snarled. "The R and R guy talked about you."

"About me?" Hugh widened his eyes, trying to keep a straight face. "Really? What'd he say? Has he heard good things? Bad things? Is it my hair? Does he hate it? Did he say that my T-shirts are so last year? Because that's just mean."

By the way Theo worked his jaw muscles, Hugh was pretty sure that his partner had ramped back up to murderous. It took Theo a few seconds to say a word, but he finally gritted out, "About who wants you dead, dumbass."

Grace sucked in an audible breath.

"Me?" That caught Hugh's interest. He'd much rather discuss which scumbag had a grudge against him than the way it hurt Theo's secretly tender heart when anyone he cared about got hurt. "Not Grace?"

"It wasn't Jovanovic. The truck bomb, the shooting, the biker, your deck… They were aiming for you. There's a hit out on you."

"What?" Grace came to her feet. "What do you mean there's a hit out on *Hugh*?"

He'd been so sure that Martin Jovanovic was trying to get to Grace that Hugh's thoughts were scattered by the unexpected revelation. He stared at Theo for a long moment before he spoke. "Who ordered the hit?"

"Truman."

"Truman?"

"Yes."

"Who's Truman?" Grace asked.

"Sit." Hugh frowned at her. She was looking pale, too pale, and he knew her arm had to be killing her.

Of course she ignored him. "Who's Truman, and why does he want you dead?"

"A coke dealer." Hugh couldn't answer the second

part of Grace's question. The man known only as Truman was a major player in the Denver area, but Hugh had never had a run-in with him. In fact, he'd never even met the guy. All Truman was to Hugh was a fuzzy surveillance photo and half a name in a briefing. It didn't make sense that Truman wanted him dead so badly that he was willing to pay a lot of money to have him killed. "Why?"

"Dresden."

"The china?"

"The town."

"In Germany?"

"Why would the... No." Theo was looking exasperated again. Grace just appeared confused and scared as she turned her head back and forth between the two, following their conversation. "Not the German city. The *Colorado* town. The one just forty miles from here. The one with a lot of rich skiers and boarders who want their coke."

Of course. He should've figured it out a lot earlier. Hugh blamed his denseness on the fact that both his leg and his hands felt like they'd been put through a meat grinder and then set on fire. "So, Truman's finally figured out what the Rack and Ruin guys have known for years. If they take Highway Six from Denver to Dresden, instead of the interstate, then they're a lot less likely to run into any state troopers who might take their nose candy away. But Six takes them right through Monroe."

"And you're the only narcotics-detection K9 team in Monroe since Denny retired." Theo started to pace the room.

"Does Denver PD have any idea where to find Truman?" Hugh asked.

"No." Pivoting around, Theo paced the other direction. "They've been trying to pin this guy down for years, but they don't even have a last name for this asshole. LT called in the FBI to help. Apparently, they've been trying to get a solid case against Truman for a while now, too." The door swung open, forcing Theo to stop abruptly so he didn't get slammed in the face. When Otto stepped inside, he looked about as happy as Theo and Grace did.

"More good news?" Hugh tried to make his voice sound light, but he didn't succeed. His burned hands throbbed in rhythm with the bullet wound in his leg, and he cursed his intolerance of pain medications.

Otto scrubbed a hand over his head. "The lieutenant and I checked out what was left of your deck."

The nightmarish image of Grace and Lexi hanging off the edge of the railing, dangling over endless space as he tried to knot the rope around his torso, hit Hugh hard. He wanted to grab Grace's hand, to pull her against him and keep her safe, but he managed to restrain himself. "Someone messed with it." His voice was dark and sure. He'd rebuilt that deck just a few years ago. It had been strong and secure; he'd bet his life on it.

Silently, Otto gave a short nod.

Theo swore, and Grace made a small sound in her throat, but Hugh tightened his jaw. Although he'd known the investigating officers would find that the deck had been sabotaged, it still hit him sharply. It was one thing to threaten his life or to blow up his truck, but Grace and Lexi had been hurt, had almost been *killed*.

Truman had declared war, and Hugh was ready to fight back.

CHAPTER 13

GRACE WOKE UP WITH A CAT PURRING ON HER HEAD.

She blinked, taking in the unfamiliar, simple bedroom, the lack of city sounds. It took several seconds before all the details of her new messed-up life came back into focus. When they did, she wished she could go back to sleep. She even tried, closing her eyes firmly, but the cat rubbed its head against Grace's cheek, squashing it. With a laughing groan, Grace gave up her feeble attempt at escaping reality and sat up.

Immediately, her arm throbbed, and she sucked in a pained breath. The doctor had told her that her shoulder was sprained, and that she'd strained pretty much every muscle in the top right quarter of her body, but nothing had been torn or broken or dislocated. Rotating her shoulder carefully, she bit back a gasp. It felt like it had been ripped off and then casually reattached, but at least she could move it. Right after the deck incident, she hadn't even been able to raise it.

Otto had invited them to stay at his place after they'd left the hospital. Hugh didn't want anyone to stay at his house until the crazy drug dealer who'd put a hit out on him was arrested and the contract canceled. She could tell it bothered him—a lot—to be chased out of his own home. Looking at the hard set of Hugh's mouth last night as they were driving to Otto's, Grace had almost pitied Truman. Hugh's expression had shown clearly that he intended to make the guy pay. She still couldn't believe that Martin Jovanovic hadn't been behind the attempts on their lives. Only she could have the bad luck to escape from one killer in California, just to stumble over another in Colorado.

Grace slid out of bed, ignoring the cat's displeased grumbles. Looking down at herself, at yet another borrowed, oversized T-shirt and sweatpants, she sighed. What she wouldn't give for her own jeans.

There was a quick knock on the door, right before it swung open. "Hey. You're up."

Why was she not surprised to see Hugh's grinning face? "You have the worst manners I've ever seen. What is so hard about waiting until you're invited in?"

"I knocked," he countered with no remorse. None. "Listen, the guys just got here, and they have some information on Truman. I figured you'd want to hear this."

"I do, thanks. Give me two minutes." Feeling like she was forty years older than she actually was, Grace moved toward the doorway...and Hugh. He was watching her with an odd look on his face, and she restrained the urge to touch her hair. It was a hideous, snaky mess, she was sure, but she was also sure that she shouldn't care what Hugh thought of her appearance. People were shooting at them, blowing things up, chasing them through print shops, and booby-trapping decks. She needed to focus on that, not her twitchy, fluttery stomach as his gaze dropped from her face down her poorly dressed body.

She reached the doorway, but Hugh didn't move, instead continuing to watch her with an unreadable expression. From what she'd learned about Hugh, he didn't do unreadable. He was either happy, jokey Hugh or serious, intent, keep-them-from-dying Hugh. "What?"

"*What* what?"

And there it was. A gleam of humor returned to Hugh's eyes, and Grace rolled her own. "Quit staring at my Medusa head and get out of the way. I need two minutes in the bathroom, impatient pants."

"Impatient pants?" Now he was actually chuckling. "That's your insult? Good one, Gracie."

With a frustrated grumble, she elbowed past him, squeezing into the hallway and stomping toward the bathroom door. "And let me pee in peace this time. Go downstairs. I'll be there in a minute."

"As if I want to stand here and listen," he huffed, although there was that constant amused undertone to his voice, as if he was suppressing laughter.

Grace paused while pulling the bathroom door closed behind her to glance at Hugh with her eyebrows raised. "I know how you are with women's restroom doors." Without waiting for a comeback, she closed the door the rest of the way. Even though she knew it wouldn't slow Hugh down too much, she shoved the button lock in with her thumb.

Through the door, she heard him make a scoffing sound. "One time. I broke into a women's restroom *one time*. Can't you just let that go? I was concerned for your safety. You'd been in there for hours."

"Minutes, Hugh." Raising her voice, she corrected him without opening the door. "I'd been in there just a few minutes. You need to grow some patience." When the only response was a wordless, cranky growl, she grinned. Despite her minor victory, she still did what she needed to quickly. After all, a serial bathroom door unlocker was not about to change his stripes overnight.

The three cops standing around the large kitchen looked at her as she came in. Lexi was stretched out in front of the stove. Although she raised her head and thumped her tail against the floor in greeting, she didn't get up. Grace figured the dog must be feeling as sore as she was.

The grim expressions on all three of the guys reminded Grace of the situation, and she felt a wave of hopelessness and homesickness crash over her. Bantering with Hugh upstairs, she'd been able to push the whole assassin thing to the back of her mind, but now, facing the three serious-looking cops, she wasn't able to think of anything but the killers who were after them. Her knees sagged under the weight of her despair, forcing her to drop into one of the chairs surrounding a wooden table.

As if he knew what she was feeling, Hugh moved behind her and squeezed her shoulders. She was glad he kept his hands, bulky with bandages, there, since the weight of them was reassuring.

"Where's your sling?" he asked, and she sighed. So much for silent support.

"Probably the same place as your crutches," she snapped back, and then immediately felt guilty. He'd saved her life over and over, and he was just concerned about her arm. Before she could apologize, though, she realized that Theo and Otto were hiding smiles. Distracted by the rare grins on Dour and Dourer, the words died before they could leave her mouth.

"Eggs?" Otto asked, scooping a mound of them onto her plate before she could answer. The smell made her stomach rumble, and she tried to remember the last time she'd eaten. Honestly, she couldn't remember.

"Thank you." She picked up her fork and started shoveling food into her mouth. With a satisfied grunt, Otto returned the pan to the stove and poured her a glass of orange juice. Dropping his hands—which made Grace have to swallow a protest—Hugh sat in the chair next to her.

"Good thing you like your eggs scrambled," he said, idly picking up a fork. "That's the only way Otto knows how to make them." When he reached toward her plate, as if intending to take a bite of her food, she held her fork threateningly above his interloping hand.

"Back off."

The hungry-puppy look was out in full force. Grace would've had more sympathy if she couldn't see the stack of dirty plates that Otto was rinsing off and placing in the dishwasher. "But…"

Narrowing her eyes, Grace gave him her most threatening glare. With a pathetic glance toward her plate and then back at her face, Hugh gave a loud sigh and pulled back his own fork.

"Cruel," he sighed.

Having warded off the threat to her eggs, she continued eating. When she'd finally had enough that her stomach's demands had quieted slightly, she put down her fork and took a drink of juice before looking at Otto.

"Thank you for letting us stay here."

He did a grunt-and-shrug combo that made her suspect her gratitude made him uncomfortable.

"I wish I'd had you come here yesterday," Hugh said, sounding unusually serious. "I hate that you were hurt because of me." His honest regret worked where his puppy face had failed. She studied him for a moment before pushing her half-full plate in front of him. Hugh gave her a surprised glance.

"Sure?" he asked, even as he was shoveling in his first mouthful.

Grace just rolled her eyes at him before turning to the other two. "What's the plan?"

They exchanged a look. Theo opened his mouth, but the door opened before he could say anything, and Jules breezed in, followed by all the kids.

Theo's expression immediately turned from grim to smitten, and he gave Jules a gentle smile as she detoured to kiss his cheek on her way to the table. Right before her lips connected, he turned his head, meeting her lips with his own. The peck turned into something a little more intense, and Grace looked away. She met Hugh's gaze, and they smirked at each other.

"Hi, Theo! Hi, Hugh! Otto!" Dee bounced over to give Otto a side hug before dropping to her knees to pet Lexi, who thumped her tail against the floor in response. "Hey, Grace. We brought you some clothes. Can I go see the animals? Where's Viggy?"

"Yes. And in the exercise yard." Otto answered both questions while giving Dee a gentle pat with his huge hand. Grace looked on, fascinated. He was such a big guy that it was odd and endearing to see him be so careful with the little girl. At the kennel, he'd been like that with the shy dog, too. "Stay away from the new horse in the back paddock, though. He's still scared."

"Okay. Thanks!" Dee ran out the way they'd just entered.

The twins exchanged a glance, and Ty nodded as if Tio had said something out loud. "We'll watch her," Ty said as the two jostled each other to be the first out of the door.

"You too, Sam," Jules said a little breathlessly, having reclaimed her lips. When her brother gave her a look, she returned it. In that moment, Grace could see the resemblance between brother and sister. "We're going to be talking about things the twins don't need to be involved in. You know they'll have at least one ear pressed against the door any second now."

After another moment of holding his stubborn expression, Sam gave an amused snort and shook his head. "An ear? T-t-too low-t-tech. T-Tio pr-probably has the room b-b-bugged."

Jules laughed. "Yeah, you're right. Now will you please go keep them from listening to our conversation? And, while you're at it, don't let them blow up anything."

"F-fine," he grumbled, and headed outside.

"Okay," Jules said as the door closed behind Sam with a thump. "So will someone please tell me why Grace can't live with us?"

"Martin Jovanovic is after her," Theo said with a growl in his voice as he jerked a chair away from the table with enough force to make Grace jump. He looked at Jules and waited until she'd settled into the chair before taking the seat next to her. It was only then that Grace realized the angry chair movement had been a courtesy. Turning her head, she met Hugh's amused gaze, and she bugged her eyes out at him. In response, he smirked and gave a tiny shrug that she translated as "That's just Theo." Holding back a snort of laughter, she refocused on the conversation.

"So?" Jules was saying.

"The FBI guys in Denver have briefed us on Jovanovic. He's a dangerous guy."

Grace barely kept from rolling her eyes at the under-statement.

"But everything that's been happening—the shooting, the falling deck, the explosion—have been targeting Hugh, right?" Jules pressed. "This Jovanovic guy still doesn't know where she is."

Theo's jaw set. "We don't know that for sure."

"Is there any sign that he does know where she is?" Jules was obviously not going to give in to Theo without an argument. Amused, Grace glanced over at Hugh and saw that his gaze was focused on her. She couldn't read the look in his eyes. For some reason, that made her feel shy, and she dropped her eyes, returning her attention to the debaters.

"If he does find out"—Theo was leaning toward Jules, his mouth set and a muscle twitching by his eye—"she'll be dead, and so will anyone who gets in Jovanovic's way."

The raw truth of that made Grace flinch. It was true, but hearing it out loud made it so much more hor-rific. This was her life now. Anyone who was around her would be in danger until Martin Jovanovic was stopped. Hugh took her hand, making her start and look down. His bandage scratched her palm a little, but she could still feel the heat of him through it. It reminded her that she wasn't alone in her nightmare anymore. Hugh would protect her with his life. She gave his hand a gentle squeeze, hoping it didn't hurt his rope burns.

From the way her mouth turned down, Jules didn't like Theo's statement, either. "So it's not okay for Grace to be around us, but it's okay for Hugh to be around her when he has that big target painted on his butt?"

Hugh flinched before dropping her hand.

"Okay," Grace said, trying to keep her voice calm. Everyone turned to look at her. "Enough playing the who-will-get-whom-killed game. I actually have an idea about how to get rid of Martin Jovanovic." That sounded so threatening, as if she was going to put a hit on him, too. "A nonviolent idea."

With all eyes focused on her, Grace shifted. The plan, which had come to her the previous night before she'd fallen asleep, seemed flimsy now that she was about to say it out loud. "Martin's nephew, Noah Jovanovic. Do any of you know anything about him?"

There was an exchange of blank glances before Hugh spoke. "Haven't heard of him. Why?"

"I...ah...dated him." There was an actual growl to her right, and she rolled her eyes at Hugh. "For about five minutes, until the whole uncle-tortures-people thing made me flee the state and killed the whole deal." When Hugh didn't look appeased, she shrugged, winced at the ache in her shoulder, and continued. "I don't think Noah's involved."

Hugh snorted, for once sounding unamused. "Of course not. I'm sure he's completely innocent."

"Maybe I'm wrong, but it's worth a shot, right? I mean, he has access to his uncle's properties. If it ends up that he doesn't know what his uncle does, he'd be able to get us proof, something we could use to put Martin in prison."

There was a silence, but it felt thoughtful, rather than like the others were trying to come up with a kind way to tell Grace she was crazy.

"What are you thinking?" Theo finally asked, and Grace let out the breath she hadn't realized she'd been holding.

"Maybe a phone call, just to feel him out?" she suggested. "An untraceable phone call, of course." Grace frowned. "Are untraceable phone calls something you can do?"

Otto sat in the chair at the head of the table, stretching his long legs in front of him. "Should we bring Shankle in on this?"

"Who's Shankle?" Grace asked.

"He's the FBI guy heading up this thing with Truman," Hugh said, leaning back in his seat. Stretching his arms out at his sides, he dropped one over the back of Grace's chair. She stared at him, still trying to wrap her brain around the fact that he'd just casually called having a hit put out on him a "thing." "That'd be a good idea. I know there's a federal investigation of Jovanovic."

The front door slammed open, and everyone jumped out of their seats. Hugh yanked Grace behind him, and she saw his hand reach for his hip, the spot where a gun would be if he'd been in uniform. She peeked around his arm to see the four kids and Theo's dog, Viggy, piling into the kitchen. Her first instinct was to relax, but then she saw their scared faces.

"What happened?" Theo demanded. Grace noticed that he'd stepped between the entrance and Jules.

Sam yanked the door shut behind them and turned the dead bolt. "Th-th-th…s-someone w-w-was w-watching us."

"Where?" Hugh asked.

"On the ridge," Tio answered. "Just north of that single, crooked tree." He and Ty had Dee squeezed between them, and Grace felt a shot of rage at Truman. Not only were his hit men trying to kill Hugh; they also didn't hesitate to take out anyone who got in their way.

Otto started moving toward the entrance to the living room. "How many?"

"Two."

"Th-three," Sam corrected Ty, who frowned at his brother.

"Are you sure? I only saw two."

Although Sam nodded, it was hesitant.

Jules shifted toward the kitchen window, as if to look out, but Theo caught her by the hand. "Stay away from the windows."

"You going to call it in?" Hugh asked, his voice and posture tight.

"Not yet," Otto said. "Sirens'll just tip them off, and they'll disappear. Let's come at them from the back way."

"Back way?" Hugh asked, but Otto didn't answer. Instead, moving surprisingly lightly for such a big man, he hurried into the living room. Grace followed, wanting to do *something*. He put his hand flat against the biometric reader on a safe, and the door clicked open. One at a time, he pulled out three rifles with slings and a pistol, handing them off to Hugh and Theo, who'd leashed their dogs.

He eyed Grace. "Can you shoot?"

Feeling a little useless, she bit her lip. "I never learned, so I think I'd do more harm than good with a gun."

When he turned to Jules, she shook her head. "Not for me, thanks."

Closing the safe, Otto looped his rifle sling over his head and one shoulder. He moved to a small door, opening it to reveal a coat closet. Shoving aside the hangers, he popped a piece of paneling free, exposing a keypad and what looked like another biometric scanner. Sure enough, he pressed his thumb to the screen and entered a code on the keypad. The back of the closet slid aside, revealing a steep staircase.

Grace couldn't hold back a choked laugh. "It's like the doomsday prepper's Narnia."

Otto gave her a quick grin, the first real smile she thought she'd ever gotten from him, before disappearing down the shadowed stairs. Theo ushered Jules and her siblings down the steps next, and Hugh waved Grace to follow them. When Otto had mentioned going out the back way, she hadn't expected something as elaborate as this. She just assumed he meant a regular back door.

Although she'd braced herself for cobwebs and creaky stairs, the steps were clean and vermin-free. It wouldn't be the worst place to wait out the invasion… if that was what the people on the ridge were planning. Maybe they were just some lost hikers who didn't realize they were trespassing?

Grace mentally rolled her eyes at her inner optimist. Sure. There were multiple people out for Hugh's blood, but the ones staking out Otto's house were just innocent nature lovers. Right.

Hugh nudged her forward. She descended the last

few steps and then looked around. They were in a mid-size, windowless room, lit by a bare fluorescent bulb. Her "doomsday prepper" comment hadn't been far off, judging by the amount of canned goods and water jugs stacked along the walls. Otto was already moving through another doorway, followed by the rest of them like a huge, gun-toting pied piper.

The corridor was narrow and shadowed, except when they were directly underneath an infrequent light fixture. Grace glanced at the ceiling. Had it gotten lower? Were the walls a little closer together? The tunnel was really long. Where was Otto taking them? And how did he oxygenate the space? Grace felt her breathing speed up, and she tried to slow it down. Until she learned how he ventilated the corridor, it would probably be smart not to suck down all the air.

Hugh's hand found her shoulder, and she jumped, clenching her teeth to hold back a yelp of surprise. Once the initial shock faded, though, the contact was reassuring, and she was tempted to reach back and squeeze his hand.

The corridor slanted uphill, and it felt like they walked for miles before Otto started climbing a ladder that was bolted to the wall.

"Anyone who's not a cop stays down here," Theo stated quietly.

Before he was even finished talking, Jules was shaking her head. Grace had been so preoccupied with her own growing claustrophobia that she hadn't noticed how pale Jules had gotten. Theo studied her for a second before stepping back so the kids could get to the ladder.

"When we reach the top, stay close to the caves."

Although he still sounded stern, he squeezed Jules's arm as she started up the ladder behind Dee. Without saying anything else, the rest of them followed, Theo lifting Viggy to one shoulder before climbing. Soon Grace was grasping the metal rungs in her hands. When Otto reached the top, he shoved open a square trapdoor that was set in the ceiling at the top of the ladder.

As Grace popped her head out of the opening, she blinked in the dimness before scrambling all the way out. Hugh emerged next with Lexi over his shoulder, and Grace hurried to get out of his way before looking around. The walls of the cave were irregular and rocky. She wanted to ask where on the mountain they were, but there was still a hush over their group that discouraged her from speaking. What if they were close to the bad guys and her question gave them away? She didn't want to be *that* person, the one who got them all killed.

Once again, it was as if Hugh could read her thoughts, because his heavy, bandaged hand landed on the back of her neck and gave a reassuring squeeze. They all started following Otto again, moving across the rocky floor. The light increased, getting brighter and brighter, until they rounded a final curve to see the mouth of the cave.

Blinking in the full, blinding sunlight, Grace peered over the edge. The cliff's rough surface reminded her of hanging off the deck, one hand clinging to Lexi as the other one grasped on to the railing for dear life. Hugh's hand rubbed her back as she fought for calm. When her heart rate finally slowed enough for her to look again, she saw Otto's house and outbuildings. They seemed surprisingly far away.

Turning her head, she looked for the ridge where the kids had seen their unwanted visitors. She saw the single, scraggly tree almost directly below her, but she didn't see any people. Just as she started to turn away, a quick movement caught her attention, and she refocused on the spot.

"Stay here," Hugh said, his mouth close to her ear. "We'll be right back."

Although Grace wanted to protest, to grab onto his arm and keep him there with her, out of danger, she managed to swallow that urge and simply nod. The three men and two dogs started down a narrow trail. Hugh glanced over his shoulder and met her gaze, giving her a secret half smile. Despite the circumstances, she smiled back. It was impossible not to. Stepping closer to Jules, Grace watched them until they were out of sight around the jagged edge of rock.

Tipping her head closer to Grace's, Jules murmured, "Half of me is relieved that we don't have to confront those guys, but the other half is kind of annoyed to be considered the helpless women."

"They're cops. Heading into danger is what they do," Grace whispered back, tilting her head toward the huddled and silent kids. "Besides, we have a different job."

"True." Jules moved closer to her siblings. "Quit looking so worried. They'll be fine." She offered the kids a reassuring smile that was met with varying degrees of skepticism.

Grace turned back to the ridge, narrowing her eyes in an attempt to watch what was happening. It was hard to be the ones left waiting, hoping that the guys returned safely. She strained her ears for gunshots—or any sound really. Something that would give them a hint about what was occurring on the ridge below.

Suddenly, there was a distant yell, and one of the dogs started barking furiously. Grace's heartbeat took off at a gallop as she met Jules's anxious gaze. Grace couldn't make out any words, but the voice, although male, didn't sound like any of their guys. It definitely wasn't Hugh. She would've known if he was the one shouting in what sounded like distress. The yells died away, and silence returned. Time seemed to crawl by as they waited for another shout, another sound that would give them a clue about what was happening below.

Above them, there was the scratch of a boot against rock, the tiny pattering noise of a pebble rolling downhill. Grace whipped her head up to find a grinning stranger on a ledge right above them. In his hands was a matte-black gun. With a sharp inhale, she reached toward the kids, instinct telling her to yank them back into the cave.

"Calm down, now," the man said, his voice casual, as if he wasn't aiming a gun at them. "If you just stay quiet and do as I say, none of you will get hurt."

He kept the weapon pointed toward them as he climbed down from the ledge. His feet slipped a few times, and Grace tensed, hoping desperately that he'd fall, giving them an opportunity to overpower him and take the gun…or at least run. To her dismay, he kept his balance—and the pistol.

Grace moved back until she was next to Jules. If she couldn't get the kids to safety, then she could at least stand in front of them. Her arm bumped Jules, who was glaring at the gunman like she wanted to rip his arms off.

"Kind of wish I'd taken Otto up on his offer now," Grace muttered under her breath. Her voice sounded strange, as if she wasn't getting enough oxygen, but she had to try *something* to bring Jules down a few notches before she attacked.

Jules's scowl didn't waver. "No." It was almost a growl. "Wouldn't have helped. I'd have just managed to shoot my foot off."

A bubble of hysterical laughter rose in Grace's throat, and she forced it down. Risking a glance behind them, Grace saw that Sam had pushed the younger kids behind him, although… She shifted slightly, trying to get a better view. Tio and Dee were there, but where was Ty? Her stomach jumped and squeezed tightly as she eyed the edge of the ledge several feet behind them. If he'd fallen, they would've heard, right? There would've been screaming, at least. At the thought, Grace gritted her teeth against a groan.

"Eyes on me, princess," the stranger with the gun ordered, and Grace whipped her head around, irrationally worried that he'd know Tio actually was half of a matching pair. The barrel of the gun was pointed right at her chest, and she squeezed her eyes closed as she fought the need to run. Even if she got away, she couldn't leave Jules and the kids to the mercy of this armed criminal.

Opening her eyes, Grace met the gaze of the man holding it. Instantly, she wished she hadn't. His expression was cold and empty. There was no panic or sympathy or remorse. In fact, there was a spark of sick pleasure. He was enjoying their fear, his control over whether they lived or died. The gun shifted to point at the group of kids, and Grace's stomach instantly cramped.

It had been horrible being the target, but having the gun directed at the children was so much worse.

Dee made a small sound, a quickly muffled whimper of terror, and Grace felt rage build, pushing out some of her overwhelming fear. How dare this man frighten a little girl, frighten *all* of them?

"Hey!" she snapped, and the word sounded painfully loud and brittle. "Quit picking on the kids."

It worked. He pointed the gun at her again, and her heart crashed to a stop. "Bossy. Why do the pretty ones have to be so mouthy?"

She opened her mouth to say something, anything, to keep his focus off the kids and delay whatever terrible thing he had planned, but a sharp pinch at her side startled her into silence. If there hadn't been a gun pointed at them, Grace would've glared at Jules.

"Why do the ugly ones have to carry guns?" Jules shot back. Instantly, Grace understood her plan. It was the same one as Grace had: get the focus—and the danger—directed at her, rather than the others. She and Jules were in the middle of a martyr-off, apparently.

The man just gave them an unpleasant smile, the gun steady in his hand. "As pretty as the two of you are, and as much fun as we could have, I'm afraid that your cop friend is worth a lot more cash. Sorry about that."

With that, he pulled the trigger.

CHAPTER 14

IT FELT WRONG TO LEAVE THEM, TO WALK AWAY FROM Grace and Jules and the kids. Even though Hugh knew they'd be safer there, it still was hard to have them—Grace especially—out of sight. He glanced down at Lexi, who was plunging eagerly forward, showing no sign of soreness and doing her very best to make his rope-burned hand shriek with pain. He'd considered leaving her with Grace and the others for protection, but he and Lexi were partners. The dog was used to working with Hugh, and he had a feeling she would've protested, loudly, if he'd left her behind. Calling attention to their hiding place would not have made them safer.

Shaking off his misgivings, Hugh increased his pace, ignoring the pain shooting through his thigh and hands—through pretty much his entire body, actually. There was no part of him that didn't hurt after pulling Grace and Lexi off the porch the day before. The thought of it made his stomach burn. When he'd seen them on the collapsing deck, Grace clinging to the railing as she clutched Lexi's harness, both of them only a second away from falling to their deaths, his mind had blanked with sheer terror. Thank God for his training. He'd gone on automatic pilot, grabbing the rope and tying it to a leg of his very heavy—thankfully—dining room table.

His boot slid slightly on some loose rock, and Theo gave him a warning glance. Hugh shook off the residual terror and concentrated on where he was putting his feet. If he didn't focus, he was going to get them all killed. He gave Lexi's leash a tug, and she quit pulling. The relief on his hand was immediate.

Otto had taken the lead, and he held up a hand as he reached a switchback in the trail. Instead of continuing down the path, he looked over the drop-off. Hugh and Theo both stopped next to him, peering down to an outcropping of rocks right below them.

There were two men, one looking through binoculars at Otto's house. The other one was focusing through the scope of a rifle. A surge of rage flooded Hugh, against Truman and every asshole who was trying to kill him. The kids had been outside. This fucker had pointed a rifle at them. His truck had been blown up, and his deck sabotaged. They'd been stalked and attacked. Lexi had almost died, and so had Grace—three times.

Fury gave him speed and courage, sending him sprinting down the trail, Lexi running in front of him. It was rough and steep, but his feet managed to find traction. They stayed quiet, and it wasn't until they were just six feet above the two killers-for-hire before the man with the binoculars looked up.

As soon as their gazes met, Hugh commanded, "Lexi, bite!" and let go of the leash. She leapt at the man. The one with the rifle gave a shout of surprise as he scrambled to get up, but Hugh tackled him. They connected with a mutual grunt, and the sniper fell onto his back with Hugh on top. The impulsion from his forward motion slid them across loose rock toward the edge of the ledge. Their heads and then shoulders dangled over the drop-off, and the distant and jagged rocks below them made Hugh instantly dizzy.

Hands grabbed his leg—his bad leg, of course—sending shock waves of pain through him but stopping both of them before they plunged off the cliff. Someone else grabbed his other calf, and he and the gunman were hauled back onto solid ground. As soon as they weren't in danger of plunging to their deaths, Hugh cocked his arm back and punched the would-be assassin in the face, knocking his head against the rock under them. The sniper's eyes rolled back, and his body went limp.

Resisting the urge to punch him again, Hugh checked for a pulse instead. It was strong and steady. Part of Hugh—a pretty good-sized part—was happy the guy would have a pounding headache when he regained consciousness. He deserved every bit of misery he would experience.

"You okay?" Otto asked, offering a hand up.

Hugh accepted it with a hand that shook with the last vestiges of rage and adrenaline. "Yeah. Felt good to hit him."

"I'm sure." With a small grin, Otto moved to the unconscious man, turning him onto his front and cuffing his hands behind his back.

The other guy was yelling, trying to pull away from Lexi, but she held on, her tail churning in happy circles. As usual, it was a game to her, whether training with a sleeve or on a mountainside with a grip on a guy who wanted to kill her partner. He, as well as everyone else, was just a playmate.

With Viggy barking at his side, Theo looked at Hugh. "Enough?"

Hugh waited another few seconds before releasing Lexi, who immediately ran over for her reward. He automatically pulled her tug toy from his BDU pocket. As Lexi grabbed the other end and started pulling on it, Hugh wanted to laugh. It was just so bizarre to be standing on a rocky ledge, playing tug with Lexi, as two men who wanted him dead looked on—well, at least one of them did. The other wasn't looking at anything except the inside of his eyelids.

"Anytime you're done having fun, Hugh," Theo muttered, his arm muscles bulging with the effort of holding Viggy back. The man Lexi had taken down was still on the ground. Every time he shifted as if to get to his feet, Viggy launched into another round of ferocious barking, and the man subsided, eyeing the dog warily.

"Good girl, Lex," Hugh praised, returning the toy to his pocket. When he automatically reached for his cuff case, however, there was nothing there, and he mentally cursed his required medical leave for the thousandth time. "Can I use your cuffs, Theo?"

"I'm on it," Otto said before Theo could respond. Even though this one was conscious, the man didn't fight much more than the sniper had. Theo hushed Viggy, and silence settled over the mountainside as the three of them eyed the two cuffed suspects.

Hugh's head was starting to throb along with the rest of his body. "Yeah. So…what's the easiest way to get them down?"

"Push them over the edge and let them roll to the

bottom," Theo stated. When Hugh and Otto frowned at him, he shrugged. "You said the easiest."

With a silent sigh, Otto bent to turn over the unconscious man. Hauling him off the ground, he slung him over his shoulders in a fireman's carry. Hugh grabbed the other man by his upper arm and helped him to his feet.

"Hey," the guy complained. "Not so rough."

Hugh stared at him for a long moment and then turned to Theo. "I say we go with your plan A. Let's toss 'em over."

His eyes bulging, the man started protesting, and Theo smirked. Rolling his eyes, Otto started down the path that Hugh assumed led into the valley. They'd only gone a few feet when there was a *crack* from above them. Hugh ducked automatically, his body recognizing the sound even before his brain caught on a half second later.

It was a gunshot.

Grace. Her name echoed in Hugh's head as a wave of blind rage flooded through him. If she'd been shot, if something had happened to her while they'd been dealing with these two, then he wasn't going to be responsible for his actions. Anger and terror clawed at his insides, shredding his logic and common sense.

With a wordless roar, he tore back up the mountain, ready to tear apart anyone who dared to harm her. He could still hear the echoes of the gunshot, and they shook him to his core. She had to be okay. She had to.

If she wasn't, he'd rip apart the pile of rocks they stood on until he found the man who'd hurt her…and then Hugh would make him bleed.

The sound of the gun echoed through the valley, bouncing from mountain face to mountain face. Grace braced herself for impact, for pain. At this range, there was no way she'd survive. There was no blow of the bullet hitting any part of her body, though. There was no searing agony of it tearing through fragile organs and tissue and muscle. There was only the echo, and even that was fading.

When she blinked her eyes open again, she saw the man's grinning face. Dropping her head, she ran her frantic gaze over her front. She wasn't hit. The first emotion that flowed through her was sheer exhilaration, but then reality returned with a thump.

If she hadn't been shot, then who *had*?

Twisting around, her eyes found Jules first. The other woman was openmouthed with shock, her gaze ripping over Grace's body, down to her feet and then back up again, with such a look of amazed disbelief that Grace knew Jules thought she'd been shot, too. There were no holes in her, though, and no blood. She quickly sought out Sam and Ty and Dee, but they were all upright and wound free.

No one had been shot. Grace took a gasping breath, her first in what felt like hours. Blood rushed to her head, sending sparks across her vision, and she swayed. Jules grabbed her arm, as if to help hold her up, and Grace straightened, trying to breathe normally.

Then anger roared through her, and she tried to surge forward, to tackle the *asshole* who'd scared her so badly, but Jules's grip tightened, holding her back. The man with the gun laughed.

"That'll bring him running," he said.

"Who?"

"The cop."

"Which one?" Grace spat out, furious. Jules might be able to physically restrain her, but Grace still had control of what came out of her mouth.

"The one who's going to pay for my retirement in Mexico." The gunman grinned again, showing off teeth that were brown around the edges.

The rage was back. This motherfucker was planning to kill Hugh. Without thinking, without considering the pros or cons of her nonexistent plan, Grace just acted, lunging forward and tackling the guy.

She'd forgotten the gun until it went off again. It roared too close to her ear, making the world fall silent, but she couldn't stop now. She took him by surprise, and her momentum carried them to the rock face behind him. They smashed against the unforgiving surface, and he grunted as they connected.

The surprise wouldn't last. Grace knew she had to be quick and thorough. Despite her too-fast heartbeat and shallow breaths, her thoughts were clear. She had to take him down before he recovered, because he would shoot her. There was no question. He would kill her and throw her off the cliff, and then he'd kill everyone else there.

Grace couldn't let that happen.

She clawed at his face, driving her fingertips into the soft parts of his face, his eyes and nose and cheeks, making him scream. A remote, strange part of her regretted her new post-manicure style of short nails. She couldn't help but imagine how much damage she could have accomplished with the talons she used to sport.

It wasn't enough. He was recovering from her surprise

attack. She could feel the strength in him, the intention of destroying her, and she had to stop it. Reaching down to his right hand, she grabbed his gun and twisted, hard.

There was another scream, and a tiny, bloodthirsty part of her was glad that she'd hurt him. The rest of her was shrieking, terrified and amazed that it had worked. His fingers loosened, and she was able to rip the gun out of his grip. As soon as Grace felt the give, as soon as the weapon was in her possession, she scrambled back, toppling onto her butt while keeping the gun pointed at the wannabe killer.

It felt wretchedly good, having the same power he'd taunted them with. She could shoot him. She didn't want to, but now she was the one with the ability to end his life, rather than him taking her life or the kids' lives or Jules's life. It filled her with heady power, and she gave him a grin—a ferocious, terrifying grin—taking pleasure when he flinched back.

"Turn over on your stomach and put your hands behind your back," she ordered, hating how her voice got squeaky at the end. She'd watched Hugh and Theo handcuff the biker, so she knew the basic position he needed to be in. The only problem was how to secure him without any restraints. "Hey, Tio?"

"Yeah?" She wasn't the only one with a trembling voice.

"In this situation, is there anything we could use to tie up this guy?"

"I have a belt." His answer was quick and sounded steadier. "There's our shoelaces, too, and our clothes and—"

"Perfect." She gave the stranger another grin, showing all of her teeth. "This is what you get for coming after a science nerd."

"Hey!"

Ignoring Tio's protest, Grace kept her gaze locked on the guy. He was looking too cocky for her peace of mind. The guy was planning something. "Over on your stomach."

"Come on, pretty—"

"On your stomach!" she said again, louder. If he didn't obey, she might have to shoot him, and she wasn't sure if she could do that. She hoped desperately, for all of their sakes, that she wouldn't fail them when it mattered. However, there was no way of knowing if she could do it until she actually pulled the trigger and put a hole in another human being.

He made a big show of slowly starting to turn, but then his muscles tensed. It was happening. The man pushed off the ground, lunging toward her in the same motion. Her finger tightened on the trigger, fear and horror zigzagging through her.

He crumpled to the ground.

Grace stared. She hadn't pulled the trigger. She'd been about to, but she hadn't actually shot him. She was sure of that.

She just couldn't figure out why he'd collapsed. She kept the gun steady, pointing it at his chest, and tried to make her brain work again.

"What just happened?" There was a strong note of hysteria in her voice, but she couldn't blame herself. The guy had fallen down before she'd shot him. Had he fainted? Had she really shot him, but just hadn't heard the noise or seen the flash or smelled the gunpowder or felt the recoil? No. She hadn't shot him.

"Very nice," Tio said, and Grace glanced at him, confused. He wasn't looking at her, though, but at a spot twenty feet above the unconscious man.

Grace followed his gaze to see Ty's grinning face peering over a protruding ledge. "What'd you do?"

"Dropped a rock on his head." He sounded surprisingly calm about it.

"Oh." In contrast, her voice was shaky. "Nice aim."

"Thanks." He grinned at her.

"Titus." Jules didn't sound calm, either. "You will climb down off that rock, and you will make your way back to us very carefully, and then you are grounded for the next five years."

Although he obeyed quickly, he was still smiling as he made his way toward them.

"I can't believe you did that," Jules said, her voice getting higher and faster with each word. Her Southern drawl thickened until it was hard to understand what she was saying. "I can't believe you hung over a cliff and dropped a rock on a man! What if you'd fallen? What if you'd missed? What if Grace hadn't done that insane thing and gotten his gun, and he'd shot you? What if—" Her words ended abruptly as she yanked him into a hug. "If you ever scare me like that again, I am going to kill you myself, understand?"

From the way his *yes* came out as a breathless grunt, Grace figured that Jules was squeezing him very, very tightly. Tio and Dee joined the hug, and a white-faced Sam hovered close by, clenching and unclenching his fists.

"Hey, everyone?" Grace said, her eyes still locked on the unconscious man. "A little help would be nice."

"Oh!" Jules and the kids ended their family hug and hurried over. "Sorry!"

"I've got this." Tio started toward the immobile form while pulling his belt free of the loops, but Jules caught him by the back of the shirt.

"No."

Sam silently took Tio's belt from his hand and moved to roll the man over onto his stomach. When Jules made a sound of protest, her brother ignored her and quickly secured the guy's feet together. Tio tossed him both shoelaces, and Sam caught them before using both to tie the man's wrists. Once the stranger was secure, Sam moved back to stand by his siblings.

"What should we do with the gun?" Grace asked. Now that the man was unarmed, unconscious, and restrained, her adrenaline was leaking away, leaving her arms shaky.

"Give it to me." Jules's voice was confident, but her face showed just how terrified she was as she reached toward the gun. Grace happily relinquished the weapon. Now that the immediacy was over, she was realizing just how gun ignorant she was. The only two times she'd ever touched a gun, she'd grabbed them away from guys who wanted to shoot her. It was a habit she really needed to stop. Once Jules took the gun and Grace's hands were empty again, she felt like a huge weight had been lifted off her mind, too.

Jules stared at the dull black weapon in her hands before cranking her arm back and hurling the gun over the cliff. In the following silence, they heard a slight *clank* as it landed on the rocks far below.

"Was that wise?" Tio asked.

Jules propped her fists on her hips. "I don't care if it was. He held that gun on us. He could've killed y'all!" Her voice got higher and higher as she flung the words at them. Grace understood Jules's hatred for the gun, but she also felt vulnerable without the weapon. The man was tied up and unconscious, but she still felt like he was a huge threat.

A flash of something in Grace's peripheral vision made her spin around, cursing herself for not keeping guard. She took a stumbling step back before she recognized Hugh, and relief crashed through her. He and Lexi charged up the trail, with Theo and Viggy close behind. They took the scene in with a glance, Hugh's frantic gaze raking Grace up and down, and then immediately headed toward the stranger. Theo checked the man's pulse as Hugh patted him down.

"Just him?" Hugh was using his rare serious tone. He hadn't looked away from Grace for more than a second or two at a time.

"Yes." Her voice came out scratchy. "That we've seen, at least."

"T-t-there's at l-least one m-more. Th-there were th-th-three," Sam said, his gaze scanning the area as if he was expecting more men to come charging from around a rock. Grace didn't blame him. She did the same thing as she moved closer to Hugh, who stood, meeting her halfway and pulling her into his arms. His hug was hard, almost bruising, but she didn't complain. It felt amazing.

"I'm okay," she said, answering his unspoken question.

Without releasing her, he turned to look at Theo. "Cuffs?"

"Good thing Otto carries two sets." Pulling them from a case on his belt, Theo secured the stranger's hands behind his back.

"We found the other two," Theo belatedly told Sam, who relaxed slightly. "What happened?"

Everyone except for Theo and Hugh looked at Grace and then Ty, who gave a modest shrug.

"Grace tackled him and got his gun." Dee pointed to the spot where Ty had ambushed the gunman. "Ty snuck up there and dropped a rock on him. Now he's grounded for *years*."

"You tackled him and took his gun," Hugh echoed, his body tensing against Grace's as his hold got even tighter. "Where's the gun?"

It was Jules's turn to point, this time in the direction of where she'd tossed the weapon. "I threw it off the cliff."

Hugh and Theo stared at her, and Hugh's mouth finally relaxed slightly, even quirking up a little. "You... threw it? Off a cliff?"

"Yes." Jules glared at Theo and then Hugh.

The absurdity of the situation caught up with Grace, and she felt hysterical giggles pushing to break free. She swallowed them down again as Jules repeated, "I threw it. Off a cliff."

Hugh snorted, relaxing the tiniest bit. "The crime scene people are going to be cursing your name."

"Sorry. It seemed like the best thing to do at the time." When Hugh just smirked at her, Jules gave a little shrug.

Grace decided it was a good time to change the subject. "Where's Otto?"

"We left him with the other two"—Hugh paused for a moment as he flicked a glance at the kids—"bad guys.

Speaking of them, we should get back." He reluctantly released Grace, and she fought down a protest. Being held so tightly against him had pushed away the fear. She stayed silent, however, knowing that she needed to behave like an adult now, rather than a needy child.

Hugh moved as if to reach for the unconscious man, but Theo shouldered his way between them.

"Jules." Although Theo usually made Grace a little nervous, with his scowls and clipped words, she had to admit that it was cute how soft his tone was when he spoke to his girlfriend. "Take Viggy?"

With a small, but genuine, smile, Jules stepped over to hold the dog's leash. She gave the unmoving stranger a wary glance and speedily returned to her original spot, although not before Theo ran a reassuring hand down her forearm. Once again, Grace was touched by the sweetness of the gesture. For some reason that she didn't want to examine too closely, she darted a quick glance at Hugh, and then immediately looked away when she saw he was watching her.

Theo hauled the unconscious man over his shoulders with impressive ease, and Hugh helped him adjust the dead weight. Theo started retracing their steps from earlier, with a still-pale Jules, her siblings, and Viggy falling in behind him. Although she told herself she was just being polite, Grace knew that she was letting the others go first so she could be by Hugh. Everything was so scary and topsy-turvy, and she felt safer with the big cop close by.

"Gracie? Where'd you go?" He was watching her, looking amused, and she realized that she'd been staring at him as the others continued down the trail. Even Lexi was eyeing her in what seemed to be a knowing way, although Grace tried to dismiss the thought. Lexi was a dog. Dogs did not mock. At least they shouldn't.

Shaking off her distraction and her embarrassment at being caught ogling, Grace hurried to catch up to the others. As she fell in behind Sam, she felt a bandaged hand cup the back of her neck, and prickles made their way from the spot where Hugh touched her all the way down her spine.

"What were you looking at back there, hmm?" he asked quietly, his mouth much too close to her ear for comfort. The prickles turned into full-body shivers. Overwhelmed by his proximity, Grace scrunched a shoulder and scooted forward until she was away from his mind-melting whispers, but it was only seconds before he was right behind her again. He sounded even more amused than before. "Could it have been…me? Were you thinking of how sexy I looked? Thinking how much you'd like a piece of me, only not in a punching way? More of a kissing and hugging way?"

Air escaped her in a laughing gasp. "No."

"Liar." It was like he was a mind reader.

"Am not. Why would I want to hug and kiss you?" *Because he's beautiful. Because he saved my life a bunch of times. Because he makes me feel safe.*

"Because I'm super fine." The edge of humor gave his words a self-deprecating cast that just added to his appeal. Grace had a soft spot for guys who could make her laugh, and Hugh could definitely do that. "And adorable. And as huggable as a puppy in a teddy bear suit."

She couldn't stand it. He really was too cute. "Eh.

I'm not really that into you. A puppy in a teddy-bear suit, though…"

With a teasing growl that made her stomach do a somersault, he poked her in the ribs. "You know you love me."

It hit her then, like a punch to the gut. He was right. It might not be full-on love yet, but she was headed in that direction. In fact, the love semitruck was tumbling down the mountainside at high speed with no brakes, about to run her over, flatten her on the pavement and leave its Hugh-shaped tire tracks all over her heart.

She frowned at the mental image. As melodramatic as it was, she knew Hugh could hurt her horribly, worse than she'd ever been hurt before, worse than she could even *imagine* being hurt. He was a good cop, a good man, and he was feeling protective. That was probably all it was on his side. While she was hurtling down the love mountain on her way to disaster, he was, most likely, just doing his job. She hated the thought that she was simply a duty to him. He didn't mind kissing her, but there was no way he felt anything stronger about her than that…was there?

He gave her another poke in the ribs that was more of a caress than anything, and she was reminded that she hadn't answered him.

With a wheezing, sad, little laugh that was not at all convincing, she forced out, "You wish."

He chuckled, and she fully deserved it. "I do." It was a gravel-filled purr, and she couldn't stop the goose bumps spreading over her skin. "I do wish."

A rock caught her toe, making her trip and jolting her out of her Hugh-induced daze. She had to get away from him, from his warmth on her back and his all-too-sexy whispers in her ear. Hurrying forward a few steps, she fell in behind Sam...*right* behind Sam, who gave her a wary look over his shoulder. Grace smiled at him, but she must've looked a bit manic, since his frown deepened before he turned to face front again.

Although he stayed a few strides behind her, Hugh's soft laugh caught up to her, bringing the goose bumps back. "Chicken."

It's not about being a chicken, she thought, biting back the retort that wanted to escape. *It's about self-preservation.* Bantering with Hugh was fun and invigorating and addictive, but she needed to call a halt. It was too dangerous to continue down the road they were on. Once people stopped trying to kill them, this—whatever *this* was—would be over. She'd return to LA, and he'd stay in Monroe, helping other people like he'd helped her. After all, that was his job.

She almost snuck a peek behind her, but caught herself just in time. She knew what she needed to do. Now she'd find out if she had the willpower to resist the many charms of Officer Hugh Murdoch.

CHAPTER 15

"I never thought I'd be happy to come back here." Grace turned in a full circle in Jules's kitchen.

Hugh watched her spin, her straight, dark hair fanning out behind her, and he couldn't help but smile. He knew he should look away, that his staring was bordering on creeper mode, but he wasn't able to do it. She was incredible. As he started to get to know her, her energy and strength and sheer Graceness shone through, just adding to her beauty. "You're just saying that because you saw Theo's place."

Abruptly turning away from the apparent amazingness of Jules's kitchen, with its mismatched, thrift-store table and chairs, its ancient appliances and crooked or missing cabinet doors, Grace looked at him. He met her gaze and immediately felt warmer. "I can't believe how tiny it is."

"I visited with Otto once—never again."

"I can't imagine how all three of you fit," she said. "It's like a dollhouse."

Hugh gave a belly laugh. It was perfect. *She* was perfect.

Immediately, he poked himself in his sore thigh, and the jolt of pain centered him. He had to stop thinking about how incredible she was, how amazing she felt, how beautiful she looked. The only reason she was in Monroe was because Jovanovic wanted her dead. As soon as it was safe, she'd run back to LA, back to her glamorous life and glamorous friends and glamorous guys. He couldn't keep her. All he could do was make the most of the short time he had with her and try his hardest not to get too attached. He had to keep things casual.

Even as he thought it, his heart laughed at his wishful thinking. Another harder poke at his thigh sent a heavy jolt of pain through his leg, distracting him.

"Why are you jabbing at your leg?" Grace asked, frowning.

"What? I'm not. That's crazy talk." When she opened her mouth, as if to argue, he quickly continued. "Agent Shankle's in town."

"The FBI guy?" All the humor disappeared from her expression, and she sagged a little. Guilt seeped through him for his part in putting that look on her face.

"Do you still want to call your boyfriend?" The last word tasted bitter as it left his mouth. "If you do, Shankle could help set that up safely."

"Ex-boyfriend, and not even that, really. Maybe for about two seconds, when I thought he was a Disney… Never mind." For a moment, she was quiet. He wouldn't have even known she was anxious except that she was drumming her fingers against her pant leg. That was her tell. He mentally filed away that fact in case he ever played poker with her. "Yes," she finally said. "I do. Well, I don't, but I want it to be over."

He winced before he was able to stop himself.

"Not you," she corrected quickly. "I don't want *this* part to be over. Just the almost-getting-killed part."

That startled a laugh out of him. "Yeah, it would be nice not to be shot at every five minutes. Maybe not, though. We might get bored."

"Right. If that happens, we can always go play paintball or have a water fight or something a little less deadly." She grinned at him, and he quieted abruptly. Her beauty was like a kick to the chest. Ever since he'd first met her, Hugh had known she was gorgeous, but sometimes he was startled by just how breathtaking she really was.

When she cocked her head, looking at him curiously, he realized that he was staring. Quickly, he cleared his throat and hunted for a comeback. "What's the fun in that?"

She rolled her eyes and then turned as Jules, Theo, and Viggy came into the kitchen. Jules still looked a little green around the edges every time someone mentioned Ty's skill with a rock, but other than that, she seemed to have bounced back with impressive resilience.

"Okay," Jules said, plopping down on one of the chairs. "The kids are upstairs and under threat of painful dismemberment if they try to listen in to our conversation, so let's talk. How do we get people to stop trying to kill Hugh?"

"Aww, you care," Hugh said, keeping his tone teasing, even as he fought the urge to peer out the kitchen window, looking for guys with guns hiding in the woods. He pulled out a seat for Grace and then took the one next to her. Stretching out his arm, he let it rest on the back of her chair. Although he wasn't actually touching her, he was reassured by the warmth of her shoulders and the occasional silky brush of her hair.

Theo didn't sit. Instead, he prowled around the kitchen, his frequent glances out the window making it obvious he was feeling as paranoid as Hugh. "I'm not happy you're involved in this."

"Yeah, I'm not too excited to be involved, either."

"I was talking to Jules," Theo growled, glaring at Hugh.

He deserved it, Hugh knew. Guilt that had been sitting in his stomach in a growing dark mass expanded, making it impossible to maintain his joking facade. "You're right," he said seriously, looking at Jules and then at Grace. "I'm going to get someone else killed. You need to stay far away from me." He turned toward Theo. "All of you." From Theo's set expression, he wasn't going anywhere. Hugh's guilt multiplied, threatening to choke him.

"So you can become a one-man army and figure this out yourself?" Grace scoffed. "Please. We don't even know for sure that it's *you* they're aiming at. It still could be that Martin Jovanovic sent these guys after me. Self-involved much?"

Despite his dark mood, that made him snort. "No. They're after me."

Twisting in her seat, she crossed her arms and locked eyes with him. "Not necessarily."

"They blew up my truck."

"Circumstantial."

"What?" He blinked at her. "That's not what circumstantial means."

"Sure it is. Next flimsy argument?"

"The Rack and Ruin member said so."

"Please." She flicked her fingers at him. "Like you can take the word of a felon who beats up his wife."

Jules made a tiny choking sound.

"That asshole at Otto's place pointed a gun at you and said he was going to kill me for the money."

With a shrug, Grace flipped her hair over her shoulder. The strands fanned out, sliding over his arm. He forced himself to focus on the argument—the *insane* argument. Even though he knew she was just trying to make him feel better, he couldn't let her ridiculous assertions slide. "One guy. There were three. Maybe the other two were there for me. We don't know that."

"Yes, we do—"

Theo's phone rang, and they all jumped. He glanced at the screen and then answered. "Hey, Otto." There was a short pause before he spoke again. "Got it." Ending the call, he headed for the hallway. "Otto's coming down the driveway." As if on cue, Lexi started barking from the front, where she was positioned in Theo's squad car. Viggy was in the kitchen with them; they'd decided Lexi would be a better alarm in case anyone trespassed.

"I'll go let him in," Theo added, disappearing into the hallway.

"As entertaining as this thing"—Jules pointed back and forth between Hugh and Grace—"is, your argument is pointless. We're not going to hide and leave you to the mercy of hired killers, Hugh. We're helping. Deal with it."

Grace smirked at him. "Exactly."

Even as their words warmed him, the enormity of the situation pressed down, threatening to crush him—crush them all. "You can't endanger yourselves like that. And the kids...they can't be involved. What if something happens to one of you because of me?"

Jules flinched as if he'd struck her, but then she lifted her chin. "We'll figure out how to keep the kids safe. I'm helping, though."

"Me, too." He'd never seen Grace look so mulish. It was a surprisingly good look on her. "We're not going to treat you like a bullet-attracting leper, Hugh. We're going to bring this Truman bitch down."

"Exactly." Jules held out her fist, and Grace bumped it with her own. They both made exploding noises as they opened their fingers.

Frustration and humor warred inside Hugh. They didn't understand that he'd rather get shot a dozen times than see one of his friends get hurt. He opened his mouth to say...he wasn't sure what exactly, but *something* that would convince them to run and hide a long way away from him and the target on his back.

He was distracted when Theo returned with Otto, however. "How'd processing go?"

"LT wants you to come in," Otto non-answered, leaning his bulk against the counter.

"I'm aware. That's why I haven't returned his fifty calls."

Grace frowned at Hugh. "Is it wise to blow off your lieutenant like that? Won't you get in trouble?"

Shrugging with a nonchalance he didn't feel, Hugh answered as lightly as he could. "If I don't answer, then I don't have to ignore a direct order. That would definitely get me into trouble. When he eventually chases me down, I can just say my phone died—which it will eventually, if he keeps calling me."

"Maybe you should go in," Grace said. Her fingers were tapping out a silent, anxious rhythm against the table, and Hugh put a gentle hand over hers, stilling them. "You'd be safe there."

"Can't hide at the station forever." The idea of cowering in safety while his partners risked their lives to save his revolted him. It wasn't an option. He'd just continue dodging his LT's calls until he fixed the situation…however he was going to manage that. "I just need to track down Truman."

"*We* need to track down Truman, you mean," Theo corrected.

With an impatient huff, Hugh opened his mouth to restart the argument, but Otto spoke first.

"Got an idea about that."

All heads turned toward Otto.

"While we were waiting for you to return, the conscious suspect got chatty." After dropping that tidbit, Otto went silent.

Hugh found himself leaning toward Otto, wishing he could physically force the other man to talk faster. It was just the way Otto spoke, considering his words before allowing them to escape, but right now, with Hugh's internal hurricane of guilt and frustration, he really just wanted Otto to spit it out. By the way everyone else was mimicking his body language, they felt the same way.

"Truman offered a bonus." Otto's face went cold and hard. "An extra fifty thousand dollars, but only if you were killed before midnight."

"Tonight?" Hugh asked, his brain processing the information as Otto nodded.

"So he's planning to have a shipment come through sometime after midnight." Theo vocalized the thought even as it took shape in Hugh's brain.

Hugh smiled, feeling the first inkling of hope he'd experienced in several days. "Should we form a welcoming committee?"

"LT won't let you within a mile of the scene," Theo warned.

"If the lieutenant doesn't know there is a scene, he can't ban me from it."

Otto and Theo groaned, but Hugh's grin widened. He knew that sound. He and Otto and Theo would be meeting Truman's shipment that night.

Hugh was driving her nuts. If they hadn't been parked next to a cliff, she would've been tempted to jump out of the car and storm off. No, it was her car. She would've kicked out Mr. Protective instead. "For the last time, I'm not leaving you here alone."

"I'm not a safe person to be around right now, not with the contract Truman put out on me."

"So?" she scoffed. "Who in this car *doesn't* have a drug lord trying to kill them?" Lexi shifted in the backseat. "Okay, so Lexi doesn't. I do, though, so quit trying to sound special."

"Special?" he grumbled. "I'm not trying to sound special. Jovanovic doesn't know where you are, so it's not the same. I almost got you killed about four times now. It's dangerous to be around me."

"That's why we're here." Grace waved an arm to encompass the mountain they were currently sitting on. "If we'd stayed in Monroe, people would've started shooting at us again. No one will find us up here. It's the safest place to be until your drug bust tonight."

"No," Hugh argued. "The safest place to be is at the police station."

"So let's go."

Hugh grimaced. "I can't. If LT sees me, I won't be leaving the station until Truman's locked up. You should go, though."

"Fine. I'll go to the station to join Jules and the kids." Grace reached out as if to turn the key in the ignition. "I'll drive this car right into the law enforcement center's parking lot and leave it there. Will you be coming with me or staying here?"

Hugh frowned at her. "Are you threatening to leave me in the middle of the mountainous nowhere without a vehicle? Call Theo or Otto. They'll come and pick you up and bring you to the station, where you'll be safe."

"Nope. No cell coverage up here. You could always come with me, though. I'm sure your understanding and easygoing lieutenant will be fine with letting you leave in a few hours to stake out a drug shipment."

His scowl deepened. Oddly enough, his cranky expression made her want to smile.

"Or you could stay here. If you and Lexi start walking now, it'll only take…what? Six or seven hours to get to town? I'm sure Theo and Otto and the others can take care of that little drug bust, though." She blinked at him innocently, trying to control the smirk that wanted to form.

After another few seconds of futilely trying to glare her into submission, he gave in. "Fine. Stay. Just cuddle right up to the guy with a target on his back. Good plan."

She rolled her eyes. There was something wrong with her that she found his fits of melodrama endearing, rather than annoying. "We are literally, as you said, in the middle of mountainous nowhere. You and Theo and Otto all agreed that it would be impossible to snipe either of us."

"Snipe?" His mouth twitched at the corners, and Grace had to hold back a triumphant grin. She knew he couldn't keep his glower for more than a few minutes. "Is that a verb meaning 'to shoot at' now?"

She waved off his teasing correction. "Snipe, shoot at, stake out, whatever you want to call it. There's nowhere to hide up here. We can see the road below us, so no one can drive up here and surprise us. Even when it gets dark, we'll be able to see headlights. If they try to drive on this road without lights, then they'll fall right off a cliff. Besides, it's so quiet up here that we'll hear their engine when they're a long way away. If anyone magically does manage to get close, Lexi'll bark, and we'll get the hell out of Dodge." As if in agreement, the dog thumped her tail against the backseat. "For the next few hours, we're safe from any and all people who want to kill you, and that includes your lieutenant."

"I doubt LT wants to *kill* me," Hugh said. His scowl had disappeared completely, and he was leaning back in the passenger seat, apparently resigned to the fact that she wasn't leaving him behind. "Maim and torture me, sure. He wouldn't go as far as actual death, though. Too much paperwork."

She laughed and then stopped abruptly.

"What's wrong?" He peered through the windshield, as if looking for threats.

"Nothing." When he didn't relax, she laid a hand on his arm. "Seriously. I was just surprised that, with everything that's happening, you were able to make me laugh."

After a moment of eyeing her closely, he eased back against his seat again. "I'm sorry."

"Sorry that you make me laugh?"

"No." His expression was serious as he reached over to link his fingers with hers. Her stomach clenched at the contact. "I'm sorry that I've put your life in danger."

"Not your fault," she said, squeezing his fingers as if she could use force to make him believe her words. "That's the awful hit men and the even awfuller Truman."

The tension around his mouth eased slightly. "*Awfuller*? Do we need to have another grammar lesson?"

Twisting, she smacked his shoulder with her free hand. "No, we do not. And quit changing the subject. I'm trying to tell you that it's not your fault. Do you think I'm to blame for Martin Jovanovic trying to kill me?"

Just like that, he was serious again. "Of course not. That's not your fault."

"And the hit out on you isn't your fault."

"I still feel guilty."

"Me, too."

They fell into silence, their hands still locked together. His grip was warm and comforting. She didn't care that it was just the illusion of safety. If he wanted her to let go, he was going to have to peel her off him, finger by finger.

The sun had dipped behind the tallest mountain peaks, dimming the light around them. The car windows were down so that they could hear, and the air cooled rapidly. In just a long-sleeve T-shirt and jeans, Grace shivered.

"Cold?" Hugh asked, his fingers tightening around hers.

"A little." When he released his grip, she wanted to complain, until he slid his arm around her shoulders. That was even better than holding hands. "It's more that I'm thinking about tonight. What if the hit man lied? What if this is a trap, so they can lure you in and kill you?" Her voice got rough with anxiety on the last few words.

"Hey," he said gently. "Come here." Before she could respond, he was hauling her over the center console.

After an initial surprised yelp, she went along with him, even helping to shift her body until she was sitting on his lap, her legs draped over the console and her feet in the driver's seat. If he wanted to hold her, she wasn't about to say no. After all, this was Hugh, and he was like a warm teddy bear with muscles and an attitude. The memory of their kiss outside the viner played in Grace's head on a frequent basis, and she had to admit that she wouldn't mind a repeat. Plus, now that she was snuggled up with Hugh, she was already feeling warmer.

Much, much warmer.

"Once this is over, you know what we're going to do?" He kept one arm wrapped around her while his other hand chafed her arm from her elbow up to her shoulder. Even with her shirtsleeve and the bandages over his palms blocking his touch, heat still flooded through her. It wasn't from the motion, but more just that Hugh's hands were on her. "Gracie?"

"What?" She jolted out of her semi-dazed state. The

man was the ultimate distractor. How was she supposed to concentrate on what he was saying when he was *rubbing* her?

"Are you paying attention now?" he asked in a mock serious way. "Because I don't talk just to hear myself, you know."

"Okay, drama queen. I'm listening. Share."

"Do you really want to know?"

"No." When he did a double take, she laughed.

Although he made a fake-sour face, he gave her an affectionate squeeze.

"Fine, okay, yes," she relented, barely resisting the urge to kiss his pouty mouth. She'd never known a guy who was so unabashedly dramatic, and she kind of loved it. The banter, his quick comebacks, his obvious adoration of her smart mouth… Talking with him made Grace feel clever and witty and so *alive*. "Tell me, please. I might die if I never know what you just said when I wasn't paying attention. Save me, my prince, and tell me what I missed."

"Fine." He gave a billowy, long-suffering sigh, and she resisted the urge to smack his shoulder. She knew from experience that it would just hurt her hand without bothering him at all. "What I *asked*, as you'd know if you hadn't been ignoring me, is if you knew what we were going to do when this is all over."

"Hmm…" The thought of not having killers chasing them made Grace wiggle her toes in glee. "I know what we're not going to do."

"What's that?"

"We're not going to get shot at. Or blown up."

"True, but you're not playing the game right." His

fake pout was back, and this time, she couldn't resist. Reaching up, she pinched his lower lip. His eyes shot open in surprise for a split second, and then narrowed. Before she could pull away, he caught her thumb between his teeth. She felt a jolt pass from her fingers all the way down to her toes. They both froze, gazes locked on each other, until he pulled away slightly, releasing her thumb.

"We're..." His voice was rough. Clearing his throat, he tried again, although it didn't sound any smoother. Grace secretly liked it. It was so easy for him to set her mind spinning, and she loved any type of proof that he was as affected by her as she was by him. "We're going on a date."

"We are?" If his voice was gravelly, hers was almost as husky. "Where? I thought the only place in town is the VFW."

"What's wrong with the VFW?" he asked. Although she could tell he was trying to tease, his gaze was heated and serious, moving between her mouth and her eyes.

"Absolutely nothing. Well, nothing except that it's too easy for some creeper to break into the women's bathroom." Instead of sounding snarky, the words came out absently. She hardly knew what she was saying anymore. The only thing she could focus on was that all signs pointed to Hugh kissing her. Although her brain still warned her to keep her emotional distance for the sake of her heart, her body was perfectly all right with the idea of kissing Hugh.

His hand slid from her shoulder to the base of her skull, and he pulled her slowly—much too slowly—toward him. Finally, his lips brushed hers, clinging for a fraction of a second before retreating. It was so different than their first kiss, when they'd gone from arguing to making out in no time at all, and this one was even hotter. Gentle Hugh, the Hugh who was taking his time, was just as appealing as the take-charge Hugh who'd initiated their explosive, spontaneous kiss.

He teased her. Of course he did; it was Hugh, after all. He used his lips and his tongue and his teeth, but in the tiniest nips and slides and touches. Every time Grace moved in to him, trying to prolong the contact, he skipped away, only to land in a new spot with the lightest brush of his mouth.

"You're driving me crazy," she groaned, turning her head to chase his lips again.

His chuckle rumbled through his chest, and she felt the low vibrations against her breasts as he touched the tip of his tongue to her earlobe. "Is that good?" The warm air expelled with his words blew against the shell of her ear, and she shivered. His teeth were next, lightly scoring the sensitive lobe.

Enough was enough. Grabbing his head with both hands, she held him still and crashed her mouth down onto his. He laughed, but only for a moment, and then he was kissing her back. It was as wild, as ferocious, as intense as Grace remembered from their earlier kiss, but this one was even more amazing. That embrace had been born of heightened emotion, but there was a sweetness now, an affection, that made things so much better.

He took over the kiss, dominating and hot, and then she took it back, loving that they passed control back and forth. It was a game, the most exciting one she'd ever played, but it felt intensely serious at the same time. Hugh grinned against her mouth as she twisted around, wriggling until she had a knee on either side of his hips, straddling him. She felt him flinch, just a tiny movement. Worried that she'd hurt his injured leg, she started to pull away, but he chased her lips with his, not letting her escape. Soon, she was lost in the kiss again.

His breath caught when she slid her fingers underneath his T-shirt, stroking the soft, hot skin that overlaid ridges of muscle. With a groan, he pulled her closer, trapping her fingers between them so she couldn't have moved her hands from his belly, even if she'd wanted to.

Their kiss grew in intensity, heating until it reached a flash point and they both burned with an incredible fire that turned everything to ash except the two of them. Hugh's fingers kneaded the back of her neck as his other hand wrapped around her hip, pulling her closer with each motion, until they were pressed together so completely that she wasn't sure where she ended and where Hugh began.

She slid her hands to his sides and then to his back, wedging them between his shirt and skin in the small space that the seat back allowed. It felt like she couldn't get enough of him, of kissing him, touching him. *More*. She needed more of Hugh. Gripping the bottom of his T-shirt, she started tugging it upward. It needed to come off.

As she pulled at the fabric, wishing it and all the rest of their clothes would just disappear, he groaned and kissed her harder. Distracted, she clenched her fingers around handfuls of his shirt and lost herself in his kiss.

Something cold and damp touched the side of her neck. With a startled cry, she jerked backward, turning her head to see a close-up of Lexi's muzzle.

"What?" Hugh asked, his voice hoarse, and immediately began scanning the growing darkness outside the car.

The ridiculousness of the situation made her snort, which made her laugh. Hugh stared at her, bewildered by her amusement. "Lexi," she finally managed to explain. "Her cold nose on my neck kind of killed the mood."

As if on cue, Lexi licked Hugh's ear before lying down in the backseat again. With an amused wince, Hugh rubbed his ear. "I have to admit that it's sexier when you do that."

Grace got the giggles again. "Sorry, but I'm not going back in that territory until after you shower."

"No?" The devilish gleam in his eyes should've made her run, but she was too caught up in the remains of her laughter to realize what was about to happen. Surging forward, Hugh held her head still and covered her cheek and ear with sloppy kisses.

"Ew!" she complained, still laughing, as she tried to rub off the dampness with her shoulder. "That's just gross."

"Sorry." He didn't *look* sorry. He didn't look sorry at all.

"Uh-huh." Now that they'd stopped kissing, Grace started to feel awkward straddling Hugh's lap. She shifted, planning to return to the driver's seat, but he caught her hips, holding her in place.

"Stay." When she met his gaze and raised her eyebrows, he shrugged but didn't loosen his grip. "You're keeping me warm."

Since she wasn't that excited about returning to the cold, Hugh-less driver's seat, she complied, although she twisted around until she was sitting sideways again. "If I sit the other way, my feet will fall asleep."

Hugh's response was a rumbling sound in his chest, but Grace wasn't sure if it was a sign of acknowledgment or contentment. His arms wrapped around her, protecting her from the chilly mountain air drifting in through the window. Relaxing against his solid chest, she yawned.

"Forget my feet. My whole body might be falling asleep soon," she admitted.

"No problem." He sounded almost gentle, and the way he was stroking her hair was incredibly soothing. "Get some rest. I'll keep watch."

"Okay." Her eyes were already drifting closed. "Wake me up when it's time to go. Or if anyone shows up here."

"I'll do that." Hugh sounded as if he was about to laugh yet again, and she opened her eyes to glare at him…or at least squint blearily at him. Once she focused on his face, her mild irritation dissolved. Just the sight of him made her happier. Although she'd met him only a short time ago, it had been long enough for Hugh to become precious to her. All of her efforts to stay detached and protect herself had failed miserably, and it was too late to turn back. He was now permanently blasted into her heart. Turning her head, she pressed a kiss against his bare throat. His hand stilled on her hair for a moment, and she saw him swallow before he began stroking her head once more.

Grace's eyes drifted closed once again. The last few weeks had been rough, and she was comfortable here. Even when multiple people were trying to kill him, Hugh made her feel safe.

CHAPTER 16

HUGH GROUND HIS PALMS INTO HIS EYES. IT WAS FOUR IN the morning, and he needed sleep desperately. At eleven the night before, he'd reluctantly woken his sleeping beauty and they'd made their careful—much more careful than if he'd been driving—way down the mountain. Although she wasn't thrilled to be excluded from the action, Grace couldn't argue about her lack of law enforcement skills, so she'd reluctantly stopped at the police station to join Jules and the kids for the night.

It had felt wrong to leave her there, to not have her with him for the first time in several days. Hugh hoped she was sleeping, that she wasn't worrying, but he doubted it. At least she'd managed to doze for a few hours before they'd had to leave their mountain hideout.

His phone beeped, and he grimaced. Although he assumed it was Lieutenant Blessard, leaving his one-hundredth message, he checked just in case it was Grace or Theo or Otto. It was none of those people. Instead, it was the final death knell of his cell phone battery charge. Sliding the phone back in his pocket, he figured the lack of a charge was for the best. Now when he told LT that his phone was dead, he wouldn't be lying.

He shifted his weight, rubbing at his stiffening thigh, and then hopped up and down in place a few times, making sure to keep his weight on his good leg. It didn't work. He still felt like he was going to fall asleep standing up. By his feet, Lexi was stretched out on the ground, snoring.

They'd been staking out Main Street for more than four hours. During that time, only thirteen vehicles had passed. Theo and Otto had stopped every one, since they'd all been traveling over the twenty-mile-per-hour speed limit that the city council had pushed through a few years earlier. Hugh had walked Lexi around each car, SUV, and truck, but she hadn't signaled that there were drugs on any of them. All the drivers had been let off with a warning, except for one who'd been texting as he came through town. The oblivious guy had almost driven right on top of Theo, who seemed grimly pleased to write the citation for that one.

Hugh swayed with exhaustion. His knees softened, and he had to catch his balance on the tree next to him. He needed to move, to do something, or he'd be on the ground, snoring right along with his dog.

"C'mon, Lex," he said, his voice rough with lack of sleep. What he wouldn't give to be curled up with Grace on a bed somewhere, even if it was a cot at the police station. "Let's go bug Theo. Or Otto. No, Theo. He's more fun to aggravate."

Yawning, Lexi stood and stretched. Although she seemed to be taking the sleep interruptions well, her tail drooped a little.

"Sorry, girl." Hugh rubbed the top of her head and behind her ears. "Just a few more hours to go and then you can sleep for a week." He did his own stretch-and-yawn combination. "I know I'm going to." The mental image of Grace sharing his bed made that plan even more appealing. As soon as they took care of Truman, and then dealt with Grace's problem, things were going to be peaceful in Monroe. Hugh set his jaw. They'd better be. After all this, everyone involved—Hugh, Grace, Theo, Jules, the kids, Otto, Lexi, and even the lieutenant—deserved some rest.

As Hugh and Lexi approached the driver's side of Theo's car, he didn't look at them. Instead, he stayed focused on his MCT—mobile computer terminal—screen, only reaching with one hand to raise the window.

"Funny guy," Hugh muttered, starting to grin. When Theo blocked his efforts, Hugh had to get creative. Crouching down so his face was level with the window, his bad leg extended to the side, Hugh kept his unblinking gaze on Theo's averted head. It took several minutes of concentrated staring before Theo broke and lowered the window a half inch.

"What?" he snapped, although he kept his voice low. They were going to have enough complaints about all the overhead light action that had been happening on Main Street during the wee morning hours. Hugh wasn't sure how they were going to explain their unofficial sting operation to the lieutenant. Hugh saw a lot of menial tasks in his professional future…if he still had a job with MPD, that was.

Hugh gave Theo his most innocent look. "What?"

"What's with the creeper act?"

With a laugh, Hugh asked, "Who's acting?"

Turning to face the window, Theo frowned. "I have reports to finish. Did you need something, or are you just bored?"

"Bored."

"Figures."

"I'm tired." Hugh stood, catching his balance on the top of Theo's car when his leg wobbled. The muscle weakness was even worse than the pain sometimes. He could deal with the pain, but it usually took him by surprise when his leg gave out on him. "You need to keep me awake."

"You're not going to let me finish my reports, are you?"

"No."

Theo's answering growl cut off when they saw the gleam of headlights in the distance. Adrenaline flowed through him, and Hugh was suddenly not so sleepy. He moved back to his spot in the shadows of a couple of pine trees. If it was Truman's shipment, Hugh didn't want to risk that the driver would recognize him. Having a shoot-out in the middle of Main Street would be a bad thing.

The vehicle got closer, and Otto's brake lights flashed. *Good*, Hugh thought. *Otto's ready*.

As the incoming SUV drew closer and then passed Theo's squad car, Otto turned on his overhead lights and pulled in front of the SUV, forcing it to stop. Theo immediately blocked it from the back. The two cops got out and approached the SUV from opposite sides, with Theo on the passenger's side and Otto on the driver's.

From Hugh's vantage point, the driver looked like a woman in her forties. He couldn't see a passenger. As he and Lexi approached the rear of the SUV, he heard the woman's nervous prattle. "...don't think I was speeding, Officer. I take this route every morning, except for my days off, and I know it so well I could drive it in my sleep. Oh! Not that I'd fall asleep while I was driving or anything. Just, you know, I *could* drive it if I... Where is that darn insurance card?"

As Hugh walked Lexi around the back of the SUV, he had a sinking feeling that this would be their fourteenth wrong vehicle. The woman could just be a really good actress, but it was more likely she was exactly who she said she was—a nurse with a two-hour mountain commute to the orthopedic clinic in Dresden where she worked. He doubted she ran drugs on the side.

Lexi agreed. She checked where he indicated, but she didn't signal that she'd picked up on traces of any narcotics. She didn't even hesitate anywhere. As they rounded the front of the SUV and finished the search along the driver's side of the vehicle, the woman sucked in a sharp breath.

"Why do you have a dog here?" she demanded, her voice going shrill. "Is it going to smell my car? Do you think I have drugs? Oh my goodness."

Hugh dredged up a grin. "Morning, ma'am. Don't mind us. I have a dog we're training, and I saw that these officers had you stopped, so I thought Lexi here could get some experience. Don't worry. We didn't find a thing."

It wasn't his best work, since a lack of sleep didn't do much for his charm, but the woman seemed to soften a little. "Oh. Well, you could've *asked* first before you gave me a heart attack."

"Sorry about that, ma'am." With a final, forced smile, he retreated to Theo's squad car.

After a few more minutes, the woman was on her way to work again, and Theo and Otto joined him.

"Is this pointless? Are we wasting time here?" Hugh asked, rolling his sore shoulders. "Bad information, maybe? Or Truman was giving himself a few days of cushion, and the shipment won't be coming until next week?"

Otto shrugged. "Could be. Theo and I still have four hours of our shift. Might as well stay on this."

"Yep," Theo agreed.

Leaning on the roof of Theo's squad car, Hugh bit back a torrent of frustrated curses. He took a few deep breaths, trying to think rationally. Exhaustion made everything seem impossible, especially when his entire body was aching. "Okay," he finally said, shoving every jab of pain into a box in his head. Just four more hours. He could do this. "I'll be by the trees."

Grace tapped her fingers on the side of her leg and fought the need to pace. Looking around the interview room, she sighed. It'd been only a few weeks since she'd barely escaped from one police station with her life, and now she was back in another one.

She clenched her hands and then relaxed them, shaking out the tension in her fingers. This wasn't the same. She had allies with the police now, and even, thanks to those cop friends, with the FBI. This time, she wouldn't have to run from one of Martin Jovanovic's henchmen.

It would've been nice to have someone there with her. Her brain screamed *Hugh*, but she resolutely ignored it. She needed to get used to doing things by herself. After all, if this worked, she'd get to go home to California.

Grace waited for the usual flare of excitement at the thought of returning to her life, but it fizzled. She'd be thrilled to see Penny, but other than that… To her surprise, she'd miss parts of Monroe. Jules, Hugh, the kids, Hugh, Theo and Otto, Hugh, Lexi, Hugh, even that old mess of a house, and Hugh.

With a groan, she let her forehead rest on the table. It was time to stop pretending she could just wave goodbye and leave Monroe—and Hugh—without any heartbreak. A part of her wanted to stay, wanted to see what would happen if they did go on a real date, even if that was just to the viner. Hopefully, that date would not include Hugh picking a bathroom lock. Grace couldn't help but smile at the thought, but then she gave herself a mental smack. She had a life—an incredibly wonderful, hard-won life—in California. Was she seriously considering giving up all she'd worked so hard for? She was probably just caught up in the moment. Once she got back to LA, she'd forget all about a certain gorgeous, clever Colorado cop.

Lifting her head, she sat back in her chair with a sigh. If she couldn't have Hugh with her for moral support, she wished at least Jules had been there to talk to. The previous night, after Hugh had dropped Grace off at the station, the kindly desk sergeant had shown her where the women's locker room was and then led her to a storage room where cots had been set up. Jules and the kids had occupied five of the cots, and there had been an empty one for her.

Jules and Sam had sat up when she'd entered. Once they saw it was her, Jules had given a sleepy wave, and both had fallen back asleep quickly. After a quick trip to the bathroom, Grace had collapsed in her cot, her entire body aching with the need for sleep. Unfortunately, her brain hadn't cooperated, spinning with worries and scenarios that blended into her dreams and jerked her out of a light doze several times.

There hadn't been any other extra cots, so she wasn't really expecting Hugh to join them, but a tiny part of her had hoped he would stop in to let them know that the bust had gone well and that he wasn't hurt. The hours had crawled by, however, and then it was early morning, and still there was no sign of Hugh. Jules and the kids had headed to the viner with a police escort, and Grace, after a quick shower in the locker room, had been shown to the interview room to wait for FBI Special Agent Shankle to arrive.

The door opened abruptly, and Grace jerked back, making the chair scrape against the floor. The memory of Officer Jovanovic escorting her toward the stairway and her possible death ran through her mind, and she stood, ready to flee. As soon as she got a good look at the man in the doorway, however, she calmed, recognizing him as the cop Theo had been talking to at the Rack and Ruin bust. She could tell just by his rigid posture, wiry form, and thinning gray hair.

He was frowning at her. In fact, that was an understatement. He was scowling ferociously at her. Grace stared back with wide eyes, not sure what she'd done to deserve the glare.

"Why is he not answering his goddamned phone?" the man demanded.

Comprehension dawned, and Grace smiled as she figured out who the angry man in front of her was. "You're the lieutenant?"

"Lieutenant Blessard," he snapped. "Do you know where he is? Will he answer if you call him? You have a phone on you? Call him right now. No, actually, give me your phone." He held out a hand, palm up.

She dug her phone out of her pocket and handed it to him even before she realized what she was doing. The man had a commanding presence. "I'm pretty sure his phone is dead."

"Yeah, that's what he always says," the lieutenant muttered, jabbing at the buttons. His heavy eyebrows drew together as he held the phone up to his ear. Almost immediately, he moved it down and stabbed his finger to end the call.

He tossed the phone back to her. She fumbled as she caught it but managed to keep it from hitting the floor.

"When you talk to him, you tell him that he needs to get his ass in here yesterday. Got it?"

"Got it." As he turned away, she added, "What's going on? Is he in danger? I mean, more danger than the Truman stuff, which I know is a pretty big danger, but…"

His glare made her words dry up, and she fell silent. "Yes. He's in danger. What do you know about Truman? That's an open investigation."

"What kind of danger?" Her anxiety spiked as she thought of him being out all night, searching cars for the drug shipment. Was he okay? Had something already happened? Theo and Otto were there, though. She reassured herself that they would've called for help if anything had happened to Hugh…unless something had happened to them, too. Fear squeezed her stomach. "What's wrong?"

The lieutenant's face softened slightly. "Don't worry about it. I'll track him down and drag him in by the scruff of his neck. He'll be fine."

With that perfectly useless platitude, he left, closing the door behind him with a sharp bang. Letting out a frustrated sound, Grace plopped back down in her chair and stared at her phone, wondering if she should call Theo and have him warn Hugh that…what? He already knew that his lieutenant was looking for him, and Hugh was well aware that he was in danger, thanks to the hit Truman had out on him.

If Blessard knew of something else, however, if there was a new danger that Hugh needed to watch out for, then it was worth a call to warn him. Decided, she found Theo's number on her sadly short list of contacts. Before she could dial, the door swung open again, less violently that time. Although Grace startled again, she managed to stay in her chair.

A short, stocky, disheveled man stood in the doorway, holding a paper cup of coffee balanced on a short stack of files and notepads. His receding hairline and ill-fitting suit fit every television cliché, down to the visitor pass clipped to his jacket that had FBI printed in large letters. "Miss Robinson?"

"Yes?" She lowered her cell phone to her lap.

"Special Agent Josh Barrett from the FBI." He placed the pile of papers on the table and held out the coffee cup.

"Thank you." Grace accepted it eagerly, immediately taking a sip. It was some of the worst coffee she'd ever tasted, but she forced herself to take another drink. After her short, broken sleep the previous night, she needed caffeine desperately. "I thought I'd be talking to Agent Shankle."

"He'll be here shortly," Barrett said, taking a seat across the table from her. "Lieutenant Blessard requested a word with him first."

"Ah." His answer reminded Grace that she needed to call Theo, but she couldn't do that with the FBI agent in the room. She avoided glancing at the phone in her lap, taking a sip of coffee instead.

Barrett pulled a small digital recorder from his pocket. "Do you mind if I record this?"

"I don't mind." Exhaustion flooded Grace at the thought of having to tell the story of that terrible night, and she mentally shook herself. If she lived through it, she could talk about it. This would be the easy part. "I assumed it would be. Aren't the police videotaping this room?" She glanced around, looking for a camera, but there were just bare walls.

Barrett chuckled. "Not in Mayberry—I mean, Monroe. This is just an office turned into an interview room. For these tiny towns, surveillance cameras aren't in the budget."

There was a smugness to his tone that made her frown, offended on behalf of Hugh and the other Monroe cops. The town might be small, but they worked hard. She could tell they really cared about their jobs. She started to defend them, but a wave of dizziness flooded her, and she lost her train of thought. Grace blinked hard, trying to bring the room back into focus.

"Miss Robinson, are you feeling okay?" Barrett's words had a strange echo to them, and she stared at his blurry form. What was wrong with her? She'd thought it was just lack of sleep, but this was different. Fog rolled over her brain, and she fought to keep her eyes open. "Miss Robinson? Or do you prefer Kaylee?"

Her alarm was muted, her panic smothered under a thick blanket. *Drugged.* The realization came slowly, even as the room darkened and tilted sideways.

"It's such a pleasure to meet you, Kaylee." The agent's voice was distorted, the words stretched and blurred. "You can call me Truman."

Grace woke up unable to move. Panic flushed through her, and her eyes popped open as she immediately started to struggle. Her muscles strained, but her arms and legs were restrained. She tried to yell, but something in and over her mouth stopped the sound. As the haze of unconsciousness started to clear, Grace realized that she'd been gagged and hog-tied, with her wrists and ankles bound together.

She blinked, trying to figure out where she was. The memory of the FBI agent—no, *Truman*—coming into the interview room, giving her coffee… Grace groaned, and the sound was absorbed by the gag. He'd drugged her. He'd drugged her and somehow moved her to wherever she was. Fear accelerated her heartbeat as reality returned. Where was she?

Her eyes slowly adjusted to the dim light. Twisting her head back and forth, she realized that she was lying on her back in a small, rectangular space. *Like a coffin.* Her panic started to return, and she firmly shut it down. Light was coming from between the slats of a metal air vent next to her head. If the enclosure she was trapped in had been a coffin, there wouldn't have been any light, and there definitely wouldn't have been any air.

Even so, the horror of her situation was starting to sink in, and her breath came hard and fast. *Stop!* she commanded mentally, reining in her building terror. Giving in to fear would not solve her problem. She wasn't sure what *would* solve it, but she knew for certain that getting hysterical wouldn't help.

Turning onto her side, she twisted her hands so she could feel her bonds. Her fingers slid across a slick, familiar surface—duct tape. Her wrists worked, her fingers straining to find an edge, to pull and work at the tape, but the angle was wrong. Giving up on freeing her wrists, she reached for her feet. A rope of duct tape connected them to her hands, and she arched her back and pulled her bound ankles closer to her.

The front of her thighs screamed a protest at her awkward position as Grace picked and tugged at the tape. There was a *thunk*, and the light from the vent brightened, making her go still. Releasing her ankles, she craned her neck to peek through the slats.

She was in the back of a van, one that had been converted into…something. She could see a large, low sink and a table with a rubber, textured surface. The table looked familiar, and she remembered that Nan had a similar one at the kennel that she put the dogs on for grooming. Confusion added to Grace's fear. What was this place?

One of the back doors was open, and Special Agent Barrett—no, *Truman*—climbed inside. Grace froze, not moving, not breathing. What was he going to do? Kill her? Torture her? This was the guy who put a hit out on Hugh, a *cop*, just to make it easier to run drugs. That kind of monster could be capable of anything.

He looked at the vent, and a cold smile crept over his face. "You awake in there, Kaylee?"

In a couple of strides, he was right next to her. With a click, the top of the enclosure—*not a coffin, not a coffin*—opened, and Truman stood over her, grinning. Trying to hide her shaking, she forced back her fear and packed all her rage and disgust into her glare.

"Comfortable?" he mocked. "I made it myself. From the outside, it looks like a water storage tank and heater, but it's actually a very convenient hiding place." His expression was expectant, as if he was waiting for her to rave over his cleverness. When she just continued to glower, Truman gave a tiny shrug. "I usually use it for…other things, but Jovanovic asked so nicely that I couldn't refuse. When I told him a woman wanted to talk to the FBI about Martin Jovanovic, he guessed it was you right away. I must say, the photo he sent does not do you justice." His reptilian eyes ran over her, and she fought the urge to cringe away from him. "He was quite desperate to know where you were hiding, but I'm keeping that to myself. I don't want Jovanovic to send one of his goons to pick you up just so he won't have to pay me. He's cut me out of deals before. Fool me once, and all that."

As much as she wanted to keep her tough expression, Martin's name sent a surge of fear through her. Truman might not torture her, but he was delivering her to Jovanovic, and *he* wouldn't have any qualms about causing Grace pain. She had firsthand evidence of that.

The men's bloody, battered faces filled her mind, and she forced them back. She couldn't panic, not now. She tried to move, to pull free from her restraints, but all she managed was to bump her knees against the side of her enclosure.

"None of that." Truman gave her a casual shove that rolled her onto her back, crushing her hands and feet painfully beneath her. "No one can hear you anyway. This auto shop is closed for the winter, and Monroe is like a ghost town. Just be a good girl, and I'll deliver you into Jovanovic's loving arms lickety-split. Well, *I* won't be the one driving, but I'll pay someone to get you there. How about that?"

He patted her on the head, and her rage returned, smothering the worst of her fear. If she hadn't been gagged, she would've bitten his condescending, evil hand. Straightening, he lowered the top of her cage, and she heard a snap as something locked into place. Grace had a feeling that Truman hadn't built in an emergency release lever for someone trapped in his drug hiding place.

Twisting onto her side again, she peered through the vent, watching as Truman hopped out of the back, leaving the door open. Grace felt a surge of urgency. She had to do something to take advantage of his absence and the open van door. Soon, they'd be in motion, and escaping would be that much more difficult. Once she was back in Martin's hands… Squeezing her eyes closed, Grace blocked out the panic that followed. *Think!* There had to be some way to escape.

Her cell phone had been on her lap when she'd lost consciousness, so it was probably still in the interview room, unless Truman had grabbed it. Calling for help was out. Hugh's face filled her mind, and she desperately wished she was with him, teasing him, joking with him, feeling safe. It hurt to think about him when she might never see him again, and she banished the thought. *Plan!* she ordered her brain. *Think of a plan!*

Her mind just spun in helpless, useless circles. Needing to do *something*, she reached for her ankles again, starting to pick at the tape while she thought. Truman had said they were in an auto shop. The only one that came to mind was a squatty little place perched on the very edge of town, a good distance away from any other buildings. Even if Monroe hadn't been mostly empty, the shop was isolated. If she managed to make noise, no one would hear—no one except Truman. Her fingers dug at the tape more and more frantically, and she forced them to slow. Panic wouldn't help. It only made it harder to think.

Truman climbed into the van, and she went still. Even though he knew she was there—he'd *put* her in there—she still instinctually tried to hide in place. As she stared through the vent, he carefully placed what looked like a canister vacuum on the shelf under the grooming table. His movements were so tentative that she examined the vacuum more closely, wondering why something labeled Pet Vac-N-Blow required such careful handling. She didn't notice anything obviously off about it, though.

Once the vacuum was in place, Truman backed away, sending a grin toward Grace's vent. "A little present for your cop friend, just in case he decides to stop your delivery today."

Grace's eyes went wide, and her body involuntarily jerked, thumping her bound feet against the side of her cage. *Hugh?* Her heart pounded as she stared at the innocuous-looking vacuum.

"Smells like coke," Truman said, his tone slightly amused. "Officer Murdoch's ever-so-talented dog will lead him right to it."

It was hard to hear Truman with her blood roaring in her ears, so Grace tried to force herself to calm down so she could listen. Air tore in and out of her lungs in frantic gasps as Truman smiled.

"Don't tell him, but there's a surprise inside. One that goes *boom*."

Grace screamed into her gag.

As the van rolled into motion, jostling her back and forth in her tiny prison, Grace lost control of her panic. She fought her restraints wildly, not even feeling her muscles shriek as she pulled against her bonds. Her fingers scrabbled to grip the tape, and two of her short nails bent back past the quick, but it didn't matter. She needed to get free before Hugh stopped the van, before Lexi found the drug-laced explosives, before the bomb went off, killing them all. Bound as Grace was, there was no way to warn them. She'd just have to lie there and watch, helpless, as everyone died.

With each second, they rolled closer to the street where she feared that Hugh, Theo, and Otto waited, and with each second, Grace prayed frantically that they'd already left, given up, gone back to the safety of the station. She'd still be sent back to Martin and killed, but at least Hugh and Lexi and the other cops wouldn't die along with her.

Flashing red-and-blue lights lit up the back of the van as it rolled to a stop. A sob jerked through Grace, and she choked on the wad of fabric in her mouth. This was it. She renewed her struggles, but then paused to listen as a stranger's voice said from the driver's seat, "Was I speeding, Officer?"

Otto's low rumble responded. "Yes. License, registration, and proof of insurance, please."

"Sorry about that." The driver gave an unconvincing chuckle. "These small mountain towns come up so fast. I'm on the highway, going fifty-five, and then suddenly I'm on Main Street. Takes a while to adjust."

Grace shifted, moving her lower body into place so she would be ready to bang her knees and feet against the wall of her enclosure as soon as there was a second of silence. Unfortunately, the driver continued to babble.

"I drive this route all the time, since the Dresden ladies love their fluffy lap dogs to be clean, but I've never been pulled over here before. Didn't even know you guys *had* cops in this town." That awkward half laugh came again, and Grace gritted her teeth. If only the guy could shut up for five seconds, she could slam her legs against the wall hard enough for Otto to hear. If the cops found her first, before the bomb was activated, then she could warn them.

The faint sound of Hugh's voice made Grace stop breathing. She strained to hear, but his words were unintelligible. Otto must have heard what he needed to hear, though, since he interrupted the still-babbling man. "Step out of the car, please."

"What? Why?" The guy sounded panicked. He must have obeyed Otto, because the van bobbled slightly as he climbed out of the driver's seat, and his babbled excuses and bluster grew fainter.

The back door jerked open, and Lexi hopped inside, followed by Hugh. *No!* Grace screamed, but the gag took away all of the sound. She swung her lower body as best she could, hitting her feet and knees painfully against the side of the small space, but an arriving squad car's siren gradually grew louder, muffling the sound. With a glance toward Grace's vent, Lexi went straight to the grooming table and sat in front of it, her attention locked on the pet vacuum.

"Good girl, Lex!" Hugh said. He limped toward Lexi, pulling a braided tug out of his pocket, but the dog didn't grab on to the toy. Instead, she spun around and started sniffing Grace's vent.

Good girl, Lexi! Grace made a grateful sound in her throat. Hugh was watching the dog curiously.

"What's up? Bored with Mr. Tugs already?" he asked, his words barely audible above the siren. "Too many dog smells in the pet-mobile to resist?" After a few moments, he turned back toward the pet vacuum and pulled a pair of gloves from his pocket. As he lifted the rigged, deadly appliance, Grace screamed at him, but the sound was lost in her gag and the multiple sirens gathering outside.

Over and over, she slammed her body against the side of her enclosure. Tears of terror and frustration filled her eyes, turning Lexi into a blurry brown-and-black blob. Grace blinked, desperate to see, to know what was happening, and tears ran sideways across the bridge of her nose and down her face. Lexi started to paw at the vent and bark.

Frowning, Hugh put the vacuum on the grooming table and moved to crouch next to Lexi. The sirens went silent, and Grace's knees hit with a dull thud. Hugh jumped back, drawing his gun. "Lexi, here!"

Lexi reluctantly moved to his side, her tail low and her attention still on Grace's vent. "*Thank you, thank you, thank you*," Grace babbled silently, rolling so her shoulder hit the side this time.

"Who's there?" Hugh barked, and Grace thumped her knees in response. He moved toward her, but slowly, too slowly with the bomb sitting right next to him. Who knew where Truman—in his Agent Barrett guise—was, or if he had a way to detonate the explosives remotely. They didn't have much time. Grace knocked into the side with her head. It was the loudest sound she'd made so far, but it hurt the most, and her vision grayed slightly. She gritted her teeth, blinking rapidly. If she passed out and couldn't talk, then Hugh would never know about the bomb, even if he got her out in time.

As Hugh cautiously crouched by Grace again, her head cleared. Obviously taking Hugh's movement as permission, Lexi resumed scrabbling at the vent. Hugh peered through the opening, and Grace pressed her face against the other side.

"Ah!" He jumped back slightly before his eyes widened. "Grace?"

She stared at him, making useless sounds in her throat. *Get out! There's a bomb!* her brain was screaming, but he couldn't hear her, couldn't read her mind.

"Otto! Theo!" he shouted, standing.

No! Don't call them! Her mental shouts were useless, though. All Grace could see of Hugh were his lower legs, but she heard him tapping and thumping on different parts of the fake water tank. She squeezed her eyes closed. He was trying to figure out how to get her out when he and Lexi should've been running away as fast as they could.

"What is it?" Otto asked, sticking his head inside the van.

"Grace is in here." His voice was grim and frantic at the same time.

"What?"

There was a click. "Got it." His voice was thick with satisfaction as the top swung open.

Grace stared at him, desperately saying, *"Bomb!"* over and over, but it came out as incomprehensible, muffled sounds.

"I've got you, Gracie," Hugh crooned, his voice gentle although the look on his face was ferocious. He pulled out a pocketknife and cut through the tape rope hog-tying her. Her legs straightened, her muscles protesting, and she groaned. He carefully started slicing through the tape on her wrists, but Grace shook her head adamantly.

The gag! Take off the gag!

He was obviously a terrible mind reader, because he ignored her and continued separating her wrists. As soon as they loosened, Grace yanked hard, pulling her hands apart.

"Careful!" Hugh warned, pulling back the knife.

Ignoring him, she reached up for the tape covering

her mouth, scratching her skin as she tried to peel up a corner.

Hugh frowned and reached out with the hand not holding his knife. "You're hurting yourself."

She didn't care. A few scratches were nothing compared to what would happen to all of them if the bomb detonated. Finally, *finally*, she managed to get hold of the edge of the tape, and she yanked it off. It was painful…very painful. Despite her desperation and adrenaline, she still felt the sting, but she ignored it and spit out the wad of damp fabric.

"Bomb," she croaked as soon as her mouth was clear.

"What?" Hugh and Otto said in unison.

Grace swallowed, trying to moisten her throat. It was so dry that she retched, but she forced herself to speak again, to get the words out. "Bomb!" Her voice was harsh and cracked, but at least it was understandable. "The vacuum is a bomb!"

There was barely a half second pause before the cops sprang into action as smoothly as if they'd rehearsed. As Otto grabbed Lexi's leash, Hugh snatched up Grace, slinging her over his shoulder.

"Agent Barrett is Truman," Grace gasped. "Is he here?"

"Yeah, and he's on his phone." Otto's voice was grim as he leapt out of the van with Lexi.

"His phone?" Her words were shrill, but Grace couldn't help it. Was Truman using his phone to remotely set off the bomb? They had to get out—now.

Hugh grabbed the vacuum in his right hand, and rushed toward the door behind Otto and Lexi.

"Are you crazy?" Every word tore at Grace's throat,

but she didn't care about the pain. "That's the bomb! The vacuum is the bomb!"

"Yeah, I got it," Hugh grunted as he leapt out of the back. "Don't want the van to be an even bigger one. Gas tank and nasty shrapnel and all."

As he landed, Grace's body thumped down hard where she was folded over his left shoulder, and he staggered before catching his balance. Lifting the vacuum, he hurled it, football style, into the air. Arching her back, Grace craned her neck to watch. It seemed to move in slow motion, arcing high with hose and cord fluttering behind like the tail of a funny-shaped kite. It tipped down, returning to the earth, dropping over the embankment and into Big Creek.

Hugh dove, bringing Grace to the ground, his body covering hers, just as the sky turned impossibly bright. The *boom* came later, seeming to go on and on until everything went quiet. The silence felt worse than the earlier cacophony.

Grace opened her eyes, blinking away the splashes of light that popped up, blocking her vision. When it finally cleared, she couldn't see anything except for Hugh's shoulder. He was on top of her, his body heavy. He wasn't moving.

"Hugh?" her voice came out scratchy, and she coughed, trying to clear her throat. It was hard to get enough air in her lungs, and her mouth was still painfully dry. "Hugh?" She tried to roll, to push him off so she could see his face, but his body kept her pinned. "Hugh!"

What if he's dead? Oh God, what if he sacrificed himself to save me? Her breaths started coming in short pants at the thought of Hugh being gone, of him never

teasing her, or laughing, or picking the lock on a bathroom door ever again. She let out a gasping sob.

"I've got you, Hugh," a male voice said, sounding muffled, and the weight on top of her lightened.
Strangely, after nearly being crushed by it, she didn't
want it gone. What if that was the last time she could be
that close to Hugh? As soon as he was lifted enough that
her arms were freed, she tried to push off the ground so
she could follow wherever they were taking him.

"Hang on, Grace." That was a different voice, but it
had that same strange, underwater sound to it as the first
one did. Gentle but firm hands held her still. "Let's get
you checked out before you move."

She struggled, but the hands were too strong, or she
was too weak. Her ears began to clear, that odd muffled
sensation easing, and she started to hear other things,
like sirens and people crying and Lexi whining and
voices shouting urgently and truck engines and even
more sirens.

Grace tried to turn her head to see what was happening, where they were taking Hugh, but those hands held
her in place.

"Better not move until they make sure your neck's
okay." She finally recognized the voice—it was Theo.
He crouched behind her, his hands surprisingly gentle
as they supported her head, keeping it still. "Should just
be a minute."

"How's Hugh?" she asked, her voice still coming
out rusty, little more than a croak. A flash of stark fear
crossed Theo's face before he blanked his expression.

"They're taking him to the hospital," he said.

"He's not dead?"

He gave her a little smile. Grace was sure it was supposed to be reassuring, but having serious Theo smile at her unnerved her more than if he'd burst into tears. "No. He's not dead."

Her body went limp in relief as she closed her eyes. Hugh was hurt, but he wasn't dead. There was hope.

"Grace?" Theo sounded worried. "You still with me?"

"Yeah." She opened her eyes and smiled. "Hugh's alive."

"Yeah." This time, when Theo smiled back, it wasn't scary at all. "Can't kill that stubborn bastard. Death would get so annoyed with him that he'd get tossed right back into the land of the living."

"Otto? Lexi?"

"They're okay. Check out Otto." His grin was fierce as he helped her roll to her side so she could see without turning her head. Emergency vehicles were scattered around, with more pulling up to the scene. All the flashing lights and sirens were disorientating, especially with the emergency services crews rushing around, adding to the confusion and turmoil.

Otto strode through the chaos, cutting a path as people automatically moved out of his way. When Grace saw the target of his ferocious focus, she sucked in a harsh breath. Phone clutched in his hand, Truman was walking quickly around the perimeter of the crowd toward the parked FBI vehicles.

"It's okay," Theo said, sounding darkly satisfied. "Otto's got this."

When he spotted Otto heading his way, Truman started to run. He dropped the phone, reaching into his jacket for what Grace feared was a gun. Shifting into a sprint, Otto quickly overtook Truman and grabbed his arm, jerking him to a halt. He twisted the gun out of the FBI agent's hand and tossed it to the side in one smooth motion. Truman's smug expression changed to shock and then fear—and then Grace couldn't see his face anymore because it was pressed into the dirt after Otto dropped him to his stomach on the ground.

Pressing a knee into Truman's back, Otto handcuffed him with jerky motions that showed his anger. Despite how much her body hurt and how worried she was about Hugh, Grace managed a tiny smile. It felt incredibly good to watch the bastard who'd put a hit out on Hugh—and kidnapped her and tried to blow up everyone—get tackled and arrested. *Score one for the good guys.*

"That's Truman?" Theo asked. He sounded almost clinical, but his face showed his true rage.

"Yes." Her voice was still rough and shaky.

"Otto's a better person than I am. I would've hit him at least once."

"Me too." All the horror of the past days came rushing back as she stared at the man who'd caused so much of it. "In the junk."

Theo barked a surprised laugh. "You know, Grace, I didn't think I'd like you at first, but you're growing on me."

Still smiling, she watched as Otto hauled Truman to his feet. The agent's front was covered in dust, and fury emanated from him, but Otto just dragged the smaller man toward one of the squad cars. "Thanks. You Monroe cops aren't too bad yourselves."

CHAPTER 17

THE HARDEST PART OF GRACE'S SHORT HOSPITAL VISIT WAS waiting to see Hugh. With only a mild ankle sprain, bruises, tape burn, strained muscles, quite a lot of scrapes, and a couple of bruised ribs, she felt like she'd gotten off easy, thanks to Hugh blocking the blast with his body.

"Hey, Grace." Jules hurried over to where Grace was sitting in the waiting room, her leg jiggling up and down endlessly. Standing despite her sore body's protests, Grace gave Jules a hug. "How are you? How's Hugh? Have you heard anything?" Jules asked.

"I'm fine, but I'm not sure about Hugh. They won't tell me anything because I'm not related." Grace sat down again. As soon as she did, her knee started bouncing at warp speed.

Jules groaned. "Right! I forgot about that rule. You should've told them that you were his wife."

That almost made Grace laugh. "We're in Monroe. Everyone knows whenever Hugh changes his socks, much less gets married."

"True, although you could've eloped."

"When?"

Waving a hand as if to brush away Grace's words, Jules said, "Logic, smogic. True love finds a way."

Flushing, Grace ducked her head. The thought of "true love" was painful when utter despair at the thought of losing Hugh was still fresh in her mind. Even now, she had no idea what was wrong or if he'd be okay. Tears pressed for escape, and she forced them back with a huge effort. "Where are the kids?"

"Home with a couple of nice officers. I wasn't sure how long we'd be here, and I knew they'd be happier there."

Grace nodded, and they both were quiet. After a few minutes, she said, "Tell me what happened."

Jules gave her a sideways look. "Uh, you were there."

"I was trapped in a box, and then I was focused on Otto being awesome. Besides, things were a little chaotic."

With a huff of humorless laughter, Jules said, "That's true. Just so you know, I might not have all the facts right. Things were pretty crazy from my vantage point, too."

"Understood."

"So," Jules started, eyeing the ceiling as if for inspiration. "Theo and Otto were entertaining the viner customers by pulling over any out-of-towners going through town. When asked, they tried to say it was an attempt to reduce Main Street speeding, but everyone knows that the twenty-mile-an-hour limit is a joke. Most of the locals go forty, and none of the cops look twice."

Grace resisted the urge to make a hurry-it-up gesture.

"They also knew it wasn't a speed thing when Hugh was taking Lexi around every car. Pretty soon, customers were calling their friends and family members, so the viner was packed by eight. People were making bets on whether a car they stopped would have drugs or not. They pulled over the dog-mobile, and no one thought there'd be drugs, except for Sam. Sam's the master at reading body language. That boy has a future in law enforcement, if he ever wants to go that route. Anyway, the driver was pretending to be casual, but Sam could tell he was nervous."

As she listened, Grace's stomach twisted. It was almost harder to hear the story when she knew the terrifying ending.

"Sure enough, Lexi got all excited about the back of the truck, so Theo had the driver get out of the cab. He tried to run, but Theo caught him in, like, two steps. He put handcuffs on the guy, and that's when everyone at the viner started pushing and shoving for a better spot at the windows, so we all went outside. I never thought that there'd be a bomb." Her mouth got tight at the corners. "I didn't even consider the danger, or I would've made the kids hide inside or run or something, rather than just let them stand there and watch."

"I know." Grace gave Jules's arm a pat. "You're great at protecting them. Even Hugh didn't expect a bomb, and he's a cop. It was just a crazy thing, and everyone— almost everyone—is okay." She got a little choked up when she said *almost*.

"Yeah." Jules's smile looked forced. "So we were watching, and then Hugh and Otto pulled you out of the back of the van?" She looked at Grace for confirmation. "I didn't see that part, but someone else was yelling about it, and then everyone was yelling 'Bomb!' and I couldn't figure out why Theo had just left the handcuffed guy and was running toward us. Hugh threw what looked like a vacuum into the creek, and then it exploded. It was mass chaos, and then Otto did his Hulk imitation and tackled the FBI guy, who ended up being the drug dealer who put a hit out on Hugh and kidnapped you—and oh my goodness, it was insane. Are you okay?"

Realizing that her hands were clenched into fists on her lap, Grace flattened them out and ran her palms up and down her thighs. "Yes. It's just hard to hear."

"I know." Jules made a face. "I've had more than my share of explosions over the past couple of months."

Grace grimaced sympathetically. "One is more than enough for me. Was anyone else hurt? Is Lexi okay?" She'd been so focused on Hugh that she'd forgotten to check after Theo had first assured her that the dog wasn't hurt. Guilt coated her insides.

"Everyone else is fine. There were a few cuts and bruises, mostly from breaking glass and people throwing themselves onto the ground. Theo said the explosion was fairly small, as explosions go." She rolled her eyes. "Which is something no one should have to say. *Oh, it was just a little explosion. Nothing to get worked up over.* Ugh. Theo said it would've been much worse if the bomb had been in the van when it went off. Hugh's a hero, and the poor guy got the worst of it. Lexi has a few nicks, but that's it. She's staying with the kids while Hugh is stuck here. There was some property damage, and the bridge over the creek is completely gone."

"Whoa." Grace sat back in her chair, suddenly exhausted. Hearing about the explosion made her feel like she'd lived through it twice, and every sore spot in her body ached. Her glance moved to the admissions desk. "I wonder how Hugh is."

"Still think you should've married him." Jules smiled

at her, but Grace couldn't dredge up a happy look. Slapping her palms against her thighs, Jules stood. "Come on. Let's figure out what's going on with him."

As if she'd summoned him, Lieutenant Blessard came into the waiting area, striding toward the admissions desk. Grace hopped up, wincing as her ankle and her ribs throbbed in unison, and hurried over to him. Jules followed.

By the time they reached the desk, the lieutenant was already heading into the corridor that led to the patient rooms. Grace's shoulders sagged as she watched him disappear.

"It's just a short delay," Jules consoled her, wrapping an arm around Grace's shoulders. "He'll know even more about how Hugh is doing after he sees him in person. Plus, if Hugh's getting visitors, that's a good sign, right?"

"Right." There wasn't any conviction in Grace's voice, though. She returned to her chair, trying to keep from imagining the absolute worst.

She waited impatiently for Blessard to return, her knee bobbing up and down like a sewing machine. Finally, she couldn't stand sitting any longer, and she jumped up to pace the waiting area. It hurt her ankle and her ribs and every sore muscle in her body, but it was better than trying to sit still when all her anxiety was raging to get out.

When the lieutenant returned to the waiting room, he looked even more cranky than usual, and Grace's stomach turned sour. Was there bad news? She hurried over to him.

"Lieutenant Blessard?"

He scanned her as if checking for visible injuries. "Ms. Robinson. How are you doing?"

"I'm fine," she said dismissively. "How is Hugh?"

Blessard continued to eye her skeptically, but he didn't press the issue. Grace wondered if that was because he could tell how close she was to a complete meltdown. "He'll be fine. Concussion and a broken arm—just a simple fracture of his radius. He's asking to see you."

Relief filled her with helium, making her so light that she felt she could float right up to the ceiling. "Good. That's so…good. Can I go now? To see him?" She knew she sounded like a ditz, but Grace didn't care. Hugh was going to be fine, and he wanted to see her. For the first time all day, she could breathe again.

The tiniest of smiles crossed the lieutenant's face. "Go ahead. We need to talk to you immediately afterward, though, to get your statement."

She winced, not wanting to relive it, but knowing she didn't have a choice. "Okay."

"Jesus Christ, what a mess. The feds are going nuts… Never mind." Looking incredibly tired, Blessard rubbed a hand over his face. "Better go see Hugh now, before he drags his stubborn, injured ass out of bed to look for you. He's in Room Eight."

"I'm going. Thanks, Lieutenant." As she hurried down the corridor toward Hugh's room, Grace marveled that there was a hospital with single-digit room numbers. When she reached the right door, she knocked, shifting impatiently during the half second it took for Hugh to yell, "Come in!"

She burst into the room and took in Hugh sitting up

in bed, a bandage on his head and a cast on his forearm. A furious-looking Theo leaned against the wall. She eyed Hugh's too-healthy-looking form lounging—yes, *lounging*—on the bed, and her relief was shoved aside by anger. Propping her hands on her hips, she gave him her best glare. He laughed. He actually *laughed*.

"Hey, Gracie. Thanks for coming to see me."

"No." She strode forward until her knees were almost touching the bed. It was better to loom over him so he could see how deadly serious she was. "I'm sick of this. You do not get to throw yourself on top of me like some kind of hero anymore. I am not a damsel. I get to save you from life-threatening events at least as many times as you've saved me. Until I'm caught up, there will be no more heroics from you, understand?"

His lips were twitching, and she knew he was about to laugh. Grace was tempted to smack him. Maybe he'd be serious then. "Not sure what to say to that. Sorry?"

"It's not enough. You have a bullet hole in your leg, a broken arm, and a bruised brain. No. More. Hero. Crap. Got it?"

He laughed, but then immediately clamped his mouth shut. "Sorry." He kept his sober expression for almost three seconds. "You're funny, though. You have to admit that you're funny."

"The situation is not funny," Theo chimed in. "If you are hurt seriously again, I'm going to kick your ass."

Grace gave Theo an approving nod. "Me, too."

"Aww, Gracie. Your threats are really sweet, as well as exceptionally hot, for some reason." Reaching out his unbroken arm, Hugh caught her hand.

The rough feeling of the smaller, more professional

bandages now covering his palms reminded her of his rope burns, and she glared at him again. "And your poor hands, all ripped up while saving me and Lexi. No more. I'm sick of worrying about you."

He gave her hand a squeeze and smiled. It was his adorable puppy smile, and she knew she was going to fold in a matter of seconds. There was just no way to resist Hugh when he grinned at her like that. As if he could read her mind, his smile widened, and he tugged her closer. With her legs already pressed against the side of the bed, her upper body started tilting toward him. Although Grace knew that she should resist, that Hugh wasn't taking her seriously, and that she needed to get him to promise he wouldn't almost die for her ever again, she was unable to stop herself from leaning in until their faces were just inches apart.

"And I'm out," Theo said. Startled, Grace tried to jerk back, but Hugh's grip tightened, holding her in place. Despite his injuries, he was surprisingly strong. Theo gave Grace a reproving look, and she dropped her gaze.

"I know." She shot a quick glance at Hugh before sheepishly meeting Theo's eyes again. "I folded. Sorry. It's that puppy-dog look…" When his disapproving scowl didn't waver, Grace, like the chicken that she was, tossed out a guaranteed distraction. "Jules is here."

With a shake of his head that expressed his disappointment in her lack of staying power against Hugh's puppy eyes, Theo stalked to the door. "I don't need to watch what's coming."

"Not when you can go find Jules and have a make-out session of your own, right?" Hugh said slyly.

Turning, Theo gave Hugh a severe look. Grace would've crumbled under that glare, but Hugh merely met Theo's gaze with raised eyebrows and a smirk. Their stare down lasted an uncomfortably long time before Theo's mouth twitched.

"Maybe." He left the room, closing the door behind him with a sharp thump.

As soon as he was gone, Grace tried again to extricate herself from Hugh's grip.

Hugh didn't let her go anywhere. In fact, he reached over with his casted arm and awkwardly caught her free hand in his protruding fingers. "Where do you think you're going?"

"Theo's right." Despite her words, she stopped attempting to pull back, telling herself that she didn't want to jostle his broken arm. The reasoning part of her brain scoffed at that, but she ignored it, as she usually did when it came to Hugh. "I gave in too easily. I should've held firm until you promised to never do stupid hero stuff or almost die again."

His laugh was low and husky, running up and down her spine like a physical touch. "Can't promise that, Gracie. It's kind of part of the job description." He cocked his head as if thinking. "And dying is kind of part of the *life* description."

His cheek looked scruffy with a few days of stubble, and she was tempted to stroke it. Since she didn't have a hand free, she closed the distance between them and brushed her lips against his jaw instead. He sucked in an audible breath.

"Is this you punishing me?" he asked, his voice even lower, even rougher than before. Grace shivered.

"Because I have to tell you, I'm going to want to be punished all the time after this."

"Want me to tie you to the bed?" she asked huskily, moving so she could nip at his earlobe. It was his turn to shudder.

"Yes, please." His response was so quick that she almost laughed. She *would've* laughed if she hadn't been so turned on.

With a huge effort of will, Grace shifted back so she could look at him. "Well, too bad. For as long as you're stuck in this hospital, all rope-burned and shot and concussed and arm-broken, we can't do anything. This is your punishment for being reckless and almost getting killed."

Tipping his head back, Hugh groaned as if in agony. Grace had a second of anxiety when she worried that he was really hurting, but then he peeked at her, and the corner of his mouth quirked up. "You're so mean," he said.

He gave a gentle tug on her hands, one that she could've resisted if she'd actually put forth an effort. It was too hard, though. He drew her in, as if he had his own gravitational pull. His lips touched hers, lightly brushing before returning with a little more pressure. To her surprise, he didn't try to deepen the kiss. Instead, he kissed her sweetly, almost chastely.

Breaking the contact, Grace pulled back and studied him closely. The muscles in his face were tight, strained. She kissed the bridge of his nose before asking, "How badly does your head hurt?"

Immediately, the lines between his eyebrows smoothed, and he gave her an easy grin. "You take away all my pain."

With a sigh, she brushed her lips against his bristly cheek a final time. "I wish that were true." Carefully detaching herself, she pulled a visitor's chair closer to the bed and sat. "Tell me when you need to sleep, or if you need more drugs or water or anything."

He laughed and then winced ever so slightly. "Thank you, Nurse Gracie, but just having you here is all I need."

"Uh-huh." She didn't believe that for a minute. She'd had a concussion when another girl had kicked her in the head during a high-school soccer game, so Grace knew the drill. "How much do you feel like you need to hurl?"

Surprise flickered in his eyes before he smiled again, more honestly that time. "Don't worry, Grace. I'll give you at least a second of warning so you can get out of the way."

Her nose wrinkled. "Please do." Despite her teasing, seeing Hugh injured was horrible. Her mind replayed the day's terrifying events, and she shuddered.

"Thinking about bomb stuff?" he guessed, his tone gentle.

"Yeah. Bomb stuff." Even after everything, he made her want to laugh. "So no one at the FBI knew that Barrett—Truman—sold drugs?"

"So they say. We've worked with Shankle before, and I believe he's honest. How do you not know something like that, though?" His forehead creased as he reached for her hand again. Although she worried that he'd pull her back in for more kissing, she allowed his fingers to close around hers. It was reassuring to touch him, to feel his living warmth, after her terror just a few hours ago. He absently ran his thumb over the back of her hand as he continued to speak.

"Truman's in jail, and he's been denied bail. We should be able to go outside without people taking pot-shots at us now."

Grace sighed. Her current situation—involving hit men and drugged coffee and exploding drugs and a dirty FBI agent—was a long way from her previous peaceful, even slightly humdrum, existence. "Will everyone know the contract is canceled, or are you still in danger?"

"His arrest is all over the news, so word will get around quickly. No one will want to kill me anymore." Hugh made a wry face. "Well, at least no one will get paid for it. I can't honestly say that *no one* wants to kill me."

Ignoring that last bit, which Hugh meant to be joking but Grace still found terrifying, she asked, "So we're safe?"

"Except for the situation with Martin Jovanovic." He gave her a serious, intent look as he said the name. "Agent Shankle is anxious to talk to you about him."

Swallowing, Grace said in a small voice, "Oh. So, Uncle Martin is a big deal?"

"A really big deal."

The idea of leaving Hugh to go to the police station to face a judgmental Blessard and an FBI interview was not appealing. "Do I have to go right now?"

"Want to have them come here? I could sit in on the interview." It really seemed like Hugh could read minds. Although it was tempting to take him up on the offer, she could tell he was flagging. His face had paled under his tan, and there were white lines bracketing his mouth. He was hurting and tired, and he didn't need to be put-ting on a show of strength for her and the FBI agents.

Leaning close, she pressed a kiss to his furrowed forehead. Although she meant it to be brief, she couldn't help but linger. The feel of his skin under her lips was addicting, especially when, a short time earlier, she'd been terrified that she wouldn't be able to kiss him anymore. At that thought, she moved to press her mouth to his. He enthusiastically participated. If not for the knock on the door, Grace might never have stopped.

Dazed, she pulled away from Hugh as the door swung open and Otto stepped into the room. He lifted an eyebrow, as if asking if he was interrupting, and she gave him a smile in response.

"I'd better get to the station, then," she said, trying to sound enthusiastic. By the way Hugh smirked at her, she was pretty sure she'd failed. "Get some rest. I'll be back tonight." Glancing at the clock on the wall, she saw it was almost four in the afternoon. With a final squeeze, she released his hand and stood. Her abused muscles protested, although not as loudly as her ribs, and she held back a wince.

"Ribs hurt?" Hugh asked.

She made a face. "Is it that obvious?"

Instead of making his usual joke, he regarded her seriously. "Yeah, but just to me."

That struck her as sweet, so she bent to give him yet another kiss. Otto cleared his throat from where he was still standing just inside the door, and she smiled against Hugh's mouth before pulling back slightly.

"I should go."

"Sure you don't want Shankle to come here?" He stroked her cheek with his thumb.

Forcing herself to step back, she gave him a final

smile. "Of course I do, but you need sleep, and I need to act like an adult. Therefore, I'm going to the station, Otto's going to tell you something and hang out for a while…I assume?" She glanced at Otto for confirmation, and he gave a short nod. "And then you're going to take drugs and sleep."

He made a face. "No drugs."

"Hugh." Grace gave him her most serious face. "Your arm is broken. You need drugs."

"They make me puke, and I'm close enough to losing my cookies without them." His expression lightened as he teased, "You already asked me to hold back on the vomiting."

She shrugged with a casualness she didn't feel. "I won't even be here, so hurl away."

Hugh laughed and then stopped abruptly, wincing.

"Sorry."

"You can't help being funny."

Although she was ready to fall right back into their easy back and forth, Grace knew she needed to leave. Delaying wasn't making it any easier, but walking out of his room was incredibly hard. Just a short time ago, she hadn't known if he was going to live. Even if he was going to be sleeping, she wanted to stay right there, holding his hand, watching him breathe, confirming with each lift of his chest that he hadn't left her alone. Now was not the time to unleash her inner creeper, though.

She needed to go. Walking toward the door with feigned breeziness, she said over her shoulder, "See you later, alligator." Immediately, she wanted to suck that back inside. Seriously? Was she five?

"Later, alligator?" Of course Hugh couldn't just let it

go. She felt equal parts evil glee and guilt when he laughed and then looked pained. "Okay. In a while, crocodile."

Shooting Otto a quick smile of farewell, she slipped through the door but then stuck her head back into the room. "See you soon, you big baboon." Without giving Hugh a chance to respond, she headed down the hall, the sound of his short-lived burst of laughter following her.

CHAPTER 18

"Ready?"

Agent Shankle was not what she expected. He was not the cookie-cutter, blue-suit-wearing, side-part-combing FBI agent that years of watching television and movies had prepared her for. He looked more like a bouncer for a seedy bar. Shankle was a big guy, with a barrel chest and acne-scarred skin. Although he didn't have any official facial hair, his five-o'clock shadow would have made a pirate proud. There was a suit, but it was rumpled, as if he kept it wadded up in a drawer when he wasn't forced to wear it. He looked like he'd be more at home wearing BDUs and a T-shirt as he constructed bombs in the basement of his bunker than he was wearing a wrinkled suit jacket in a police-station interview room. She would've assumed that Shankle was a criminal way before she'd have suspected innocuous-looking Agent Barrett was Truman.

Shankle cleared his throat, and Grace jumped a little. She realized that, while she'd been mentally redressing him—and giving him a few illegal hobbies—he'd been waiting for an answer. "Oh! Sorry. It's been a long day. Yes, I'm ready."

It was a lie. She wasn't ready. She'd never been so un-ready in her life. Even when she'd called Corban

Dabbs in eighth grade to ask him to a dance, her hands hadn't shaken this hard.

Shankle clicked a few times on his laptop touch pad and then looked at her expectantly. She dialed the old-school landline phone that they'd hooked up to the laptop. If everything worked as it was supposed to, it would record her conversation with Noah and keep anyone on the other end from tracing it, while at the same time tracking Noah's location.

Slowly, Grace dialed his number, a number she'd memorized right after he'd first given it to her. She'd had such a huge crush on him initially that she'd been illogically worried she was going to lose his number by dropping her phone in a puddle or something. Thinking back on him, though, he seemed like a pale shadow, just as inconsequential as the cartoon prince he resembled. Hugh filled her mind now with his teasing and stupid heroics and muscles, so there was no room for Noah anymore.

That's probably a good thing, she thought semi-hysterically, listening to the phone ring on the other end. *Family reunions would've been awkward.* As she turned a nervous heave of laughter into a cough, the ringing stopped, and so did her breathing.

"Noah Jovanovic," he said coolly. Instead of a rush of nostalgia, all she felt was fear. His voice brought back that terrible night in vivid detail—the blood, her terrified escape, Martin dragging her toward the front door. Her throat closed, and she couldn't speak.

As Noah said his name again, this time impatiently, Shankle made impatient "talk!" gestures. With panic gripping her voice box, the words wouldn't come. Why hadn't she taken Hugh up on his offer to sit in on the interview? He gave her courage, and this wouldn't have happened if he were there, holding her hand.

Shankle kicked her in the shin. It hurt. More than that, the kick was so juvenile, so Hugh-like, that it startled her out of her frozen fear, and she blurted out, "Noah?" Only then did she glare across the table at Shankle's smug face.

"Kaylee?" Noah sounded startled. "Is that really you? Where are you? Are you okay?"

"Yes, it's me." Her voice shook a little. Now that her indignation had faded, reality had returned and so had the tremor in her voice. Maybe she should ask the FBI agent to give her a wet willy or something so she could be startled into regaining her composure again. Rather than helping, the thought just made inappropriate giggles start to build in her lungs.

"Are you okay?" he asked again. "Where have you been? We all thought you were d— that something bad had happened to you. The cops have been here a bunch of times, asking about you. Why didn't you call? Forget that, why didn't you tell me you were leaving that night? Did I say something wrong? Did something happen?"

"I'm okay." Noah's babble eased a few of Grace's nerves. He was normally so self-confident, so composed, and his flood of anxious questions made her hopeful that he wasn't a bad guy—or at least not as bad as his uncle. "Something did happen that night."

"What was it?"

Grace took a deep breath and flicked an unsure glance at Shankle, who gave her an encouraging nod. "How much do you know about Martin's business?"

"What?" Noah sounded completely confused. "Uncle Martin's business? What does that have to do with anything?"

"I'll explain. I just need to know if you're part of…" Grace attempted to think of a noninflammatory way to say *torture*, but quickly gave up and rephrased the question. "Do you work for Martin?"

"No." His answer was immediate. "You know that. I'm a mortgage broker."

She did know that. He'd told her on their first date. What she didn't know was if she believed him or not. "Do you know what Martin's business involves?"

"Not really." Noah sounded as if he was getting frustrated. "I know the basics, but his business is pretty diverse. He owns a couple of restaurants, some laundromats, a few apartment buildings. That's all I can think of right now." He made an impatient sound. "Why are we talking about Uncle Martin right now? Where have you *been*? I've been worried about you! And poor Penny…"

Grace stopped breathing. "What about Penny?"

"What?"

"You said 'poor Penny.' What did you mean? What's happened to her?" As she spoke, her voice rose higher and higher until it broke on the last word.

"Nothing!" Noah said harshly, and then dragged in an audible breath. When he continued, he sounded more subdued. "Nothing happened to Penny, except that you disappeared and scared us both out of our minds. Penny's fine. Worried, but fine. Where *are* you? Do you need me to come and get you?"

Despite the fact that his tone was filled with concern, his last question made Grace physically recoil.

"No! I mean, no. I'm safe for now." She gave Shankle a questioning look. He frowned and then held out his hand, turning it side to side. *What does that mean?* Grace wondered, staring at him. Widening her eyes, she made a *what-do-I-do* face, and he lifted one shoulder in a shrug. Nice. It looked like it was up to her whether she spilled the beans to Noah. The more she talked to him, the more she thought he was telling the truth. He was too concerned about her, and his worry—even his frustration—seemed honest.

"Kaylee? Are you still there?"

"Yes." Her fingers tapped on the table as she tried to think, to decide. For the hundredth time, she wished Hugh was there for moral support. She shook off the thought. With or without Hugh, she needed to get this done. If Noah really wasn't connected with Martin's business, he could help the FBI, give them information that might help convict the senior Jovanovic. If Noah was playing her, though, he already knew what she'd witnessed. Martin would've told him that she let those men out of that terrible room. She wouldn't be giving away anything that he didn't know.

There was a pause before Noah spoke again. "Talk to me, Kaylee. I've been so worried about you. I haven't slept since you disappeared."

The concern in his voice confirmed her decision. "I got lost on the way to the bathroom," she blurted.

"O-kay," he said slowly.

"I just started opening doors, trying to find the right one. One led down some stairs, and I was just about to shut the door when I heard someone call for help. I went down there, and… It was awful, Noah. There were three guys, tied to chairs, and they'd been tortured." Her voice caught. Somehow, it was worse telling the story to the nephew of the torturer than it had been to share it with Hugh or Agent Shankle. "One was unconscious, and there was another who'd been beaten so badly that he didn't even look human. Then there was one whose eye…" She couldn't finish the thought. "It was awful. I cut them free, and they went one direction, and I left out a back door."

"Kaylee." There was so much horror and disbelief in that one word that tears sprang to her eyes. Was this going to be when he told her he didn't believe her? That she was crazy? After all, the only witnesses were the men who'd escaped, and she didn't even know their names. She'd asked Shankle about them, but he'd said the FBI didn't have any information about their identity. "You think that Uncle Martin was involved in something like that? He's a good man, Kaylee. I can't believe you'd think that."

"He grabbed me. When I was trying to leave, he grabbed me and dragged me back toward the house." She didn't need to see Shankle's frown to know that she was telling the story all wrong. It was hard to stay reasonable and orderly when Noah sounded as if his uncle would never do anything wrong.

"I'm sure he was just trying to talk to you." Noah's soothing, patronizing tone put Grace's teeth on edge. Oddly enough, though, the shot of irritation helped calm her slightly. Taking a breath, she let it out slowly and silently, using the pause to get her thoughts in order.

"No, Noah." Her voice wasn't even shaking anymore. In the back of her mind, she was proud about that.

"He wasn't. He isn't a good guy. Do you know that he's being investigated by the FBI?" Belatedly, she checked in with Shankle, unsure if she should've shared that information with Noah. The agent rolled his eyes, and she made an apologetic face, but he just made a "keep going" gesture. Grace hoped that meant she hadn't just ruined years of the FBI's work.

Noah was sputtering on the other end of the line. "What are you talking about? Uncle Martin? What kind of investigation? Is it because of those guys you saw? Because I'm sure you were mistaken. I can't even conceive of my uncle *torturing* people."

It was Grace's turn to roll her eyes as she wondered what she'd ever found so entrancing about Noah Jovanovic. If he was telling the truth, then he had to be the most unobservant, naive person ever to walk the earth. If he was lying, if he was perfectly aware of all the bad things that Martin Jovanovic had done, and Noah had just accepted them, helped hide them... Grace's stomach turned. It was hard to believe that she'd dated a monster. She hoped that Noah just had a huge blind spot when it came to his family.

"Noah, I saw it. I saw *them*." She tried to keep her tone even, but the tremor was back in her voice. The image of the men's injuries, of the bloody, empty spot where the one's eye had been, rose as vivid and clear as if she was back there, seeing them for the first time. Shankle reached over and gave her hand a quick squeeze before retreating to his side of the table. That contact, as short as it was, returned her to the present. "There's no way to innocently explain this away. Martin is not a good guy. He's never been a good guy. That

FBI investigation started a long time before the dinner party. I tried to report what I saw, but Martin sent Logan Jovanovic after me at the police station."

"Logan?" Disbelief was still thick in Noah's voice, but she took slight comfort in the fact that he hadn't hung up on her yet. After all, if he truly didn't believe her, didn't think in his heart of hearts that his uncle could do those terrible things, then he would've ended the call by now. "My weird cousin Logan? Are you sure? He's kind of…awkward socially. He might have been trying to ask you out, and you just misunderstood."

"He wasn't trying to ask me out, Noah." Shankle's silent presence was the only thing that kept her from thumping her forehead against the table in frustration. Grace had expected some disbelief, probably some yelling, but she hadn't predicted this obtuse refusal to see the truth. How could he have grown up with Logan and not know that the guy wasn't just "awkward," but actually capable of killing on Martin's orders?

"This is all so crazy," Noah exclaimed after a long moment of silence on both ends of the call. "After you disappear for weeks, I get a call out of the blue, and you tell me that you ran because Uncle Martin—my uncle Martin, who's like a dad to me—is torturing guys during a dinner party. Not only that, but he sent Logan to kill you. Sorry, but this is a little tough for me to wrap my brain around."

"I know it's hard." She felt a tiny spark of sympathy. After all, she had a tough time believing everything that had happened, and she'd lived it. "It's true, though. Why would I make this up?"

"I have no idea."

Grace wasn't sure how to take that. She grabbed a pen and notepad lying next to Shankle's computer and scribbled "meet?" on the paper before turning it toward the agent. He studied her for a second before nodding in a sideways motion that Grace interpreted as "yes, as long as you're okay with it." She wasn't okay with meeting Noah, a guy who was either criminally naive or just… criminal. Before she could decide, Noah spoke again.

"Why are we having this conversation over the phone?" he asked, sounding calmer. Grace wasn't sure if that was a good thing or not. "You never told me where you are. Give me your address, and I'll pick you up. I want to be able to see with my own eyes that you're okay."

Her brain raced. This was it. She could turn him down and hope that Shankle's program worked and that Noah wasn't able to track her. If so, she could hide in Monroe for the rest of her life, spooking at shadows.

Even as the thought passed through her mind, she rejected it. How could she endanger her new friends, her new…Hugh, whatever he was to her, by keeping that target on her back? Martin Jovanovic had contacts everywhere. He'd find her eventually. Even if the meeting was a mistake, if Noah was lying through his teeth and couldn't be convinced to help them find evidence of Martin's crimes, at least she was doing something, trying something to fight her way out of the fake life she was living.

She took a deep breath and blew it out, meeting Shankle's serious gaze.

"Okay," she said, proud that her voice didn't shake at all. "Let's meet."

"You're doing *what*?"

Grace winced, more for Hugh's concussed, newly released-from-the-hospital head's sake than for her own ears. "I'm meeting Martin Jovanovic's nephew in Denver tomorrow to try to convince him to help us find evidence against his uncle."

Hugh glared at her, and she gave a tiny shrug in response. She knew it had been a rhetorical question, but her answer was the truth, and no amount of bellowing was going to change anything.

"I need to do this, Hugh." Grace met his gaze evenly. "You know exactly what it's like when someone's gunning for you, putting other people in danger. I can't just hide and do nothing."

He paced his living room, and she watched him. It had only been a day since she'd been trapped beneath him, terrified that he was dead, and she couldn't get enough of just looking at him. He'd caught her staring several times and teased her about checking him out. Instead of rising to the bait, she'd just smiled. Hearing him joke and laugh was a gift, and she was going to enjoy every second.

Listening to him bellow wasn't quite as enjoyable, but he was alive, and that's all that mattered. Hugh stomped across the floor and then pivoted around. When he saw her smile, he stopped and demanded, "What's funny about you meeting up with some ex-boyfriend who just happens to be related to the guy who wants to kill you?"

"Nothing." The reminder sobered her somewhat, although she couldn't help but smirk a little. "You reminded me of Theo just now, with the pacing and the frowning."

She walked over and grabbed his hand, pulling him down with her as she sat on the couch. "Sit. Your Theo pacing is making even me tired, and I'm not the one who just got out of the hospital."

He allowed her to tug him down. When they landed, he immediately reached over and hauled her into his lap. Startled by the quick movement, and by how easily he manhandled her with only one fully functioning arm, she stiffened for a moment. Soon she relaxed, leaning against his chest. It was much more comfortable to sit that way on a couch than in a car. Her head fit nicely between his shoulder and neck, and his hand stroked her back, releasing tension she'd held on to fiercely for the past stressful weeks.

"It's kind of weird being here after the deck...incident." She stared across the open lower level at the sliding glass doors that had opened to the now-destroyed deck. The doors were still strung with police tape.

He tensed. "Yeah." After a short pause, he asked carefully, "Are you okay being here? We could go to Otto's instead. Or Jules's. Or Theo's clown car of a house."

"No." Her reply was immediate and honest. "I feel safe here. It's just odd to see empty space where your deck used to be. Will you rebuild it?"

"Yeah. I'll use concrete and rebar this time instead of wood. Make it harder on any bastard who wants to kill me." She flinched, and Hugh's arms tightened around her.

"You smell good," she said, snuggling more tightly against him. "I think I'll stay here forever. You're like aromatherapy in a strong, warm, mouthy package."

He did his usual post-explosion laughter that was quickly capped, and Grace frowned, reaching up to stroke the side of his head. "Still hurts?"

"I'm fine," he said, and she rolled her eyes and pinched his belly, making him yelp.

"Liar."

"Sadist."

"Please," she scoffed, although her hand was stroking instead of pinching now. She couldn't help herself. He was just so…washboard-y. "You love my sadist tendencies. Weren't you begging me to tie you up?"

He pulled back a little, tucking his chin so he could glare down at her. "I didn't beg."

"Sorry," she mock apologized, using her nails instead of her fingertips to scratch lightly against his abs. Although he tried to keep his pretend offended expression in place, his eyes went to half-mast, making his pleasure obvious. If he were a cat, he'd be purring. "So you *don't* want me to tie you up."

He shifted beneath her and cleared his throat. When he spoke, his voice remained husky. "I'm not saying that."

Laughing low in her throat, she slipped a hand under his T-shirt. Although he'd just been at the hospital for twenty-four hours, it felt like longer. It was nice to have the freedom to pet him without being interrupted by a nurse or a doctor or a crabby lieutenant—or an even crabbier Theo. "Yeah? So what are you saying?"

"I don't want you to go to that meeting tomorrow."

With a groan, she turned her head so her forehead

was resting against his collarbone and then rocked it from side to side. "Hugh. Hugh. Hugh. *Hugh.* I have to go. I'll be careful, and a bunch of FBI agents will be watching out for me, and we're going to be in a busy mall filled with people. Even if Noah is involved in Martin's business, he's very concerned with his reputation and things like, you know, staying out of prison. He won't do anything to me with all those shoppers around, ready to be witnesses. If he isn't willing to work with us to nail Martin to the wall, then we part ways, and I go back into hiding. We're not going to lose anything by giving this plan a shot."

Lifting her head, she saw his frown hadn't eased. If anything, it was even deeper than before. What worried her more was his silence. Hugh was a talker, she'd learned. The only time he went quiet was when he was either in pain or very serious about something. She had a feeling that, right now, he was both.

Changing tactics, she leaned in to kiss his neck. When she pulled back to check his reaction, she saw he was still scowling. Grace took this as a personal challenge. Returning to a spot right under his jaw, she kissed him again, a light peck, and then licked the bristly skin. He shivered, and she couldn't hold back a devilish grin as she met his gaze.

"Did you just lick me?" he asked. Although she could tell he was attempting to sound grossed out, laughter underlay his words.

"Yes." Just for fun, and because he tasted good, she did it again. "It's like when you're with a group of people, and there's only one cookie left, so you grab it and lick it in order to claim it."

"You're"—he paused, his breath catching as she ran her teeth lightly over his jawbone—"claiming me?"

"Yes." Her answer surprised her, and she went still, thinking about it. It hadn't been very long since she'd first met Hugh and dismissed him as an ass, but it had been an intense few weeks. When she thought he'd been hurt, even killed, by the explosion, she'd been terrified, even more so than she had been in Martin Jovanovic's house. She wasn't exactly sure what her feelings were, since they were roiling around inside her like a whole nest of agitated snakes, but Grace knew she'd never felt this strongly before about anyone. She had a strong suspicion—a *very* strong suspicion—that she was in love with this man. It was enough to make her consider trading her wonderful, hard-won life in California for the tiny, often-cold town of Monroe, just so she could stay close to Hugh. "If that's okay?"

Hugh cleared his throat. "So you're basically slapping an I-belong-to-Grace sticker on me." His good hand stroked from her shoulder to her wrist and then back up again.

"Basically."

"Okay. Sounds good." He ducked his head so he could reach the side of her neck and give it a long lick. Giggling, she attempted to twist away, although she didn't try too hard to avoid his tongue. "And now you belong to me, too."

Hearing it out loud made her go still, her ticklish laughter dying in her throat. It sounded so *nice*. "I like that."

"Yeah. I do, too." They smiled at each other for a second before Hugh grew serious again. "I'm going with you tomorrow to the meeting."

"Okay."

"Okay?" He sounded surprised. "That was easy."

With a snort, she responded, "Of course it was. I'm glad you'll be there. I wish you were there when I called him. You make me brave."

His face softened. "You're already brave. I just remind you of that fact."

That was just too much. She had to kiss him. Shifting to straddle him so her knees pressed into the couch cushions on either side of his legs, she cradled his face in her hands. His un-casted hand stroked up her side, from her hip up to her arm and back down again.

His mouth turned up in that devilish way that both exasperated and amused her. "This reminds me of a couple of days ago. Weren't we in this very position?"

"Hmm…" She pretended to think, even as her thumbs slid over his cheeks. It was wonderful being able to touch him like that. If this was the reward for claiming him, she wished she'd licked him days ago. "I vaguely remember something similar to this, although I recall a cold, wet dog nose more vividly than anything. I nearly jumped out of my shorts."

He started laughing, and Grace was immediately fascinated by how that made his face move under her fingers. "Good thing the owner of that cold, wet, interrupting nose is spending another night at Jules's house."

Grace smirked at him. "Because Dee looked at you with big, hopeful, pleading eyes, begged you for one more day with Lexi, and you totally caved."

"What can I say?" He shrugged, not looking at all bothered about being a total softie. "When a lady begs, I give her what she wants."

Her eyes immediately narrowed in challenge. "Oh really?"

His gaze grew wide in response, and he immediately defaulted to his adorable puppy look. "It would be rude of me not to."

This time, Grace didn't cave. "Oh, Hugh," she said breathily in her best phone-sex-operator voice. His eyes got even rounder before lowering to half-mast. "Please, *please*, give me what I want. I'm begging you." What started out as teasing turned into something completely different as his gaze, intent and hot, met hers. The barely banked fire inside her roared to full, flaming life, and her brain turned off. She couldn't remember what she'd just been saying. All she knew was that she had to kiss Hugh...right now.

She didn't know who moved first. It felt like there was an invisible signal, a silent starting-gun blast that sent them lunging toward each other. Their lips met with an almost painful force, but she barely noticed, too intent on getting as close as she could to Hugh. Her hands slid over his head and clutched the back of his neck, pulling him even tighter in to her. It wasn't enough. She needed to touch him, to feel his muscles moving under his heated skin.

Her hands dove under his T-shirt, finding that bare flesh she craved as they kissed hungrily. She forgot to breathe until dark crowded the edges of her vision, and then, struck by what she was doing, Grace pulled back, ripping her mouth away from his. They stared at each other, panting.

"What's wrong?" Hugh asked, his voice little more than a growl. His pupils were dilated, and his mouth was already swollen. She stared at it, mesmerized by his full lips, desperately wanting to kiss him again.

"Your head," she said, tearing her gaze off his mouth with a huge effort of will. "And your arm. You're hurt. I shouldn't be taking advantage."

He laughed—a short, sharp sound—as he slid his unbroken arm behind her back to pull her impossibly closer. "I'm not feeling any pain when I'm kissing you," he said. He seemed as fascinated by her mouth as she was by his, if his staring was any indication. "So, please, take advantage of me." Tipping his head down, he paused with his mouth less than an inch away from hers. "I'm begging you."

Grace stopped breathing again for a second before she grabbed his head and closed that tiny gap between them. Her lips, already tender from their previous kiss, throbbed at the pressure, but she didn't mind. Everything—that tiny ache, the heat rushing through her like lava, the feel of his chest in front of her and his iron-hard arm behind her—came together in a rushing flood of need. If she could've managed to say a word, she really would have begged Hugh to keep kissing her, to touch her, to undress her and complete her and never leave her alone again.

The magnitude of her feelings overwhelmed her, and she fell deeper into his kiss. Now wasn't the time to think, she told herself, yanking up his shirt. Now was a time for kissing and touching and stripping down to bare skin.

Hugh pulled back just far enough for her to work his shirt up over his chest, breaking the kiss to yank the fabric over his head and pull one arm free. The other sleeve caught on his cast, and Hugh let it go, leaving the fabric to drape over his casted arm. Grace was fine with that. In fact, with the wide, gorgeous, wonderfully naked male chest in front of her, she was fine with pretty much anything, as long as she got to keep Hugh.

She touched him, stroking across his pecs and strumming her fingers over his abs. It was like touching a work of art come to life, an almost-too-perfect sculpture made from warm, moving marble. The best part was the way he sucked in a breath when she brushed his side beneath his ribs, or when he groaned with pleasure as she lightly scored his nipple with her thumbnail. It was even better when she used her mouth to map his favorite places.

As she explored, discovering all of his secrets with her fingers and lips, he leaned back, watching her with hooded eyes. His hand wrapped around her side at her waist, his grip tightening whenever she found a sweet spot. The bottom hem of her shirt had worked its way up to her ribs, bunching right under her bra. Even his casted arm was in play, his fingertips tracing an invisible pattern on her lower back.

Her clothes felt hot and restrictive, and she abruptly slid off his lap to stand in front of him. His eyebrows bunched in concern in the moment before she yanked her shirt over her head and dropped it on the floor. Then his worried look dropped away, replaced by one filled with raw desire.

As she fumbled to unbutton her jeans, her hands shook. It wasn't fear that caused the tremor this time, though—it was excitement. Reaching for her, Hugh gently brushed aside her unsteady hands and finished unfastening her pants. He looked at her, as if to check whether she wanted him to continue. Instead of answering out loud, she hooked her thumbs in the waistband of her jeans, stripped them down her legs, and stepped out of them, taking off her socks at the same time.

She straightened, standing in just her panties and bra, wishing that she had one of her cute, matching sets from home instead of her desperate purchase at Grady's General Store. Then she saw Hugh's expression, and all of her insecurities dropped away. His gaze moved ever so slowly up her legs and over her body before meeting hers. She'd never seen anyone look as hungry as he did right then, and her entire body flushed as she realized that it was all for her. It was obvious that he wanted her…badly.

The fascinated, heated look in his eyes gave her the courage to reach for the back fastener of her bra, but he placed a hand on her hip, stopping her.

"Wait right here," he ordered, standing up so quickly that she took a step back to catch her balance. "Don't move. Don't go anywhere. Don't put on any clothes. Please. I'll be right back." He hurried up the stairs with an odd gait, a sort of run-and-hop favoring his injured leg.

Grace watched him go, completely confused. Why was he running off in the middle of everything? He'd told her not to get dressed again, which sounded like it meant they were going to start up where they'd left off as soon as Hugh finished his mysterious errand, but it was weird standing there in just her underwear—weird, and a little cold.

Crossing her arms over her chest, she debated whether

to ignore his request and get dressed or not. Without his hands and hungry gaze keeping her warm, her skin prickled with goose bumps. She rubbed her arms briskly. *This is dumb*, she thought. *Why am I just standing here?*

Bending down, she reached for her shirt.

"No!" he cried from the bottom of the stairs with such intensity that she straightened abruptly, yanking her hand away from the shirt as if it were radioactive.

"What?" she asked, holding up her hands, palms out, as if to prove she wasn't touching any article of clothing.

Without slowing, he jog-hopped the rest of the way to her, returning to his spot on the couch. He hooked her with an arm as he passed, pulling her onto his lap after he sat. Startled, she tumbled down on top of him. It took a few seconds to orient herself, and then she moved into her earlier position straddling his waist. It felt different in fewer clothes, more…naked. Shoving her hair out of her face, she smoothed it over her shoulder. She must have missed some strands, because Hugh imitated her action—only his hand lingered, his fingers rubbing in the best way against her scalp.

"Where'd you go?" she asked, more curious than offended.

In response, he pulled a wrapped condom out of his pocket. Giving her a sideways glance, he promptly started babbling. "Not that we have to actually do anything, or go any further, unless you want to, of course. I just thought, well, you were almost naked, so it seemed like a good idea to be prepared." He paused, sending her another quick glance. "Just in case."

That last look did it. She broke into uncontrollable giggles.

"What?" he asked, appearing baffled and offended and more than a little adorable. "I didn't think it was *that* unlikely. I mean, is the idea of having sex with me that funny?"

"No, no," she choked out, trying to get her laughter under control. After a couple of deep, hiccupping breaths, she finally managed to talk. "That's not it. I mean, it was kind of cute how you got all flustered, but I was mostly laughing because you went into the bedroom to get a condom."

He paused, as if waiting for her to continue. When she didn't, he threw up his hands in an exasperated gesture that made her want to start laughing again. "So? What's wrong with that?"

"Nothing," she said, pressing back fresh giggles. "It's just that you left me here, mostly naked, in the living room, while you went to the bedroom to get a condom. And then you came back here." He still looked confused. "To the living room. Most people would have just, you know, both gone to the bedroom at that point."

"Oh." His expression lightened as he appeared to consider that, and then he shrugged and pulled her close with his operable arm. "True. Since we're here now, though, we might as well make the most of it."

That made her laugh again. Who would've thought that she'd be laughing just weeks after fleeing from a vindictive mob boss? She ran her hands over his biceps and onto his shoulders, shocked by her happiness. Despite the residual shock and horror, and her worry about the meeting with Noah tomorrow, she really was surprisingly content, all thanks to the man she was currently straddling. Grace smiled at him. "True."

"So…" His eyebrows wagged teasingly. "Wanna make out?"

"With you?" she purred, using her phone-sex-operator voice again. "Anytime." She started leaning toward him, but then she looked over her shoulder.

"What's wrong?"

"Just making sure a dog isn't going to stick her cold nose in my ear this time."

Despite the bullet hole in his leg, the broken arm, the concussion, and God knew how many bruises, Hugh tilted back his head and laughed out loud. Unable to resist that happy sound, Grace grabbed the back of his head and pulled him into a kiss.

CHAPTER 19

IT WASN'T LIKE HUGH HADN'T THOUGHT ABOUT IT, BECAUSE he had. A lot. He'd even dreamed about it. The reality of kissing a mostly naked Grace Robinson, however, was better than anything he could have imagined. When she'd stood in front of him and stripped down to her underwear, he'd thought his heart—among other body parts—was going to explode.

She was gorgeous, tall and sleek, with olive skin and that silky, dark hair that he couldn't stop touching. The only frustrating thing was his cast. He wished that he had full use of both arms, both hands. At least the pain from his headache had all but disappeared with the initial rush of endorphins during that first frantic kiss.

Using his good arm, he flattened his palm in the middle of her back, tucking her even more tightly against him. Her skin was unbelievably soft—so soft that he felt bad about his callused hands. He worried that he'd hurt her, that he'd be too rough, but she didn't seem to mind the abrasive contact. In fact, she made little noises in her throat and pushed into his hand every time he touched her.

As if she'd read his mind, Grace hummed and wriggled, working her body until she was plastered against him. He couldn't seem to catch his breath, but he honestly didn't care about getting enough air. As long as he could keep kissing her, all was right in his world. Oxygen was overrated, anyway.

Her hands were everywhere, touching his ears and his neck and his chest and his belly. They even flitted down to work at the button on his BDUs. His whole body jerked when he realized where her fingers had landed. When he tried to break the kiss, she followed him, and he soon gave in with a groan, meeting her lips. A faint warning bell rang in the very back kiss-drugged corner of his brain, just loud enough to catch his attention. Before he could get sucked back into their explosive make-out session, he pulled back.

"Wait a sec," he gasped, sucking in air. Grace made a tiny disappointed sound and leaned into him, her lips seeking his. Although he was tempted to give in—very tempted—he resisted the siren call of her mouth. "Are you okay?"

Her answer was a distracted murmur that meant nothing as she struggled to get his pants unbuttoned. He slapped a hand over her working fingers. If she managed to get his BDUs undone, then he'd be undone as well.

"Hang on." His voice was even less than a gasp. It was more of an exhaled breath. He tried again. "Are you okay with this?"

She glared up at him with her dark eyes narrowed. "I'm literally trying to get into your pants, Hugh. I think I'm fine."

His laugh was little more than a pathetic wheeze. "Okay, then. Carry on. I was just checking."

He thought his heart was going to stop when her hands paused. This time, when she looked at him, her expression was a great deal softer. "I know. Thank you for that. Now, quit asking. Okay?"

"Got it." He laughed again, but it was quickly cut off as she dragged his unfastened pants down. Lifting his hips, he helped her tug his pants and boxer briefs until they were down around his thighs.

Their kisses gained urgency, and he nipped her lower lip as he struggled to unhook her bra using one hand. With a throaty chuckle that sent a shock wave of lust through him, Grace reached back and unfastened the bra. Drawing it down her arms, she revealed her breasts, and Hugh stared as if he were a thirteen-year-old boy who'd never seen a naked woman before.

"Wow," he said, cursing himself for how not-smooth he sounded. It was Grace's fault, though, for being so heart-stoppingly beautiful that his brain refused to work right. Bending his head, he lowered his mouth to one of her breasts, and Grace sucked in a breath. Worried that she was nervous or self-conscious, he went soft and gentle at first, placing tiny, light kisses all over her chest. When she started to make eager sounds and arched toward him, he got a little more intense, nipping and sucking and teasing her nipples with his tongue.

"Hugh," she moaned, raising her hips toward him. "Please!"

Grinning against the soft skin, he gave a final lick before raising his head. "What's that I hear? Is it…begging?"

She went still for several seconds before giving him a shove that teetered between playfulness and true annoyance. "No!" she lied, sticking out her lower lip in a pout that made him tempted to bite. "Jerk! Just for that, we're stopping what we're doing, getting dressed, and wearing

Snuggies while we watch a chick flick." She glared at him, and he felt a little wrong thinking that she looked really hot when she was mad.

Then her words sank in, and his heart fell into his stomach. "Oh. Really?"

"No." Her scowl couldn't hide the teasing glint in her eyes. "But I should."

"Thank God," he sighed, making her giggle. Before she could say anything so horrible again, he yanked her toward him and kissed the laugh off her lips. The kiss instantly ignited, and all teasing was forgotten as their urgency grew. Once again, he wished for two working hands as he stroked her body, petting all the silky bare skin that he could.

When she slid off his lap, he groaned in protest, but reluctantly let her go. To his relief, she just shimmied out of her panties and moved to rejoin him on the couch.

"Wait," he said, his voice a low rasp. "Let me look for a minute."

"Hugh," she complained, color rising from her chest to her face. Her gaze darted around, her atypical shyness somehow endearing, as much as he didn't understand it.

Reaching out, he traced a line from between her breasts to below her belly button. "I didn't mean to embarrass you," he said, feeling her shiver and twitch under his light touch. "I just wanted to look at you. You're so stinking beautiful."

Her laugh sounded a little choked. "Thank you?"

"Why the question?" Leaning forward, he laid a chaste kiss on her belly. "I didn't say 'stinky and beautiful.'"

She gave his shoulder a shove, but there wasn't much conviction behind it. "You'd better not." Her voice caught on the last word as he kissed her hip. His pants dug into the side of his thighs, and he remembered that he was still partially clothed. He shoved at his BDUs and boxer briefs, mentally swearing at the awkwardness of his casted arm, and Grace bent to help. With three working hands, they made short work of removing the rest of his clothes.

Naked Grace caught his attention again, and he brushed his knuckles along the underside of her breast before running his thumb ever so lightly over her nipple. Her eyelids lowered to half-mast, and she swayed. Hugh caught her, wrapping his arm around her waist and dragging her back onto his lap for the third time in the past hour. He expected her to complain about his manhandling, but she came easily, and their mouths met again.

Hugh didn't think he could ever get enough of kissing Grace, touching Grace. The only reason he was able to tear his mouth away from hers was that there was so much more to explore, so many sweet, soft places. When she pressed against him or made a throaty sound, he made a mental note to remember that spot below her earlobe or on the side of her neck or the high point of her shoulder.

Her thighs were strong with lean muscle, and he ran his good hand along the side, enthralled and a little pleased with himself. After all, he'd made those sturdy muscles shake with need. Switching back and forth between her upper thighs, he teased and tormented until she pleaded with him to touch her—to really touch her.

This time, he kept his mouth shut and didn't point out the begging. That didn't mean that he wasn't utterly thrilled that she desired him that much, though. Nipping at her lower lip, he touched her center, finding her hot and wet and wanting.

She was amazing. Their mouths battled back and forth, giving and taking, and he loved that she took control when she wanted it. Once again reading his mind, Grace made a frustrated sound and grabbed the condom packet from where it had fallen on the couch next to them.

With fumbling, impatient fingers, she opened it and rolled it on him. Her touch forced Hugh to squeeze his eyes closed and fight for control. Grace raised her body and lowered herself on him. The feel of her around him, so hot and tight and *alive*, was the best thing he'd ever felt in his life. If he could've stayed buried inside her forever, he would've done so happily.

Then she moved, settling him more deeply inside her, and his hard-won restraint was gone. Grasping her hips, holding on as best he could with his casted hand, Hugh started to thrust. He watched her face, listened to the sounds she was making, and memorized what she liked. His hips rose and lowered, his movements gaining in speed and power, and Hugh knew that he'd pay for it later, that his leg and arm and head would all take their painful revenge. At this moment, though, buried inside Grace, he knew that everything was worth it. *She* was worth it.

As he sped up, her kisses grew in ferocity, until they were wild and rough and a perfect complement to the storm building between them. He watched her face, fighting to pay attention when his body wanted to lose control, to drop off the cliff into the raging water below.

Grace was more important, though. He wanted to make

her happy—needed to make her happy—and his own pleasure was secondary. It was easy to see what she liked, what drove her higher. She was loud and unrestrained, and he loved that. That was his Gracie, not afraid to say what she was thinking, what she was feeling.

Her face flushed, and her eyes grew glassy as her body tightened around Hugh. Once again, he was struck by her beauty as she moved above him, her hair mussed and tumbling down her back, the muscles shifting beneath her skin. His thumb rubbed her hip, and he was amazed that he could touch her like this, feel her like this. Now that he knew how incredible it actually was to be this close to Grace, he knew he could never let her go, not without fighting everything inside him that urged him to keep her.

With that resolve, his fingers tightened around her hips, and he pounded into her. She cried out as she orgasmed, her back arching and her head falling back, letting the ends of her hair brush his legs. He could feel his own climax approaching, but he held it off, wanting to watch as pleasure flooded through her. As she slowly recovered, a huge, slightly drunken smile took over her face, telling him exactly how she felt.

Intense satisfaction flooded him. *He'd* done that. Hugh had made her feel that amazingly good. If she let him, he wanted to keep her this happy all the time. With a final upward thrust, he slid his arm around her back and pulled her close. They kissed as he climaxed, ecstasy radiating from his spine to every cell in his body. Hugh had been so focused on Grace, on making her feel better than she ever had before, that his own pleasure took him by surprise. He drowned in it, letting it strip away everything until he was raw and naked inside.

Breathing hard, he collapsed backward. Since his arms were wrapped around her, he pulled Grace with him, toppling sideways until they were sprawled full-length on the couch. She giggled, sounding a little punchy and a lot happy.

With a groan, he forced himself to release her and pushed himself off the couch. When she clung to him, her arms around his neck, Hugh gave into temptation and hugged her, hard. Then, he gave in to another temptation and kissed her thoroughly before finally pulling away.

"I'll meet you upstairs," he said, heading for the bathroom.

"Oh?" Her tone was too sweet, and he grinned, knowing what was coming. "I'm staying over, then?"

"Yes." If he had his way, she wasn't going to be out of his sight until Martin Jovanovic was either dead or behind bars. He stopped and turned, bracing for the argument he knew was coming. "I'll give you a toothbrush."

To his surprise, she just grinned at him. "Deal. Will you cook breakfast, too?"

Hugh made a face. "If you want. It won't be good. Also, I don't think I have any eggs or...well, any ingredients."

"Never mind, then. We can just have cereal."

"Sorry. I don't have any."

"Bread for toast?"

"Nope."

She blinked at him. "Pop Tarts?" When he just winced and gave her his best apologetic, *I-know-I-suck-but-don't-you-love-me-anyway* smile, she sighed. "How do you not starve?"

"The viner. And Otto brings me eggs."

"The viner it is, then." Standing, she stretched, showing off all her naked glory, and he could only stare. His brain shut off completely. In fact, he was pretty sure he'd just forgotten his own name. Grace sauntered over to where his T-shirt had landed when he'd finally worked his cast free. She pulled his shirt over her head, and only then could Hugh think again. Blowing out a hard breath, he made his way to the bathroom. Apparently, Grace could short out his brain anytime she wished. If that meant he'd get to see her naked on a regular basis, however, he was okay with that. He'd give up just about anything—including the ability to think—if it meant keeping Grace. In just a few weeks, she'd become the most important part of his life.

It was one thing to be confident and sassy when Hugh was staring at her with hungry eyes, but her confidence faded a little as she lay in his bed, alone. The silence of the room made her thoughts too loud. After everything they'd been through, her worries seemed silly, but she couldn't shut them off. Would things be different between them now? Would they be stiff and awkward with each other? With a groan, she flopped onto her back and covered her eyes. *Shut it, brain.*

Hugh walked in, and she quickly yanked her hands from her face and pretended that she hadn't been freaking out. "Hey."

"Well, *hello* there," he said in such an over-the-top smarmy voice that she immediately relaxed.

Crawling into bed, he scooted over until he was right next to her. After wiggling his arm under her head, he draped his casted arm over her waist. "That okay?" he asked.

"Sure." The fiberglass cast was lightweight and smooth, so it didn't bother her. "Why am I not shocked that you're a snuggle bunny?"

"Why would you say that?" he asked, pulling her closer and tucking his face into her neck.

She chuckled softly and reached up to give his head a pat. "Good night, Hugh."

"'Night, Gracie."

As she was dozing off, Hugh asked quietly, "You worried about tomorrow?"

Grace started slightly. With everything that had just happened between her and Hugh, she'd actually forgotten about the meeting with Noah. "Not until you said that." She struggled to keep a teasing tone. "But thanks for reminding me."

"It'll be fine." He sounded like he was reassuring himself, rather than Grace.

"I know." Even she could hear the uncertainty in her voice.

"It'll go well." When she didn't respond, he asked, "Know how I know?"

"How?"

"Because you'll be amazing. Know how I know?"

Her smile grew more genuine. "How?"

He kissed her neck, making her shiver as warmth spread from the spot. "Because you're always amazing. It's impossible for you to be anything else."

She ran her nails lightly over his head, and delighted

in the fact that she could make him shiver, as well. "Thanks, Hugh."

"Also, I won't let anything happen to you."

Sleep was creeping up on her again, and her eyelids slid shut. "I know." This time, she actually meant it.

She was almost asleep again when he said, "Grace?"

"If you woke me up to tell me 'good night' again, I'm going to punch you in the junk, John Boy."

His husky laugh was warm against her neck. "Sorry. I'll let you sleep."

"Okay."

"Just one question."

"Junk. Punch."

"Please?"

"One question, and then I can sleep?"

"I promise."

She huffed out an exasperated breath. Now that she was curious, she wouldn't be able to sleep without knowing what his question was anyway. "Fine. What?"

"When Martin Jovanovic is arrested, are you planning on moving back to California?"

Grace went still. Everything had been so crazy recently that she hadn't wanted to think about what she'd do if she didn't have to hide anymore. Over the past weeks, it had been enough just to survive. Now, when she thought about returning to the life she'd left in California, she felt a little flat. Even though she missed Penny and her home and her job, she couldn't imagine leaving Hugh and Jules and the kids and even Theo and Otto. This weird little town had become home.

She must've been silent too long, because Hugh spoke again. "That's fine if you want to." She sucked in a breath as the words stabbed her heart. "I'm sure I'll learn to like it there. Maybe I can be a motorcycle cop like in that eighties show. It might be fun to be able to grow oranges in our yard, too. Whatever you decide, we'll work it out." He pressed a kiss to her neck as he tucked her closer to him.

Giving his head another stroke, Grace blinked back surprised—but happy—tears. She hadn't expected that he'd offer to move to California with her, rather than make her choose between him and her old life in LA.

That one gesture pushed her over the line, and Grace knew beyond a shadow of a doubt that she loved K9 Officer Hugh Murdoch.

CHAPTER 20

As she glanced around the food court, Grace gave a humorless huff of laughter. Yet again, she was sitting on a hard, uncomfortable chair, scared out of her mind as she waited to talk to someone she really didn't want to see. At least it wasn't at a police station this time. She took a tiny sip of her lukewarm coffee, trying to ignore how the cup resisted leaving the sticky surface of the table. Food court or police station—it was a toss-up as to which was worse. At least this coffee wasn't drugged.

Her knee bounced up and down, and she pressed her hands against her thigh to stop the nervous motion. It would be fine. Even if Noah *was* part of Martin's evil empire, he couldn't do anything to her in the middle of a busy Denver mall on a Saturday afternoon. Besides, the FBI agents would be listening from their surveillance van in the parking lot, and Shankle had promised that there would be undercover agents nearby.

Hugh had lobbied to be one of them, but Shankle had told him to count his blessings that he'd be allowed to stay in the van. Grace wasn't sure how Hugh had finagled his way onto the FBI team, but she was intensely glad that he had. Knowing that Hugh was just a two-minute sprint away was the only thing that kept her in her seat. If he'd hadn't been there, Grace was pretty sure that she would have called the whole thing off and run, tail tucked, back to the van.

As she scanned the crowd again, Grace tried to turn *spot-the-FBI-agent* into a game. Was the woman frowning at her phone, shopping bags piled around her, one of Shankle's colleagues? Grace cocked her head thoughtfully, but then dismissed the possibility. The woman's knee-high boots were too nice to be part of a government agent's disguise. Grace turned her attention to a couple of men a few tables away who were holding hands and whispering to each other, ignoring their plates of fast-food Chinese. Were they on the FBI team? Her fingers drummed on the table as she mentally filed them as definite maybes.

"Kaylee."

Her pulse, which had settled a little while she played her game, took off again at a dead run. Jerking her head around, she looked at Noah, who was standing right next to her table. How had he gotten so close without her noticing? She'd picked an out-of-the-way table intentionally, and there wasn't anyone else sitting nearby. She kicked herself for being oblivious to his approach.

His smile faded, turning quizzical, and Grace realized that she'd been silently staring at him with what was probably a horror-stricken expression.

She gave herself a mental slap. This was it. She needed to get this done. If she wanted any semblance of a normal life, if she wanted Hugh and Jules and the kids and everyone she came into contact with out of danger, then she had to go through with this meeting.

She forced a smile. "Oh! Noah, you startled me. Hi." Trying to hide a wince, she widened her grin, knowing that she sounded—and probably looked—strange. It was just so odd to see him, in all his Disney prince–like glory.

"No hug?" he teased, holding out his arms.

Hug? Her brain rebelled at the idea, but she didn't want him to think she'd already decided he was Martin Junior. Standing on shaky legs, she reached out to give him a stiff embrace. Although she tried to keep it quick and as casual as a hug could be, he wrapped her in his arms and pulled her stiff body flush against his.

Noah wasn't nearly as muscular as Hugh, but he was only an inch or so shorter than the cop and had a fairly solid build. Grace used to love Noah's long, tight hugs, but now she only felt panicky and trapped. Fighting down the urge to struggle wildly, she pushed against his chest with both hands until he shifted back slightly.

"What's wrong?" he demanded, still not fully releasing her. Twisting out of his hold, she offered him another insincere smile as she turned back to her seat. Although she hoped that she hid her fear, Grace knew it had to be obvious to Noah. After all, she used to sink into his hugs, enjoying the feeling of being safe. She almost laughed out loud at the thought that she'd believed that *Noah* would keep her safe.

"Nothing," she said as she slid back into her chair. "This whole situation just has me really spooked."

His posture relaxed a tiny amount, and he sat in the seat across from her, immediately leaning across the table. "Understandable. From the little you've told me, that had to have been terrifying."

A small, irreverent part of her wondered if she should warn him about the mysterious sticky spots adorning the table, but she quickly wrenched her brain back on topic.

"Yes. It was definitely terrifying." She fought the urge to play with her necklace. Although she'd borrowed most of her outfit from Jules, the pendant—and its tiny, hidden video camera—was on loan from the FBI. They'd also hooked a more traditional wire to her bra, and the location was such a movie cliché that it had made her choke out a laugh. To keep her hands from drawing attention to the necklace, she lowered them to her legs, digging her fingers into her thighs right above her knees. "You didn't tell Martin that you were meeting me, did you?"

His look of horror appeared authentic, but she wasn't going to take anything from Noah at face value anymore. "Of course not. I still think you're mistaken about him, but I kept your confidence."

"Thank you." She stared at her hands again, wishing for a better poker face. If Noah was involved in—or even knew about—Martin's crimes, then he was a much better actor than she was.

"Tell me what happened," he urged, bringing her gaze to his again. "I've been so worried about you. Are you okay? Do you have someone you can stay with, or are you alone? You need to come back to California with me. We'll figure this thing out with Uncle Martin. He's a reasonable guy. You'll see when you get to know him." Leaning across the small table, he reached out to brush his fingers across her cheek.

It was an effort not to jerk away from his touch. Noah seemed so sincere, so caring, but Grace couldn't bring herself to trust him. That aura she'd always noticed about him—that sense of confidence and self-assurance—was still there, but it seemed hollow now. His standard good looks paled in comparison to the thought of Hugh. The cop had shown her what a true hero was, and it wasn't this faded copy of a Disney prince who could very possibly be hiding his uncle's deadly crimes.

"I'm okay," she said, not sure which question to answer first. Picking up her coffee cup, she pretended to take a sip to give her an excuse to shift back enough that Noah's hand dropped from her face. She didn't want to give him too much information. As close as he was to his uncle, she didn't trust that Noah wouldn't slip up and give something away. "I'm in a safe place."

"You mentioned the FBI earlier. Are they protecting you?" he asked, sitting back. He didn't seem offended that she'd moved away from his touch. "I'd feel better knowing that you had someone watching out for you, at least. Do they have you in witness protection?" He glanced around the food court and frowned. "If so, they're doing a poor job of it. Did you come here by yourself?"

Hugh's face immediately flashed in her mind, and she had to push down a sappy smile that wanted to emerge. *Focus!* "No, not witness protection. It's nothing official, but I do have friends who are helping me. I'm not alone." *Not anymore.* "Plus, I'm meeting you. It's not like I need the FBI to protect me from you." Her small, disbelieving laugh was mostly honest.

"True. I just don't like the idea of you being afraid and alone."

She waved her hand to brush off his concern. "I'm fine. It's you I'm worried about. Your uncle is a dangerous man. You're not planning on confronting him with what I told you, are you?"

Staring at the sticky table, he blew out a short breath.

"I don't know what to do. I don't even know what to think. Tell me again what you thought you saw that night at my uncle's house."

Grace frowned. "I didn't just imagine this."

"No, of course not." Although his tone of voice was smoothly apologetic on the surface, she heard a slight hesitation. "All I meant was that we all see things differently. That's why eyewitness accounts are considered to be the least reliable evidence. People filter everything through their own experiences. I didn't mean to say you were making this up. I know you better than to think you'd ever invent a story like that."

It took her a second for his comments to sink in, for her to realize that he was trying to make her doubt herself, to question whether she really did see those three battered, bloody men. Swallowing the angry words she wanted to let fly, Grace pasted on a syrupy-sweet smile instead. "I'm glad that you know me so well that you realize I wouldn't make up a crazy story about your uncle torturing people." When he frowned, she dialed back the saccharine gratitude. As much as she wanted to tear into him for trying to gaslight her, that wasn't the purpose of the meeting. "He's like a dad to you, isn't he?"

"Yeah." Noah looked a little startled by the change of subject, and his answer sounded bluntly honest.

Reaching across the table, she laid her hand on his. "I'm sorry. This must be so hard to hear."

Just like that, the mask was back. "Thanks, Kaylee. I just want to be here for you. What do you need?"

"Help me understand." It was much easier to try to pump information from Noah-bot, with his fake platitudes and barely hidden condescension, than it was from honest Noah, who reminded her too much of the man she'd dated less than a month ago. "You know Martin so well. Is there any reason for him to be involved in this? Could he have fallen in with some bad company? Maybe he got mixed up in illegal things and realized too late that he was stuck."

Noah's eyes cooled as he pulled his hand out from under hers. "Uncle Martin is not a weak man. He wouldn't blindly *follow*"—he spat out the word—"some criminal. My uncle is a leader."

Grace wondered if Noah realized that he wasn't helping his uncle's case. "What about his friends or business partners? Do any of them seem like they could do something like this? Maybe your uncle didn't even know about what was happening in the basement." That wouldn't explain why Martin had tried to drag her back into the house, but she was hoping to get Noah talking.

"Uncle Martin wouldn't associate with someone who'd condone torture, much less use it." Noah's hands fisted for just a split second before he flattened them out again. That small flash of obvious anger made her stomach clench. The meeting hadn't produced any helpful information, and, by the way Noah was shifting in his chair, he wasn't going to be staying in the food court much longer. If she didn't get him to give her *something*, this would be a waste—all the work that went into arranging it, all the FBI agents' time, all of her anxious moments leading up to the call and this meeting. Hugh should be home in bed, recovering from his injuries. Instead, he was here, just in case she needed him to save her.

Resolve hardened in her. Noah might not volunteer anything that could help them in the case against Martin Jovanovic, but she was going to try her hardest to get him to spill. For the FBI agents and for the tortured men and for Hugh and for her future, she was going to push until he walked away from her.

"If Martin didn't do it, and none of his acquaintances did it, then why were those men being tortured in his house?" she demanded, dropping all pretense of sweetness.

Noah's eyes narrowed as he leaned forward. "How do you know they were tortured?"

"Their injuries were pretty obvious," she said, mimicking his posture so that they were face-to-face. "So were the chairs they were tied to, and all the knives and pliers laid out next to them. Oh, and the blood. There was a lot of blood."

"Did you actually see them being tortured?"

"Just the aftermath." Her nervous stomach settled, and all she felt was calm. "You don't need to see a house burn. If you see the smoldering ruin, you'll have a pretty good idea about what happened."

He made a scoffing sound, his gaze so cold that she would've cowered if she hadn't been so focused on making him say something to implicate Martin. "You don't know who those guys were. They could've staged it. Every successful business owner has enemies."

Her laugh came out as a humorless bark. "Right. Because an empty eye socket is easy to fake. This wasn't pretend blood and Halloween party favors, Noah. If your uncle has enemies, it's because he *tortures them*."

His face turned white, a muscle ticking at his jaw,

and Grace fought the urge to escape. All the fear she'd pushed out of the way came rolling back in, and she struggled to hide it as she held his gaze.

"I think we're done," he said coolly. "I can't be with someone who says such terrible lies about my uncle."

Several things tried to escape her mouth at once. She wanted to yell that they weren't lies, and that his uncle was an evil man. The logical part of her wanted to convince him to stay a little longer. If she could keep prodding at him until he lost his cool, there was a chance he would blurt out something the FBI could use. One glance at his face, however, told her that pushing any further was useless. He was locked up tightly, and her gut told her that she wouldn't get anything else out of him that day.

A tiny, petty voice in her head also really wanted to tell him that *he* couldn't break up with *her*, because they hadn't been together since his uncle tried to kill her. Besides, now she was with Hugh, who was fifty times the man that Noah could only hope to be.

But that would get them nowhere fast.

"Fine." She stood and picked up her barely touched, now-stone-cold coffee. It was an effort to not crush the cup in her fist. "Thank you for coming all this way to meet with me. If you do notice something suspicious about Martin, please tell someone—the FBI or the police. He's hurting people, and he needs to be stopped." Dropping her coffee cup in a trash can, she paused and glanced over her shoulder. "Goodbye, Noah."

He didn't say a word. His face was hard, cold, and she was baffled at how she ever could have thought that he was one of the good guys. Noah Jovanovic had "villain" written all over him. Penny had been so right not to trust him, and Grace couldn't wait to hear her friend say "I told you so."

Looking straight in front of her, Grace walked away from the table…and the last wisps of her Disney prince fantasy disintegrated. When she reached the edge of the food court, she finally gave in and glanced back at their table. Noah was gone.

A wave of sadness and frustration and worry crashed over her, and she ducked into a women's bathroom. She was relieved to see all three stalls were open and empty, and no one stood at the sinks. This way, she could have her nervous breakdown in peace. A sob wanted to escape, and she clamped her hand over her mouth to hold it in. She wasn't sad that she and Noah were finished. It wasn't that at all. Hugh was all she wanted, and she intended to keep him. His declaration that he'd go to California with her and grow oranges was the most amazing gift she'd ever been given. If she decided that she truly wanted to return to her Los Angeles life, Hugh would be there with her. She didn't have to choose, didn't have to split her happiness in order to keep him. He'd offered to leave his partners and his department and the house he'd grown up in, all to be with her. The thought made her want to do a happy dance, squeal with excitement, and burst into tears, all at the same time.

Instead, aware of the video camera hanging around her neck and the mic attached to her bra, she pressed her palms to her closed eyes and mentally counted to five. Taking a deep breath, she calmed, and the tears receded. The FBI—and Hugh—were waiting. With a final shaky exhale, Grace dropped her hands and opened her eyes.

Just in time to see a fist flying toward her face.

———————

He'd never been so tempted to punch a fed, and that was saying something. As a rule, FBI agents could be almost as aggravating as firefighters.

"Let me listen. Just for a minute."

Agent Shankle didn't look up from his old-school notebook where he was busy scribbling notes on the conversation that Grace—*Hugh's* girlfriend—was having with her felonious ass of an ex-boyfriend. Shankle was acting like he couldn't hear Hugh, thanks to the headphones the agent was wearing, but Hugh knew he could hear the other people in the van just fine. In fact, he'd responded several times to Contares, the woman who appeared to be responsible for the tech equipment, all while not missing a beat in his eavesdropping and note-taking.

"So…" Hugh tried again. "What are they saying? Anything? How close are they sitting?"

Contares's cough sounded suspiciously laugh-like, but Shankle didn't even twitch. It was like he was Hugh annoyance–proof, and that wasn't a good thing. Hugh wished they were watching the video feed, but the necklace camera just recorded; it didn't transmit. The wire, on the other hand, was streaming in real time, right into Shankle's ears. Pretending to stretch, Hugh moved so he could look over the agent's shoulder to read what he'd written. Shankle shifted, hunching his shoulder so that his body hid the contents of his notebook.

Scowling, Hugh sat back and absently rubbed his

thigh. Being stuffed in the van for the hour-plus drive to Denver, plus hanging out in the back of their spy mobile while Grace and the ass talked about who knew what… *Oh wait! Shankle knows what. Too bad he's a greedy bastard and doesn't share his toys*. Hugh glared at the agent's back, but it didn't slow the man's continuous scribbling. At one point, he underlined something several times, and Hugh nearly went out of his mind with his need to know what had been said, as well as the need to punch Shankle in the back of the head.

Suddenly, the agent paused. Even his constantly moving hand went still.

"What?" On high alert, Hugh straightened from his slouch. "What is it? What's wrong?"

Finally, *finally*, Shankle turned to look at him. He was smirking a little, and Hugh relaxed. If something bad had been happening to Grace, the agent wouldn't be smiling like that—at least, Hugh hoped he wouldn't. "Grace left the table without Jovanovic. Now, according to Swanson, she's in the ladies' room."

"Oh." Hugh slumped back in his seat, relieved. "So, it's done? Does she sound like she's okay? Did you get anything useful?"

To Hugh's surprise, Shankle actually answered. "She's fine. We're…"

After a silent moment, Hugh prompted, "You're…?"

Instead of responding, Shankle appeared to be listening to something, either from Grace's wire or one of the other agents. He frowned, lines forming between his eyebrows, and Hugh immediately went back on full alert.

"What's the situation?"

"We lost our eyes on Jovanovic," Shankle said,

before he started barking orders to his agents. "Li and Novak, keep searching for him. Kandeski, head to the mall security office. See if you can find footage of him, and keep Li and Novak in the loop. Swanson, get in that bathroom and stay with Grace. Murdoch, where are you going? Get back in here. She's fine. We have this under control."

It was Hugh's turn to ignore the FBI agent. Jumping out of the van, he hit the ground running, mentally cursing himself the whole time. He'd known the meeting was a bad idea. He should've convinced Grace not to go. Hell, he should've locked her in his bedroom for the next fifty years. She would've been pissed, but at least she would've been safe.

He weaved his way through the grid of parked cars and sprinted for the mall entrance. Tires screeched against the pavement as someone braked hard, and an SUV came to a stop just a few feet away from him. Ignoring it and the insults the driver was shouting, Hugh ran for the doors.

Once inside, he slowed, dodging mall shoppers and looking around to get his bearings. Before Grace had gone inside, they'd studied a map of the mall, but Hugh hadn't paid too much attention to where the women's bathroom was located. He spotted a sign for restrooms and took off in that direction, barely avoiding crashing into a stroller.

"Hey!" the woman pushing the child called after him. "Slow down! Someone's going to get hurt!"

Not Grace. Not if I can help it, Hugh thought grimly, running faster through the food court. The tables and chairs seemed to be arranged in the most obstructive way possible, forcing him to pivot and dodge. Vaguely, Hugh was aware of people staring, of a mall security officer yelling something at him, but he was focused on one thing—the bathroom door.

A woman stood by the door, tugging at it. She turned as he approached, and, by her concerned expression, he guessed that she was Agent Swanson. "It's locked," she said. "I heard what sounded like a struggle."

Without answering, Hugh dug in his pocket, pulling out his lockpick set. As he opened it, his hands shook from adrenaline and stark fear. He fumbled the torque and pick, almost dropping them. Gritting his teeth in frustration, he sucked in a deep breath through his nose. He needed to calm down. Losing it would not help Grace.

"Stop!" the security guard called as he jogged toward them. "What are you doing?"

Swanson stepped forward so she stood between Hugh and the guard. Hugh felt a moment of gratitude for the block as he eased the torque and then the pick into the lock. The familiar feel of the motion calmed him slightly, steadying his hands. "FBI," she said. "Do you have a key for this door?"

"A key for the bathroom?" The guard sounded uncertain now that Swanson had identified herself as a fed. "I think so?" There was a jangle of keys, but Hugh ignored it, focusing on pressing the pins into place. The dead bolt turned, and Hugh ripped open the door.

Noah Jovanovic was dragging a limp Grace by her ankles across the bathroom floor toward an open supply closet. He looked up, startled, and then released her. His right hand moved behind him, toward his lower back. Grace's legs flopped to the floor, and Hugh felt a tearing pain in his heart at how limply she lay there. She looked like a lifeless rag doll. Her hair tumbled over her face, hiding most of it, but what he could see was covered in blood. With a roar, he charged.

The move startled Noah into taking a backward step, but he didn't hesitate in raising the gun he'd drawn. Time seemed to slow, and Hugh knew he wouldn't make it before Noah could shoot him, especially with Grace's limp body lying between them. It didn't matter. He'd take the bastard down or die trying.

The gun rose, the barrel almost level, and Hugh braced himself for the shot he knew was coming. Hell, he'd been shot before and survived. He could do it again. Maybe it would give Agent Swanson time to take Noah out before he could hurt Grace any more than she already had.

Before Noah could fire, Grace's leg shot up, and her booted foot caught Noah square in the crotch. Noah's expression changed, his eyes going wide and his mouth rounding in a surprised—and pained—grimace. The gun tumbled from his grip as both hands clutched his groin. Grace rolled out of the way just before Noah, letting out an agonized groan, swayed and fell to his knees.

Hugh tackled him, taking Noah the rest of the way to the floor. The gun went flying, skidding across the tile until it disappeared under a stall. Hugh punched Noah in the face twice, fast and hard, holding the image of Grace's precious, bloody features in his mind. Noah went limp under him. Staring down at the man who'd terrorized Grace—*his* Grace—Hugh fought the temptation to slam his fist into Noah's slack face over and over.

"Hugh." Grace's voice was shaky but strong, and he

turned his head to look at her. She was sitting up, and blood streaked the lower part of her face. It looked like it had come from her nose, and a fresh surge of rage jolted through him. Hugh was starting to turn back to Noah with the intention of destroying the man when Grace spoke again. "Did you see that? I totally nailed him in the junk."

Hugh's head snapped around so he could stare at her. Even bleeding and rumpled and scared, she was smiling at him. He forgot about planning Noah's bloody, violent death. All he wanted to do was hold Grace. Scrambling to his feet, he moved to crouch in front of her. Peripherally, he was aware of Agent Swanson rolling Noah over so she could cuff his hands behind his back, but Hugh's attention was fixed on Grace.

He cupped her face as gently as if he were holding a baby bird. It looked like the blood had stopped flowing from her nose, but he still frowned. "Never thought I'd wish that I were the kind of tool who carried around a handkerchief."

Her laugh was short and strangled, but it was still a beautiful sound. Reaching up, she circled her fingers around his wrist. "Never wish that. Snot rags are gross."

It was his turn to bark out a laugh. Unable to restrain himself anymore, he gathered her against him, not caring how awkward it was with his casted arm. He needed her close. With their bodies pressed together, he could feel the quick strum of her heart, and he wondered if his was beating as quickly. Judging by his post-adrenaline jitters, he would guess that it was.

The bathroom was filling up with agents and mall security. Shankle gave them a swift, narrow-eyed look, as if checking for bullet holes, and then moved to help Swanson with Noah. Despite his resentment that Shankle's orders had kept him away from Grace when she needed him, Hugh grudgingly appreciated that the FBI agent was giving the two of them time. After seeing her limp form on the floor, Hugh needed to hold Grace, to touch her, to find the reassurance he needed that she was okay.

Her arms wrapped around him, and she clung to him as tightly as he was holding her. "What took you so long?"

"Sorry." Guilt roared to life inside him. Why hadn't he fought to stay closer? Why had he listened to Shankle's order to stay in the van? "I had to pick the lock."

She pulled back just far enough to look at him. "You're kidding. You actually used your talent for breaking into women's bathrooms for good, rather than evil?"

His scowl was mostly put on. "I never use my talent for evil. I'm, like, a poster good guy."

Instead of laughing, she stroked his cheek. "Yeah, you are. You're the *best* good guy."

"And you're a junk-kicking badass." His words were thick with satisfaction. "You were so still and limp. I thought…" He had to stop and swallow hard to clear the obstruction in his throat.

Grace gave him a proud grin. "I was totally faking it."

"I'm impressed." He was. "Impressed, and proud, and grateful, and so happy you're okay." Frowning, he gently swiped at a streak of blood on her chin. "Mostly okay. Did he hit you?"

"Yeah. I ducked the first one, but he got me with the next one." She looked so disgruntled that it made

Hugh want to laugh—and swear and hit Noah a few extra times. "I pretended to be unconscious, and he started dragging me toward the closet, and that's when you showed up." Her bravado faltered, and she looked incredibly vulnerable as she met his gaze. "I think he was going to shoot me once I was in there. He muttered something about not getting blood everywhere."

Rage filled Hugh. Why hadn't he killed that bastard when he'd had the chance? He saw Grace's eyes get glossy with tears, and he shoved back his anger, tucking her more closely against his chest. "Bet he regrets it now."

He was rewarded by a watery chuckle muffled in his shoulder. "Yeah, he does."

The feel of her filled him with relief and gratitude. "You know I love you, right?" The words spilled out in a rush. He'd almost waited too long to say them. If things had gone wrong, it would've been too late. He needed her to know how he felt, because the last few weeks had given him reminder after reminder that life was incredibly fragile.

She went still for a moment, and Hugh held his breath as she raised her head to meet his gaze. "You'd better."

His laugh was more of a choke. "That's all I get?"

"Fine." Her smile shook around the edges, but it was still beautiful. "I love you, too. Even when you're being annoying."

He made a scoffing sound, trying to hide the obstruction in his throat. "Please. I'm never annoying."

Special Agent Shankle laughed. When Grace raised her eyebrows at Hugh in wordless triumph, he frowned.

"He wasn't laughing at that."

"Yes. I was," Shankle corrected him, making Grace smother a giggle.

"Don't you have something else to do besides eavesdrop?" Hugh grumbled, although he couldn't work up any true annoyance. After all, Grace loved him. How could he be anything except happy?

CHAPTER 21

"ARE YOU SURE ABOUT THIS?"

She shifted, turning to face him. Hugh stared straight ahead as if watching Dee's movie selection intently, but Grace was pretty sure he wasn't that interested in the cartoon penguins dancing on the screen. "Are you pouting?"

"No."

"Then why is your bottom lip sticking out like that?"

"I can't help it if I have the mouth of a model."

She laughed so hard that she tipped sideways against the back of the couch. Lexi, curled on the floor next to the couch, raised her head briefly and then went back to sleep. "I love it when you say ridiculous things like that, Mr. Badass Cop."

"My friends just call me Badass." Although she could tell he was fighting it, a smile curled the corners of the mouth under discussion. "You didn't answer my question."

Her laughter fading into a sigh, she lifted his arm and snuggled underneath it. "The question of whether I'm sure that I want to live in a house with five other people and one bathroom? Yeah, I'm sure."

"I have the past four years of *Tattered Hearts* on DVD."

Sitting up, she sucked in an excited breath.

"At my house."

Slumping down again, she gave him her best hungry-puppy look. It wasn't as effective as his, but it seemed to get her what she wanted from Hugh a little over half the time. "Can you bring them here on a day I'm not working at Nan's? Please?"

"No. They're for residents of my house only."

She widened her eyes even more.

"Fine. I'll bring them tomorrow." He scowled at the waddling birds on the TV screen, and she poked him in the side.

"Quit sulking. You should be glad I'm not moving back to California, instead of just living five minutes away."

Rather than flinching away from her prod, he squeezed her closer to his side. "I am glad. I'd just be gladder if you moved in with me."

"I'd love that." She really, really would. In the past two weeks following Noah's arrest, she'd realized how much she'd undervalued privacy when she'd lived alone. Jules, the kids, and even Theo acted as an effective and entirely frustrating chastity belt.

Because of Hugh's casted arm, he'd hired some people to help him reconstruct the deck, so his house was a beehive of activity during the day. Several times, Grace and Hugh had ended up parking his new pickup in some remote spot and then making out like teenagers despite their various injuries and the confines of the truck cab. The only reason they had the couch to themselves at the moment was that Jules and the boys were at the high school for an informational meeting about new safety measures implemented since the shooting, and Dee had gone to bed. Grace was reveling in the rare alone time with Hugh.

"Everything just happened really fast with us, and I want to give normal a chance, I guess. It'll be different now that I know we're both safe here, with the Jovanovics and Truman locked up."

He frowned. "You always were safe. Noah and Martin had no idea you were here. If it hadn't been for me…"

"Stop." She gave him her best glare, but it only made him smile at her. "That's all on Truman. Your only fault in all of that was being too good at your job. We've won, good has prevailed over evil, and there's nothing the bad guys can do to us anymore. We get to live normal, boring, uninteresting lives now."

"We could live a normal, boring, uninteresting life together at my house."

"Nice try," she retorted, "but you don't get to skip the dating part."

What she didn't mention was that her confidence in her man-picking abilities had been shaken to her core. The FBI had searched Noah's house and office, and what they'd found had led to eight other arrests—including Martin Jovanovic's. Not only had Noah known about his uncle's illegal pursuits, but the younger Jovanovic had actually been the leader of their expansive criminal organization—and the one who'd ordered the three men's torture. Both Jovanovics were now in jail, waiting to be tried on charges ranging from drug trafficking to money laundering to murder.

Grace felt like an idiot. How had she mistaken the head of a crime family for a Disney prince? She suddenly had sympathy for the baffled people who were interviewed on the news after a serial killer was exposed, saying how they didn't understand it because he seemed like such a nice man. Noah had seemed perfect, but he'd actually been as far from perfect as a guy could be. Although Grace trusted Hugh completely, and loved him so much her heart hurt, her trust in herself was a little shaky. Plus, she wanted a little more time to get to know her new *Grace* self outside her relationship with Hugh.

"So…we date?" Hugh scrunched up his face.

"Yes." Shoving Noah's perfidy out of her head, she laid her head on Hugh's chest. "We date."

"Do we have to?"

"Yes."

"Why can't we just skip to the good stuff?"

She pulled away slightly so she could frown at him. It was hard to hold a straight face when she saw his pout had returned. "No skipping to the good stuff. We'll plan a date, and then you'll drive here, and you'll stand uncomfortably in the entry while Theo and Sam glare at you and Jules lectures you on responsible behavior. Next, I'll sweep down the stairs, looking glamorous, and you'll be struck speechless by my beauty, and then you'll give me flowers, and we'll go on a nice date. At the end, if you're on your best behavior, you might get a kiss good night."

"Huh." He looked like he was trying not to laugh. "I'm not sure I'm capable of most of that, especially all the parts where I don't talk. Theo glaring sounds about right, though." Pulling her close again, he tucked his face in her neck. "I know I'm not capable of good behavior when I'm around you."

At the touch of his lips, Grace lost the ability to think. She tipped her head so that he had better access to the side of her neck, and he immediately took advantage, kissing and nipping lightly at the sensitive skin. When he lifted his head abruptly, she made a soft sound of complaint until she followed his gaze to where Dee hovered in the doorway, watching them uncertainly.

"What's wrong, Dee?" Hugh asked.

"I can't sleep."

Grace shifted over to open a space between her and Hugh. "C'mon in. Want to watch the end of your movie?"

"Okay." Smiling, Dee rushed to snuggle into the gap between them while Lexi thumped her tail against the couch in approval. Hugh gave Grace a long-suffering look over the little girl's head, and she had to swallow a laugh. Dating Hugh was going to be fun.

"When does your friend get here?" Dee asked.

"Penny?" Saying her name made Grace's smile widen. That had been a fun phone call to make, even if she had to admit that her friend had been right about Noah's lack of princely virtues. Another almost-as-wonderful call had been with her supervisors at St. Macartan's. They'd agreed that Grace could continue working for the college by telecommuting from Monroe. Getting to keep both Hugh and her beloved job felt almost too good to be true, and now Penny was going to visit. Even while talking to her friend, Grace hadn't doubted her decision to stay in Colorado. She'd carved out a new life, become a stronger person, and now that the threats to her life had ended, she was incredibly happy in Monroe. It was where she wanted to stay. "Tomorrow."

"Are you excited?"

"Yeah." Grace gave Dee a teasing nudge. "Especially since she's bringing all of my shoes."

Hugh snorted. When Grace mock glared at him, he

gave her an innocent look and leaned over Dee's head to whisper in Grace's ear. "Fine. We'll date. But I'm not promising good behavior."

She met his eyes and smiled. "Perfect."

EPILOGUE

THE BUZZ OF JULES'S CELL PHONE VIBRATING AGAINST HER nightstand brought her out of a really nice dream about Theo to the reality of her half-empty bed. Theo was working nights, and she missed him horribly. Scowling, she reached for the phone and answered it with a snap. "Yes?"

"Ms. Jackson."

She was immediately wide awake. "Mr. Espina?"

"Another…school friend of yours needs a safe place to stay. She'll be arriving tomorrow."

Jules closed her eyes.

"Motherf—"

Read on for a sneak peek of the next book in the
Rocky Mountain K9 Unit series from Katie Ruggle

SURVIVE
THE NIGHT

CHAPTER 1

"ALICE!"

Jeb's shout made her jump, the tiny zipper tab slipping from her fingers. Alice glanced at the closed door. "Just a moment!"

"Hurry up." Jeb sounded tense, making Alice's fingers tremble in response. "Your brother is waiting."

Her gaze darted to the clock. It was just past eight, and Aaron had told her to be ready by eight thirty. It didn't matter that she wasn't actually late, though. The punishment would be the same. "I'm almost ready."

Alice fumbled for the zipper, only to have it slip from her fingers again. Gritting her teeth, she sucked a silent breath in through her nose and closed her eyes, willing her body to stop shaking. It would only delay her, and that would make everything worse. Opening her eyes again, she grasped the tab and slid it up until it touched the back of her neck.

Something scratched at her skin, and she frowned as she reached inside the collar. Had she forgotten to remove the dry cleaner's tag? Her fingers closed around a small piece of paper, and she tugged it free. Taking the two steps toward the small trash can next to her vanity, Alice absently glanced at the now-crumpled scrap. It wasn't the usual red tag the dry cleaner used, though.

Smoothing it out, she saw there was something written in a slashing, aggressive hand.

Be ready to escape. Soon.

Alice froze, staring at the words. What was this? A joke? Why had it been attached to her dress? It couldn't be meant for her, even though the wording made her desperately hope it was. How wonderful it would be to have a friend, one who would be willing to help her. She didn't have any allies, though. Not in Aaron's world.

"Alice, for Christ's sake." Jeb swung open the door and stormed into the room. "It's like you're *trying* to piss off your brother."

It had taken years of practice to keep the guilty anxiety from showing. Closing her fingers around the slip of paper in a way she hoped looked casual, Alice glanced at her bodyguard over her shoulder. "Almost ready." Her voice sounded calm, not revealing how hard her heart was pounding. "I just need to use the bathroom, and then we can leave."

"No time." Jeb grabbed her arm, his fingers pressing into old bruises, making it hard to hold back a wince. "You can go at the restaurant."

Alice twisted free, despite knowing that he would make her pay for that small act of disobedience. Still, whatever Jeb's punishment would be, it couldn't be as bad as what would happen if Aaron found that message. "I can't wait. I promise to be quick." Without hesitating, knowing it would be impossible to escape Jeb's grip if he caught her a second time, she darted for the bathroom.

The lock was something a five-year-old could unlatch with a piece of wire and some luck, but it would give her a few seconds, and that was all Alice needed. She allowed herself one last quick glance at the message, just long enough to convince herself that it was real. The words were still there, exactly the same as before, and her heart sped up again—this time, with hope.

Jeb's heavy fist pounded on the door. With sweaty fingers, Alice shredded the note, allowing the bits of paper to fall into the toilet. She flushed and watched the tiny pieces spin in circles until they were sucked down the drain. After a last check to make sure every bit of evidence was gone, she pulled up her sleeves and washed her hands.

As she dried them, the lock popped out, and the door swung open. Alice adjusted her sleeves so they reached her wrists, hiding the faded and fresh oval bruises that dotted her forearms. She turned to Jeb, keeping her expression blank, but inside she braced for his anger.

"Let's go," he grunted, and she relaxed slightly. Obviously, Jeb wasn't willing to delay them any longer, even if he was irritated with her. He rushed her out of the bedroom and down the stairs, staying so close behind her that the thud of his footsteps was almost painfully loud.

"Alice!" The impatience in her brother's voice made her want to run back up to her room, but that would be futile. Not only would Jeb stop her, but her bedroom wasn't a sanctuary. There wasn't a safe place in the entire house—or in Alice's entire life.

The promise scrawled on that note flickered in her mind, but she quickly banished it. It could be a joke or a trick or meant for someone else or…who knew. She couldn't get her hopes up. If she did, and whoever it was didn't come through, the disappointment would crush her.

As she reached the bottom of the steps, Aaron was already charging down the hall toward her. "Alice! Where is that—oh, there you are." He stopped abruptly, frowning as he took in her appearance. Even though she knew he could find no fault—that he himself had chosen the blue dress for its nun-approved neckline and concealing sleeves—her stomach still soured with nerves. "What took you so long?"

It was futile to protest, to tell him that she wasn't late, that she was, in fact, fifteen minutes early...so she just stayed quiet.

Besides, he wasn't really interested in what she had to say.

"Come on, then." He turned to the front entrance. "The car's waiting."

With Aaron in front of her and Jeb behind, Alice made her way out of the house. The driver holding open the car door was Chester, and he gave her a subtle wink as she slid into the back seat of the SUV. She raised her hand in a tiny return wave, hoping he saw it but not daring to do more. When she was younger, she'd spent as much time as she could with Chester and his wife, Gloria. He'd taught her how to drive and take care of the horses, and Gloria had taught her how to cook and take care of herself. Both of them had showed her how to be a decent human being. After her father died, Aaron took over as head of the family and assigned Alice full-time bodyguards. It became impossible to sneak away to the kitchen or the barn. Surreptitious waves were the closest she'd gotten to talking to Chester or Gloria in years.

Jeb circled the car to climb into the front passenger seat as Aaron sat next to her. Chester closed Aaron's door, and Alice had the almost irresistible urge to scramble out of the car and run. Only the knowledge that she'd barely get ten feet before Jeb tackled her stopped her from trying. *They said to be ready*, she reminded herself, fingers clutching the leather upholstery on the side away from Aaron, where her brother couldn't see her bone-white, desperate grip. *What if there really is a plan? I just need to wait a little longer.*

Aaron glanced at her sharply. For one terrified second, Alice thought she'd actually said the words out loud. Then reason returned, and she was able to smooth her expression into its usual placid lines.

"Best behavior, Alice," he warned, settling back in his seat. "This is an important meeting. First impressions matter. Make a good one, or there will be consequences."

Fire flared in her belly, working its way up to her cheeks. With a huge effort, she kept her rage locked inside and gave Aaron a small nod, hoping that he'd mistake her red face for embarrassment. Turning her head, she stared blindly out the window, not seeing the irrigated lawns or brassy, overdone homes they passed. *Just a little longer*, she repeated, turning it into a chant in her head. *Just a little longer. If the note is real, if it's meant for me, if there's an escape plan...so many ifs. Wait and see and be prepared, just in case it's real. It won't kill me to wait a little longer.*

Why did it feel like she wouldn't survive another second?

When Chester pulled the SUV up to the entrance of Mod fifteen silent minutes later, Alice swallowed a groan. Of all the Dallas restaurants, they had to go to the most pretentious one? She shook off her annoyance.

Of course they did. Aaron had chosen the place after all, and he was easily swayed by flash over substance.

"Miss?" Jeb held her door open. With a deep, soundless breath, she climbed out of the SUV.

"Thank you," she said quietly, waiting for Aaron to circle the vehicle and step to her side. Instead of offering an arm to her, he strode ahead. Alice hesitated, the temptation to turn and run so strong that it almost overwhelmed her. A nudge from Jeb brought her back to reality.

"Miss," he said again, gesturing for her to follow Aaron. Straightening her shoulders, Alice walked into the restaurant after her brother.

As she approached the hostess stand, she heard the tail end of his question. "...the Jovanovic party arrived yet?"

Her heart skipped at the name, and she sucked in a quiet, shocked breath. As shady and unethical as her father had been—and now Aaron was—the Blanchetts were angels compared to the Jovanovics. The Jovanovics, according to everything Alice had heard, were the worst of the worst.

Alice had always been quiet, even as a small child, and people tended to forget she was in the room. She'd heard dozens of horror stories about the Jovanovic family, and she wondered which of the demons they'd be meeting tonight. From what people said, Noah Jovanovic was the true head of the family now, although his uncle Martin was the false face of their empire.

She'd gotten a glimpse of Martin one day five years ago. Breathless and with bits of hay in her hair, Alice had been hurrying inside from the stables, hoping to clean up before her father caught her. She may as well not have bothered. Not only had he spotted her, but so had his guest. Her father had introduced them, and Martin had shaken her hand for a bit too long as he stared intently at her face. Alice had to fight not to yank her hand back, not to rip her captive fingers from his grip and run to her room. Even now, five years later, those eerily light blue eyes were burned into the memory. His gaze had been cold, as calculating and predatory as a snake's. Even if she hadn't heard whispers about Martin Jovanovic and his family, Alice still would've recognized evil at a glance.

Now she was going to have to sit and have dinner with them. Alice briefly considered faking sick, but she was too afraid of the consequences. Aaron didn't like it when things didn't go as planned. It was either sit with the Jovanovics for a few hours or deal with the fall-out. Her stomach churned until she thought she was going to vomit for real. Whatever she did, Alice knew it was a lose-lose situation. Once again, she was trapped.

The hostess began to lead them into the dining area, making the decision for Alice. She'd endure dinner. At least this way, she knew it had to end. Aaron's anger never did. Alice flexed her shoulders, trying her best to stand straight and not cower as she followed the hostess into a private room that held a single round table surrounded by four chairs. Four men in dark suits stood around the room, and Alice knew they were most definitely armed to the teeth.

The two men who were seated at the table rose, and Alice's heart thumped in her throat. The elder of the pair wasn't Martin, thank God, but rather a slightly older and more faded version. Despite his slightly cruel smile, he didn't have the same aura of menace. Alice's muscles relaxed slightly. Dinner might not be quite as torturous as she'd expected.

"Judd," Aaron greeted the white-haired man, shaking his hand. "Good to see you again." He moved to greet the younger man, tall and gangly, with a sparse mustache, who looked to be in his late twenties. "Logan. This is my sister, Alice Blanchett."

The two strangers eyed Alice with a similar expression: smarmy avarice tinted with lust.

"Miss Blanchett," the older man—the one Aaron had called Judd—said, his voice low and smooth and much too slippery. "What a pleasure to meet you."

"Hello." Alice managed a slight smile as she shook his hand. "Please call me Alice."

The courtesy slipped out almost of its own volition. Manners had been drilled into her from the time she could speak, and it was as easy as breathing to go through the motions, even with Jovanovics. Then she turned to Logan, and the gross way he flicked his eyes up and down her body immediately made her stiffen. It wasn't even the rude, sexual perusal that bothered her. It was the possession in his gaze, as if he'd already paid the asking price and she was being delivered for his pleasure, that truly made her skin crawl

After she shook Logan's hand and greeted him politely, her smile slipped away. He pulled out her chair, and she sat at the very edge of the seat, hoping to avoid any accidental touches. Logan slid the chair beneath her, brushing his fingers along her arms and shoulders as he straightened. Even through the fabric of her dress, Alice felt the sticky heat of his caress long after he'd moved back and taken his seat again.

"Any news on the case?" Aaron asked as soon as they were seated and a discreet server poured their wine. Alice was careful not to let her interest show. There had been a few whispers about a raid on the Jovanovics' place—one that had led to several arrests—but this was the first time she would hear any of the details.

Judd made a face. "Nothing good. For the amount we pay the attorneys, you'd think they would've made these charges go away by now. Noah and Martin are getting...antsy."

"I'm sure they are." Aaron lifted his wineglass. "Here's to a quick dismissal of all charges, so that things can go back to business as usual."

The others lifted their glasses in response, and Alice followed suit, pretending to take a sip afterward. She'd always hated wine, but she knew better than to refuse with Aaron watching.

"Business as usual can't come soon enough," Judd agreed, sounding completely sincere. "I'm ready to hand the reins back to my nephew and brother."

Aaron raised his brows slightly, as if the idea of giving up power was inconceivable. "Any luck finding the witness?"

If the dinner continued to be this interesting, it would almost make up for the way Logan was staring at her. His gaze felt as if it left a sticky film on her skin wherever it touched. She felt a rare moment of appreciation for her Aaron-chosen, not-at-all-revealing dress. At least she had that thin layer of protection between Logan's slimy gaze and a good portion of her body.

Judd cast a quick glance at Alice, and Aaron waved

a hand. "Don't worry about her. She's family." He gave Judd a knowing glance that Alice wasn't sure how to interpret before continuing. "She's aware of what the consequences would be if she ever even thought about betraying us."

The threat made Alice shiver, but his words seemed to convince Judd. "We're working on it. The witness met Noah in Denver, but she could've flown in from anywhere. Our guy in WITSEC can't find any mention of her, which is strange. Since the FBI was involved, we assumed she was in witness protection, but we're starting to wonder."

Aaron made a small, skeptical sound. "Isn't she just some nobody that Noah hooked up with a few times? How hard could it be to find one woman?"

"Harder than you might think." Although Judd's voice was still mild, he'd stiffened at the implied criticism.

"I'm sure it is," Aaron agreed quickly. "It's just surprising that a person without any connections can disappear so completely."

Although his frown remained, Judd settled back in his chair, partially soothed. "Even Logan hasn't heard anything."

Alice shot Logan a curious look.

"I'm a police officer in LA," Logan said, catching her glance. He brushed at the front of his jacket. The motion reminded Alice of a puffed-up rooster. "The information I collect is invaluable for the family."

With a small bob of her head, Alice searched for some way to respond. "I'm sure it is."

Leaving him to his preening, Alice turned her attention back to Judd. "We're watching a friend of hers," he was saying. "With Noah and Martin in jail, we're hoping she will relax and possibly contact her friend."

Noah and Martin Jovanovic are in jail? Alice felt her eyes widen. As hard as she tried to keep her face blank, this news was just too amazing. She sent a mental message of thanks and good luck to the missing witness who'd apparently had a hand in getting those monsters locked away.

"Alice." Hard fingers grabbed her chin, jerking her head around until she was looking at Logan's annoyed face. "Quit ignoring me."

His touch was so sudden, so rough, that she tried to pull away before she caught herself. "I wasn't ignoring you." Her voice sounded strained, and she tried to soften it. "I'm just...shy."

Still gripping her face, Logan studied her for a long moment. Alice stared back, clinging to her most earnest expression, not daring to let her fear show. Finally, he released her and sat back in his chair. "No need to be shy with me."

As he looked away, reaching for the bread basket, Alice risked darting a glance at the other two men. They were both watching, but their silence told her that there would be no help from Aaron or Judd.

"Bread?" Logan asked, low and intimate. He leaned toward her, bread basket in hand.

"No, thank you." Despite her best efforts, her polite smile was stiff around the edges. All she wanted to do was listen to Judd and Aaron's fascinating conversation, but now she was afraid to take her eyes off of Logan.

"No?" He placed the basket back on the table. "That's probably for the best, anyway. As small as you are, you probably can't eat too much without tubbing out."

"Tubbing...out?" she repeated, blinking at him.

"You know." Logan blew out his cheeks. "Getting fat."

"I knew what you meant. I just couldn't believe you said it."

"Alice," Aaron snapped, making her jump and turn toward him. "Don't be rude."

A rush of righteous indignation crashed through her, nearly burying her fear. She opened her mouth to protest, but the warning narrowing of Aaron's eyes made her close her mouth before she said anything at all.

"Apologize to Logan," Aaron ordered, as if she were a five-year-old who'd just kicked a fellow kindergartner in the shin.

She turned a blank face toward the man sitting next to her. "I apologize if I seemed rude."

"Alice..." Aaron said, low but sharp, and she had to hide a wince.

"I don't think you were rude," Logan said. "You just didn't understand what I said."

Forcing a smile, Alice said, "Thank you, Logan."

With a pleased grin, he reached over and patted her back. As he withdrew his hand, his fingers lingered, stroking down her arm. Clenching her teeth, Alice took back everything she'd thought about the dinner not being so bad. It was going to be horrid.

"That was disappointing," Aaron said after a chilly two minutes of silence.

"What was?" A cramping stomach told Alice that she

knew perfectly well what was disappointing Aaron—she was. After he'd rebuked her, the conversation had taken a more general—and less interesting—turn. Alice had endured three hours of pretending to drink wine and eat overpriced, badly cooked food while attempting to evade Logan's groping hands. It had been hard to put him off when every movement had been monitored by Aaron. After Judd and Logan had left the table, Aaron hadn't said a word or even looked at her until they were in the SUV, heading toward home.

Aaron reached out, as quick as a striking snake, and backhanded her across the face. Her head jerked to the side, and she heard the slap of skin against skin before the pain registered, sharp and horribly familiar. "Don't play stupid. You know how to behave. You just chose not to."

Pressing her hand against her stinging cheek, Alice said nothing. Any attempt to defend herself would just enrage her brother more. Instead, she watched him warily, fighting the urge to press against the door. There was no way to escape. She was trapped. Her gaze met Chester's in the rearview mirror. The helpless fury in his eyes made her want to reassure him. It wouldn't help if the driver tried to defend her. It would just make things so much worse for all of them.

"This is my chance," Aaron said, jerking her attention back to him. "The Jovanovic family is in chaos right now. Eight people—eight!—were arrested, including Noah and Martin, and they'll be locked away for years. Judd is no leader. That's obvious. There's a huge power vacuum, and I'm going to fill it."

"So fill it!" Alice burst out. Enough was enough.

Being stuck in the middle of Blanchett family power games was one thing. She was born into that. There was no way that Alice was going to get involved with the Jovanovics, though. Let Aaron wallow in all the power he could grab, but Alice didn't want any part of it. All she wanted was the freedom to do normal things—to choose her clothes and friends and meals and job and... everything. "What does any of this have to do with me?"

He grabbed her, his fingers wrapping around her throat, forcing up her chin so she had to meet his eyes. Alice's heart thundered in her chest, her breaths coming in short gasps. Although Aaron's grip wasn't tight enough to cut off air, the threat was there, that he could close his fingers and end her if he wanted to. His eyes were the exact same dark brown, same round shape as hers, but they were as cold and hard and pitiless as marbles. Alice tried to swallow and choked instead.

"This has everything to do with you," he said, fingertips digging in just a little more until Alice knew he was leaving small, round bruises. He'd left them before. "You're my in."

"Me?" she tried to echo, although no sound emerged. All she could do was mouth the word.

"You." Aaron tightened his grip just enough that Alice couldn't breathe. She tried to hold back the panic by pretending she was underwater, that she was perfectly safe, that she could surface for air at any time. Eventually Aaron would let her go. He'd just said that he needed her. If he killed her, he wouldn't succeed.

Even so, she felt the panic rising as her lungs pinched with the need for air. Her thoughts went fuzzy, fear creeping in until she couldn't focus on anything else.

She grabbed his wrist with both hands, instinct forcing her to fight. His arm was rock-hard under her grip, solid and unmovable. Despite knowing that it was futile, she yanked and pulled, trying to pry his hand off her throat. *Maybe he really will kill me this time.*

Just as her vision started to go dark around the edges, Aaron let go of her throat. Bending at the waist as far as her seat belt would allow, Alice sucked in deep breaths that rasped her throat and made her cough.

"What do you mean?" Her voice was hoarse and breathless as she forced herself to straighten, and she wished she were better at faking nonchalance. It felt like weakness to show her brother how much he'd hurt her.

"According to my sources, Logan is gaining something of a bad reputation with the California ladies." His mouth curled up at the corner—a mouth that looked just like Alice's. She hated that they looked so much alike, hated seeing bits of him when she looked in the mirror.

"What kind of bad reputation?" Her hands wanted to rub at her aching throat and rest against her swelling cheek, but she forced them to stay in her lap. This was important. She had to get all the information she could from Aaron. The more she knew, the easier it would be to figure out how to avoid falling in with his plan.

He waved a hand in a dismissive gesture, and Alice flinched before she could catch herself. "That doesn't matter. What does matter is that his dad—Judd—and the rest of the Jovanovics are sick of spending money paying off these women, not to mention the doctors and judges."

"Paying off doctors and judges?" Her stomach twisted as she tried to process his words. "Why? Did he hurt those women?"

"I said it doesn't matter."

Alice dropped her gaze, trying to force her brain past the idea that Logan—the same creep who'd just sat next to her all through dinner, who had touched her multiple times—had abused women in some way. That he'd done something awful enough that the Jovanovics had been willing to pay off his victims and bribe the authorities. She swallowed, her sore throat complaining. "What do Logan's…issues have to do with me?"

"The Jovanovics are hoping he'll settle down with a nice woman." He smiled, and it was terrible. "Someone that will keep him home, away from opportunistic whores."

Her pulse was going wild again. Aaron's plan was a simple one, but Alice was still having a hard time putting it together in her mind. It was just too horrific. "You…" she finally stammered. "You want me to date Logan?"

"No." For a second, his answer made her sag with relief, but Aaron wasn't finished. "You're going to marry him."

CHAPTER 2

Ever since that night, Alice had been waiting for rescue—hoping for it, praying desperately for it even as she searched for another way to escape. The days ticked by, and she fought to hold on to hope, keeping alert for any hint that her unknown friend had finally come through. When the first sign of rescue came, however, it took a form she hadn't expected.

She never dreamed they'd blow up her house.

The explosion knocked her out of bed, startling her out from an uneasy doze. Her insides felt battered, hurting more than her elbow or head where they'd connected with the hardwood floor. Her brain ran through crazy, illogical explanations—it had been an earthquake or a kick from Aaron or a poltergeist that had sent her flying.

She pushed up to her hands and knees while trying to sort out her thoughts. All the chaos made it hard, though. Alarms blared, shrill and ear-piercing, competing with shouts and heavy, running feet. Suddenly, it hit her— was this it? Was *this* the escape the note had promised?

Even as Alice climbed to her feet, she hesitated. What if this wasn't part of the plan? What if the house was on fire, and Alice was about to be burned to death because she'd waited for some mysterious savior to arrive? She sniffed. There was the smell of smoke hanging in the air, but it wasn't heavy—not yet, at least.

Either way, if it was a disaster or if someone had come to help her escape, she needed to be ready to run. Alice hurried over to the closet. Ever since she'd found the note, she'd been preparing for this. Shoving aside designer dresses hung on satin-lined hangers, Alice grabbed a full backpack and the stack of clothes that were sitting at the very back of her enormous closet. She yanked on jeans and a long-sleeved T-shirt, topping it off with a black hoodie while jamming her feet into hiking shoes.

Heaving the pack onto her back, she hurried out of the enormous closet, not feeling a single pang for all the expensive clothes she was leaving behind. They'd been chosen for her by her father and, over the past few years, her brother. To her, the clothes were just costly prison uniforms.

Back in her bedroom, Alice hesitated again, still not sure if she should try to escape or wait for someone to arrive. The smoke was thicker, and the voices were more urgent, although still muted, blocked by at least one level and the heavy door to her room. She moved to try the door, but it was locked from the outside, as always. Every night, from ten until six in the morning, she was bolted into her room.

Her already thrumming heartbeat picked up even more. What if her unknown friend didn't realize that she was locked in? What if they'd only been offering a distraction, an opportunity, and this was it? She could be missing the only chance she'd have to slip away, to escape from her brother and Logan and a future that was heartbreakingly close to her present.

Someone knocked.

Dropping her hand from the handle, Alice backed away, staring at the door in horror. Who was it—friend or foe or, even worse, family? The knock came again, a sharp *tap-tap-tap*, and she realized with a jolt of surprise that it wasn't coming from the door.

Whirling around, she stumbled back a step, swallowing a scream. A dark silhouette filled the window. Someone was outside, their dark-clad form just a few shades blacker than the night sky.

The lurker leaned closer, the dim light from the room illuminating his harsh features, and Alice recognized him. Shock gave way to disappointment mingled with fear. It was Mateo Espina, one of her brother's colleagues, a man who was as firmly entrenched as Aaron in their criminal empire. Alice berated herself for building so much hope on the shaky foundation of an anonymous note. Of course there was no one willing to help her, not in her tiny world of liars and thieves and abusive assholes.

Mr. Espina tapped again. Outside her room, the alarms still shrieked, and the shouts were getting closer and louder. The man outside the window watched her, still and serious, and Alice tried to figure out what was happening. Why was he outside? If he was on her brother's side, why sneak into her bedroom? She wondered if there was a chance, even a slight one, that Mr. Espina could be there to help her. Although she quickly shut down that thought, she moved toward the window. Mr. Espina, dressed all in black, stood on the ledge outside her window, over thirty feet from the ground.

"What do you want?" she asked.

"Didn't you get my note?"

With the window closed and the alarms blaring, she could barely hear him, but that didn't stop her heart from taking off at a gallop. She'd thought she'd beaten down all hope, but there it was again, trying to break through her doubt. With enormous effort, she kept her expression blank. "What note?"

"Do you want to get out of here?"

Yes! her brain screamed, and she took an automatic step closer to the window, to the freedom Mr. Espina was offering. She pulled herself up sharply. Knowing her brother, it could be an elaborate trick, a test of her loyalty and obedience.

"I'll get you out of here," Mr. Espina said.

"Why?" The word burst out of her, revealing too much, but Alice needed to know. "Why would you help me?"

He pressed a small, creased photo to the glass. In the low light, it was hard to make out many details, but Alice could see that it was a picture of a dark-haired, smiling girl. "The Jovanovics killed my sister."

Alice studied him, looking for any twitch, any tell that meant he was lying to her. There was nothing. He returned her gaze steadily, the picture still flattened against the window. In that moment, she made her decision. Maybe it was a trick, a cruel set-up engineered by Aaron. If it was, she'd take the punishment. It wasn't worth turning down this opportunity, this possibility of escape.

Alice fumbled to unlock the window but then paused. Opening it would cause an alarm to go off. Mr. Espina made a hurry-up gesture, and she shook herself. With all the alarms blaring, no one would notice another one... she hoped. Taking a deep breath to steady herself, she jerked open the window.

There was a quiet, repetitive beep. Alice knew she had four minutes. After that, if the correct code wasn't entered into the keypad in Aaron's office, the alarm would start shrieking. It might be ignored, since all the other alarms were also going off. It might not. It could bring Jeb or Aaron tearing into her room, catching her and Mr. Espina in the middle of their escape.

"Let's go," Mr. Espina said, pulling her out of her frozen fear.

With jangling nerves that worsened with each shrill beep of warning, Alice swung a leg over the sill. She glanced down at the narrow ledge and immediately jerked her gaze back up to Mr. Espina's. The decorative molding protruded a mere six inches, not nearly wide enough for comfort.

"Hurry. We don't have much time."

Choking back her terror, she fumbled around with her foot until she had it planted as securely as possible on the too-small ledge. Inhaling a deep breath, she let it out in a rush as she swung her other leg over the sill. With both feet on the ledge, she felt a wave of dizziness rush over her, and she clung desperately to the edge of the window.

"Let's move." Mr. Espina covered her hands with his, detaching her desperate grip with ease. He shifted her hands over next to the window, where the stucco facade offered very little grip. Alice bit down on her tongue, holding back a sound of protest as she clutched at the too-smooth stone. Releasing Alice, Mr. Espina slid the window closed.

The dark made it harder for Alice to keep her balance. Flattening herself against the wall, she closed her eyes and prayed.

"Let's go."

She looked at him, confused. There was nowhere to go. Instead of answering her unspoken question, Mr. Espina wrapped his hands around her waist and lifted her up.

She stiffened as the ledge disappeared from under her feet and the rain gutter appeared right in front of her. Automatically, she grabbed it, needing to hold on to something to anchor herself.

"Up," he grunted, and she boosted herself onto the roof. A push from underneath sent her even higher, and she managed to get a knee onto the red clay tiles. Scrambling, she hauled her other knee onto the roof and crawled toward the peak. There was barely any sound over her shoulder, just the softest brush of fabric on tile, the quietest exhale. When she looked behind her, Mr. Espina was there, gesturing her forward.

The clay tiles were painfully hard under her knees, but she didn't try to stand. The roof was steep and slick, and crawling was hard enough. Thunder rumbled as she made her slow way toward the first peak, and she glanced at the dark sky. If it rained, this would all get that much harder.

A tile cracked under her knee. She jumped at the sound and started to slide. Grabbing for a hand hold, she caught a metal exhaust flue, bringing her body to a jerky halt. Alice paused, trying to catch her breath, looking ahead at the mountain she still had to climb. The thought that she'd have to make up those painful feet she'd lost in her slip made her want to cry, but she'd learned long ago that tears didn't solve anything.

Clenching her teeth, she started to crawl again.

Finally, she reached the peak. She hurried to throw a leg over before she started slipping backward again. Mr. Espina moved up beside her, turning so he was sitting with his feet out in front of him. Without hesitating, he pushed off and slid down the roof like it was a playground slide. As soon as he reached the valley between the peaks, he started climbing the next slope.

Breathing too fast, Alice forced herself to follow his lead. She turned so her feet were forward and slid down the slope. The tiles were painfully bumpy under her, especially as she started moving faster. By the time she reached the base of the next rise, Mr. Espina was nowhere to be seen. Fear built in her chest as she peered through the darkness, trying to spot his dark figure.

"This way," a voice whispered, and she gratefully started to climb toward where Mr. Espina lay on his stomach at the top of the next peak. As Alice scrambled over the top, she came to an abrupt halt. They were at the edge of the roof now. If she tried the sledding trick again, she'd go sailing off the edge and fall to the ground below—far below.

A hand on her arm made her jump and then freeze, terrified that she was going to lose her balance.

"Stand up," Mr. Espina whispered, and she stared at him. *Stand?* She could barely sit straddling the ridge without completely losing her nerve. He must've read her thoughts, since he urged her to move across the ridge line to the spot where a stone chimney jutted out past red tile. Using it for support, Alice carefully stood on shaking legs. The weight of her pack pulled her backward, and she bent slightly at the waist to counter it.

As soon as she was upright, Mr. Espina buckled some

sort of harness around her waist and each of her thighs. Hooking a cable to one of the front straps, he wrapped the line around the chimney and held the other end in both of his gloved hands. He gave her a nod.

Confused, she looked at him.

"Go."

"What?"

"*Go.*"

"Where?"

"Over the side."

"Over the side?" Alice knew she sounded like an idiot, but the idea was crazy. She was supposed to throw herself off the roof with just a thin cable and a moody all-but-stranger to keep her from hitting the ground like a mosquito on a windshield? It was insanity. "I'm sorry. I don't think I can do this."

Mr. Espina's hatchet-carved face softened ever-so-slightly as he moved closer to her. "You can." So quickly that she couldn't even brace herself, he gave her a tiny push.

It was hardly a shove, but it was enough to put her off-balance. She took a step backward to steady herself, but the roof sloped dramatically and her backpack didn't help matters. Her one step turned into two and then three, faster and faster until she was almost running backward off the roof. Alice knew that if she tried to stop, she'd pitch backward and slide the rest of the way on her back. The thought was too terrifying for words, so she continued her reverse, shuffling run until the roof ended and nothing was underneath her feet.

Time seemed to stop for a second. Alice felt like a cartoon character who'd run off the edge of a cliff, hesitating in midair while the realization of what was going to happen hit her. Then she dropped, free-falling for an infinite moment before the cable tightened and the harness caught her.

The tension tipped her back, and she swung toward the house. Just in time, she yanked her knees to her chest so that she didn't put her legs through the quickly approaching window to Aaron's study. It was located at the back of the house because, as her brother liked to say, it was far away from all distractions. Dizzy with adrenaline, Alice wondered if that was the real reason, or if it was isolated so that no one could hear people scream. She'd had several bad visits to that room.

Yanking back her wandering thoughts, Alice struggled to turn upright. She managed to straighten and get her feet underneath her as Mr. Espina lowered her slowly toward the ground. The alarms were suddenly silenced, and she couldn't hear voices shouting anymore. The quiet made her uneasy. If everyone was running around, trying to fix whatever Mr. Espina had done, then they most likely wouldn't be looking for her. The silence, though... Aaron could be checking on her right now.

As her feet touched down on the concrete patio bordering the pool, the cable hit the ground as well, coiling like a snake at her feet. Hitching her backpack higher on her shoulders, Alice gathered up the cable, looping it with shaking hands before clipping the coiled line to a carabiner on her harness. She unbuckled the belt and then the straps around her thighs, the dark and her fumbling, nervous fingers making it harder than it should've been.

By the time Alice had gotten free of the harness, Mr. Espina still wasn't next to her. Craning her head, she stared up at what she could see of the roof, although it wasn't much. Alice backed up several steps until she stood next to the pool, but there still was no sign of Mr. Espina. She wondered if he'd gone a different way. Now that she was out of her room, maybe his part was done, and she had to escape on her own.

If she waited here to find out, it may very well be too late.

She started to turn, to run around the pool toward the perimeter fence, when a loud boom rocked the ground. Alice crouched instinctually, her arms wrapping around her head. As two more blasts echoed through the night, a motion above her caught Alice's eye, making her flinch down again. It was Mr. Espina, flying through the air. Her first thought was that he'd been caught in the explosion, tossed off the roof like shrapnel, and fear for him made her lungs tight.

He hit the deep end of the pool just as yet another explosion shook the ground. When he began swimming toward the far side of the pool, Alice realized that he was fine. His leap must've been intentional, a quick way of getting off the roof. She had a brief moment of thankfulness that he hadn't made her jump with him. It would've been terrifying. Not only was she not a strong swimmer, but there was a long stretch of concrete between the house and the pool's edge. If she hadn't jumped far enough, she wouldn't have had to worry about escape— she would've been lying broken on the patio.

Shaking herself out of her shocked daze, she ran around to the other side of the pool, reaching the edge just as Mr. Espina was hauling himself out. He barely hesitated long enough to get his bearings before running toward the back perimeter fence. Alice followed, just as two more bangs echoed from inside the house. The silence afterward was terrifying. Everything sounded horribly loud—her pounding heart, her breaths tearing in and out of her lungs, her footsteps, the crack of every branch as she tore across the decorative landscaping. Even the harness buckles jangled as she ran, still clutching the assortment of straps in one hand.

Alice couldn't stop herself from checking over her shoulder, expecting at any second for Aaron and an army of guards to come tearing after them. Aaron would like that, to give her hope that she'd escaped before reeling her back in at the last moment. Alice wasn't the only one with something at stake, though. Aaron would make her life miserable, but at least he'd keep her alive and relatively undamaged. After all, he needed to use her to secure his entry into the Jovanovic family. If Aaron caught them, she might survive, but he'd kill Mr. Espina in the longest, slowest, most painful way possible.

When she tripped over a newly planted lacey oak, Alice forced herself to focus on the ground in front of her. Mr. Espina pulled ahead, the distance between them growing, and Alice had to hold back a plea for him to wait. She knew logically that he wouldn't abandon her at this point, but her anxiety was still thrumming through her. Without his help, there was no way she could get over the ten-foot wrought-iron fence.

He stopped at the fence and pulled something out of his small pack.

When Alice reached him, she saw that Mr. Espina

was removing the bolts securing the brackets on the top and bottom crossbars of the fence. As she bent over, gasping for breath, he moved to the other post and did the same on that side.

A shout from the house made Alice twist around in panic. Someone with a flashlight stood right outside the French doors by the pool. The beam of light crossed the backyard and flickered over her. She hurried to turn her face away, but it didn't matter.

"Stop!" the man shouted, and with sinking dread, Alice recognized Jeb's voice.

"Time to go." Mr. Espina gave the fence a shove, and the whole panel fell over with a heavy thud. Grabbing Alice's wrist, he ran across the panel and over the scrubby grass toward the wooded ravine that ran the length of the property.

There was an odd popping sound, and a clod of dirt kicked up a few feet away. It took her a moment to realize that Jeb was *shooting* at them. Mr. Espina pulled her to the side, leading her on a zigzagging trail. The ground was rough and uneven, and Alice caught her toe, but Mr. Espina pulled her right out of her stumble and back into a sprint. Jeb kept shooting, but Alice couldn't think about that, not when she was trying to breathe and run.

Fear kept her heart racing, and their mad dash made it beat faster and faster until she felt like her whole body was trembling with the effort. Lightning flickered overhead, making everything too bright for a second before plunging into darkness. Thunder rumbled, shaking the ground and blotting out the sound of her pounding heart and rasping breaths.

At first, Alice didn't realize that it was raining, that the droplets were pounding against her head and running down her neck to soak into her hoodie. Then it started to pour, falling in heavy sheets of rain, just as she and Mr. Espina entered the trees. The ground immediately fell away in front of them, dropping into a yawning ravine with a creek rushing along the bottom.

Alice tried to automatically brake, but Mr. Espina kept running, and his grip on her arm kept her in motion, as well. A cry escaped her as they flew off the edge, landing three feet down the slope. The dirt had already turned into mud, and they sank into the muck with each step. With Mr. Espina hauling her forward, Alice couldn't do anything but keep moving her feet, sprinting and sliding and only staying upright thanks to the hand on her arm and her continuous forward motion.

The rain was loud, too loud to hear if Jeb was still shooting. Alice couldn't look to see how close he was, though. She was too concerned with her high-speed downhill sprint. The slope started to level off, and Alice looked away from her footing for a moment. They'd reached the bottom, and she gave a gasping sob of relief. Splashing through the small creek, she risked a quick glance at the top of the ravine.

There were so many flashlights now—at least ten—bobbing and moving as Aaron's men climbed down after them. Jeb was the closest and closing the distance quickly. He grabbed a small tree, bringing himself to a sliding stop, and then lifted his gun.

Alice sucked in a breath, trying to force her legs to run even faster. They started to climb the other side of the ravine, but there wasn't anything close by that was big enough to hide behind, just brush and small trees and lots of weeds. Jeb had a clear shot.

The incline sloped up dramatically, and their run turned into more of a scrambling climb. Mr. Espina released her in order to use both hands. Alice grabbed a clumpy weed, but the plant pulled out of the ground. She started to slide down the slope, and she fumbled to grasp a half-exposed root. That one held, and she reached for the next handhold.

Every second, she expected to feel one of Jeb's bullets pierce her skin. Her breathing, already rough from fear and exertion, sped up even more. Closing her fingers around a thick vine, she shot a quick glance over her shoulder.

Jeb was standing in the same place she'd last seen him, his flashlight hand supporting his gun hand. The light turned the rest of Jeb's body into a silhouette, but Alice could clearly see the gun. The rain poured over him, but he stood perfectly still, his head cocked to the side as he aimed.

Then, the ground crumbled under Jeb's feet. The flashlight and gun went flying as he fell onto his back. He started to slide, traveling several feet before his body ran into a pair of tree trunks that brought him to a rough stop.

"Move!" Mr. Espina's command broke her paralysis, and she started climbing up the slope again. Temporary rivulets of water coursed down the side of the ravine, and Alice's feet slid through the muck as she pushed herself forward and up. The tree coverage became heavier, and there were more saplings and roots to grab. Alice sped up, not wanting to look to see if Jeb had gotten up or if the other guards were closing in. She just climbed.

Alice didn't notice that she was at the top of the ravine until she reached for the next handhold and there was nothing there but grass and weeds. She looked up to see that Mr. Espina was already on his feet and jogging toward an older-model sedan parked on the shoulder. Alice stood and tried to run for the car, but her head spun and her stomach threatened to expel its contents.

Swallowing down bile, she had to settle for a shambling jog. It felt like it took forever to reach the passenger door of the car. She was sure that, any second, Jeb—or, worse, Aaron—would pop out of the ravine. That would be the end of any escape attempt. Aaron would never let her out of his sight until he'd married her off to Logan Jovanovic.

Her hand caught the handle, and she jerked open the car door. In the back of her mind, she mentally apologized to the car's owner, since she was head-to-toe mud, but that didn't slow her down. Alice threw herself into the seat as Mr. Espina shot them forward. The door swung shut, slamming with the force of their acceleration, and Alice wiggled out of her backpack, dropping it onto the floor by her feet as she grabbed for her seat belt. By the way Mr. Espina was driving, she had a feeling she'd need it.

She turned to face him as they flew down the road, the windshield wipers working at their fastest speed. "Thank you," she said.

His only response was a slight upward tilt of his chin.

"I dropped your harness." She glanced at her muddy hands as if she'd find the missing equipment hanging from herself. "Sorry."

The corner of his mouth quirked. "I have others."

"That doesn't surprise me." She settled back in the seat, her muscles easing slightly one by one, leaving her feeling limp and shaky. They were both still alive, though.

They were alive, and she was free.

ABOUT THE AUTHOR

When she's not writing, Katie Ruggle rides horses, shoots guns, and trains her three dogs. A police academy graduate, Katie readily admits she's a forensics nerd. While she still misses her off-grid home in the Rocky Mountains, she now lives in a 150-year-old Minnesota farmhouse near her family.

ALSO BY KATIE RUGGLE